FURY CONVERGENCE

CHRYSOULA TZAVELAS

For Ailsa, who tracked down Shatiel.

This one may not be appropriate for the kids.

Previously in the Senyaza Series

THE FAERIES, an offshoot of fallen angels, were released into the modern world. Branwyn, a human artist, learns a rare human-only magic from the faeries called Artificing, which lets her enchant and 'wake up' mundane objects with the assistance of celestial Machine shards.

In Divinity Circuit, she discovers just how what she creates can be abused when her sister Rhianna recruits her to recover a lost artifact. Rhianna works for both an angel and the government, neither of which Branwyn likes. She's also entangled once again with the murderous schemes of the monster Severin, her least favorite ally. She ends the story angry at both of them.

Meanwhile, the Wild Hunt, bound to hunt down corrupted souls and their haunts, was reformed with a werewolf, a zombie, a vampire, a mage, an artificial person and an ordinary girl. They quickly discovered that simply destroying corrupted souls wasn't very palatable and have since been searching for a way to redeem those yet redeemable. They also discovered that the ancient magical horses of the Wild Hunt are violently against 'office romances,' blaming mortal passions for the corruption of the previous Wild Hunt.

———

PREVIOUS STORIES relevant to **Fury Convergence** (and briefly recapped above) include **Wolf Interval**, **Divinity Circuit**, and "The Wild Hunt Goes To School" (in **Etiquette of Exiles**). The stories "Stainless," "Her Daughter Pinned To The Sky," "Endless Silence of Forgotten Things" and "Wicked Stepself" may be considered bonus material.

Part I

1

Recruited

WHEN A 10-MINUTE REMINDER chirped at her, Branwyn put down the tablet she'd been using to plan one of her artificing projects and looked at her agenda. Not because she didn't know her schedule, but because she did. She'd been thinking about this appointment all day. It was... unexpected. Unusual. She'd gone along with it mostly out of curiosity.

And now... Ten more minutes until she found out what exactly was going on.

Ten minutes... but she probably didn't have to wait that long. She'd played along this long, but why wait when she didn't have to? She stood up, strode to the front door of her cluttered studio, and yanked it open.

Her sister Rhianna, slumped against the opposite wall, jerked upright and stared at her with wide eyes. Her shoulder-length red hair was shaggy and her green eyes had makeup carefully applied to hide the natural shadows, but her pantsuit was beautifully crisp.

"You might as well come in," said Branwyn. "There's no point in both of us staring at the door for the next ten minutes."

"All right," said Rhianna meekly. "Thank you for agreeing to see me." She picked up her messenger bag, walked past Branwyn into the studio, and stood beside the chair in front of the battered wooden desk.

Branwyn narrowed her eyes. "I saw you at Christmas, and in April, too. You didn't make an appointment then." Ever since they'd disagreed over the disposition of one of Branwyn's creations a year ago, the relationship between the sisters had been cooler than normal. They still spoke, they still enjoyed the same family activities, but they no longer trusted each other the same way. It hurt.

"Well, that was personal time." The roguish smile Rhianna flashed at Branwyn was so familiar that her nebulous worries eased a little.

She reached out to tweak her younger sister's nose. "And this isn't? Sit down, then. I'll sit down too, and we can discuss your business like civilized women." She did just as she said, but she also leaned back to put her feet on her desk, because that was the kind of civilized she was.

Rhianna sat primly. "This is business, yes. I wanted you to understand that from the beginning, which is why I went through your appointment calendar."

Branwyn studied her, trying to read between the lines, before giving up. "I wasn't sure. Because you already know I won't work for your little government agency. I mean, we've discussed that and everything. So I figured maybe you had some other reason." She paused as an idea occurred. "Did you want me to refuse to meet you?"

Rhianna looked pained. "No. I want to hire you on behalf of OX. Branwyn, I'm not being tricky. There's no secret goal here."

"Then why did you make an appointment?" said Branwyn triumphantly. "You've never made an appointment before. You're my sister."

"That's why," said Rhianna quietly. "You wouldn't have given me a chance to say anything if I just showed up at your door again. Not after last time."

"Aha! That's your plan!" Branwyn said, but her heart wasn't really in it. "Rhianna..." She wanted to say her sister could always talk to her, would always be able to ask for help. But there were some kinds of help Branwyn would simply never give her now. Probably never. Almost certainly never.

It really did hurt. She said, "Well, I'm not making anything for OX, unless something has seriously changed behind the scenes."

Rhianna hesitated before leaning forward. "Bran, what I've been doing lately... No, nevermind. We don't want you to build anything. My Advisor wants you to come with me to investigate something. We're trying to track down some missing kids."

Caustically, Branwyn said, "Of course you are. Has anybody asked you to track them down or did you just make it your business?" Tracking people was a big part of what she hated about Rhianna's Office of the Unexpected.

Rhianna's mouth thinned, and she sat up straight. "Have you ever heard of Tucker, Idaho?"

"No."

"No, of course not. It was a tiny, isolated town with slightly more than four hundred people. Nobody's heard of it, except in passing. We were very careful about that."

The back of Branwyn's neck prickled. *Was.* She swung her feet off the desk and leaned forward. "Rhianna...."

Rhianna kept talking flatly as if Branwyn hadn't said anything. "On May 12, a little over a year ago, Tucker was destroyed by a firestorm. We initially thought there had been no survivors. It took us a little longer than expected to discover we were wrong. Seventy children vanished in the inferno. We want them back."

Branwyn's hands felt cold. "A firestorm."

Rhianna nodded. "A firestorm with a notable respect for town limits."

"And you covered it up?" Branwyn asked slowly.

"Oh yes. The details, anyhow." Rhianna set her shoulders like she was ready for a fight. "Do I need to explain why?"

"Rhianna… a fire that stopped at the edge of town. Who did it?"

"Ah, see, I knew you'd understand. Who, not what. And we don't know. We have theories, but our investigators keep running into problems in the remains of the town. It's been hard to gather much evidence, which is one of the reasons we're keeping it quiet. We don't want anyone jumping to dangerous conclusions."

Branwyn put her head in her hands, thinking of times past when she'd worked hard to prevent similar atrocities. She'd pushed herself to her limit to pull people out of the path of a potential supernatural rampage, and that had… worked, mostly. Once. Then.

And since then she'd chosen not to make weapons. Surely this couldn't…

After a moment, Rhianna said, "Would you like a tissue? A bottle of water? Some vodka? I brought all three."

Branwyn looked up. Her sister had carefully laid out a packet of tissues, a half-sized water bottle and a miniature of vodka in a row on the desk. A smile trembled on the corner of Branwyn's mouth. Then it faded away again, swallowed by her inner turmoil. "No. Are you asking me for help because something I created was involved?"

Rhianna's eyes widened. She shook her head energetically. "No. We think whoever controlled the fire didn't need an arti-fact's help. But my Advisor believes you'll be useful for tracking down the children."

"Seventy missing children. And you know they're missing? Not just…" She trailed off, her tongue twisting around the grim words as she visualized her youngest sister, bright and vibrant and so very small.

"Not just too small for there to be remains? That was an early theory, but it's too consistent. Somebody took them."

Branwyn thought about all her sisters, right up to Rhianna, and her brothers when they'd been kids. She didn't particularly enjoy children, but as the eldest of seven, it was hard-wired into her to care about them. The idea of somebody burning down a town and stealing seventy of them made her skin crawl.

But something niggled at her. Rhianna simply didn't work like this, by making appointments and offering jobs, and Branwyn trusted her precious Advisor not at all. There was a trick here, and she wasn't seeing it.

"Why me? I won't make anything for OX, even as part of a different task."

Rhianna shrugged. "I don't know. My Advisor doesn't usually tell us his reasons, but they're always good ones. It may be because of who we suspect, but I can't tell you anymore until you've agreed to help." Rhianna dropped her gaze and drew circles on the desk's surface with a finger.

Branwyn frowned and then shook her head. "That's not enough. I don't trust your Advisor."

Rhianna winced but kept her gaze on the table. "He thought you'd want to help find the children. And we'll pay you." She glanced up. "He insisted I mention that."

"That doesn't make it better!" Branwyn snapped, then caught herself. "And you know that. I know you know that. I assume you told him. And you trust his reasons for his instructions." She shook her head again and rose. "What are you supposed to do if you can't get my help?"

"I didn't get a flow chart. I was instructed to hire you and provided those details—would you like to examine the contract? After that, we go on to Tucker and report back once we've turned up something." Rhianna also stood up, packing her bag again.

"I'm working on making better decisions but in this case I'm a little stumped. I suppose I'll go to Tucker by myself."

Rhianna turned to the door and then leapt backward in a respectable imitation of a frightened cat, kicking her chair forward at the man who was unaccountably leaning against the studio door. "Holy crap—!" She scrambled backwards, around the desk and behind Branwyn.

Branwyn scowled as the man caught the chair and neatly moved it out of the way. "What the hell are you doing here?"

He had dark hair and shadowed eyes, wore a plain black t-shirt over old jeans, and his rugged face was far too familiar to Branwyn. Not a 'man' at all, but Severin, a fallen angel, a monster, and Branwyn's own personal nemesis.

He straightened up and stepped away from the door. "Oh, I was in the neighborhood and I happened to overhear your little sister. You know, I think this is a job you should take, cupcake."

Branwyn growled, "In the neighborhood. I worked hard so —" but the mark he'd placed on her collarbone itched, and her teeth clicked together as she was reminded once again that it was more than an ugly, unwanted tattoo.

Severin looked at her, unsmiling. She preferred it when he smiled. It was a surefire tell that he was being evil somehow. "Take the job, Branwyn."

"What?" Branwyn stared wildly between Rhianna and Severin. It involved some twisting because Rhianna was still hiding behind her. "Why are you both telling me this? I'm not going to work for the feds and I'm certainly not working for you."

Severin spread his hands. "Missing kids, cupcake. And you can't say somebody else will deal with it. Nobody in the world can do what you do. You know it, Umbriel knows it." Umbriel was the angelic name of Rhianna's Advisor.

"Potentially true," Branwyn conceded. "But now that you've shown up, my moral responsibility might be to keep you away from wherever those kids might be."

Severin's jaw tightened almost imperceptibly, but Branwyn, so attuned to his every move, noticed. "You couldn't. But you might make recovering them run more smoothly."

Rhianna, peeking over Branwyn's shoulder, said, "What do you know about those kids?"

"Ah, little sister. As I said, I overheard what you told Branwyn." He gave Rhianna his widest shark-like smile. "Very worthy."

Rhianna shuddered against Branwyn's back and asked softly, "He has a soft spot for kids?"

Staring hard at Severin, Branwyn replied, "Not that I've seen." He'd once claimed he'd saved her youngest sister from being run over, but Branwyn was convinced even now he'd engineered the situation to insinuate himself into her mother's household for an evening.

Severin's smile twisted. "Umbriel is more cunning than I've given him credit for. Come on, cupcake. Find the missing children and I'll consider your debt to me paid."

"I don't owe you anything," Branwyn snarled. "And if you think I'd trade a kid to pay off any debt I might owe you, you don't remember our walk through Faerie together."

"Why do you even care?" added Rhianna.

"Let's just say that whoever stole them sounds like somebody I'd like to meet." Severin's gaze flicked back to Branwyn. "Are you honestly going to abandon these kids?"

"Go to hell," Branwyn said.

His mouth twisted further. "As delightful as always, cupcake. Fine. Your choice. I have bigger fish to fry. Little sister, come here. I can take you directly to this town the faeries burned and help you investigate. If you do a good job, I'll even mention it to those of my siblings who want your head."

Rhianna came out from behind Branwyn, but she said, "My name is Rhianna. I didn't tell Branwyn faeries did it."

"Very well, Rhianna," he said, with a mocking lilt. "Yes, I've heard of the place. It's a memorable event when a faerie wipes out a town. People gossip. Well, when I say 'people'... But this is wasting time. Save your boss the price of a plane ticket and come along." He held out a hand to Rhianna.

She glanced at Branwyn, squared her shoulders, and took Severin's hand.

Branwyn said urgently, "What are you doing, Rhianna? His friends want to kill you. You can't trust him."

Patiently, Rhianna said, "I need magical help for this investigation, Branwyn. And I'm harder to kill than I look."

Branwyn wanted to shout at Rhianna not to be stupid. Instead she clenched her fists in helpless frustration. Her mind raced. There had to be something else she could do...

Severin glanced at her with an appreciative little smile. "If you show up in Tucker sometime tomorrow via plane or bus, I'm going to be very annoyed." He held out his other hand to her.

Branwyn, who had been formulating that very plan, said a bad word as she realized just how far she was considering going to prove nobody was the boss of her. Instead, she grabbed Severin's hand.

———

SEVERIN'S FINGERS closed around Branwyn's hand and wrist and he *yanked* her toward him, pulling her into the crook of his arm. Blackness dropped over them, close and tangible, and then they were floating in a vast dark space, orbited by windows of light.

Branwyn had been here twice before, but both previous times, she'd been too shocked and traumatized by the preceding events to notice much. This time, she managed to observe that the windows of light each opened onto a different place, and one of them was her studio. From the corner of her eye, she caught a flash of color, and turned to look at her sister, clinging to

Severin's other hand. Rhianna glowed like a Pre-Raphaelite painting, complete with brushwork.

Branwyn blinked and tried to refocus, but one of the windows of light rushed toward them. Once again she was *yanked*, despite already being loathsomely nestled against Severin's arm. Then her feet touched the ground as afternoon light filled her vision.

They stood on an old road, facing a scrubby, debris-filled field. Forested mountains loomed in the distance, and there was a trickle of water from a culvert nearby. The sky was clear and blue, but Branwyn could smell lightning, and the faintest whiff of long-dead fires.

Rhianna gracefully twirled away from Severin. "Huh. That wasn't nearly as smooth as my Advisor's travel."

Branwyn, far less elegant, tried to jerk herself away from Severin. He let her step away from his chest but his hand continued to clasp hers as he said, "Well, you don't belong to me like you belong to him."

Rhianna turned a sunny smile on him as she took another step away. "And thank God for that, don't you think?"

Severin smiled back as if he was oblivious to Branwyn spasmodically driving her nails into his palm. "Does he take you inside him often?"

Rhianna pivoted to scan the field before saying, "That sounds so naughty. Oh, that must be the investigator's camp. We might as well start there." She set off across what had to be the ruined town, following the cracked pavement.

Branwyn stared at her sister's back and forced her fists to unclench. If her sister 'belonged' to the angel Umbriel in any way, she'd chosen it herself. Probably. Almost certainly. People were entitled to make their own choices even if Branwyn hated some of them.

She only realized when he moved into her line of sight that

Severin had released her. "Any time you'd like to murder an angel, cupcake, just say the word."

"Oh, and..." He held up the hand she'd been gripping, showing the blood welling from three crescent punctures. "Next time you make me bleed, I'll expect you to kiss it and make it better."

Branwyn refocused her rage and frustration from Umbriel to Severin. "You're the one who wouldn't let go of my hand. You got what you deserved."

He looked at her for a long moment, his dark eyes fathomless but not swallowing her down as they so easily could. "I hope Umbriel knows what a distraction you are," he finally said softly.

"Hey! Are you two coming or what?" Rhianna shouted.

Branwyn shook herself and plunged past Severin, leaving him to follow behind her or not. She'd come here to help find some missing kids. Everything else was irrelevant.

The 'field' was easily visible as a ruined town as soon as she paid a bit more attention. In the year or so since the fire, hardy vegetation had taken root here and there. Nobody had done anything to clean up the remnants of the structures, although there was evidence they'd been moved around. Bricks and roofing tiles and melted metal were piled haphazardly in the street. Vehicles burned almost beyond recognition collapsed on themselves. In the distance, beyond the cluster of tents Rhianna was exploring, there was a bulldozer.

On one level, the ruins reminded her of the beginnings of the recycled art she worked on before she'd learned artificing. She absently wondered if she could make something new from it, if the foundations of the town created a matrix she could rebuild on.

Then she realized why there were piles of debris in the road and pulled back hard on creative musings. Rhianna had said four hundred people had died here a year ago. And she'd been considering inspecting the ruins with her magical Sight, letting herself think of it as nothing more than a potential art project.

Branwyn wasn't the only magically-endowed person in her family these days. Her middle sister Brynn was the Master of Horses for the Wild Hunt, a group sort of like the Ghostbusters. It was irritating to admit it, but she knew things now that Branwyn didn't, and sometimes she shared them.

Recently she'd warned Branwyn against close study of the sites of recent violent deaths. Shuddering before a family dinner after a Wild Hunt gig, she'd said, "I don't know if it'll hit you like it hits me, but… it's not something you want to stumble into accidentally. Sometimes there's nothing, if the soul moves on cleanly. Sometimes… just be careful, okay?"

Branwyn remembered that, remembered the people who had died, and pushed away her desire to create, or even evaluate creatively.

"Branwyn?" said Rhianna, approaching her. "Are you all right? Where did your monster go?"

"*Please* don't call him my monster." Branwyn looked around, but sure enough, he'd vanished.

To her surprise, Rhianna blushed, something she normally only did when she revealed something secret about herself. "Sorry. I won't do it again. Has he abandoned us?"

Branwyn sighed. "We can only dream."

"Because if so, it'll make getting home harder. I doubt ridesharing comes out this far."

Branwyn shook her head, thinking of her own Veil-tearing charm, and all the wizards she knew. "I'm not worried about that. Look, where are those investigators you mentioned?"

Rhianna said, "It's just the investigators' campsite. There aren't any people. All the investigators assigned here keep quitting."

"Have they all been ordinary investigators? That is, conventionally trained, without magic?"

"As far as I know." Rhianna turned, and they walked over to the cluster of tents together. "There's more camping supplies inside the tents."

"How about a journal they left behind meticulously documenting their descent into madness?"

"Oh, only one of them quit because of mental health reasons. Another one broke his leg, and his partner developed some sort of lung disease. And the last one didn't say anything about Tucker but he got himself reassigned pretty quickly." Rhianna pulled a camp stove out of one tent.

Branwyn peeked into another, spotted a folded camp chair and dragged it out. After unfolding it and dropping into it, she stared off over the ruins, thinking about Rhianna's news. "Well, that certainly sends a message. I wonder who's sending it."

"A faerie," said Severin, stepping out of the air between Branwyn and Rhianna. He was frowning and holding Branwyn's hammer loosely in his left hand.

"Hey! Give me that." Branwyn grabbed her hammer's handle. He released it without argument or acknowledgement, and she pulled it into her lap, wondering why he'd fetched it. She'd left it behind, true, but only because she was pretty sure she could fetch it herself anytime she needed it.

"I've been looking around the Backworld here. There's active faerie glamour all over the place. And something else, too."

"Ooh, ooh, what?" asked Rhianna.

Severin bared his teeth. "I don't know. And I don't like that."

"You said back in my studio that a faerie wiped out the town," Branwyn said. "Is it more than that?"

"Yes." Severin looked down at her. "You're probably going to need that hammer, cupcake. Whatever happened here isn't over yet."

Branwyn tapped her fingers on her hammer's head. "It's not a weapon." Severin only shrugged in response.

Rhianna clapped her hands together like a kindergarten

teacher. "All right. Let's start by looking around. Severin, you can figure out what's going on in the Backworld while Branwyn and I go over the ruins. Later, we can see if any of the neighbors are still around."

Severin gave her a chilly glance. "I am not going to be ordered around by an overconfident angel's pet."

"No, no, of course you won't," said Rhianna soothingly. "You're going to do that because you feel like it, not because I'm the boss of you. See, I understand. Branwyn *is* my sister."

Severin's little appreciative smile flickered on and off. "And don't you forget it." He vanished.

Branwyn stood up quickly. "What did you say about neighbors?"

Rhianna exhaled slowly, her gaze still focused on where Severin had been. "Neighbors... oh, right. The fire stopped at the town limits. There are, or possibly were, people living beyond them. They're the ones who originally described the 'fire tornado'. But they live out a couple miles in various directions, so let's see what we can learn here first."

2

Tucker

RHIANNA AND BRANWYN picked their way through the ruins together. After a time, Rhianna asked, "Do you need to call anybody? We left so quickly and I don't know if Mr. Congeniality will get you back by curfew."

Branwyn shrugged. "Mom doesn't expect me for dinner until next week, and Marley and her entire entourage are off on a private island somewhere in the Caribbean. You're lucky I'm not with them."

Rhianna raised her eyebrows. "You were invited?"

Branwyn rolled her eyes. "Oh yes. I do mean 'entire entourage'. The cat, Marley's family, me, and Penny. Zachariah also invited a friend of the twins, along with his mom. I think, if I'd asked, he would have flown our family out there too."

"It must be so *nice* to be rich," said Rhianna wistfully.

Branwyn stopped to inspect a solitary rosebush. It had somehow survived the flames that consumed the ranch house behind it. Now it was twisted and thirsty, with only a few leaves lingering in the heat of summer. "You're in the wrong career if you want money."

"I was doing all right before… well, never mind that. I *was* doing all right, but not 'private island' all right." They walked on. "Did Corbin go too? How are he and Marley doing?"

"Yeah, see, that's the main reason I didn't go. Corbin and Marley are great. Marley and her boss Zachariah are all right, even if Zachariah is an authoritarian asshole. But Corbin and Zachariah together put my teeth on edge. They snipe at each other. They can't seem to stay away from each other. There's all this drama throbbing under the surface." Branwyn flexed her fingers. "If I was trapped on a tiny island with them, I'd just end up getting out my chisel."

"And then the island would explode," Rhianna guessed. "Probably a good decision."

They walked along in silence until they reached what had been the center of town. Rhianna raised her eyebrows at Branwyn, who said, "Let's keep walking. To the other side, and then we can do a perimeter circuit."

"Just like old times," Rhianna said, and started walking again.

They used to go on long strolls when they'd been teenagers, exploring some new part of Los Angeles. Branwyn didn't have the investigative training to pick any details out of the overall mess of Tucker, but exploring was an important first step in figuring out what to do next.

On those teenage rambles, she'd discovered she could learn more about a place by focusing on a single element than by trying to take in everything. The graffiti, or the trash receptacles, or the parked cars. This time, she noticed the plants.

As they finished their silent circuit, she said, "The roses survived the fire somehow, but they're not surviving the summer heat. I'll have to get them water from that creek I heard."

"Oh?" said Rhianna. "Since when did you have a green thumb?"

When Branwyn just shrugged, Rhianna added. "I noticed the roads. They're in terrible condition." She nibbled on her lower lip. "Which fits. This really was an isolated town. Not just geographically, but politically. They didn't ask for much from the state, and any services they could manage themselves, they did."

Branwyn looked around at the burnt foundations and resisted any snarky remarks about Rhianna doing her research. Of course she had. In her situation, Branwyn would have too. "Any idea why a faerie might have hated this town in particular?"

"We don't *know* anything," said Rhianna cautiously. "I'm not sure I should contaminate your opinions this early."

Branwyn's brows drew together. In theory, she appreciated this kind of evidence-based approach to judgement, especially from a government agent. But it was unlike her whimsical sister.

Severin stepped out of thin air once again. "Have you spotted the glamour yet?"

"No?" said Rhianna. "Ooh, what did you find?"

"Take another walk, and this time don't be fooled," he responded, and vanished.

Rhianna pursed her lips, staring at where he'd been. "I'm not entirely sure I like him."

"Good," said Branwyn, and started retracing their route.

Rhianna jogged after her. "You say that, but suddenly you're doing what he says."

"I've decided not to be petty right now. He knows something, and he wants us to find out what it is."

Rhianna looked askance at her, but all she said was, "I do wish they wouldn't do that. My Advisor loves making me dig up information he already knows."

"Aren't you doing the exact same thing by not telling me what you know about this place?" Branwyn pointed out. "Except I have no way to dig up anything about this town, except maybe with an actual shovel."

"That's true." Rhianna blew out her breath. "Well, this may or may not be relevant, but Tucker was an extremely homogenous town. 98% white at the last census. One post office. One school. One bowling alley. One bar, which was incidentally also the bowling alley." She paused as Branwyn shrugged. It sounded exactly like she imagined a tiny town in Idaho would be. "One church."

That made Branwyn raise her eyebrows. "Not very religious? I'd expect more bars then."

"Well, it's hard to say now, but it was a big building, with several full-time employees." Rhianna scuffed her feet in the dirt. "There have been problems elsewhere stemming from isolationist communities clashing against the Extraworlder phenomenon."

Extraworlder: the term used for the faeries by those who disliked the original word. The faeries themselves had gleefully embraced it, holding Extraworlder conferences and starting Extraworlder businesses and sending an Extraworlder lobby to DC. Branwyn preferred the old term.

Eventually, Branwyn said, "That's interesting but I don't know that it explains anything. Unless some of these other isolationist communities have also been going up in flames."

"No," said Rhianna. "Not that, although the faeries have certainly caused other kinds of trouble. But this was… destruction, not mischief."

"Except that seventy kids escaped somehow. Speaking of which, have you noticed any of this glamour yet?"

Rhianna shook her head. "I don't even know where to start. I was really hoping you did."

Branwyn grimaced, contemplating her options for not being 'fooled'. The Sight, which her sister Brynn had warned her not to use at the sites of catastrophes, would show her the lines of the Geometry that underlaid everything, along with the auras of any celestials around. That didn't help with glamour, though, because faerie magic convinced the world to lie to itself.

On the other hand, a while back she'd made a deal to share her eyesight with a Faerie Queen. Other than letting her escape with her life, it had never been the slightest bit useful to her. She wondered if it might be now. Could the Queen of Stone under-stand the same visual data differently? And if so, how would Branwyn know? It had always been, as far as she could tell, a one-way stream. But who really knew? She'd stay alert, just in case the Queen was watching and felt like making a contribution.

Concentrating on trying to see what might be hidden, she walked along, only paying half attention Rhianna's grumbling about celestials who wouldn't just spill the beans. When Branwyn finally did notice something strange, she stopped dead and Rhianna bumped into her back.

"What?" said Rhianna. She glanced around and said, "Look at that pothole. It needs a bridge."

"Let's go get some water," Branwyn said, staring hard at the wilting rose bush growing in front of the entrance to a burned-out house right at the edge of town.

"Whaaat did you see?" wailed Rhianna. "Don't you dare do this, Branwyn Lennox. I will beat you."

"Catch me first," Branwyn suggested, and took off running back through the town.

Branwyn wasn't in terrible shape. She walked a lot, and some of her work required wrestling with bulky or recalcitrant mate-rials for long hours. But Rhianna trained daily, and long gone were the days when Branwyn's longer legs made up for her sister's explosive energy. After only a moment of shocked outrage, Rhianna caught up with Branwyn and passed her, slowing down just enough to give her sister a disgusted look. Then she sped past, running like a nymph.

Having achieved her primary goal of buying time to consider what she'd spotted, Branwyn was tempted to drop to a brisk walk again. But her pride made her keep running, even when she began to puff.

By the time she arrived at the investigator's camp, Rhianna had four buckets filled and waiting beside the culvert that flowed under the road. As Branwyn staggered up to her, she impassively picked up one of the buckets and sloshed the contents onto her sister. "There, I beat you. Now tell me what's going on."

Branwyn, who had expected and even hoped for the drenching, wiped water from her face. "The rose was growing in the wrong place. It stood out. I thought we might as well water it and some of the other ones while I figured out why."

Rhianna stared at her expressionlessly for a moment, then filled up the newly emptied bucket and handed it to Branwyn. Then she picked up two more. "All right. Let's do this."

Self-consciously, Branwyn grabbed the fourth bucket. Once upon a time, she would have refused to give such a fuzzy answer. Once upon a time, Rhianna wouldn't have accepted it if she had. They'd both changed.

"Do you think the monster could have magicked this water to the plants?" asked Rhianna after a few minutes, a little wistfully.

Branwyn resisted her first reaction and actually thought about the question. Eventually, she said, "I don't know. Carried it faster without spilling it because he's stupidly strong and fast? Probably. Done it without muscle? I've never seen him create anything." She remembered shattered glass fusing into a molten ball over his palm and corrected herself. "Not from scratch."

She stopped and tilted a bucket over a scraggly rosebush entangled in the skeleton of a house. The water puddled on the dry ground before sinking. When Branwyn touched the earth, it was barely damp.

"Branwyn," said Rhianna in a hushed voice. Branwyn glanced up and watched as the faded, curling leaves of the rosebush darkened and straightened. It didn't do much to make the bush look healthier, but it was a *very fast* response to the watering.

"I see," said Branwyn. "Well. That's a thing. Let's go on."

They watered five more plants before arriving at the ruins at the edge of town. Branwyn walked over to the rosebush she'd noticed. "It's where the door of the house would be. I thought it was... odd."

Rhianna shrugged and emptied one of her buckets over the twisted branches. Like the other bushes, this one shivered as its leaves responded to the water, but nothing else happened.

Rhianna looked puzzled. "But there's two more bushes, you see?"

But Branwyn didn't see until she joined Rhianna at the house's foundation. Then she could see the two withered bushes that had been hidden by debris.

No, probably not hidden by debris. Hidden by something else, hidden by something that tried to twist Branwyn's thoughts even after she saw the truth.

Rhianna emptied her other bucket on the two new plants, and they shuddered. Leaves unfurled from dead twigs and the main trunks straightened.

"And now there's two more," Branwyn said. "Yeah, something's hiding here." She looked around the ruins. The house had been tiny, with a square floor plan. "Come on out, we know you're here."

Nothing happened. Thoughtfully, Rhianna used the rest of the water on the newest bushes and watched as yet more appeared. "How much water do you think we need?"

"More than another four buckets' worth," Branwyn said, and added conversationally, "*Can* you create water, Severin?"

He stepped into the world behind her. When he spoke, she could feel his breath in her hair. "What if I can, cupcake? Are you asking me for help?"

Branwyn turned to look at him. He was further away than she expected, regarding her with glittering eyes. "Am I? We can bring the water ourselves, but it will take us a few trips. You might get bored. But if you're keeping busy in the Backworld, carry on."

Severin's brow darkened in irritation and for an instant, Branwyn could *feel* the sharpness of his black diamond aura flickering around them. Then his mouth twisted in a wry expression. "Wait here," he ordered, and vanished again.

Rhianna exhaled. "Wow. For a minute I wondered if he was going to smite you or something."

Branwyn pulled her mouth to one side. "It's a little worrying that he didn't even say something nasty." Rhianna gave her a quizzical look, and Branwyn shook her head. "I just keep wondering why he cares about this town. I know he doesn't like faeries, but I don't think that's it."

Rhianna stirred the dirt with her shoe without responding. After a moment, she said, "Bran, do you have any kind of protections? You know, in case whatever or whoever destroyed this place tries to hurt you?"

Branwyn shifted her hip, feeling the weight of the hammer she'd slung through a belt loop, and thought of her few utility charms. The only self-defense magic she had was more of a party trick than anything else. She couldn't imagine two-inch claws doing much to fend off somebody who would obliterate a town. "Not particularly. Do you?"

"Yes," said Rhianna. "I do." She took a deep breath. "So outside of handling your monster, please let me do the stupid stuff."

Branwyn squinted at her little sister. "This is a sudden topic shift. Why does anybody have to do the stupid stuff?"

There was a low thrum and Severin appeared, carrying a large, blackened steel drum. Water sloshed over the rim as he deposited it. "A family curse, perhaps? Here's your precious water. Now get a move on."

Rhianna gave Branwyn a conflicted look she perfectly understood and chose to ignore. She couldn't promise her sister she'd stay in the back seat if anything dangerous appeared. She'd faced too much by now, present company included, to even consider it.

Instead she watered rose bushes, observing closely as they appeared, twining themselves all around the perimeter of the ruined house. At last, she and Severin and Rhianna stood within a completed square of rose bushes, each one a couple feet apart. They were all verdant green, but flowerless.

"Now what?" said Rhianna reluctantly.

"The next part's up to you," said Severin, crossing his arms.

"What is it?" Rhianna demanded, but Severin just raised his eyebrows at her. She muttered, "I wish I could beat you, too."

Branwyn walked back and forth between a pair of bushes, exiting and re-entering the ruins. Then she walked around the edge, looking at the plants.

"What are we even doing?" Rhianna complained. "Are we trying to take apart a spell? Solve a riddle? Cast a spell of our own?"

"If only it was that rational. I wish Marley was here," said Branwyn absently.

"I'd rather not go get her, cupcake," said Severin. "It'd take time and her boyfriends would annoy me. Try your best without her."

Branwyn gave him a sharp look and then wished she hadn't. Instead she pivoted toward Rhianna. "In my experience, faeries follow rules. The rules aren't always... sane, sometimes they're... well... fairy tale rules, but they follow them anyhow. There are rules at work here. If we can understand them, we can make them work for us."

Rhianna tilted her her head, lifting her chin in that way she'd always had. "A riddle, then." She joined Branwyn in staring at the bushes. "Oh. They don't have any flowers."

"Well, they were nearly dead an hour ago," Branwyn pointed out. "But I think you're right, and I have no idea how to make them bloom."

"I do," said Rhianna lightly. She knelt before the bush growing in the door, brought her hand to one branch, and firmly pressed her the pad of her ring finger into a thorn.

Branwyn's breath hissed between her teeth. But Rhianna

stayed still, almost serene, as blood welled up around the edges of the puncture and was absorbed by the thorn. The bush shivered again, though the thorn biting Rhianna remained embedded in her finger. Buds swelled on stems, then burst into crimson bloom with a sound like the snap of a sheet.

"All right. Why are you still sitting there?" demanded Branwyn. "Come here, so we can talk about how you shouldn't go giving your blood to random magic plants."

Rhianna held up a 'wait' finger on her other hand and remained sitting on her heels. After a few heartbeats, Branwyn realized the blossoming roses were slowly spreading around the perimeter.

"Ah," said Rhianna in satisfaction. "I thought if it was one piece of magic, I wouldn't have to feed them all individually." A moment passed, and she added, "I wonder how much blood a rose garden of this size requires."

"Stop and let me take over," ordered Branwyn.

Rhianna gave her a small smile and shook her head.

Branwyn gritted her teeth. Why hadn't she thought of this first? It seemed obvious now. But she hadn't wanted to see it, hadn't imagined her sister would do so instead. It was such a stupid, self-sacrificing, storybook act. And what if it wasn't even the right thing to do? Would the roses drink Rhianna dry? All because Branwyn hadn't gotten there first?

Severin's hand curved around her hip and she felt his, "Shhh," in her ear. Infuriated, she turned toward him—and froze. Despite the strong sense of his presence, she'd expected him to still be near the steel drum at the center of the ruined house. But instead he was right behind her, his burnt-sugar scent tickling her nose, his head tilted down and his face perilously close. His dark eyes met her own, as drowning as the sea.

Fight, flight, and something else engaged in a paralyzing three-way battle. She abruptly remembered when he'd given her the mark on her collarbone, and his lips brushing across her skin.

Rhianna made a small sound behind her and Branwyn couldn't *think*. She had to *do something*. Fight, flight…

"Look away if it helps," Severin whispered, and finally 'fight' won.

She pushed away from him. "What the hell is wrong with you?" She didn't even try to hold back. "Why are you even here, anyhow? Are you sick? Have you added 'ghoul' to your hobby list? Does this awful place turn you on? Or are you so stupid now you think I'd let you at those kids when we find them? You are such an asshole. I can't believe I—"

Branwyn stopped herself abruptly and stared at him, her eyes burning and her fists clenched. Behind her, Rhianna said faintly, "I think that will about do it. Ouch."

Severin lifted his eyebrows, looking almost cheerful. "You'd better watch yourself if you want to finish this job, cupcake. It wouldn't do for us to get too distracted." Then he strolled past Branwyn, saying, "Would you like me to fix that finger of yours, little sister?"

Branwyn turned as he passed. It was bitterly unfair that he seemed to have gotten the benefit of her moment of catharsis while she just felt hollow and frustrated.

Rhianna, her skin pale, said, "Healing doesn't seem like your field. Can you really do that?"

"Yes," he said calmly. "Now, say yes quickly before the mood passes."

"He can," confirmed Branwyn, rubbing the heel of her palm against her eyes. If her venting somehow inspired Severin to help her sister, maybe it wasn't a total waste of emotional energy.

"Please do," said Rhianna, and held up her hand. The hole in her ring finger was disturbingly large and ragged. "I didn't think it'd be able to take so much via a fingertip. Not quite sure how it did…" Her voice faded, and she swayed on her knees.

Severin caught her hand and pressed her fingers to his mouth. Rhianna's eyes flew open. She sucked air through her teeth and tried to yank her hand free before sagging into near total relaxation.

Branwyn remembered when Severin had healed her before and what had come along with it. "No marking her," she said sharply.

Severin released Rhianna and placed his hand on her hair as she leaned forward to rest her head against his leg. He gave Branwyn his shark smile. "You do so like making demands you can't enforce."

Branwyn narrowed her eyes. "I have a hammer."

"And I hear Umbriel has a new Sword," said Severin agreeably. "Honestly, she's not really worth the fight, cupcake."

"Fuck you too," said Rhianna sleepily, lifting her head. "Maybe I'm worthless but I'm the one who did that." She waved vaguely.

Branwyn realized the final roses in the perimeter were slowly blooming. Severin took Rhianna under the shoulder and lifted her to her feet. "Well done." His mouth curled derisively. "And there he is."

3

Gale

DEBRIS NOW CLUTTERED the interior of the perimeter of roses, including a broken washing machine, a chipped kitchen sink and a small but carefully arranged cairn of stones beside a camp cot with a masculine figure flopped haphazardly across it.

Releasing Rhianna to wobble on her own, Severin strode to the figure and pulled him up by his wildly tangled dark grey hair. The man—the faerie—wore the shreds of a vest and mostly intact jeans, with a musculature that would have been impressive if he wasn't such a skeletal wreck.

"...Imani?" muttered the figure, eyelids fluttering over brilliant blue eyes.

"No," growled Severin. "No. I'm Imani's guardian, and you're the boy I warned her against, and now she's dead and *where the hell is Charlie?*"

Branwyn caught Rhianna around the waist and hugged her close, staring at Severin in shock. At first she barely processed his words. She'd never before heard him sound *angry*. Bored, disinterested, amused, even irritated, yes. But the rage underlying those words reminded her of the black diamond Machine fragment

31

she'd worked into the construction of her hammer—a Machine fragment Severin had previously owned.

The faerie squinted at Severin like he was seeing double, apparently oblivious of the way he was being shaken. "You sure you're not Imani? That's what she keeps saying too..."

Severin froze, staring at the faerie, then dropped him in a heap like a rag-doll. He looked around warily as he stepped back from the groaning person pile. "Something else is here. Something... very bad."

Branwyn glanced casually at her surroundings. Except that they were now in a bower of blood-drinking roses, everything seemed quiet. It was an ordinary summer afternoon, but Severin was reacting like the soundtrack had just turned sinister.

Rhianna squeezed Branwyn in a silent one-armed hug before pulling away and extending her clasped hands out in front of her in a stretch. "Let's ask the faerie more, shall we?"

A muscle flickered in Severin's jaw. "Yes." He knelt down and turned the faerie flat on his back, arranging his limp arms over his head. Then he put his palm on the faerie's chest and pressed down hard.

Torture doesn't work, thought Branwyn, but bit the words back until she knew more. It didn't matter that she stayed silent.

That depends on the goal, whispered Severin's silent voice in her ear. *But I'll make time for fun and games later.*

Then he fully released his celestial aura.

An invisible hand tried to press Branwyn to the ground as needle-like black rain danced across her vision. A sharp pain entered her forehead and left through the back of her neck. But after a gasping breath, the aura receded, compressing around Severin and his victim.

"Holy crap," whispered Rhianna, rubbing her neck. "Ouch. That was like the Battle of the Bookstore all over again. What's he doing?"

Branwyn unclenched her aching jaw. "Getting the faerie's undivided attention, I suspect."

The faerie struggled weakly under Severin's hand, no more effective at freeing himself than a pinned butterfly. But the light flickered as unexpected clouds started tumbling across the sky.

"*Where is Imani?*" asked Severin, with the icy precision of a scalpel.

The faerie blinked at him. "Here. She's always here. She sleeps sometimes. That can be good or bad. Who are you again?"

"Somebody who knew Imani. You say she's here but I can't find her. Why?"

The faerie strained against the pressure and then relaxed. "Oh. You're the other one she's angry at."

Severin's hand on the faerie's chest clenched into a fist as his eyes widened. Then his neutral expression turned bleak. Tension grew in the lines of his crouched form, like he was about to lash out. But he didn't.

"If you stay here, she'll find you soon," added the faerie. "She can punish you too. It won't help much, but it's something."

Severin said nothing, although his other hand curled tightly as well. He stared, unseeing, at where he pressed on the faerie's chest.

The silence dragged out for a long moment as the sky darkened. Rhianna seemed content to watch and wait, but Branwyn felt the silence pulling her forward. She had no idea what was going on, but the tension was building again and she had to break it before somebody else did.

She joined Severin and put the head of her hammer on the faerie's chest, right above the monster's clenched fist. The faerie hissed and his sleepy eyes dilated. The Machine shard Branwyn had incorporated into her hammer made it more than an ordinary hammer from the perspective of celestials. Nothing like a heavenly Machine Sword, no—after getting bitten by one of those, Branwyn was clear on the difference. But celestials and faeries still didn't seem to enjoy it.

"I told you it'd be useful," said Severin, in a voice that made Branwyn think of cracking glass. Then he vanished.

Rhianna joined Branwyn and sat on the faerie's legs. "So what happened here, Mister?"

The faerie craned his neck, trying to see Rhianna, before giving up and staring at Branwyn instead. His eyes, grey now, were bloodshot and his dirty face was tear-stained. "You're both mortals. I sent the other mortals away. But you snuck in while I was sleeping and fed the roses. I'm sorry."

His gaze shifted to the flickering sky above Branwyn. "Ah. And I'm sorry if the fire returns. You probably mean well. I don't think it can unless she wills it. I'm giving her almost everything. But that's the thing about the weather. You can never be completely sure."

"What happened here?" Branwyn asked sharply. "What destroyed the town?"

The faerie shook his head and closed his eyes. "I did."

───────

SLOWLY, Branwyn sank down onto her heels. The wind picked up, flinging dust into the air and spreading the sweet scent of the roses. The late afternoon sun was again swallowed by a cloud.

"We did think it was a faerie," Rhianna said quietly.

"One like this?" Branwyn asked tiredly, gesturing down at the filthy, limp figure between them.

Rhianna rubbed between her eyes. "No. I should have, though. When my Advisor cared more about finding the kids than catching the perp." She paused. "He seems drunk. Can faeries even get drunk?"

"I don't know. I suppose it's up to them. Rhi, I need to think for a minute. It's been a long day, and I wasn't really prepared for any of this."

Rhianna said, "Yeah. I'm sorry about that."

Branwyn stared down at the murderer on the ground. *Why* trembled on her lips, but the answer wouldn't help the people who had died and she wasn't ready to go down that rabbit hole yet. If ever. No, the people who'd lived here were dead, and nothing she could do would undo that. It was a tragedy, but it wasn't what needed her attention now.

She swallowed around the lump in her throat and tried to move on to what was currently important. It took a moment before she could. Finally, with a deep breath, she pushed down the useless anguish and moved on.

Severin worried her, even more than usual. The faerie held down by a hammer was not presently a threat. But Severin, always dangerous, had been... *wounded* somehow by the faerie's words. Branwyn had watched Severin die a year and a half ago to a monster hunter blade, witnessed his body crumble to dust as his celestial spirit fled the premises. She hadn't particularly enjoyed it. Seeing his fist clench on the faerie's chest bothered her far more than watching his throat cut.

Instinctively, she knew Severin was even more dangerous than usual right now. She had to understand why, so she could fix it.

"Who's Imani?" she asked the faerie, nudging him with her toe when it seemed like he'd fallen asleep again.

His stormy eyes flickered open. They exactly reflected the sky. "I loved her, but they hated her. They killed her. So I killed them."

Branwyn shook her head in frustration and crossed her arms over the tightness in her chest. The answer she hadn't wanted, and no further insight into why the name had so affected Severin.

"Was she a nephil?" Rhianna asked. "His child, maybe?"

The faerie frowned. "How could she be? She *came back*, angry. She was... so beautifully human."

Branwyn shivered. She'd heard something like that before from a different faerie. She hadn't liked it then, either. She didn't like any of this: the dead town, Severin's peculiar reaction, or how she would have to let Rhianna and her angel deal with the culprit. He was, no question, way out of Branwyn's league.

But she couldn't stop thinking about how once she'd argued in favor of freeing the faeries. Once she'd declared the innocent shouldn't be imprisoned alongside the guilty, that the guilty could be dealt with as individuals.

"Rhianna, ask him about the missing kids. I need to..." Branwyn shook her head. "I need to take a walk or something."

Rhianna waved absently and Branwyn walked past the rose perimeter into the town. Not too far, not so far she couldn't hear Rhianna scream. It would probably be too late by then, as it was too late now for this town. But she had to do something, or she was going to break down in a way she wasn't sure she'd fully recover from. Severin would love it.

Severin. She could do something there. She knew she could, and if she couldn't, she might as well fall apart, because why the hell not?

"Here I am," she said softly. "This is a whole new brand of feeling awful and you're not going to swing by and sample the bouquet?"

Nothing happened. The dusty ruins were still. Severin didn't appear, and the absence was worse than she'd feared. There was nothing to distract her from the awfulness, no reason to hold back her tears except her own worthless pride.

A helpless sob choked its way out of her and she clenched her fists in her hair, pulling as if the pain could clear her heart and mind. She *had* to get it together, but she felt overwhelmed, surrounded as she was by the remnants of the faerie massacre.

Then Severin touched the back of her neck and said, "Shh," just as he had earlier. Mockingly, he added, "Such a sad little voice. But hush. You've distracted me enough right now."

Branwyn closed her eyes and chose not to turn around this time. Instead she swallowed her tears and focused on her balance. After a long, slow breath, she asked, "What's going on?"

"There *must* be ghosts here, but I can't find them." His touch remained against her skin, under her hair. "I don't like that."

The wind picked up, dust stinging Branwyn's cheek. A moment later, Severin's touch faded, and she opened her eyes to see him standing in front of her, his head low as he looked at her. His gaze was inscrutable and his hands were in his pockets.

Branwyn had long ago learned that in a crisis it was never helpful for people to say, "Now what?" This *felt* like a crisis even though she didn't understand why. And doing something, *anything*, was better than waiting around.

"Is this Imani why you came along? Or are you still hoping for some kids to eat?"

Severin's eyes narrowed. "You aren't encouraging me to devour children, are you? Cupcake, that's almost… sweet."

An almost-typical response. Full attack now. "I'm not letting you *near* any kids, but you'd better not try to back out of helping us now." And the best part was, it was all true. All she wanted was his help, and for him not to eat anybody. Simple, straightforward goals.

"No," cried the faerie. Rhianna stood over him as he struggled against the weight pinning him. Branwyn was surprised the hammer was that effective. It hadn't hindered Severin at all when she'd tried to do something similar. Was the faerie so weak? How had he destroyed a town so quickly, so comprehensively?

Rhianna was using her phone, and apparently the faerie didn't like it.

"No, you can't take me away," he shouted. Lightning jumped from cloud to cloud. "I won't let you."

Prickles ran down Branwyn's back. She took a step toward her sister and Severin caught her wrist. "Wait."

The sun slipped below the cloud layer, crimson light pouring through the narrow space between storm and night. The wind dropped and picked up again. Then, with a jangle of bells Branwyn felt more than heard, somebody stepped into the world between Branwyn and Rhianna.

"That's enough," he said in a voice of bronze that pressed against Branwyn the same way Severin's aura had. Dust swirled around him, then followed him as he stepped forward, caught within the wind in his wake.

He had dark hair, and he wore an untidy black suit with the sleeves rolled up. His face was young and handsome, but celestials so often looked young and handsome that it meant nothing at all. She had no clue who he was.

But Severin did. His hand tightened on her wrist as he said, "*You.*"

The celestial gave Severin a half-smile. "Hello—"

"Don't you fucking dare," said Severin, maintaining his grip on Branwyn's wrist. She stood at an awkward angle between him and the newcomer, and she wasn't quite sure how to fix it without turning her back on the newcomer or executing a dance step that would leave her in a differently awkward position.

Still smiling, the newcomer said, "Whisperer? Ah, yes, *Severin.* I've protected her this long, Severin. But it can't go on. You're here now, so you can solve her problems. Or not, as you choose."

"No," howled the faerie, kicking his legs.

The celestial ignored him to add, "She's extremely angry. And powerful. Well done."

"I didn't make her that way," Severin said, and once again his voice reminded Branwyn of cracking glass.

The celestial shrugged as if it didn't much matter who had, and went to the faerie. "If you'll excuse me, Rhianna...."

Her eyes big and round, Rhianna stepped back with a convulsive 'feel free' gesture. Her phone slipped from her hand and the newcomer handed it back to her as he knelt beside the writhing figure.

Branwyn realized she'd followed the newcomer halfway back to the square of roses, hauling Severin behind her, clutching his wrist as tightly as he held hers. Her shoulder ached.

The newcomer picked up the hammer in the same absent way he'd returned the cell phone, setting it aside on the ground. Freed, the faerie scrambled to his feet and dashed behind his camp cot as if it was a safe barrier. The newcomer watched him while sitting on his heels.

"You promised you'd help us," gasped the faerie, compulsively rubbing his chest.

"Come now, Gale. I said I'd help you *for a time*. But this has to end, or your Court will fall. You don't want that."

"I want to *die*," wailed Gale. He looked around wildly and then darted south down the edge of town. He ran so quickly that there was no time to even consider chasing him.

The newcomer stood up, brushing off his jacket. "Don't worry. He won't leave town. Though, in fact, untangling him from Imani will be an important task if you want to preserve her."

"Where is she?" growled Severin.

"I've hidden her under my mantle," said the celestial, far too nonchalantly in Branwyn's opinion. "I'll remove it presently. But first—"

"Wait. Stop," said Branwyn. "We're going to back up here. Apparently you know all of us. But I don't know who you are." Then she added, "Severin, if you don't stop holding onto me, you're going to get more puncture wounds."

Severin's fingers loosened around her wrist, then tightened again before he released her. She rubbed her wrist and sensed him at her back, but kept her eyes on the celestial.

He nodded at her. "Branwyn Lennox. Artificer. Mother of the artificial intelligence Titanone." His tone was friendly, almost breezy as he voiced that final disturbing descriptor. "I am Shatiel. You helped save my children at the start of your career, and for that you have my gratitude." He hesitated, his pleasant expression fading. "Though I'd appreciate it if you wouldn't tell their current guardians you met me. My daughters have a good family now, and I have no desire to disrupt that."

"A deadbeat dad, eh? Well, we'll see," said Branwyn, her mouth on automatic. She knew exactly who he was talking about. Her thoughts went to the young twins that Marley protected. The super-rich half-fey rebel nephil Zachariah Thorne was their legal guardian. As much he annoyed her, he took very good care of the powerful children.

Shatiel's eyebrows flew up in surprise. "I don't think Zachariah Thorne would accept my support if I offered it. I was… rather abrupt with him the last time we met."

Branwyn waved a hand, putting that subject aside. "All right, Shatiel. Now, *who are you?*"

Shatiel paused, then curled one hand around his mouth, as if pondering a hard question.

"A new experience, Shatiel?" rasped Severin. "I just bet. He's the angels' executioner, cupcake. Every dreamborn faerie that exists has had their name and their connection to our source severed by him. Some of my siblings, too."

Shatiel looked beyond Branwyn at Severin, something old burning in his gaze. It was a long moment before he pulled his mouth to one side. "Well, now that's answered. Shall we move on?"

Severin answered before Branwyn could recapture control of the conversation. "Yes. Let's. Why did you hide Imani?"

The smile Shatiel flashed was cool and mocking. "Are you distressed, little brother? I owe you as well for your role in preserving my children. And here I thought you might appreciate me returning the favor by doing what you couldn't."

With a violent jolt, Severin's aura snapped free. Branwyn's vision filled with black needles, joining the uncomfortable pressure of Shatiel's voice on Branwyn's person. Suddenly it was hard to breathe, let alone turn her head to see what Severin was doing.

But Shatiel didn't seem to notice at all. Still smiling, he said, "Careful, little brother. You'll hurt your toys, and for nothing." Then his smile faded, and he tilted his head. "Hmm. So close to the edge. I see. Is that what's going on?" His mouth formed a word Branwyn couldn't hear and as quickly as it had appeared, Severin's aura vanished.

Branwyn took advantage of the moment to stumble out of the direct line of fire, for whatever that meant. Severin stood where she'd left him, but deep darkness spiraled around his feet, far more vivid than any other shadow in the overcast twilight. He was flexing his hands and his eyes were like black holes... but only for a moment. He shuddered, exhaled and when his gaze flicked to Branwyn and away, he seemed almost himself.

"The stories we tell ourselves, fences along the chasm," he said softly. "Why did you do that?"

"Because I shouldn't have teased you," said Shatiel. "I apologize. And because you *can* still save her, and I cannot. It would have been stupid of me to destroy the very opportunity I sought."

"Save her how?" Severin asked. He stretched his shoulders and stuffed his hands in his pockets.

"Her soul is at risk. If I hadn't hidden her, she would have been destroyed months ago." Shatiel's expression had relapsed into what seemed to be its default of pleasant interest, but Branwyn didn't buy it. The bells behind his voice were flawed.

"Are you really going to fucking lie *now*?" she demanded loudly.

Severin gave her a sidelong glance. "It doesn't really matter, cupcake—"

"Shut up. And you," Branwyn pointed her hammer at Shatiel. He blinked and glanced at the empty spot on the ground where he'd placed it. "I don't know what game you're playing but you haven't been hiding this soul out of the kindness of your heart. What have you been doing to her?"

There was a moment of possibly shocked silence. Then Rhianna whispered, "Does Grandma know you use that kind of language?"

"You know, I watched her grab Belial by the blade with her bare hand and win," said Severin, conversationally.

Branwyn ignored the peanut gallery, keeping her gaze locked onto Shatiel. She *had* won that encounter with the Sword Belial, although she'd carried the wound for months after. She was pretty confident that the angel couldn't do a damn thing to her sense of identity.

He could, of course, do a number of other awful things to her.

Instead Shatiel put his hands up in surrender. "A sin of omission, not deception, Miss Lennox. I don't talk about my work much."

"Your 'executioner' work?" she asked suspiciously.

"No," he said in a clipped tone. "Different work. Sheltering Imani and seeing what she grew into was one of my projects for a time. That time is over. The project has to end. I'd rather it not end tragically."

Branwyn shook her head, struck by the absurd dissonance. In the world she'd grown up in, this woman's death was the tragedy, but Shatiel barely seemed to register it had happened.

"Very generous of you. Bring her out," said Severin acidly.

"Soon," said Shatiel placidly.

"What are you waiting for?" Rhianna asked, in a sweet voice far removed from Severin's acid and Branwyn's frustration.

Shatiel looked at her from the corner of veiled eyes and smiled like he knew her. "The right moment, so the next moment follows after." A responding smile crept across Rhianna's face, and Branwyn wanted to vomit.

"We're taking a little breather, are we? Nobody's going to try to kill anybody for the next ten minutes? Good. Rhianna, we're overdue for a talk." Branwyn took her sister by the arm and pulled her away, a block into the town.

Rhianna followed willingly enough, raising her eyebrows at Branwyn when she finally stopped and faced her. "This isn't about the roses, is it? I warned you I was going to be doing the stupid stuff. Although I'd *hoped* you wouldn't turn it into a competition."

Branwyn didn't take the bait. "Rhianna, do you *know* him?"

Rhianna shook her head. "Nope."

"Are you sure? He seems to know you. He seems to *like* you."

Pursing her lips, Rhianna said, "Well, that could be because I was the only person not screaming at him. Or maybe my Advisor's mentioned me." Her neck and chest flushed pink.

"You love that thought," Branwyn accused.

"Well… yes. Everybody wants their boss to say nice things about them, right?" Rhianna gave her a canny look. "He's pretty hot, too."

Branwyn groaned. "Rhianna, you can't—"

Rhianna's face hardened. "Sleep with a celestial? Yes, Branwyn. I can. You should start coming to terms with that. I'm not a little girl."

"You might as well be!" Branwyn snapped and then clenched her fists in her hair again. "Rhianna, you heard him. We're *toys* to them. I know they're attractive, but—"

"Yes, you certainly do," Rhianna cut in.

Branwyn blinked. "What's that supposed to mean?"

Rhianna paced in a tight little circle. "I used to wonder why you were so certain I was about to jump into bed with my boss. It hurt, you know? But I understand now. You're *projecting*."

"*What?*"

"Oh, come on, Branwyn. I have eyes. You and your monster are all over each other. You want to screw him so badly that I'm stunned you haven't already."

"I do *not!*" Branwyn ended her denial on an unintended shout. Her vision blurred, her chest hurt and her face burned. "I don't."

Rhianna curled her lip in a skeptical sneer, raising one eyebrow in that way she'd practiced in the mirror for months. "Always sniping, but you can't stay away from each other. All that *drama*. Do I need to find a chisel?"

Branwyn stared at her sister, her head throbbing. Rhianna had practiced everything, every expression, every emotion, and yet for all that practice she never seemed to think past her immediate gratification. She couldn't begin to understand how Branwyn felt. There was no point in explaining.

She tried anyhow. "It's different."

"Yes, neither of you are dating Marley," countered Rhianna. "But otherwise?"

"You really think that's the only way it's different?" Branwyn asked incredulously. "You don't see anything a teensy bit problematic with just throwing yourself into the bed of any attractive *whatever* that happens along? No matter the consequences?"

Rhianna sighed. "And there you go again. You know what? I'm sorry I mentioned it. I thought—but never mind. You keep on looking at the big picture and refusing to see what's right in front of you."

Branwyn bit her lip so hard she tasted blood. "You think I don't see it? I do. But I also know the difference between what I want right now and what I'll want tomorrow." Rhianna's tired, knowing expression didn't even flicker, so Branwyn angrily finished with, "Clearly that's more than you've ever learned."

She regretted it as soon as she said it, and couldn't take it back because it was true all the same. Instead she dropped her gaze and walked past her sister into the rising night.

4

Haunt

IN THE DEEPENING TWILIGHT, Branwyn walked to the center of the ruined town and sat on a debris pile. She held her head in her hands, listening for the sound of anybody coming after her. When nothing stirred, she took a long, slow breath.

Then she dug out her phone. She flicked through a few messages from Titanone, that skyscraper she'd awakened to, yes, artificial life. So like a child, and her responsibility, and definitely not somebody she could talk to right now.

She sighed, flicked over to Marley's temporary number at her island paradise, and dialed it before she could convince herself it was better to huddle miserable and alone in the dark.

It rang twice before Corbin answered, half-asleep. "Yeah?"

"Hi, Corbin. It's Branwyn. Can—" Branwyn's voice broke, and she clenched her fist. "Can I talk to Marley, please?"

And now he sounded wide awake. "Branwyn... Is everything —okay, okay, here you go."

"Bran," came Marley's breathy phone voice. "Are you all right?"

"Oh, Marley," Branwyn sighed. "I've had a really shitty day, and it just keeps getting worse."

"What's going on? Where are you? I can come—"

"No!" said Branwyn. She loved the concern, loved knowing that whatever happened, Marley was on her side. But— "No. Please don't. I've got so much to track already. Stay there where it's safe. I just wanted to… talk. Please?"

"Of course!" Marley's voice was warm, but Branwyn knew her best friend well enough to understand the calculations going on under the words. She knew Marley hadn't missed one word of what she'd said, and it was so comforting she wanted to sink into it.

Briskly, Marley said, "Do you want to tell me what happened, or hear what you've been missing here?"

"Maybe the latter for a bit?" Branwyn suggested.

"Absolutely. Actually, here's Penny. I'm going to let her fill you in. We've both missed you a ton."

"That's fine, too." Penny wasn't the warmth of a childhood security blanket, but she was poise and confidence and survival. Survival, even when she'd wanted to embrace her own destruction. Branwyn hiccuped as the other end of the line changed hands.

Penny's soft voice said, "Hey, Bran. It's a good thing you called late or we probably would have missed you."

"That was absolutely on purpose," Branwyn said. "Tell me what the island's like. What am I missing?"

Without an instant's hesitation, Penny launched into a beautifully presented description of the tropical island: its art installations, its food, a glassblower's studio in the village. She'd been keeping a journal again, Branwyn could tell. She listened with half an ear as she tried to wrap words around her own thoughts.

Halfway through a description of a snorkeling trip, she blurted, "I had a fight with Rhianna, Penny."

Penny paused, then said, "Should I put this on speaker so Marley can talk too?"

"Sure," muttered Branwyn. Then, as it clicked and the sound changed, she added, "Wait, is Corbin still there?"

"Yes," said Corbin. Branwyn hesitated long enough that he said, "Fine, okay, I'll leave. But Branwyn?"

"Yeah?" she managed.

"I'll figure out how to kill him permanently if you need me to."

Branwyn put the phone on the debris heap and rested her forehead on her knees, wondering why she'd never mastered the trick of sinking into the earth as a teenager. She told herself that Corbin had access to special insights through his nephil magic, but that didn't help at all.

"Corbin…" said Marley.

"Fine, I'm going. I'm gone."

"He's gone," confirmed Penny.

"So. You were saying?" asked Marley.

Branwyn picked up the phone again. "I had a fight with Rhianna."

"Oh?" said Marley encouragingly.

"About Severin."

"Oh…" repeated Marley, in a different tone.

There was a pause before Penny said, "There's more, isn't there."

"Yeah. Kind of a lot more, but I don't want to talk about it. It's awful, but it's just stuff. I can handle it."

"All right," Marley repeated, more thoughtful than encouraging this time.

"I screamed at her like I was still in elementary school, Marley. I think I may have stomped my foot."

"About… Severin?"

"Yeah," sighed Branwyn.

"Did she suggest—?"

47

They both knew what Rhianna was like. Branwyn cut her off quickly. "Yes."

Penny asked carefully, "Are you… involved with both of them right now? Or did this come out of nowhere?"

"Something came up and I'm working on it with them. That's all the other stuff. And it's *weird*, guys. Severin has not been… *normal*." She realized something. "He didn't even get involved when I was fighting with Rhianna and he must have heard every bit of it. Oh God."

"Maybe he was being polite? Or smart?" Penny suggested doubtfully.

Marley snorted. "Him? No way. Branwyn, you're really upset. What are you more upset about: fighting with Rhianna, or… thinking about Severin?"

Branwyn's heart squeezed twice, and she said, "Both."

"Wow. No wonder you called us," said Penny.

Marley shushed her. "But you're working with them on something. Okay." She went silent for a long moment, and Branwyn wondered if she was taking notes. She always seemed to take notes.

"All right." Marley started up again. "Bran, I can't help you with Severin. I know you can handle that yourself, because only you know what's best for you. Rhianna is… harder."

"I don't understand how she can be like this," managed Branwyn, without wailing. "One minute we're walking along and it's just like old times and the next minute she's making eyes at a celestial and telling me she's going to sleep with them."

"Do you think she's changed?" Marley asked.

"Yes!" Branwyn's own words came back to haunt her. "I don't know. Maybe she hasn't. Maybe she's never been who I thought she was."

"Ah," said Marley, as if Branwyn had given her the key to a riddle. "All right. Branwyn, you're on a project. Rhianna is a long-term problem; getting that project done is not. If you don't have to be Rhianna's sister to do it, don't. Just be her coworker. Deal with who she *is*, not who you thought she was."

Branwyn stared at her phone unseeing. Somebody on the other end covered the speaker and a muffled argument ensued, but Branwyn hardly noticed. She was Branwyn, Action Girl, and she got things done. Yeah, she was shaken by her argument with Rhianna, and the stress of Severin's strangeness was a pressure on her psyche as powerful as his aura. That was stuff she'd eventually have to confront.

But her relationships with Rhianna and Severin had nothing to do with the stolen kids. They weren't relevant to solving the problem with the faerie and the dead woman and the angel's executioner. She had to put them aside. She *could* put them aside.

Marley knew it. Maybe Branwyn's sense of herself had been wounded by Rhianna's accusations, but Marley believed she was sound. Marley trusted her judgement.

And Marley, clever Marley, was saying *exactly* the right things. The muffled argument continued and Branwyn said, "Uh, guys?"

Somebody uncovered the mic. Marley was speaking. "—I know, but she needs to get there on her—oh."

Branwyn noticed but decided not to mention it. Because even if Marley's feelings were more complicated than she was sharing, she was, in fact, saying the right things. Marley was reminding Branwyn that Branwyn believed in herself. "Thanks."

"Are you feeling better?" asked Marley.

"I'm feeling more like me. It'll have to do."

"Wait a minute—" Penny began.

"Penny, she's—"

"No, you hush, Marley. You made a very nice speech and now it's my turn. Bran. When was the last time you ate? Drank? Did all the other things human bodies need to keep functioning?"

Branwyn blinked. "Uh." Lunch had been a long time ago, and it had been a warm afternoon full of exercise and empty of drinking water.

"I thought so," said Penny grimly. "You always do this. Do you have access to those things?"

Branwyn thought about the abandoned campsite, with its boxes of supplies. "I can probably find something…"

"You'd better. I understand why you don't want us there right now but if I don't get a better report when I call again in twelve hours, I'm sending out the Marines, and then I'm calling your mother."

Branwyn went cold. "Don't you dare."

Penny was unmoved. "Eat something.

"Branwyn?" called Rhianna in the distance.

"And there she is," sighed Branwyn. "I will, Penny. Thanks." She disconnected the call before it could get drawn out any further, and took a few breaths. Then she called back, "I'm here," and waved the glowing face of her phone overhead.

But she didn't get up to go meet her sister, didn't even turn her direction. It was weak and cowardly, but she wasn't ready to start the conversation. As her sister scuffed towards her, she kept her head down, trying to be ready for anything.

Something cool pressed against her neck, through her hair. "Thirsty?" asked Rhianna. The chill against her skin disappeared and a large, frosty bottle of water appeared in front of Branwyn.

She took it and opened it and drank a third before saying, "Thanks." Then she frowned. "Where did this come from?"

"I made the monster and the angel go get supplies," Rhianna said, as if it was an ordinary thing. "There's hot food at the rose house, too. If you come now, you can eat something before Shatiel does whatever he's planning on doing." She glanced at the horizon, which only had an echo of crimson staining the clouds.

"Made?" asked Branwyn suspiciously, mostly to hide her relief that Rhianna didn't want to continue their earlier talk. But of course, Rhianna was a professional.

"Well, I suggested it to Shatiel, because he seems nice and he does know my Advisor, and he was clearly just killing time. I told him how we'd come kind of spontaneously and how the camp supplies were old and would take a while to prepare, and we'd *probably* be fine but if he wasn't doing anything, I knew my Advisor would really be happy he was looking out for me, though he'd definitely scold me for getting into this situation in the first place—and around that point, Severin came back with the water bottles and fast food bags and told me to shut up already."

Rhianna paused for breath and then kept going in a rush. "And then Shatiel laughed, and *he* disappeared and almost immediately came back with one of those emergency preparedness backpacks and handed it to me. And then Severin got this annoyed look on his face and he disappeared again and when he came back, he had your overnight bag, although I think he packed it by sweeping your entire bathroom sink into it because it was overflowing."

"It was mostly packed already," said Branwyn faintly.

"Yeah? Oh, right, they invited you to that island thing. Anyhow, I grabbed the water and left them staring at each other. Shatiel kept smiling but Severin was *not*. I figure if we stay away long enough, we might come back to one of those portable showers." She gave Branwyn a hopeful look.

"You said there was food," said Branwyn firmly. "I need that. And I don't want to miss whatever the angel is going to do."

"All right then," said Rhianna agreeably, and walked beside her in silence back to the rose-covered ruins.

Shatiel stood in the center of the ruins, watching their return, while Severin stalked around the perimeter of the house like a tiger in a cage. There was no camp shower. Rhianna sighed her disappointment loudly.

"Look. They're back. On their own. Because it's *safer* here. *I want to see Imani.*" That was Severin. Branwyn shook her head and darted past him to the fast food bag on the faerie's cot. French fries and a fish sandwich: not her favorite but anything would do.

"Perhaps not safer right now, but it will be once I uncloak her," said Shatiel. "It's time, in any case. She'll be less confused now that the sun has set." He gave Branwyn, stuffing fries in her mouth, a speculative look, and she gave him a 'get on with it' gesture.

In response, he lifted his head. The breeze that had never stopped making whirlwinds behind him expanded like his aura, blowing gently in every direction at once. Silent silver lightning traced lines in the clouds overhead.

No, not in the clouds. It was much closer. The light flickered again and again in a jagged, toothed pattern. The silence became oppressive, and Branwyn opened her mouth to see if she could hear herself speak. Then the sky cracked open, and a nightmare poured out.

It was bright instead of dark, but it was a strange brightness, the brightness of death. It was light that made everything it touched darker: withered and wounded and lost. Discordant tones echoed in the air, stealing the flavor of screams and mad laughter. The shadows of the burned town stretched across the ground. In each house, the windows had eyes and hands against the bars. The smell of blood and char assailed Branwyn. She dropped her bag of food and tried to keep down what she'd already eaten. Swallowing hard, she looked around.

The sky was ink and the world beyond the rose house and the edge of the town vanished into the same blackness. Shatiel had said he was revealing what he'd hidden, but this felt instead as if he'd taken them into a secret place, a bubble set apart from the world.

The rose house had a ghost shadow just like the other buildings. But in its shadow, flames flickered at the windows. "Imani," called Shatiel.

The random tones in the air fell silent. Then the flames flowed together, and a woman gowned in fire and carved of light rose out.

"I feel the wind, Shatiel," she said. Her voice was musical and vibrant. "Where is my lover? What have you done?" Her gaze wandered around the rose house, passing over Branwyn and Rhianna as if she didn't see them. When she got to Severin, standing just outside the rose perimeter, she said, "Oh...."

"Hello, Imani," he said softly. "I'm sorry I was late."

The stench of blood grew stronger, and a burning wind whipped the flames of Imani's ballgown into an inferno. "Sev... er...in..." she whispered. "They came for me, but you didn't. I've been waiting for you ever since."

Imani's flames reflected in Severin's eyes like dying suns. "That wasn't a good idea, little star. It looks like you've gotten yourself trapped."

"Not trapped," breathed Imani. "Anchored. Growing." She held out her hand to him and all the shadows leaned toward him too. "I'm so angry, Severin. You know about anger. Let me punish you."

His face remote, Severin said, "Another bad idea. You've spent too much time in the wrong company."

Imani hissed and the shadows lunged toward him. The black vortex around his feet sprang into spinning motion and held the shadows away. He put his hands in his pocket and leaned forward as if pressing against a barrier.

"Stay in the rose house," said Shatiel quietly, suddenly standing right between Branwyn and Rhianna. "You're relatively safe here. If you step outside, she'll make you part of her nightmare without ever realizing you exist."

"What happening with him?" asked Rhianna in a tiny voice. "Where are we?"

"I'm monitoring my little brother. Don't be afraid there." Shatiel probably intended to be comforting, but at least for Branwyn, he failed utterly.

The shadowy forces beating at Severin slackened, although Imani still blazed brightly. "You always say no," she said bitterly.

"Every time I conjure you. Why are you here? To taunt me more? To tell me I should have listened? I hate you. Go away and let me burn in peace."

"I only came here for Charlie." Severin had scarcely said those cold words before the whole shadow town outside the rose house exploded into flame.

"Gale! Gale! Come out, my love!" shrieked the spectre. Real lightning crackled, driving itself into the earth at the center of town and the edges of the nightmare world. A figure formed out of the sparks and walked to the rose house, head down. The tones in the air began again, and every scream and laugh and chime became words: *Charlie, Gale, burn.*

"Gale! Where's Charlie, Gale? I can't find her. Did you burn her, too?" The ghost's voice was a blade and Branwyn covered her ears instinctively. She couldn't hear what Gale said, but she didn't need to hear to understand the miserable little shrug.

What are we supposed to do about this? she wondered. Soothe the ghost and send her off, she supposed. But ghostbusting was another sister's job—

That was when the clarion sound of a horn echoed in the nightmare space and once again the sky cracked open. With a rushing, jangling percussive noise, dogs and horses and riders spilled through the hole and the Wild Hunt flew to earth.

5

Hunt

"AND NOW THE PROBLEM ARRIVES," said Shatiel in his pleasant way and walked out of the rose house to meet the Wild Hunt.

Branwyn shook her head. The Wild Hunt had a vibrant, intense reality that made the shrieking of the ghost no more than tinny sound from a screen. The breath of the horses and the shifting of their tack was almost overwhelming in comparison.

Branwyn's younger sister Brynn's voice was another splash of creek water as she said, "*Branwyn?* What are you doing here? And Rhianna too?"

Branwyn had to shake her head again. She knew what Brynn had become although she tried not to think about it very much. She'd been there at the beginning, but she'd never seen Brynn in working clothes, metaphorically speaking. The superrealism was disorienting.

...Although in this case, Brynn's actual working clothes seemed to be her summer pajamas. All six of the riders were in some state of undress. The two young men were both shirtless in pajama bottoms; blonde ex-vampire Amber was in a short, silky nightgown, teenage AT was in a rumpled long t-shirt and unbuttoned cut-offs, and Jennifer, the eldest of the group, wasn't wearing much more than a man's button-down shirt.

Amber covered a yawn as she looked around. "Wow. This is… how did we miss this?"

Severin said in a low voice, "No fucking way this is happening."

"This is bad," said Jennifer, holding the Horn. She dismounted and her horse dropped its head to nuzzle the dogs around AT. "Hello, Branwyn. I'd love to know what you've been doing here. We may have to make sure you can never do it again."

"I just got here today," said Branwyn, with an artificial calm. Severin was circling the rose house again, and the ghost Imani hovered high above Shatiel. The air tingled with tension. "I think you're better off talking to the angel here."

Jennifer refocused on Shatiel, whom she'd apparently simply overlooked to accost Branwyn. "Oh. Not just a tourist, then. Who are you?"

"I know who he is," said Cat, who was himself the remnant of an angel. "We were all wondering how a haunt this powerful manifested so quickly. But it was you, wasn't it, Shatiel?"

"Yes. I hid her for a while," said Shatiel.

"That's not okay," said Jennifer. Her calm was otherworldly. "Do you have any idea what's happening here?"

"I do," said Shatiel. "Which is why it has to end. One way or another."

"Jen, this is a mess," said Yejun, the younger of the two men, who was staring up at Imani and the brightness behind her.

"Yes. Well, Shatiel, we'll have to deal with you after we deal with this. Don't go anywhere."

"Jennifer," said Shatiel quietly, and some of the shine vanished off Jennifer's superreality. She blinked and sudden tension hunched her shoulders.

"Shatiel, don't make this harder than it has to be," said Cat. "You are who you are, but we're a lot more than that."

"Cat," said Shatiel, even more softly, and the blond man lost a portion of his shine. "This is not yet a fight. All I want you to do is… wait a little."

With an edge to her voice, Jennifer said, "I don't think we can. I think we need to destroy this *now*."

Severin's low voice said, "*Bad idea*," but nobody but Branwyn seemed to hear it because the three younger members of the Wild Hunt burst out with their own protests.

Yejun said, "Whoa…."

"We can't—" said AT

"We have to at least *try*, Jen," said Brynn. Then she added, "Branwyn and Rhianna are here. We can probably do something." Her faith would have been touching if it wasn't so frightening.

"People," said Amber, who had also been watching Imani. "This ghost is furious. I don't know if waiting is a good idea."

"We're in the middle of nowhere," pointed out AT. "Who can she hurt? Not us. Not the angel."

"Well, those two are still mortal," said Amber, pointing at Rhianna and Branwyn without looking at them. "And there's all those other souls she's keeping locked in torment."

Jennifer pressed her forehead to the Horn. "Let me see how bad it is…" The horses shifted around and most of the rest of the Hunt dismounted. Only Amber remained on her horse, staring up at the ghost above them.

Then Jennifer's eyes snapped open. "What the *hell* have you *done?* This isn't a haunt, it's… an abomination. This will eat through the world if we don't deal with it."

Shatiel said, "Yes," and then added as an afterthought, "I'm sorry, I thought you already knew that."

Through gritted teeth, Jennifer said, "I know it now far better than you do, asshole."

With a little shrug, Shatiel said, "Possibly true. Nonetheless, I wish for you to release rather than destroy this soul."

"You are insane," said Jennifer. "Kids, I don't know how it happened, but this abomination has more power than some gods, and it's right on the edge of going critical in a way we'd all regret. I know you want to save her, but that almost never works and we do not have the time to argue about it."

"*Make time.*" Suddenly Severin was right in front of the Wild Hunt, rippling with darkness. Judging from their group recoil, they hadn't realized he was there. "Or you'll have a brand new problem on your hands."

Imani started singing, and the distant beauty of the song was completely untouched by lyrics of blood and rage. It made Branwyn's skin crawl.

"Yeah, that's no good," said Yejun, after a quick glance up.

"Good doesn't enter into it, kid. There's just smart, and stupid." Severin's eyes were wide and his pupils pinpoints.

Jennifer said, "Yes, this is stupid. You can't stop us. I'm making this happen." Her superreality flickered and returned, stronger than before. The dogs milling around AT looked up, fixing their gaze on the ghost above Shatiel.

AT whimpered and Yejun took her hand. "We always knew we couldn't save all of them."

Brynn said, "We hardly save any of them."

"Stupid, stupid," muttered Severin. When he reached out to grab Jennifer, his hand passed right through her, as if he was a shadow himself. His face twisted with frustration and rage.

The dogs surged into the air in a sudden convulsive leap. Gale, who had been no more than crouching scenery near Shatiel, looked up. "No, no, no… no, no!"

Lightning flared around Imani and her song became a thunderous chant. Suddenly she wasn't faded and distant anymore, but a blossom of fire in the sky. The dogs barked, sprang and fell away, cringing from the flames. The living shadows of the ruined houses sprang into sharp relief and then yawned open, reaching for the Wild Hunt.

A golden glow sprang up around them in response. Amber's horse reared and Cat said, "She *is* strong. And growing fast."

"We're stronger," said Jen grimly, and blew the Horn. A bright, intense sound emerged, higher than the sonorous notes that had brought them into the nightmare. The shadow edges shivered and started to dissolve. Imani's song stuttered.

Severin's eyes emptied, becoming flat and shark-like. He looked up at the ghost and raised a hand. "*Imani,*" he said, and the sound of his voice caused Branwyn's nails to bite into her palms.

"Ah, and there he goes," said Shatiel, quietly conversational. "Rhianna, Branwyn, you must absolutely stay close."

The black vortex around Severin's feet climbed up his body and followed his outstretched arm. Gale, moaning nearby, switched to shouting, "Yes! Yes! Do it!"

Imani reached down a flickering hand.

AT shuddered. "He's helping her grow faster!"

"Uh," said Yejun. "I don't think it's a good idea to let him do that."

Amber and her horse lunged forward, trailing golden sparks. She swept her hand down on Severin like it was a hammer, but all it took was a single step to avoid her.

"It doesn't matter anyhow," he said flatly. "You aren't built to stop *me*." A distortion wavered between him and Imani, and the brightness around Imani flared painfully.

Lightning crackled all around them. Branwyn saw the look of horror on Jennifer's face and her baby sister Brynn clinging to AT. Rhianna was holding onto Branwyn's back, giggling hysterically. Severin reached out to the ghost like a hellscape version of the Sistine Chapel ceiling.

Somebody's description of Severin came back to Branwyn: "He wants to destroy *everything*. That's just his nature." A hated voice, a distrusted speaker, but at that moment, Branwyn was sure he'd been telling the truth. The ghost would burn a hole in the world and Severin was *helping* her.

"They *aren't* built to stop you, are they?" said Shatiel. He held out his hand and the wind at his back swirled in. The ghostly inferno above dimmed once again. "But I am." He said something. A name. It vanished from Branwyn's mind as soon as she heard it, but she knew it had been a name. Then Shatiel's outstretched fist closed.

Severin sagged, staggered, and collapsed to his knees like a puppet with its strings cut. His darkness and his aura vanished completely as his eyes closed. His head drooped. Branwyn wasn't even sure if he was breathing. He was like a machine that had simply been switched off.

———

BRANWYN STARED at Severin's body in blank shock until Rhianna smacked her on the back and she remembered to breathe herself. Then horror overtook the shock, as she understood, on an extremely visceral level, what made Shatiel so dangerous to celestials.

"Now," said Shatiel in his bronze voice. "I cannot take what makes the Wild Hunt the Hunt, but I can take what makes you each individuals. Please stop attacking my charge for a moment, or I will do so."

"The abomination is still growing," hissed Jennifer.

"Yes," agreed Shatiel. "But perhaps there's something we can do about that. Miss Branwyn Lennox, would you mind looking? You have a unique insight."

While Branwyn tried to pull her gaze away from Severin's slack face, Jennifer said, "I already looked. She can't see nearly as deeply as we can. Not here."

Rhianna, who finally had her giggles under control, squeezed

Branwyn's hand. Branwyn dragged in a breath and tried to push past her own distress at Severin's collapse.

She just... he'd been *right there* and now he *wasn't*. It wasn't like when Simon had killed Severin's previous vessel. There'd been a clear cause and effect there: knife, throat, poof. But all Shatiel had done was close his hand, and Branwyn had no idea whether it was permanent.

She shouldn't care if it was or wasn't. He'd been trying to help Imani hurt the world. She shouldn't care... but she did. They'd been *working together*.

That had to be it. It was just the phenomenon known as *misattribution of arousal*. People in tense, frightening situations together felt closer, but it was a trickery of increased heart rate and adrenalin. It made haunted houses popular for dates.

This was one hell of a haunted house. And she'd been caught in the middle of high-powered supernatural spats before. She ought to be used to this by now.

She wasn't, though.

"Can't she? Let's find out. When you're ready, Branwyn."

She stretched her neck, letting herself be calm. "What exactly do you want me to do?"

Shatiel gave her a friendly smile, still holding his fist in front of him. "Due to her own native gifts, the context of her death, and the power of her lover, Imani has become something other than an ordinary ghost. The structure of the world cannot bear the weight of what she is growing into. The Wild Hunt would solve this by destroying her. I think that's an unnecessary tragedy. But it's true she is a clear and present threat to a world we are all —almost all—of us bound to protect. It's my theory you can grant us an extension. Build us a cage, Branwyn. Or reinforce the world. Whichever you choose."

"Or we just end it now," said Jennifer. "What you're suggesting can't be done here." She glanced quickly at AT and Brynn, still hanging onto each other, and added, "Maybe another time, with an ordinary corrupted ghost rather than an abomination...."

"No, I think we'll try it here and now," said Shatiel. "Or, if you prefer, I'll release my little brother and let him get on with his business. You could have a race to see if he can pour his strength into her faster than you can devour it." His mouth curved in the same mocking smile he'd given Severin before. "Fair warning, though. My brother was an angel of growth once upon a time."

Cat sighed and spread his fingers. "Shatiel, don't try to coerce the Wild Hunt."

"Is that what I'm doing?" Shatiel looked amused.

Amber leaned down from her horse, annoyed. "You don't rule *us*, angel."

"Of course not," Shatiel agreed. "I rule other things." He glanced down at his fist.

Branwyn glanced at the inert vessel of the erstwhile angel of growth and sighed. She was already tired of the bickering and posturing. "Look, you kids argue it out while I see if I can do anything. If you do decide to shatter the world, give me a shake so I can see the fireworks." She knelt down and drove her fingers into the ashen earth. Then she activated the Sight she'd resisted using thus far.

She wasn't entirely surprised to discover that things mostly looked the same. The ghost's nightmare had torn a hole through most of the layers of the world. Here, the Backworld and the normal world had merged into one, and the Geometry underlying it all had warped it into frayed and knotted strands.

She still heard the argument going on over her head: sound without meaning, but still too much distraction. She pushed herself into the Geometry as she'd only previously done with Titanone. Titanone was so big it was all but required for deep work on the skyscraper, but despite its size, it was a bounded, cohesive entity. Unexpectedly, she found this place was too.

Part of the cohesion arose from the nightmarish haunt, and

part of it echoed from the fire that had destroyed the town, but there was... something else too, something much older. It was nothing she'd seen before, so all she could do was take note of it.

Branwyn recalled Rhianna pointing out the isolation of the town. Touching the thin lines that bound Tucker to the world beyond, she wondered if it had been easier than expected to downplay the death of the town. It would, she decided, be so very nice to sit down Rhianna's Advisor and pry answers out of him.

The Geometry shivered around her as the powerful entities arguing in Tucker spread their powers. It ruined her brief fantasy of extorting answers from Umbriel, and she sighed and turned her attention back to the nightmare itself.

The self-containment of the town made it easier to see the whole thing from her otherwise limited perspective. The nightmare world was rooted in the earth, and in the human-built structures whose patterns lingered even after the original buildings had burned down. They formed the horrible shadows. But they were all tied to a crimson fire at the core, and somehow the crimson fire was hurting the world.

She brushed over the knots on the strands that ran through the town. They could become nodes of sentience if she wanted, but she shuddered away from that. Waking this place would bring something fundamentally broken to life, and to pain.

She thought about that for a moment, and realized it wouldn't even be a very long life, because the world truly would break rather than contain it. The Wild Hunt hadn't been exaggerating. She wondered if that breaking point was what Shatiel had been observing, in his mysterious illicit project.

Branwyn traced more significant strands, finding where Gale had woven himself into the pattern. She saw he was more than he seemed. But he'd put so much of himself into his lover's haunting that he was barely a fragmentary person now. She saw other elements, too: hints at stories she didn't have a key to interpreting, and materials she'd never shaped. Sometimes she was so proud of her skill as an artificer, at being *The Artificer,* but as soon as she stepped outside her studio, she found more she didn't understand than did.

Build a cage, Shatiel had said. But that couldn't be her first choice, or her second choice, or possibly any choice except her last one, her last action. *Or reinforce the world. Your choice.* Branwyn didn't know how to do that, either. She wasn't a wizard; she wasn't a celestial. She was an Artificer; she worked on bounded objects, and 'the world' was far, far too big for her.

She studied the knots and frayed parts of the pattern again, then tried to reach into the closest knot. In her normal work, she pinched Geometrical intersections into nodes, but as part of that, she could also smooth unfinished nodes away again. What were these knots but unfinished nodes? And if she smoothed them away, the fraying parts of the pattern ought to stabilize, at least for a while.

But while she could perceive the nearest knot, she couldn't touch it. Titanone's existing nodes and self-awareness made the whole bounded structure more accessible. Here, if she wanted to touch the natal nodes, she'd have to walk to them.

"Shut up," she said out loud. "Haven't you argued enough? I think I *can* slow down what you're afraid of, but I need some kind of transport so I can get around this town while working."

A chorus of voices demanded to know what she was going to do: Yejun, Cat and Jennifer, she guessed. The knots in the pattern swelled. "How about I explain after I'm done?"

"I'd like that," said Shatiel. "Arrange transportation, Wild Hunt. I will stay here and contain my brother and the ghost for a while longer. But the sooner Branwyn does her work, the better."

Amber said, aghast, "You mean he might get up again?" and then, "Uh, why are you smiling like that?"

"Come on!" Branwyn snapped. Then something big and warm knocked into her back.

"Oh!" said Brynn, and Rhianna said, "You get to ride the pretty pony, Bran."

Branwyn blinked, completely losing her perception of the town's Geometric pattern. Her sister's horse stood beside her, and another horse was pushing her from behind. Over her head, Amber was looking with real concern between Severin and Shatiel, while Shatiel gave her a smile that was disturbingly similar to Severin's. Above, AT's dogs prowled around and around the faded form of the ghost.

"Here, I'll help you mount," said Brynn briskly, making a step with her hand. Branwyn, a little dazed from the perceptual switch, put her hand on her little sister's head. Rhianna was shorter than her too, but Rhianna was very definitely grown. Brynn was still going through puberty. She was tiny.

"You put your foot here, not your hand there, Bran," said Brynn with exasperation. "Please help us save this ghost. It's important to us."

When Branwyn did put her foot into her sister's clasped fingers, her sister boosted her with an unsurprising but depressing strength straight up into the horse's saddle. The horse shifted to make sure she didn't fall as she caught her balance and slung her legs into the right position.

"Yejun, Cat, go with her," said Jennifer.

"AT, Yejun, go with her," said Cat, and Jennifer threw him a frustrated look.

"That's fine," said AT, and she and Yejun remounted.

Brynn said, "Hey, what about me? I was going to go."

"You're staying here in case something goes wrong," said Jennifer. "You're the Master of Horses, and you're a distraction to Branwyn."

Branwyn had nothing to add to this, so she nodded at Yejun and AT. All three horses moved away from the rose house into the town, and Branwyn concentrated on making sure she wouldn't fall off. She patted the horse's neck. "Sorry I'm not a better rider…"

"Where do you need to go, Branwyn?" asked AT.

"I need to follow the pattern of the town and interact with parts." She glanced at the ground, which seemed awfully far away given that the horse's feet were on it. "I can touch them from here, I think…" She focused on the Geometry again, pushed herself into the vision, and reached out for the line underneath her. To her surprise, it was easier to reach than when she was touching the earth. It was something about the horse, she thought. It had as many nodes as a human, each filled with some-thing she couldn't parse, and arranged differently.

Well. That was an interesting bit of trivia to share next time she needed something from a wizard. She filed it away and returned to focusing on the pattern of the town. When she spotted the nearest swelling self-knot, she waved. "That way."

Once she was close enough, she reached down and stroked the line. The knot was hard, like an inflamed cyst. It resisted being smoothed out; it was far denser than she had expected. She looked closer and recoiled so hard she almost fell off the horse. "Oh my god."

The knot was a *person*, or at least the pattern of a person. Another ghost, she realized, bound very small and tied into the nightmare. And there were hundreds throughout Tucker.

The horse backed up and sidestepped beneath her, and then AT caught her elbow. "I don't want to say *what?* because I can probably guess, but don't fall off, Branwyn."

"No," Branwyn managed. She leaned forward, wrapping her arms around the horse's neck. It was probably rude, but she needed the support. Then she watched as the knot pulsed again. She'd thought she could just smooth them out—they'd knot back up again as time passed, but that would take time, time they could spend finding another solution. But she couldn't smooth out a soul in torment.

She'd *said* she'd do this, though. She'd promised a client, without even making sure it was possible. Once again, she'd set herself up to fail, and this time, what would fail with her?

Severin. Severin would, at the very least. Severin, who should have heard those thoughts and laughed at her, pushed her, teased her, distracted her. Inflamed her. She hated him, yet she wished he was there now, pushing her past her limits instead of slumped like a broken toy on the ground.

From somewhere, she thought she heard her great-grandmother clearing her throat. Her great-grandmother: who had died when she was a teen, who had been sweet and dreamy and unstoppably fierce in her own way. She'd raised Branwyn's feminist grandmother alone, and the two of them had raised Branwyn's mother, and all three of them had raised Branwyn. Suddenly she was furious at herself.

Rhianna and Brynn were here. Her little sisters believed in her.

Hah, she said to herself. *Look what he's done to me. I don't need some sadistic bastard to get stuff done. I can go past what's sane all on my own. Right, Mom, Grandma?*

The last time she'd been this frustrated, she'd grabbed a Machine Sword by the blade and used the forge of her soul to invert it. She'd fought a battle for her name, and tiny fragments of the sword had leached into the wound. She suspected they were still in her now.

And what had she learned from that? Before that experience, she'd only ever used fragments of the celestial Machines to make things *more.* But when she'd first learned of Machines, she'd been told they ordered the structure of the universe and devoured celestials that got too close. And she'd used a bespoke Machine shard to repair Penny's soul once.

Somehow, they could bring power to inanimate objects, but they also *ate* angels. They could inject energy into a system, and they could take it away.

Some things couldn't be solved with a gentle touch. She *knew* that.

She slid off the horse's back and took her hammer in the hand Belial had marked. Then she focused on the knot and brought down the hammer.

It wasn't a violent blow, but it shivered through the twisted soul. The nameless Machine fragment in her hammer couldn't actually damage a mortal soul, but she didn't want it to. All she wanted to do was temporarily remove energy from the system. So she used the hammer to *unlock* the soul while she reached out with her other hand and *squeezed*.

The swelling knot diminished, the energy that inflamed it flowing into the black diamond on the hammer. The transfer happened quickly, and when it completed, the knot was only a lump, and the black diamond was warm and dizzy in her mind.

Branwyn rubbed the stone. A moment's evaluation told her much more than she needed to know. She picked out the important details: the energy of the corrupted node would only remain a brief time, and the black diamond could not possibly hold all the energy she had to extract from the nightmare system.

"I need something," she rasped. "Quickly. A battery. I need a battery that can hold souls. And I'm going to have to walk so I can swing the hammer.."

"Oh *hell*," said Yejun.

"Um," said AT. "Yeah. Yejun, stay with her and I'll go get Brynn."

Brynn.

Branwyn remembered, on that troubling Halloween when the Wild Hunt had been reborn, that Brynn had been covered in tattoos, tiny dark marks like writing that had unfolded into souls when the time had come.

Branwyn bit her lip hard, then shook her head and walked to the next knot. Some things couldn't be solved by a gentle touch. She still knew that. She *knew* that. No gentle salvation for lost souls, no shelter for her own feelings by keeping Brynn from what she'd been remade to do.

She went through four knots before AT returned with Brynn. The black diamond on the hammer was sparking fitfully as it tried to make room for a fifth charge. Rhianna came with them, her hands behind her back like she was out for a stroll.

Brynn eyed the sparking hammer. "AT said you needed me to hold some souls."

Branwyn ground her teeth. "I need *something*. I don't know how to load them into you though."

"I've been watching you," said Yejun. "I think I can do it. I'm not actually sure anybody else could."

"Great. How do I get them to you?"

Yejun grinned at her. He was disturbingly cute in a far-too-young-for-her way. "You don't have to. You just squeeze those babies and I'll catch what's released. AT, you and the dogs have to help me."

No gentle touch. No time to argue, or even be skeptical. Branwyn said, "Fine. Keep up," and ran to the next node.

And Yejun's plan seemed to basically work. He had to adjust parts, and when he did, AT's dogs chased down bright energy streamers like they were Frisbees. Over and over, Branwyn swung her hammer and squeezed knots. Dark marks shimmered onto Brynn's skin, while Brynn looked more bored than troubled by the proceedings. At one point Branwyn thought she saw Brynn glancing at a phone. Later she looked again and there was no sign of it.

That was the point at which Rhianna tripped Branwyn as she dashed to the next node, then tried to catch her as she fell. Branwyn tumbled down anyhow, pulling her sister down with her and bruising her shoulder on the shaft of her hammer.

Stunned, Branwyn lay still as Rhianna sprang to her feet. "Sorry about that. I felt like I should tell you this isn't going to work."

She glanced around, seemed to realize everybody was semi-stunned, and kept going anyhow. "Look, it comes down to math, doesn't it? I've been timing you, and I know how many people died here, and Angel back there, or, uh, Not-Umbriel as I keep reminding myself, uh, anyhow, that guy said we'd have at least until dawn to sort this out, which means 'at most until dawn' for *this* plan. I mean, we all heard him. But Branwyn doesn't hear anything when she's focused. Which is why I had to trip her. And you guys didn't tell her. Even though I bet you can do math, too."

Branwyn frowned. Her first thought, that Rhianna was unusually nervous, was quickly superseded by the news of the deadline nobody had told her about. She sat up, around the same time the stunned kids started moving again. But all they did was glance at each other in some silent communion and listen to Rhianna.

"So anyhow, you just don't have the time. Too long per stop, too many stops. Too much running." She paused significantly. "Way too much running. Because way before dawn, Branwyn would die of exhaustion. Interval training isn't meant to be done for hours on end, guys, especially not 3x interval training targeting aerobic, anaerobic, and Geometric systems!"

She stopped and dragged in another breath. "Right! Right, so anyhow I thought I should stop you and ask a question. It might be important, and if it's not, we're not losing much, are we? Mathemagics. So. Um." Her eyes were very bright as she looked around. "Why are you running to the souls rather than making the souls come to you?"

Branwyn frowned, trying to parse the question, but once again, the three younger members of the Wild Hunt exchanged looks.

"We're the *Hunt*," said AT.

"We do have to hunt them down," agreed Brynn apologetically.

"The Horn doesn't have any real range, ma'am." That was

Yejun, politely charming and so wrongly attractive. Branwyn rubbed her face and tried to climb to her feet. It took a few tries.

"Why would it need to? You were going to tear down this whole hellscape down from the south edge. Do whatever you were going to do, and just stop before you swallow. Er, or substitute the right metaphor there."

"It's not that easy!" AT looked annoyed. "It'd only work... on..."

Yejun picked up where she'd trailed off. "But we'd need help. Something to slow it down suddenly..."

"A plug for the horn." Brynn's eyes widened, and she jumped up and down. "A mute. Like what Tia did in our first episode!"

Branwyn blinked again and shook her head. She simply couldn't follow what they were talking about. The night sparkled and sang around her, and in the distance she thought she saw a line of ghostly dancers. She said, "Are things are getting weird?"

Rhianna rubbed her arms and watch the Wild Hunt jabber at each other. "Yeah, I kind of noticed that too. There was a lady in a princess hat earlier..."

Suddenly all three Huntsfolk turned and ran back to the rose house, waving and screaming in excitement, the dogs chasing them. Branwyn and Rhianna stared after, until Rhianna said, "Uh. Do you think they liked my idea?"

A moment later, Brynn came running back, still waving her arms and screaming. She skidded to a halt in front of Branwyn, her hands clasped for a boost. "Come on, come on," she panted. "Get up, let's get back there." Somehow Branwyn found herself half on a moving horse that seemed to fly back to the edge of town.

When she fell off the horse at the rose bower, there was a four-way argument going just outside the perimeter. As Brynn pounded up and dived into it, Branwyn realized it wasn't an argument, it was a *collaboration*. Only AT stood apart. She smiled as she helped Branwyn to her feet. "You're so bruised already,

Branwyn. I wanted to thank you for trying this, but I can't thank you enough. Take it easy for a few minutes. We *will* make this work, somehow, and we'll need you then, too." She squeezed Branwyn's hand and pointed her at the cot in the interior of the rose house.

Then she grabbed Rhianna's hand with both of hers, bringing it to her chest. "And you! I will *never* be able to thank you. If we can do this… oh my God. We could really make some progress. Come explain it to the others, won't you please?"

As Branwyn sank down onto the cot near Shatiel, AT pulled Rhianna into that massive, insane collaboration.

"What… what is going on?" Branwyn asked. She realized everybody else was over in that huddle. It was just her and Shatiel, and of course the living corpse of somebody she—of a monster.

"Several things. Good job, by the way. Out there. Figuring this out."

Branwyn snorted. "I didn't figure out a winning solution, so you might hold off on the praise."

He smiled. "Didn't you? Well, I'm not disappointed. When you ask what's going on, what are you really asking?"

Branwyn gestured at the collaboration in progress. "Why are they suddenly so excited?"

He dropped his voice in a confiding way. "Well, my theory is that they've been puzzling over a way to non-destructively deal with corrupted souls and their haunts, and something your sister said gave them the missing piece of the puzzle."

"Oh," said Branwyn, slowly.

"I could tell that with you, they had hope. But it was such an unlikely idea and they've found so many other ways to fail."

"Oh," Branwyn said again, still watching the huddle.

"That's just my theory, and honestly, it may draw too much on my own experiences."

That finally pulled Branwyn's gaze away from the cluster. She glanced up at him. He continued to occupy the same position he'd been in when she left: one hand out, clenched in a fist. But he smiled again. "When you ask what's going on, what *else* are you asking?"

"Uh. How long do we have? I've got a whole list."

"Good question," Shatiel murmured, and that was all.

It made Branwyn smile though. He was peculiarly likable, even with his strange experiments that would never pass any reasonable ethics board. She studied him. "You're somehow suppressing both the ghost and Severin, right?"

"I am," he said, glancing at her. "It was all I could do to stop him. All I *would* do. We both have our limits." He shook his head wryly. "Accelerating Imani's growth clearly wasn't his first choice, but when it was the only choice he had left, my choice was also made."

"Why did he—" Branwyn cut herself off, pressing her lips together.

But Shatiel answered anyhow. "Oh, he couldn't endure watching her destruction, not when he'd already failed her once. I hadn't realized how much of his remaining ability to care he'd invested in her, or I would have been more careful about reintro-ducing them and reminding him of what he'd lost. Perhaps I ought to have left well enough alone? But I really don't like my research partners destroyed unnecessarily."

Branwyn listened to Shatiel's musings, her gaze on Severin's shuttered form. She realized what a different—and alien—perspective Shatiel had on his 'little brother,' and shook her head.

"So how long can you keep that suppression up?"

Shatiel inspected his fist. "As long as I have strength to do so. Unfortunately, both tasks are challenging, so I expect my strength will run out around dawn."

"Thought so," said Branwyn. She eyed the Wild Hunt. There they were, trying to build some kind of soul engine. But going faster wasn't the only way to make the impossible possible. You could also change the deadline.

"You'd have more strength if you freed him, wouldn't you? And he might be handy if you do run out of juice. As, you know, lunch for the angry ghost. He'd probably slow her down for at least a few minutes."

"Would he? You know, I'm actually stronger with him. I'm actually not suppressing him so much as *containing* him. An idea of mine, another theory getting tested. It isn't the, ah, executioner's cut, but I think it may be like what you were doing to those souls out there. And while I hold his name, his unsundered energy has to go somewhere. It bounces around within me. It is... tiring in its way. But also strengthening, just as your hammer is now stronger."

He glanced up at the ghost. "Probably not as strong as I think, though."

"Um," said Branwyn, alarmed.

He looked down at her again. "Ah, I shouldn't have said that. I've scared you. I'm sorry. You'll have a better warning than that when that moment comes." His fist turned over. "For one thing, you'll again have my little brother to deal with. Even if freeing him would strengthen me, Branwyn, I couldn't do so. Bringing him back won't bring back that last spark of preserving nature he lost. That will require something more than just telling him everything is now okay. I'll deal with him presently, but... after the current crisis."

Branwyn scowled. That sounded just as bad as she'd imagined it could be. "Who *is* she? Why does he care so much?"

"Hmm. I could answer that, but I won't. I've already betrayed him enough. Ask him yourself, once I've brought him back?"

"Hey!" shouted AT. "Branwyn! We need you!"

THE WILD HUNT did things only they understood. In the end, most of them clustered around Jennifer and the Horn, all except for Yejun, who followed Branwyn like a shadow. The Hunt communicated in that creepy silent way they had, and then Jennifer blew the Horn. The sound was different, but the nightmare world still trembled.

"Yes, I do think it's best my little brother is sleeping through this part," murmured Shatiel.

The nightmare world trembled, and knots in the Geometry slid down the pattern toward the belling of the horn. Strange things happened, but that was when Branwyn had her own work to do, so she didn't pay much attention.

For a long time, too long, so long, the knots along the pattern of the ghost town came to her, and she unlocked them with her hammer and pulled the energy out. Yejun took the energy from her and passed it back and somehow it ended up stored on Brynn rather than swallowed by the Horn. It was hard and exhausting, and even though it was much faster than Branwyn's original approach, it still took hours.

But when no more knots approached, and the nightmare world was crumpled around them and blotting out half the Hunt, dawn was only the faintest glow on the horizon.

Branwyn collapsed onto the ground and waved at Jen. The woman had been playing all this time. That was definitely some inhuman stamina. Branwyn needed some of it.

That weird ripple of communication travelled through the Hunt, and Jen stopped playing, releasing the nightmare world to expand to its full size once again. There it was, just as it had been before, but now it was… simplified.

Cat collapsed into a heap just like Branwyn, and she gave him a prone thumbs up. He gave her a sleepy smile and closed his eyes. Everybody else sat down.

Everybody except Shatiel. He rolled his shoulders and stepped forward, a statue come to life. "Very nice. You'll be able to do something with this and really get down to work. Oh, Branwyn. Don't sleep yet. I need to return him now, and I'm going to need something of you to make it work.

"Do you have to?" said Amber wistfully. "Do you really have to return him? He's such a jerk."

Shatiel laughed. "You don't think you're redeeming Imani without him, do you? Now, Branwyn, you can lay there, but lift your hand."

And Branwyn, fool that she was, did.

6

Fools

SHATIEL CLASPED his cool hand to Branwyn's and sleep instantly closed over her.

After a time, a bright presence moved in the darkness upon her mind. She was aware, but not awake.

Thank you. Now, I'll need one of your nodes. Do you care which? Oh no, I see the charm to replace. This will be much better than those claws. Stay calm. This won't take long.

Branwyn struggled helplessly to wake herself, and Shatiel paused. *You're really the only option I have. But I promise: it's only temporary. Unless you die, of course. Then, well, it will still be temporary for you, but also far too late for him. And meanwhile, you'll be able to influence him.*

Why?? Branwyn shouted silently.

Why? The bright presence paused again, then moved around her. *Remember when I said bringing him back would take more than kind words? The truth is, I don't know how to return him to what he was. I don't even know if he wants to come back. But he's needed all the same. So I'll use your soul as a limiter for a while. If he starts going the wrong way, you'll be able to stop him, hold him near you until the urge passes.*

Oh my **god**.

It's not the least bit permanent.

Branwyn broke into a blind panic. But what did that mean, in dreams?

———

SHE WOKE up under the grey skies of full day, in the place of honor on the filthy cot in the rose house, and she knew Severin's true name. It had been written into her soul by an angel. Instead of freeing his 'little brother,' that pleasant, terrifying angel had decided to give *her* the keys to Severin's prison.

Branwyn shuddered, kicking off the sleeping bag that some-body had tossed over her. Then she sat up. The ghost Imani was no longer hovering overhead, but Branwyn remained in the ghost's haunted nightmare world. In the light of day that appar-ently meant everything came in two shades: overcast and shadow. The shadow houses still stretched across the ground, but an odd assortment of structures no more substantial than tissue paper—woodland cottages, a tiny palace, an alpine lodge—stood atop those shadows. Just beyond the rose house, the inkiness of a disconnected world swallowed the land and sky, but it was curi-ously easy for her eyes to slide away from the blot and toward the flicker of movement in the town.

AT's three dogs had placed themselves around Branwyn's cot, and they all faced at her as she moved. The middle one, with the grey-brown curly coat, gave her a friendly woof, and she held out a hand for it to sniff. It skipped straight to pushing its ears under her fingers. Absently, she scratched as she looked around.

Except for the dogs, she was alone in the rose house. No, not alone. A figure sat across the threshold, camouflaged by the unnatural shadows. Brynn.

She bounded to her feet when she realized Branwyn had woken. The illustrations of the horses were back on her arms while tiny characters covered her chest and hands. But her legs under her pajama shorts were unmarked.

"Hey!" said Brynn. "Want some water? Rhianna says there might be coffee later."

"Sure," replied Branwyn, accepting the offered bottle. "Uh, how are you holding up? I see you're wearing horses again, too."

Brynn glanced at her arms. "They got bored because there's nothing nice to eat here. But I'm fine. This isn't nearly as bad as the last time I did this. That was… thousands of souls, I think."

"Yeah? How long can you hold them?"

Brynn bit her lip. "I don't know. I didn't have to hold them long before. I don't think they'll go all at once, though. I'll have a better idea of how long once they start draining off."

"All right." Branwyn exhaled, then held out her arm to her little sister. Brynn joined her on the cot and for a moment they leaned into each other.

"It's really cool to work with you and Rhianna, but I wish we'd planned it in advance," said Brynn happily, nestling against Branwyn's shoulder. "Why didn't you tell me you were ghost-hunting?"

Branwyn frowned. "Didn't Rhianna explain any of this?"

Brynn wrinkled her nose. "She said she didn't want to steal your thunder, and it was probably classified anyhow. Then she ran off to the other side of town."

Steal my thunder? "Oh. Well… we didn't come here for a ghost. I didn't even know there was one. We're investigating some missing kids. The ghost and the angel were an unexpected twist. Where did they go, by the way?"

"The ghost is wandering around yelling at people. AT's trying to talk to her." Brynn glanced at where Shatiel had been standing. "And the angel left with Sevvy. Neither of them have come back. Uh, do you know what happened there? Yejun said the angel put a new spell on you."

Branwyn bared her teeth. "Yes, I saw what the angel did and

I don't like it. I don't know where Severin is. I wouldn't mind never seeing him again."

She felt his presence behind her as if he'd sat on the cot. Judging from the lack of reaction from Brynn or the dogs, she decided he hadn't.

Never, cupcake? I wanted to get your current take on murdering angels.

"Unfortunately, I'm pretty sure he hasn't gone far. He's probably just sulking somewhere because he got taken out so easily." Branwyn stood up, brushing herself off, and the sense of Severin's presence faded.

She wasn't going to think about it. Her eyes still burned with tiredness; she couldn't have had more than four or five hours of sleep and it hadn't been restful. She was still hungry, still thirsty. Still human.

"They're moving that investigator camp over here," Brynn said, watching her with wide eyes. "Your overnight bag's over in the corner."

"Brynn, why *are* you wearing pajamas?"

Brynn looked down self-consciously. "Well, I was sleeping when the Horn picked up the haunt and woke us. We didn't expect it would take long. And we didn't think there'd be an audience. Jen went back to the farmhouse for real clothes already. She's going to bring me something of AT's."

"Hmm," said Branwyn. "And… while I'm thinking of it, did I hear you refer to 'our first episode?'"

Brynn curled around her knees. "That's what Amber and I call that Halloween. It's just a joke."

"Just checking." Branwyn twisted her mouth wryly. "Things were… weird last night."

"They're still pretty weird." Brynn unfolded and hopped to her feet, suddenly all lanky arms and legs.

"Yeah? Well, I have to stretch my legs and stuff. Why don't you come along and fill me in?"

Brynn did. The dogs did too and Branwyn concluded they'd been guarding her rather than lazing around hoping for scritches. She wondered what the biggest threat was. Then she stopped wondering. For fifteen minutes, or maybe even until coffee appeared, she would let ignorance be bliss.

According to Brynn, the ghost town was "kinda sorta real, kinda sorta not." The Wild Hunt could come and go safely with magic, but from the outside it was clear the haunt really had consumed the town, tearing a hole between world and Backworld that looked like a town's shadow scorched into the earth. There was no way to return to the dusty, empty ruins Tucker had been before Shatiel had released Imani, and anybody mortal who wandered into what Tucker had become would be trapped.

"I mean, if we weren't here. Obviously we'll help you and Rhianna leave," Brynn added. "That'll be easy."

"So what makes it not real?" Branwyn asked, strolling along the edge of the town. A block over, a shadowy gardener weeded among the now-blooming roses in front of her shadowy house. In the distance, Imani wailed, but the gardening ghost didn't seem to hear. "I mean, ghosts are real, right?" She hadn't always believed that, but there was no point in belief now. It was a simple fact.

Brynn pulled her mouth to one side. "AT says this is the *happiest* haunt she's ever seen, though I don't think that's the right word. And Yejun said everything's been *simplified*. I haven't seen much of that myself because when I arrive the complexity ratchets back up." She touched the marks on her arm. "These guys, I guess. I don't understand how it works. But, like, listen to Ghostlady Imani. She's literally just floating around complaining. She can't hurt *us*, of course, but she's not even trying to hurt Rhianna. She's not doing much to the other ghosts that have popped up, either, except screeching and zapping them, and her zaps don't seem to hurt much."

"You're right, that *is* weird." Branwyn thought a moment, then found her phone. "You know what? I need you to leave a message for Marley and Penny. Tell them you're here too, and I'm taking care of myself. They're not going to believe a message from me."

Brynn took the phone but gave Branwyn a skeptical look. "Are you?"

"I'm doing my best. But more importantly, if you don't convince them everything's fine, more of us pesky mortals will be showing up to make life difficult."

Brynn frowned and took the phone. As she called Penny, Branwyn walked away and leaned on a surprisingly solid black and white stone fence in front of a tissue-paper cottage from a different part of the world.

She focused on Severin, recalling the first time she'd talked to him, when she'd summoned him and he'd terrified her, told her she wasn't interesting enough to bleed for. He'd toyed with and tormented Tarn's servants, and he'd tried to kill Tarn. She'd hated him so much for that, but she'd hated him more after he saved her from a mess she'd walked into with her eyes open.

He'd showed up, unwelcome, at her family's house to rope her into another scheme. She'd gone along, suspecting him, desperate to beat him at his own game, only to find out she'd never understood what it was. She'd gotten what she wanted in the end, and he hadn't cared at all.

Ah, he whispered in her ear. *You've got a whole scrapbook. Would you like to go through it together?*

"How can you be sulking in the Backworld if the Backworld is part of the haunt, anyhow?" Branwyn muttered.

I'm not, he said. Something *yanked* on Branwyn and she stumbled forward, into a world of velvet darkness and high, bright windows. There was nothing under her feet, but she didn't fall.

Severin sat in what looked like one of her own armchairs in

the center of the windows, slumped low, his head leaned on one hand while the other draped bonelessly over the overstuffed arm. "I expected that would work," he said flatly. "Well, here we are, cupcake. You're inside me and I'm inside you. Isn't this cozy."

"Oh, so you're sulking here instead," said Branwyn, taking the opportunity to finally get a good look at the strange space. But there simply wasn't much to see. The windows had lifted above her eye-level, and the velvet blackness was the world outside a spotlight. When she looked over her shoulder, she thought she saw a flash of aurora.

She wondered if there was a way out other than Severin's windows and decided she could always make one if there wasn't. Her Veil-parting charm was very powerful, if a bit messy.

"I wasn't in the mood for the prattle of children."

Branwyn turned back to him. His mouth was thin with annoyance. "I know your name now. Your original name."

"My true name," he corrected her. "Say it."

"What? Why?"

"I want to know what it feels like when you say it. Don't be tedious, Branwyn."

"Fine," she said. "Ramiel." It was just a word, an unfamiliar name on her tongue, but the velvet darkness *rang* like the interior of a bell.

"Hmm," said Severin née Ramiel, only his eyes moving as he took in the shivering windows. "I'll certainly hear that. But I'll hear you say Severin, too, so let's stick to that, shall we?"

Branwyn tamped down the surge of annoyance that made her want to immediately respond with his original name. He just *presumed* she'd agree—but no. He had every reason to know she'd agree. She respected everybody's right to define themselves. Mostly. She *tried*, anyhow.

He smiled and lifted his head. "Next...." With a flick of his dangling hand, Branwyn was yanked forward once again. This time, she fell into his lap. Quick as he ever was, he caught both her hands in one of his and held them under her back. Already emotionally off-balance, Branwyn stared up at him, too confused to be frightened.

Then her confusion abruptly grew much worse as he slid his other hand under her shirt. White hot fire flooded Branwyn's nerves as his fingers made slow patterns on the skin of her stomach. Gradually, they inched their way up her torso. After a moment of aching, mindless paralysis, thoughts started trying to fight their way through the heat.

He'd never... but it felt so *good*... She wanted both his hands all over her, and his mouth—

But he'd never... if he just moved his hand a little more, he'd be...

He'd never touched her like this before.

The voice in her mind, his hand to hers, and that strange touch on her neck sometimes; his hands on her hips, and once, his mouth on her collarbone. That was all, the limit of the ways he'd really touched her.

All the other ways he'd touched her had been in her dreams.

There had been so *many* of those. She'd tried to forget them upon waking, wrote them off as the whims of a sleeping mind. But she remembered too much. And now, with his fingers trailing over her sensitive skin, she wanted even more.

His eyes were very bright as she looked up into his face. "Tell me to stop," he whispered.

"Stop," she repeated softly, unthinkingly.

He laughed, his fingers still moving. "You don't mean that. I wish your sister could have held her tongue a while longer, cupcake. You can't imagine how annoyed I was that she'd provoked such a delicious meltdown when I couldn't enjoy it." His teasing fingers unlatched her bra.

Remembered shame and humiliation overtook the heat

making her boneless. "Stop it," she said. Sharply, firmly. What she wanted right now wasn't what she would want tomorrow, or even in ten minutes. She was *more* than her physical cravings.

Severin's fingers slowed, then stilled. He bent his head so his forehead was resting against hers. "Ah. Bad news, cupcake. That's not going to stop me at all. If you want to tighten my leash, you'll have to call my name, over and over and over again."

He lifted his head, withdrew his hand from Branwyn's shirt and released her hands all at once. She sprang to her feet and staggered a few feet away before sitting down abruptly on the velvet darkness.

"I don't want to be anywhere near your stupid leash," she said bitterly, her heart pounding. Her bruises and muscle aches had faded under his burning touch and stayed gone now. That seemed deeply unfair.

"Yes, it's a pity Big Brother Shatiel doesn't take requests," Severin responded, his voice once again cold and flat. "Whether you want it or not, there's a collar around my neck and tied to you."

"Why did he do that? Why did he think he needed to?" Branwyn demanded.

Severin only looked at her, his eyes glinting as he rested his head back on his hand.

Some fucking leash, Branwyn thought. She climbed to her feet. "Come on, *Ramiel.* If I've got the—"

As the velvet darkness rang again, he was behind her, holding her around the waist, his mouth at her ear. "Each and every time you use that name, you will pay a price." She suddenly remembered, with shocking clarity, a night in Faerie: when she'd found him torturing one of Tarn's changelings. He'd thanked her for bringing the rest to him. She'd never felt so helpless, and the only way she'd saved any of them was to *beg him* for their lives.

It was a memory she'd mostly buried, even when going over

her 'scrapbook' earlier. She'd remembered what he'd done, but not how she felt, what *she'd* done. She had done her best to forget.

He released her and stepped away. "Go ahead," he said, his voice glacial. "You take the chair. Dogs sit on the floor."

Branwyn said, "What the hell?"

"Take the chair, Branwyn," he said, and every word buzzed in Branwyn's head like a suppressed exposion. Numbly, she sat on the edge of the armchair. Severin knelt on one knee in front of her, a grotesque parody of a knight before his queen.

"You asked *why. Because*, my mistress, I am a very, very bad angel and I have finally run out of what few fucks I had. I *do not care* about preserving any part of this world, especially if instead I could watch it burn."

Branwyn found herself lifting her feet under her as if the acid in Severin's voice was creeping across the floor. He watched this distantly before continuing. "Shatiel believes that, given enough time, I'll revert to an attitude he finds less offensive. Until that happens, he intends for you to restrain me from… indulging myself."

His gaze flicked over her from head to toe. "You will, too. And you'll hate it. Is that my consolation prize, or just serendipity, I wonder?"

Branwyn, already feeling a twinge of guilt for using the name he'd asked her not to use, flared up. "I'm not going to be your regulator. That's fucked up."

A familiar smile crooked the corner of his mouth. "But it will cost you so little, cupcake. You can't even feel what you're doing to me."

"Is this all because of Imani? Was she, like, the only person in the world you cared for or something?" She half-expected him to tease her about being jealous.

But instead his face shuttered again. "She was a game I'd forgotten I was playing."

"So, yes," Branwyn said.

He sighed. "It's a little more complicated than that. Are you going to *make me* talk about it, *mistress?*"

Branwyn scowled. "I'm not going to make you do anything."

Severin's head lowered. "I do love it when you lie to yourself, cupcake."

"And stop kneeling there!"

He laughed again and sprang to his feet. "Shatiel also told me you found a way to stop the Wild Hunt. Well done."

His praise slid off Branwyn's back as she regarded him narrowly. "What are you going to do now?"

With a wide-eyed look, he said. "You're the mistress. What do you want me to do?"

"I hate you *so much,*" she told him. In response he smiled at her and she remembered his fingers on her skin, and her unlatched bra. She fixed it. "So much. Severin, dear, would you please be *so kind* as to escort me back to Tucker, Idaho?"

In response, one of the windows circling above swooped down to pass over them. As simple as that, they were standing in Tucker, beside a black and white stone wall, and AT's dogs were *extremely unhappy.*

They darted between her and Severin, then leapt at the fallen angel, snapping and snarling. He pivoted and ducked, catching first the gray dog and then the black one by the scruffs of the neck. The red dog pressed against Branwyn's legs, growling savagely. Severin gave it a disgusted look.

I guess I know what they were supposed to protect me against.... "Whoa, whoa, whoa!" said Branwyn. The red dog flicked her ears, and the grey dog whined pathetically, but the black dog remained focused on ripping Severin's throat out.

"Ah, a dog after my own heart," Severin said, and maintained his grip on the black one while releasing the gray one. "Hey, AT, can I keep him?"

AT came pounding up. "Nod! No! Let him go! What are you doing back here?"

Severin dropped the black dog, and it joined its siblings lurking behind AT. "This is my fucking party, wolfchild. You're the gatecrashers, not me." He shook his head, glanced at Branwyn, and then said, "I'm going to go talk to Imani. Come along and maybe I'll introduce you."

7

Forking Roads

FOR SOME REASON, nobody wanted to let Severin find Imani alone, or even with only Branwyn supervising. "It's like they don't trust me," said Severin, and smiled like a shark when Amber hissed and followed along with AT and Yejun.

It's okay. I've got this, Branwyn could have said. It probably would have helped. But she wasn't a fucking regulator, or a limiter, or leash-holder. She was only here to rescue some kids she couldn't even name.

"Severin!" cried Imani, when he came around the corner to where she was peeling the petals from white roses. They fluttered in the wind, each one marked with a crimson fingerprint.

The roses grew outside a picturesque shadow-and-paper bistro that was as out of place as the cottage earlier. The ghost inside peeped out over low curtains, all eyes and a chef's hat. It was ludicrous and funny and wrong. This place was definitely getting stranger away from Brynn. The chef was positively cartoonish compared to the previous nightmarish hellscape.

"Severin, why do you keep coming back? It wouldn't have mattered if I'd listened, so you don't need to gloat." Scarlet skirts swirled and the fire at Imani's heart brightened as they approached.

"She's been conjuring shadows of him to stick pins in. Little dreams," confided AT. "He's definitely one of her unresolved issues. Solving it might be a little tricky...."

Severin walked right up to the ghost as she settled to earth and took her into his arms. Ruby light flared like a halo and faded as she pressed her head against his chest. He stroked her flaming hair while looking down at her. But there was no tenderness in his expression, only a cold bleakness Branwyn had seen before.

"Uh," said AT.

"That's just *wrong*," said Amber. "What the hell is he doing to her?"

"Hugging her?" suggested Yejun. "Come on, guys, let's give them some space." But neither Amber nor AT responded, too busy gawking to listen.

After a moment, the tight embrace between monster and ghost slackened. When she drew away, Imani looked nearly human. The proportions of her face were less exaggerated and her Hellqueen ballgown had become a simple dress.

"What happened, Severin? Why didn't you come? Was it because I ignored your warning?"

Branwyn felt rather than heard the creak of cracking glass. She put her hand on her chest, but remained silent.

"You spent your whole life ignoring me, little star. Why would it would have mattered that time?"

"I wish I hadn't!" cried the woman and pressed herself against his chest again. AT turned away at that point, crouching to pet her dogs.

Severin stroked Imani's hair again. "I would have come if I'd known, but I didn't. I was bodiless and... *distracted* and by the time I'd touched earth again, I was far too late." He laughed harshly. "Too late even to get revenge for you. Your lover had taken care of that."

Imani's face shifted back toward that of the Hellqueen. "Gale...." she hissed. "He burned everything, Severin. All my work. He burned *Charlie*. Won't you punish him for us? We have to punish everyone, but Gale most of all."

Very deliberately, Severin took Imani's face in his hands and rested his forehead against hers. "He did not burn Charlie."

Imani froze before exploding away from him. As she rocketed into the sky, she wailed, "Then *where is she*? How can you say that? Even he can't say that! He burned Charlie, and he *didn't even notice*. Oh, I wish I'd listened to you, I wish I'd listened, I wish I'd never come here, I wish I'd never heard the stories, I wish I'd killed him, I wish I'd killed them all. I should have listened...."

"I'll find her," said Severin flatly.

"You won't! Or you'll only find her soul, and if you bring her to me she'll be caught here. I wanted her to *live*. My Charlie."

Amber convulsively turned away, joining AT and her dogs. Branwyn remained. The ghost's high, thin wailing hurt, and Branwyn, who was weak to maternal tears, tried to focus on Severin instead. He said nothing more, but remained looking up at the grieving ghost, his eyes growing wider and his pupils constricting.

Branwyn moved beside him. "Hey," she breathed. When he didn't respond, she repeated, "Hey," and this time brushed his hand with her own. He glanced down at her expressionlessly and she said, "Let's go find her."

His hand twitched next to hers, his fingers brushing against her palm. Then his face relaxed, and he exhaled. "Yes."

After another breath, he added, "See, that wasn't so bad, was it? You're a born regulator."

"Fuck off," said Branwyn, but she was secretly proud of herself for redirecting without commanding. AT and Amber both stared at her in bewilderment and she gave a small shrug. "Where did Rhianna go?"

"She's sleeping in one of the tents," said AT.

"Oh, goodie. That means I get to wake her up."

Rhianna was instead on one of the sleeping bags, outside the single remaining tent. The other two had been removed and half the supplies hauled away. Cat sat in the camp chair Branwyn had once set up, writing in a book.

Silently, Branwyn peeked into the tent, saw it was full of strange shadows of a cramped mansion, and closed the flap again. She studied her sister. Rhianna slept curled up, except for a single leg. Ready for kicking, Branwyn had always felt. She had always been a kicker.

Her chest clenched, and she stopped herself from waking Rhianna with a wet willie. They were both on a job, not a sisterly retreat. Rhianna had approached her as a professional. She would do the same...

...even if she hadn't signed a contract, and she probably wasn't getting paid; even if she'd stuck her nose in purely as a sop to her integrity.

She wasn't even angry at herself, just wry and... sad. She'd wanted so much to wake Rhianna up like a big sister should.

Rhianna's eye cracked open, and she said around a yawn, "That's a mighty glare, Branwyn. What's up?"

"We need to have a planning session. About Imani, and our original purpose here."

"Ooh, okay!" Rhianna kicked up from prone to standing in a single smooth move. Branwyn's beautiful, talented sister....

Branwyn shook her head. "Also, I was promised coffee. Where's the coffee? I don't even smell coffee. If the coffee is a lie, I'll just go join Imani in a duet."

Rhianna ran her fingers through her hair. Uselessly, because her natural curl had taken over and was starting to knot. "It was bad coffee, and honestly, it was mostly tea. But! Before you go tap into your banshee roots…" Rhianna rolled an inquiring eye at Cat.

He'd stowed his pen, but he was still wearing the small eyeglasses Branwyn was confident he didn't need. Perhaps he thought Clark Kent had found a good disguise.

"Jen should be back any—ah. You have only a few minutes yet to suffer." He smiled.

Rhianna said brightly, "All right," and wandered behind the tent. When she returned a moment later, she had her own messenger bag, the one she'd had in Branwyn's studio during her recruitment pitch. She rummaged through it for a moment and resurfaced with some toiletries. After a glance in a compact mirror, she said, "Ugh, look at me. I'm going to run down to the creek and fix this mess. Be right back!"

Branwyn watched her go and sat on the vacated sleeping bag, resting her chin on her pulled-up knees. Severin and the rest of the Wild Hunt had followed her to the campsite. All the latter were watching her while Severin focused his attention on the non-existent fire of the fire pit he crouched beside.

"What's up with the tent interior?" asked Branwyn. "And the bistro, and the cottages?"

AT shrugged. "Ghosts don't always look like what they were before they died. Draining the energy out of the corruption seems to have given the trapped souls the freedom to… pretend they were something else."

Brynn objected. "Is it pretending, or their true selves manifesting?"

Skeptically, AT said, "I don't know if a 'true self' can be a bistro chef. That seems like it requires more work than simple self-identification."

Brynn glanced at Branwyn as if deferring to her authority, but Branwyn shook her head, unwilling to get involved and a little embarrassed than Brynn expected she would be.

Cat said, "There's a difference between wishing you were and *knowing* what you are."

"As you've discovered, cast-off?" said Severin, still focused on invisible flames.

Cat shrugged. "I started out as somebody's *wish they were* but unfortunately for them, I *know* what I am."

"And what's that?" Branwyn said. She considered it only polite to ask.

Cat's gaze raised to the sky above the campsite. "Hers," he said, and with the low song of the Horn, Jen and her horse burst through the sky.

As Jen came in for a landing, Cat returned his gaze to Branwyn. "In any case, I do think it's more pretense than truth with the ghosts, just as Imani pretended to punish *him*. But just because something is a dream doesn't mean it should be disregarded."

Ouch. Branwyn bounced to her feet and went to where Jen, now completely dressed, was dismounting. She carried a suitcase in one hand, and a gallon container of coffee in the other. Branwyn relieved her of both and said, "You're the true angel here."

Jennifer smiled at her, the lines around her eyes crinkling. "I'll take that as the compliment you intend. There're bagels in the suitcase."

Once Rhianna had returned, looking far more groomed, and the rest of the Wild Hunt donned more substantial clothing, everybody who wanted breakfast settled around the fire pit. It had gained an actual fire at that point, possibly fueled entirely by Severin's glare. Branwyn certainly couldn't see any other source for it.

"This will be tough, even with extra time," said Yejun. "This isn't simple."

"They're never simple," said Brynn.

"Did you *see* what he did?" asked Amber, waving a bagel at Severin. "He just... and he..."

"Did he?" Jen looked puzzled. "That's..."

"Yeah, it was," said AT. "But you never know. She's got other..."

Cat said, "I've been writing down... something's missing..."

Rhianna and Branwyn glanced at each other over the fire. Finally Branwyn said, "Where's Gale?"

The Wild Hunt chatter faded away. They all looked at each other, and then Amber pointed towards the center of town. "The faerie is in chains at the whipping post."

"I talked to Umbriel," said Rhianna. "He wants to turn Gale over to his own people for justice. He's part of Honeychord, which is bound to Summer and Air."

Branwyn filed that under *will make sense later* and also *the things Rhianna knows now*. "Okay." She drained the last of her coffee, and repeated, "Okay. It sounds like you guys have ideas on what to do with Imani. You've been figuring out some of her issues. It sounded like she had a few. Stay here. Work on those. It'll probably help. Meanwhile, I'm going to Faerie."

Brynn's brow furrowed in disappointment. "Why? Because of that—?"

"Because seventy kids *didn't* die in Gale's revenge spree, Brynn, and one of them is Imani's daughter. And I don't think she'll rest until she knows her kid is safe and sound. Until she sees it with her own two burning eyes."

"Oh," said Brynn, frowning. Then she looked at Rhianna hopefully.

"I'll be going with Branwyn, kiddo. Sorry, but this is actually what they sent me here for."

Brynn pouted. "You two are *always* going off on adventures without me."

The fire crackled and popped. *And that's the place we're at,* Branwyn thought. *She's an indestructible force of Creation and she still wants to tag along with us.* "You're having your own adventures. You'll be fine."

"How do you know they're in Faerie?" demanded Brynn.

"I don't know. I suspect. But there's people in Faerie who *will* know, whether they're there or hidden somewhere on Earth."

Rhianna nodded. "Plus, I bet faeries will want to sort this out rather than face the consequences of this thing going critical." She waved around the nightmare town.

"I just bet," said Jennifer darkly.

"Unfortunately, you can't take the faerie out of the haunt system until we've resolved it," said Cat. "He's a part of it as much as the mortal souls are."

"That's fine," said Rhianna. "A drunk, depressed faerie would get in the way anyhow. I'll make sure some other big strong faeries are ready to grab him once we finish here."

"What about *him?*" asked Amber, and the fire flared and brightened.

Severin raised his gaze from the flames to look at Amber until she said hurriedly, "Right, okay, of course you're going after the kid."

Branwyn frowned as he lowered his gaze again. "Is that going to work, Severin? Last time I checked, you and the faeries don't get along, and they're capable of throwing you out without talking first."

"Then I was a stray mutt, but now I'm *your* dog, cupcake. Ask AT if anybody can keep her dogs away from her." He smiled into the flames.

"Uh," said AT, looking intensely uncomfortable. "I don't think whatever you've got going on is the same—" Once again, Severin raised his head to stare at AT, and her dark skin flushed. "Uh, no. Not anymore."

"There you go," said Severin, although Branwyn didn't think much of the proof, and really hoped AT was right in that they were very different circumstances.

It didn't matter though. She'd known he would come, regardless of difficulties. "All right. That just leaves prepping for the trip and finding the right door."

Admiringly, Rhianna said, "You sound like such a pro, Branwyn."

Branwyn snorted. "You're the one going on about Honeychord and Summer and Air."

"Oh, that's just reading memos. Though… what about a guide? Don't we need a guide? I remember reading that it was dangerous to travel through Faerie without a guide."

"It is. We'll have one," said Branwyn, trying to sound more confident than she was. She might have to negotiate with whoever showed up, but she was almost certain somebody would show up.

Yejun flicked his paper cup into the fire and watched as it didn't burn. "We'll do our best here, but it might not work. Brynn's already started losing souls."

Brynn jumped and looked up guiltily as Yejun continued. "If the system powers up too much, I can't drain it again the way you can. Not yet. Maybe someday."

"How long?" Branwyn asked Brynn.

"A few days, more or less," said Brynn unhappily. "Probably less."

"Just like old times," said AT. "Hurrah."

"Plenty of time," said Branwyn. She brushed her fingers over the black diamond in her hammer, which still held a few knots worth of energy. They'd discharge too, eventually. She'd know. "But if it gets close, I'll get back here. We can keep working on this as long as we need to."

She was lying. Everybody was aware she was lying. Shatiel was gone, and it was Shatiel who had given them the time to drain the system the first time. But they accepted her lie, even Severin, because sometimes another word for lying was 'hope'.

———

BRANWYN WALKED BACK to the rose bower to figure out the rest of her plan, leaving Severin to play with his fire while the Wild Hunt did their thing nearby. She stopped along the way at the whipping post. Though Gale was shirtless now, his skin was unmarred, and the chains that bound him were shaped from lightning, from his own magic, which told Branwyn all she needed to know about his imprisonment. It was performance art, probably put on entirely for the sake of his own ego.

He cringed when he saw her. "I don't know!"

"You're hiding yourself. I saw you in the system," she told him. "I guess I'm glad you feel bad about what you've done. With a hurricane we don't even get that much."

He stared at her. His lips curled away from his teeth. "Do you think I regret burning them? They deserved every scream."

Branwyn raised her eyebrows. "All of them? Did Charlie deserve what you did, and all the other children?"

Gale's moment of rage vanished. "I don't know," he whispered. "I can't remember."

"Uh-huh," said Branwyn. "Did you burn Imani's house first or last?"

"Last… a pyre for her dreams, for all her work never to be completed. I thought I was bringing peace, but she was reborn from the flames, so *angry*."

Coldly, Branwyn said, "And no wonder. Last question, Gale. How late were you?"

He blinked at her. "Too late."

"How late was that? Was her body still on the ground? Her blood warm on the floor? Or had they moved her? Had they buried her? How late were you when you killed Tucker and chained Imani to hell?"

Gale shrank back, the lightning thinning around his wrists. "That night. It was that night. The same night she died."

Branwyn sighed. "When I think of all the ways you could have avenged her instead... Well, carry on. Enjoy your hell while you have it. I'm going to go do for your love what you didn't even think of, and I don't even know Imani."

She walked on past him, her heart pounding and her adrenalin pumping. She didn't know the details of how Imani died, she didn't know why Gale had been late, and she didn't care. Those details might matter to the Wild Hunt as they tried to untangle the mess that wretched angel had let grow like a rare bloom. But all Branwyn needed was the story around seventy children vanishing. And now that she understood the timing, Branwyn was *certain* that another faerie had been present when Tucker died, and their only objection to the massacre was the presence of kids.

At the rose house, one of the tents had been reassembled while the other was a crumpled heap of fabric and poles. Branwyn eyed them, wondering if she ought to find a way to bring one. Then she shook her head and grabbed her overnight bag and the survival backpack Shatiel had fetched from the center of the house. If they only had the time, she'd take a day or two just to make sure she had her head on straight, contact Tarn for any leads she could purchase, *make* a suitable tent, shake any missing information out of Umbriel and see if any of the Senyaza monster hunters wanted to serve as a monster therapist instead. She'd go into Faerie with a known guide, Tarn's William for preference.

But none of that was going to happen. She was going to stomp into Faerie as The Artificer and hope everybody she met wanted to curry her favor rather than own her themselves. She was going to *improvise*. And under her veil of crankiness, she was just a bit excited about it.

She met the others in the center of the town. Everybody else clustered on the far side of the street from where Severin was having a quiet conversation with Gale, still bound to his whipping post.

Branwyn ignored Severin and pushed her phone into Brynn's hands. "You have to keep that charged and answer it. Don't let anybody worry!" Brynn scowled, and Branwyn scrubbed her hair. "Good kid."

She transferred her attention to Rhianna. "Any final words of wisdom from Umbriel?"

Rhianna pursed her lips. "I don't think he realized the haunt existed, Branwyn."

"Bullshit," said Severin, joining them. "He absolutely knew something." Branwyn, involuntarily looking, saw Gale staring at the ground in a shell-shocked kind of way.

"I think he knew about the kids," said Rhianna stubbornly. "And maybe even that you cared about one of the kids, if he really did want you overhearing my chat with Branwyn."

Severin stared at Rhianna for a long moment, then shook his head and said, "Nah, I think Shatiel's still on top of the dead list, don't you, cupcake?"

Judiciously choosing her words, Rhianna said, "Anyhow, he's ready to, uh, take decisive action against the haunt if... if we don't hit our own deadline. One way or another."

Branwyn contemplated that. "Is that supposed to be reassuring?"

Brightly, Rhianna said, "Probably not. On the bright side, we have incentive to do our best!"

Branwyn bit back an acid remark and turned to the Wild Hunt. "All right. There's three ways we can get to Faerie. We can make Gale open a door—"

"He won't be opening anything for a while," said Severin.

Branwyn gave him an impassive glance and kept going, "—or I can open a door, or we can walk into that darkness beyond the town. The important question, other than whether Gale can still wiggle his fingers, is what you experts feel would be best. Doors I open don't tend to close quickly and I don't know what that will do to the fabric of the haunt."

"Where would your door go?" asked Yejun, looking baffled. "If the Backworld and the world have merged here, isn't this... sort of a very specialized part of Faerie?"

"Faerie folds on itself. It would go somewhere," said Branwyn firmly. "I could see it in the Geometry last night. I don't know where the door would go though. I'd figure it out when we arrived."

Jen said, "It sounds awful, but I suspect setting out from the edge of town is the best option for the haunt, so as to prevent energy imbalances from being introduced. It does connect to something; I saw a flicker on the way in. But I have a feeling it will be... horrible until you escape the darkness."

"Yeah? That's what I was thinking, too. Good to have confirmation. I was afraid I was losing my nerve." Branwyn inspected the Hunt one more time, then shrugged. They weren't *all* kids. Jen was actually quite a bit older than Branwyn. They didn't need her advice, which was good, because she didn't know what to say.

Finally, she said, "All right, well... bye. Good luck. See you soon." Then she turned and headed for the creek-edge of town.

Part II

8

The Court of Stone

BRANWYN STOOD at the far edge of the bridge out of town and put her hand in front of her. She could see her fingers. It wasn't a fog. But the light from Rhianna's flashlight simply... went away.

"This really leads out?" asked Rhianna.

"Yes," said Branwyn firmly. *In a way. I'm sure it leads out one way or another.*

"Get a move on," said Severin. "Hold hands if you must."

"Good idea!" said Rhianna and grabbed Branwyn's hand.

"What about you?" asked Branwyn, her calloused fingers curving around Rhianna's thin ones.

Severin raised his eyebrows. "I'll be right behind you." He grinned. "Better me than some of the other possibilities."

"You're not the worst?" inquired Rhianna. "Suddenly so modest, Severin!"

He chuckled, placed his hands on their backs, and shoved them into the dark.

Branwyn stumbled forward and when she regained her balance, it was worse than she had imagined. It was *death*. She wasn't walking, or falling, or breathing. She certainly wasn't moving. She couldn't sense the overnight bag on her shoulder, or wind on her face, or Rhianna's hand in her own.

This was a terrible mistake. She tried to tell herself it was temporary, that she just had to keep moving, and she'd reach... something else. She had not actually died. But how could she move without a body? Where was Rhianna?

Without legs, she tried to move. Without breath, she tried to scream. She'd fought the Sword Belial for her name, fought against an angel's uncloaked glory for her will. Neither had been as all-consuming as this darkness.

She was going to stay here forever and she would have paid any price for salvation from the darkness. If only Branwyn had known, she would have found another way. Jen had said it would be horrible, but she was an immortal now. She'd only been guessing.

Branwyn had been so sure there was something on the other side. But in the darkness, her Sight betrayed her. There was nothing to see. She was in a world that did not exist. Perhaps *she* no longer existed.

Something was burning.

It was *her*. A sharp throbbing pain joined the darkness. And it was *something*. She was something that could burn, that could hurt.

The pain continued, and in its throbbing, she perceived the passage of time. That gave her thoughts structure. She still couldn't remember how to breathe, but she no longer felt like all she would do with a breath was scream.

She'd had a plan.

She waited. Sometimes she contemplated walking or Rhianna. But mostly, she waited, feeling her own pulse in the beat of the burning as time crept by.

Finally a scarlet crack appeared in the darkness, and the crack became a ruby staff. Where it was planted became the ground, and the darkness retreated around it.

Branwyn stood in a dim spotlight, holding Rhianna's hand, and Severin's mark on her collarbone was burning. A tall figure in ruby armor faced her. She'd met him once before, outside the dwelling of the Queen of Stone.

"I thought you might show up," said Branwyn. Breathing felt so good. The burning on her collarbone faded.

"I have an offer for you, Branwyn Lennox," said the figure. His dark face was so beautiful, but about as expressive as a rock. "I will guide you to the Queen, and you will render unto her an equal service."

"Hmm." said Branwyn. She would have preferred, *Oh Branwyn Lennox, we love your work, let us save you from the peril you've flung yourself into.* Debts were annoying. But at least these days she had more to offer than bits of herself.

Rhianna asked, "Does she have to provide the service herself?"

The ruby knight's gaze flicked to Rhianna. "No invitation has been extended to you."

Branwyn opened her mouth to argue and Rhianna squeezed her hand so hard it hurt while saying, sweetly, "That's not an answer to my question."

A furrow appeared between the chiseled ebony features. "If another can provide what is agreed upon, that is the Artificer's decision."

Branwyn hesitated until Rhianna nudged her, and then said, "All right. Get me out of here. Rhianna… stay close."

The ruby knight turned, sweeping his lance out to cut away the darkness and walking away. The path created was exactly one Branwyn wide, but she and Rhianna stayed together anyhow by the simple mechanism of angling their bodies.

Branwyn said in a low voice, "Rhianna, I did not agree to your whole 'you do the stupid stuff' proposal. Stop butting in."

Rhianna clicked her tongue. "Bran, let the magic of 'expense reports' enter your life. You're using your skills and expertise at the request of somebody in a position of power. It would be positively *abusive* to make you pay your own expenses, especially since you never signed that contract."

Branwyn frowned. "Isn't it usually the other way around? I didn't sign the contract, so your people don't owe me anything?"

With a shudder, Rhianna said, "Don't say that to my Advisor, please. I've been lectured enough recently."

Branwyn chewed on her lip, then gave it up for now. "Are you okay? That part before our guide showed up…"

Rhianna said, "Oh yeah, I'm fine. It didn't take long, did it? I thought we'd have to go a lot farther." She shifted her backpack and added, "I did get a little worried when I lost track of your hand, but that was about when the red guy showed up, so everything was fine." She squinted at Branwyn. "It was different for you?"

"Yeah… yeah, it was." Branwyn shivered.

The ruby knight halted, turning and planting the lance on the ground. "Once again, the darkness is following you, Branwyn Lennox." His tone of voice implied this was about on the same level as not showering for a year.

Branwyn glanced back. The darkness was, in fact, following them, and Severin was nowhere to be seen. Her mouth formed his preferred name, and his voice in her ear said

Not yet. I haven't even gone anywhere.

The ruby knight stood. "Come out, darkness, so I can send you back."

Severin laughed derisively and moved forward out of the inky blackness between Branwyn and the knight. "Try it."

The ruby knight whirled his lance as once he had before, and a distortion flew out to swallow Severin. His form faded away like a bubble popping in slow motion.

"Uh," said Rhianna, as the knight once again turned away from them to march.

But Branwyn couldn't say anything or even move, because

suddenly she could feel Severin all over her. His breath was in her hair, his hands were at her waist and he was closer than he'd ever been before, even when he'd cradled her in his arms. His voice, low and purring in her ear, said, *Now you can say my name.*

Instead she found her voice and said, "Is this a good idea?"

Think of it this way, cupcake. If you don't let them know I'm right here, you're lying to them. And carrying a concealed weapon into a Queen's Court is so very rude.

The ruby knight glanced back at her, that tiny furrow once again between his perfect brows.

Branwyn sighed. "Come back, Severin." As Severin soundlessly stepped beside her, still half in the thick darkness and grinning like a shark, she added, "He's not that easy to get rid of these days, but he's not going to start anything."

The furrow became a full-fledged frown. "This is not acceptable."

"Of course it is," said Rhianna indignantly. "You invited her, and he's a part of her now."

Branwyn winced. "Thanks, Rhianna. Thanks a lot. Ruby, if you could just…"

The ruby knight stepped closer—not threateningly, but as if he needed a closer look at her. He looked at Branwyn. He looked at Severin. He looked at Branwyn again.

Then, he broke into a terrifyingly satisfied smile. "I see. It is good. We may proceed." He turned and started his ponderous tread again.

Severin's laugh faded into impassivity. He stared at the retreating figure, then asked, "Does that count as him starting something, cupcake?"

"No," said Branwyn, and started walking again, hauling Rhianna after her.

After walking a while, they reached a mirrored wall that the ruby knight passed through without a pause. Branwyn, who had walked into paintings and holes in the air, didn't hesitate as she approached it, but Rhianna suddenly dug in her heels.

"What is it?" asked Branwyn.

Rhianna was staring at their reflections with wide eyes. At first, Branwyn didn't see why: Branwyn was a little grubby, but her ponytail was freshly tied and her clothes were cleanish, while Rhianna was, if not flawless, at least an expertly put together model for cataclysm chic.

But she glinted strangely in the mirror, as if the dim light was striking angles instead of curves, and then scattering wrong.

"Is that because I wasn't invited?" asked Rhianna breathlessly.

"I don't think so," said Branwyn slowly. "Do you want me to find another way in?"

"No! No… It's probably related to Umbriel. Or maybe nightmare creek water has a future as a beauty balm. Let's go!" Rhianna tried to plunge past Branwyn into the mirror, but Branwyn body blocked her and caught her chin.

"Hmm." Branwyn looked between the reflection and the real thing. "Well, mirrors are notorious for lying. You look fine. The shine on that lip gloss is perfect."

"Very sweet, woof woof, now I'm bored," said Severin, looming up behind them, and once again, he shoved them both forward.

They emerged from a plate of stained glass in the Court of Stone, stumbling across a beautifully faceted floor. There was a snap as a velvet drapery covered the screen they'd emerged from, followed by a babble of strange voices. Branwyn was at the throne end of the huge, vaulted chamber, but the giant throne itself was empty and the many stained glass screens shrouded. Meanwhile the galleries of the courtiers spilled over with expectant fae.

"The Artificer Branwyn Lennox, and attendants,"

announced the ruby knight, and stepped back to wait beside the empty throne. Silence settled across the galleries.

One courtier disengaged himself from his peers and glided over to them. He wore a patchwork suit of metal and cloth that had nothing of the make-shift or hand-me-down to it. Every piece of copper and brown fabric was layered and twisted together so they folded and unfolded, accordion-like, as he moved. His face was dark, but surprisingly unattractive unless you liked them as craggy as the Rocky Mountains. His voice, when he spoke, was smooth and low with an odd hitch.

"Well met, Branwyn. I am Karst. So happy you've come. We're all admirers of your work."

"Where's the Queen?" asked Branwyn bluntly. It had never occurred to her that someone else might order the ruby knight to fetch her.

"I will inform her of your arrival presently, but first I wanted to—" and then he stopped, his face twisting in an expression of displeasure that was no longer human. "What is *that* doing here, Ruby?"

And, yes, *that* was Severin standing a few steps behind Branwyn, looking up at the vault and its crystalline rafters in a speculative kind of way.

"Branwyn Lennox, and attendants," said the ruby knight, without bothering to disguise his annoyance at the speaker.

Karst's eyes became slits. "We missed this episode, Artificer." He circled her, scrutinizing her the same way the ruby knight had. Then his circle turned into a figure eight as he also orbited Severin.

Severin looked down and gave Karst his shark smile, sticking his hands in his pockets.

"Oh… Oh! I see! He is leashed!" Karst clapped his hands and did a brief jig, setting his entire outfit chattering. Emboldened, he moved closer to Severin, close enough for Severin to grab, and then even closer. Branwyn's hands curled into fists and every nerve in her body thrummed with tension.

Severin's smile faded, his face returning to chilly impassivity. Karst's suit brushed against him as Karst inspected him from less than six inches away. Severin didn't even twitch.

Then Karst sprang away, laughing. "Wonderful! What a treasure you are, Artificer."

The galleries murmured and laughed as well. Then somebody called, "She holds him, but does she truly control him?"

Somebody else said, "Make him dance! I want to see the Destroyer dance!"

Karst's expression clouded. "That's true. I have seen the bond, but the Artificer's commitment to freedom is legend: Duke Tarn's favorite tale. What good the bond if she won't use it, Ruby?"

The ruby knight didn't reply. Branwyn said, "Tarn talks too much. Will you inform the Queen I'm here now?"

Karst made another of those exaggerated facial movements, this time one of doubt. "Oh no. Not without knowing you truly control that one. Risking the Queen would be risking too much."

Branwyn glanced at Rhianna in case she had one of her bright ideas, but Rhianna only shrugged.

Okay. They were in a large room full of not-very-nice faeries. If Branwyn didn't finish the negotiation she'd implicitly started with the Queen by following the ruby knight, they'd come after her. She still needed to inquire after the stolen kids, too. She didn't technically need the Queen for that part, but she strongly suspected the jerks in the galleries were a few steps lower than Tarn in the pecking order, which probably meant they had less information too.

And she didn't *want* to ask them anything. They were being cruel. Not just to Severin, who probably deserved it, but to her. It made her angry. Yet she guessed from the way they were settling in that she wasn't moving forward until they got their demonstration.

She glanced at Severin again. He stood with his hands in his pockets, his head low and his eyes black pits. She could feel that cracking in her chest. He was controlling himself of his own volition right now but that wouldn't last long and she couldn't really blame him. Maybe…

I'm not going to fucking dance for them. Let's just kill them all and keep going. I know, let's go pick up Marley's little darlings and bring them here to char their precious Faerie to its white bones. Do you think they'd give Charlie back then?

Branwyn swayed under the buffet of frustrated rage. *Stop, stop, stop! Severin.* Her lips formed his name, but she tried to keep the rest of her words subvocal. *I don't want you to dance for them.* She inhaled. *I want you to scare the shit out of them.*

He lifted his head a fraction, and something glittered in his eyes. *Ah.*

Branwyn straightened her shoulders, turning to the expectant audience. She pursed her lips. "You really want him to dance?"

The courtiers cheered wildly. Karst leaned against the end of the gallery, visibly gratified.

"Well… I'll try. Let's go over here, Rhianna, out of his way. All right, Severin. Go ahead."

It practically *was* a dance, although not the one they'd hoped for. After he'd spun and kicked, his unbelievable agility as he sprang away from the disarmed ruby knight dropped jaws. And when Severin stood over Karst with one foot on his chest and that lance, a faerie-killing weapon if ever there was one, descending towards the fae's throat, the black needles of Severin's aura looked like a curtain's fall.

Branwyn's throat worked convulsively, too dry for her to speak. "Severin," she mouthed, then "Severin!"

It was barely audible in the rumble of courtiers scattering. But the black tip of the lance stopped as it pricked Karst's throat.

Then it clattered to the ground and Severin strolled back across the hall to where Branwyn stood, his aura gradually fading away.

"As you see, he is *under control*," Branwyn coldly told the galleries. "Please tell the Queen I'm here."

As a dead silence spread over the galleries once again, Karst eased himself up and the lance returned to its owner's hand. Severin stepped behind Branwyn and seemed to instantly wrap himself around her: that pressure on her hips, his breath in her hair.

Say it again, he said. *Keep saying it, or I'm going back over there to finish the fucking job.*

"Severin," she said breathlessly. "Severin. Severin."

Karst spoke loudly, the hitch in his voice more noticeable, "Ruby! How could you be so *derelict* as to allow yourself—"

"Severin," whispered Branwyn.

"I had no reason to doubt the Artificer's control," said the ruby knight, his voice as icy as Branwyn's had been.

Karst touched the spot of crimson on his throat, then lowered his eyes. "I have informed The Queen of your arrival. Her handmaiden will escort you into her presence momentarily." He slumped against his gallery and didn't look up when the rest of the audience burst into cheers.

Branwyn glanced at the galleries once, then looked away. She would have preferred any other response.

Severin's physical presence ebbed as they waited. When Branwyn glanced over her shoulder, he was leaning against the geode wall with his arms crossed, looking at her. Their eyes met, and she wondered if she could have come up with a better plan, one that hadn't involved a 'demonstration.' But she'd been so annoyed.

It really *would* have been a great time for one of Rhianna's anger-deflecting tricks.

Branwyn became aware of movement beside her. Rhianna was bouncing on her toes, with her hands clasped and her eyes shining. "Severin, that was *wonderful*. Would you please teach me? Especially the part where you just kind of *zoomed* across the hall. And then—"

"Rhianna!" said Branwyn.

Rhianna gave her a veiled pout. "What?"

"Aren't you more—" Branwyn waved a hand. "More tricky?"

Rhianna's wide-eyed innocent look switched on. "Oh, Branwyn. I know at least twelve ways to kill a man barehanded, and three more if I have a spoon. Just imagine the raise I could get if I moved like him!"

"And a girl like you works for Umbriel," murmured Severin.

"What?" said Branwyn, glancing at Severin sharply. "She's joking. Isn't she? Tell me she's joking."

"Excuse me, Artificer," came a quiet, feminine voice. Branwyn turned to see a figure with long, pale hair and a stone visor wrapping around her head at eye-level. She had gorgeous platinum ear cuffs that Branwyn instantly coveted, and snug bronze bands around her upper arms and wrists, but otherwise she was dressed far more simply than the other courtiers in a plain long gown that matched her hair.

"I am the Queen's handmaiden. She does not choose to see her courtiers today. If you and your attendants would come with me, I will bring you to her."

9

The Queen of Stone

THE HANDMAIDEN GUIDED Branwyn and her companions through an archway that hadn't been there before and down a corridor of polished golden tiger's eye. The corridor led to a wide serpentine staircase that rose far too many flights into an aquamarine tower.

The handmaiden's steady pace never slackened, but at about the twelfth flight, Branwyn's legs started to cramp. She was bitterly unsurprised to note that neither Rhianna nor Severin seemed fatigued, and decided if they could do it, so could she. What was a little pain and heavy breathing? She needed the workout. But at the sixteenth floor, she lost her footing, landed hard on one knee, and didn't have the wind to get herself back up again.

Rhianna crouched beside her, then called, "Wait, please." Severin leaned against the inner wall of the staircase, crossing his arms. He wasn't smiling, which was a small mercy.

The handmaiden looked over her shoulder, then descended the stairs again.

Branwyn caught her breath, then said, "Is there a reason

we're climbing a tower to see the Queen of Stone? Stone is in the ground."

The handmaiden lifted her head up to the heights. "She likes to be close to the sky sometimes. But, ah yes, this path is challenging for mortals inexperienced with heights. If you can complete this flight, I will take you to her elevator." Her head turned to Severin. "If not, perhaps your attendant can carry you."

All it took was one tilt of the corner of Severin's mouth and Branwyn shot to her feet, almost pulling down Rhianna in the process.

"There you go," said Rhianna, patting her on the back. "There's always a second wind."

"Enough to get me to an elevator, anyhow." Branwyn hurled herself up the stairs, rushing past the handmaiden to the landing, where with a supreme effort of will she didn't sprawl on her face.

"This way," said the handmaiden, clearly amused. She touched an unbroken plane of aquamarine and a moment later, it split in two horizontally. The elevator beyond was very large, and also transparent quartz.

"Ooh, a glass elevator!" said Rhianna, and bounced in, going directly to the opposite wall to press her nose against the surface. Branwyn entered more cautiously, ready for the vertigo she'd experienced before in high places in Faerie.

But this time it wasn't terrible. At least, the ground and the sky were in the proper places relative to herself. The tower rose above a dark, rocky plain where only crystals grew, and several deep fissures cut through the earth. In the distance, the landscape assumed the patchwork look of Earth from high above: fields and lakes and forests and the glitter of structures.

Though... some of the structures seemed to be walking, and a lake-like spot of blue suddenly rose into the sky to sail into the further distance. Off on one horizon, something vast and dark moved over the land on many legs.

"What's that?" Rhianna asked. "Uh. Sorry. Can you see through that?"

"My eyes are not like human eyes, but I still perceive," said the handmaiden, unruffled by the question. "That is Night, wandering in search of its kindred."

"Wow," said Rhianna slowly. Branwyn, who already knew Night was a creature in Faerie, asked the next obvious-to-her question.

"Does it *have* kindred?"

"Oh yes: both the parents who abandoned it, and its cousin spirits. But it is rarely allowed to find them."

"What are its cousins?" Branwyn asked. The elevator had started moving smoothly, and she experienced a touch of vertigo.

The handmaiden, her hand on the wall, hesitated, then lifted her hand. The elevator stopped. "Is this a casual inquiry, or something you will pursue with Her Majesty?"

Startled, Branwyn said, "It's not why we're here."

"Oh? Then I would request you not mention the world-spirits, Night and its kin, to Her Majesty. It will only needlessly distress her."

"Of course not," said Rhianna promptly. "Branwyn's the soul of tact."

The handmaiden looked puzzled. "She is not. She is often very blunt."

"They've got my number, Rhianna," said Branwyn. "I won't, though."

"Well, I'm the soul of tact," said Rhianna blithely. "And none of us want to distress the Queen."

The handmaiden tilted her head, her mouth twisting. "You keep lying, and in such obvious ways. I have no doubt the other one wishes very much to trouble the Queen." Her head moved toward Severin.

"That's the tact," said Rhianna confidingly. "He may want

to, but he won't, so it's practically the same thing, and it sounds prettier."

"You sound like a courtier," observed the handmaiden, and placed her palm on the wall again. The elevator silently rose once more. "But a clever one, at least. So I give you a warning: let the Artificer talk to the Queen, for she is weary of courtiers today."

The elevator stopped once again, and the door split apart at the top of the tower. Tall, sharply crenelated walls rose but there was no roof but the blue, blue sky. The wind across the cut walls howled and sang. In the chamber's center, the Queen of Stone reclined in a chair similar to her throne in the hall. Several other attendants sat on cushions on the floor nearby, engaged in small handicrafts or games. Two of them flowed to their feet and adjusted the Queen's chair back. The handmaiden waited beside Branwyn.

"Hmm," said Rhianna, and Branwyn glanced at her. Rhianna glanced back, a frown drawing her eyebrows together, but only shook her head.

The Queen of Stone was even more like a statue than her knight or her handmaiden. Her face was scarred grey stone, and her hair was obsidian and basalt, falling free over her shoulder. She wore a gown of golden beryl, with copper pleats and a girdle of of twisted silver. Her head turned toward them ahead of her chair being rotated, and Branwyn was surprised. The Queen's eyes had been dull stone on their previous meeting, but they were now translucent cabochons, glimmering in the sunlight.

"You played a dangerous game in the belly of Death, Branwyn Lennox."

"Yes, I know. I thought maybe while I'm here, we could set up a better method of communication. Writing on the mirror hasn't seemed to work."

The other attendants giggled at this, but the Queen's impassive face didn't change. "I will consider it. But this is not why you struck out into darkness and brought a monster who does not dance into our midst." Or was that the faintest hint of a smile? Did a Queen tired of her courtiers *appreciate* the little show below? It was a fascinating thought. She certainly didn't seem concerned by it.

"One of your kind destroyed a mortal town, Your Majesty. Another faerie stole the town's children. We're looking for them."

"One of *mine?*"

Rhianna whispered, "Honeychord draws on Summer and Air, not Stone."

Hastily, Branwyn clarified. "Sorry, I meant only a faerie. It has nothing to do with the Court of Stone."

"Unless they stole the kids," said Severin. "Then it has everything to do with them." He cracked his knuckles and the attendants on the floor drew together, murmuring fearfully.

"Stolen children..." mused the Queen. "Stolen children..." She tilted her head to the sky, and the handmaiden's breath hissed between her teeth. But when the Queen spoke, her voice was almost friendly. "Why are you here, monster?"

"Woof woof," said Severin. "I go where the leash pulls me. I'm sure you noticed."

"Prevarication." The Queen's voice hardened as her gaze lowered. "Fool. Your inclusions may have been washed away, but that only makes the flaws in your nature easier to see. You are here for a child, though not a child of your own body. And you are here because you are weak and selfish. You are barely more than a child yourself."

There was a long pause, during which Branwyn tried not to blink. Clearly the Queen had a soft spot for stolen children. Why was Severin wasting this opportunity?

"Woof woof," repeated Severin, very softly.

"Useless," said the Queen, and her attendants quaked. Only the handmaiden beside Branwyn seemed unafraid, but she focused on the Queen with a sharp intensity.

The Queen's cabochon eyes were teal blue. "Branwyn

Lennox, I will not offer you information on your quest. You could not now afford it. Let us turn to the service you owe me."

Branwyn balked, annoyed at both Severin and the Queen. "We can afford quite a bit. This isn't a personal project, Your Majesty."

"That is not my concern. Your hellhound has decided I shall not advise you, and so I shall not."

"Come on, Your Majesty!" said Branwyn desperately. "Are you really going to let *him* make decisions for you? Believe me, I realize how tempting it is to punish him, but I'm sure if we work together, we can come up with something much more interesting. Something that doesn't involve stealing some kids away from their whole world."

The floor attendants stared at Branwyn, open-mouthed, and the Queen was silent. Then the handmaiden laughed out loud. "No, there is no more interesting way. I apologize, Your Majesty. The moment overcame me." And she chuckled again before covering her mouth.

Branwyn couldn't really say the Queen's face softened, but once again, there was a hint of amusement around the mouth. Hopefully, she asked, "How about it?"

The Queen's head moved from side to side. "Alas, it is no true offer. You would no more punish him at my whim than you would make him dance. But hold! It does not matter. My judgement is absolute and already given."

Branwyn's teeth clicked together, as she recalled her experience with Tarn: how he couldn't lie in his own realm without damaging it, and how his doubts caused tiny earthquakes. Ultimately, second thoughts had torn most of his domain to shreds, though he'd preserved its heart.

The Queen had already said she wouldn't help them. There was nothing more to be said. Branwyn's annoyance with Severin grew hotter, but she kept it in check. Later, after she'd learned out what body part the Queen wanted this time, she'd explain to him in excruciating detail exactly how he'd fucked up.

Still trying to resign herself, she said, "Right. Well then. That service. Let's hear it."

The Queen looked back at the sky again. "A journey for a journey...." After a moment of silence, she continued. "Soon, my handmaiden will make a journey to the Court of Summer to bring my son home from his holiday. Attend her there and present yourself to him before they depart." Her head lowered and her cabochon eyes were amethysts now. "It is well for him to interact with other mortals now and then."

Branwyn frowned, ignoring Rhianna suddenly nudging her. "That seems... very fair, Your Majesty. How soon is soon, though? We've got our own deadlines."

The Queen tilted her head. "You may work that out with my handmaiden. Goodbye, Branwyn Lennox."

As the chair tuned away, the handmaiden and Rhianna both hustled Branwyn back into the elevator, leaving Severin to follow along or not.

For a moment, it looked like he might not. He was giving the back of the Queen's chair a worrying look. Then he looked down at the floor attendants and gave them his shark smile.

Vividly remembering the fate of Tarn's changeling attendants, Branwyn said, "Severin!" before she could stop herself.

He looked over at her with glittering eyes, then strolled leisurely over to the elevator. "Starting to enjoy that leash already, I see."

Suddenly Branwyn was furious. She pulled him the rest of the way into the elevator and then hit him in the chest with her palm. "I'm doing this for you, you toxic worm. You're the one losing your mind over a kid. I'm trying to help you *find her*, not get locked in a faerie prison for the next millennia. Can't you ever think beyond your immediate gratification?"

Rhianna, who had been having a quiet rapid-fire planning conversation with the handmaiden, abruptly fell silent.

A buzz under his words, Severin said, "I used to. It hasn't paid off." Then, in a different voice, he added, "Don't worry, cupcake. Even if I make a mess, they can't keep me away from *you*."

Branwyn stared at him before pushing herself away. "They could kill me. Shatiel said that would pretty seriously inconvenience you."

"It would kill me, too," said Severin, leaning against the wall again. "But I'll make sure that doesn't happen."

This was in no way reassuring. "How kind," she said frigidly. "Why did you lie to the Queen?"

"I didn't," he said, his voice flat. "I am here because you are. I told her all she needed to know."

"She wanted to *connect*, you asshole. She wanted to *help you.*"

Severin's lip curled. "Do you think I want to 'connect' to the Queen of Stone? Do you think I want to give her any part of me?"

"Do you want to find this kid or not?" Branwyn demanded. "Because if you do, you may have to start actually communicating with people."

"Nah, cupcake," he said. "That's what I have you for. I'm just here to tear things apart."

Branwyn glared at him in mounting frustration. "You are such a… a…"

Suddenly he was too close, his black eyes boring into hers. "A monster? A nightmare? An animal?" His grin cracked across his face and he whispered, "Woof woof."

She stared up at him, and then shoved him hard. "Get away from me. You make me sick!" Branwyn threw herself into the corner of the elevator and slid down to sit on the floor, hugging her knees and hiding her face in her arms.

She was breathtakingly angry at him. Not nervous, not afraid, not even burning with hate. Just... *angry.* She was used to anger empowering her, driving her. But in this situation, what could she do? What could she build that would make things different, but not compromise her own integrity? There was nothing.

Rhianna knelt beside her and said quietly, "It isn't as bad as you think. The Queen *did* help us after all. She gave us a powerful guide to our next destination. And at the Court of Summer, Gale's Court, we'll have a better chance of finding answers."

Branwyn raised her head. Rhianna was oddly pale, but her demeanor was calm and encouraging. "Yeah," she said. "Good idea."

Severin was back leaning against the wall, his arms crossed. As far as Branwyn could tell, her rant had run off him like water off a duck's back. At least this time it didn't seem to have entertained him. His face was totally blank, but it wasn't empty.

Small consolation.

She took a deep breath. "Before we go... Severin. This is Faerie. Everything has a cost, and sometimes it's personal. Are you willing to give up *anything* to find this kid?"

"I've already given up too much, cupcake." His eyes glittered. "What I have left, I'm keeping."

Branwyn thought about that. It was frustrating, and maybe true. And yet, they had to find the kids. Her anger drained away, leaving behind only tiredness.

"Fine. Good to get that on the table. Well, I've worked with stubborn materials before." Then she let Rhianna pull her to her feet and turned her attention to the handmaiden.

10

Between Stone and Summer

RHIANNA and the Queen's handmaiden had already worked out the details of the journey to the Summer Court while Branwyn had been busy with Severin. "Kind of one handmaiden to another," said Rhianna. "It was only natural."

Branwyn was willing to wait for the handmaiden to ready herself for a journey she hadn't intended to start so soon. But she drew the line when the handmaiden encouraged her to take a bath and rest while she waited. Rest would too quickly become sleep, and sleep was too close to the darkness in the belly of Death.

Rhianna, clearly disappointed, also refused the offered bath. The handmaiden obligingly guided them instead to a room of alabaster overlooking a garden of yellow crystals and rose-gold wire, where the ranks of seating suggested that, in the Court of Stone, gardening was live entertainment.

The handmaiden *also* offered to guide Severin to the kennels. With a glance at Branwyn and a sparkle of amusement, she said to him, "Those new to ownership sometimes don't realize how much exercise their hound needs." He laughed and accepted the invitation, to Branwyn's alarm.

But *Starting to enjoy the leash already* still burned. She wasn't his fucking regulator. Shatiel should have known better. If Severin screwed this up, she'd be disappointed in him, but the sooner she found that out, the easier it would be for her to return to not caring.

When the handmaiden returned only a moment later, she was quick to reassure Branwyn. "Do not fear. Nobody in the Court will taunt him now, and I have put him in the hands of a talented faeling who shares some of his interests."

"What interests?" asked Branwyn. "Wait, never mind. I don't want to know."

"Well, I do," said Rhianna brightly. "I'm interested. Miss Maiden, is 'kennel' a euphemism for a brothel in Faerie?"

"A *brothel?*" demanded Branwyn.

"Well, if I can't take a bath…" began Rhianna delicately.

The handmaiden laughed again. "Ah, no. The kennels house the hunting beasts, and the faeling is a specialist in training the most recalcitrant. There *are* those in the Court who would enjoy coupling with a monster no matter how he used them, but I felt introducing them would not have calmed him the same way." She smiled at Rhianna. "But I do think you would have enjoyed the baths."

"Is a faeling like a changeling?" Branwyn asked, eager to move the topic away from Severin and brothels.

"Let me see… They are both of mortal origin, but only a Queen can create a faeling. As a result, they have far more independence and power than changelings. They are often quite troublesome and are thus rare. But the beastmaster is worth it despite his temper."

Somehow this didn't seem to be far enough away from the previous topic. Branwyn said, "Ah. And… I'm sorry if I missed it earlier, but do you have a name of your own?"

"I do not. I am bound to pumice, but I should not like to be called such. I am simply the Queen's handmaiden."

Rhianna caught Branwyn's eye from the other side of the handmaiden, giving her a look that meant, *Ask me about this later.*

Branwyn pulled her mouth to one side, and then said, "All right. Can I call you Handmaiden then?"

The handmaiden considered the question seriously. "To address me, that is appropriate. But to speak of me, please use it as my role rather than my name."

"So, 'Hey Handmaiden, dinnertime!' but 'the handmaiden is hungry'?"

The handmaiden inclined her head demurely. "Thank you. It would not be fitting elsewise. And while we travel, how would you prefer to be addressed?"

"Branwyn," said Branwyn firmly. "Just Branwyn. But, uh, you can introduce me to others as the Artificer, if you think it will help."

"Very good." The handmaiden curtseyed. "I will go now and arrange our travel. You will not have an extended wait here, but you may visit the garden through that door if you wish."

Rhianna asked, "Would it have been a longer wait elsewhere?"

"A hurried bath relaxes no one," said the handmaiden, and retreated from the chamber.

Branwyn turned to contemplate the garden again. "In my experience, it's perceptual rather than actual time compression. But I should have hacked together a reliable timepiece before we came anyhow." She didn't know how long they'd been in that dark place, in the belly of Death, but she had an uncomfortable suspicion it had been longer than she wanted to share.

Rhianna joined her. "Well, we're not working toward a clock time, are we? How's your hammer holding up?"

"Don't worry, I'll swear a lot when the souls start discharging."

"All right," said Rhianna, and seated herself in the first row of seats. Upholstery wasn't a big thing in the Court of Stone, but there was a single cushioned seat in the center. It seemed too small for the Queen of Stone.

"So... you were pretty upset earlier. Anything you want to talk about?" Rhianna asked, carefully casual.

Branwyn shook her head slowly. There was *plenty* she wished she could talk over with Rhianna, but she was going to stay professional on this project even if it killed her. Talking would just turn into fighting, and fighting might be deadly right now. "What did you have on the handmaiden?"

Rhianna looked down at her hands. "She's nice, isn't she?"

Branwyn narrowed her eyes. "That's it?"

"I don't think she's 'simply' a handmaiden, despite what she said. But she *is* nice."

Branwyn looked back at the crystal and wire garden again. "Sometimes people are."

Rhianna sighed. "I suppose so."

Silence fell between them, and it wasn't a comfortable one. Eventually Branwyn shook herself and went through the indicated door and down two flights of stairs to the garden. She spent some time inspecting the wire sculptures, trying to focus on the art. But she kept glimpsing Rhianna leaning on the window edge above, her head on her hands like she was a little girl. It was distracting. It hurt. She wanted her sister back, and she didn't even know how she'd lost her.

When it was time to go, Branwyn was standing in front of three crystals with wire woven thickly between them. It was positioned as a base for a complex secondary structure, but the woven wires weren't able to to catch and support the burden. She was trying to decide if she could turn it into a metaphor for her own relationships when Rhianna called to her from above. *No*, she decided. She'd have to make her own sculpture if she wanted to portray that, and it would involve a lot more than crystals and rose-gold wire.

In the viewing room, the handmaiden awaited. Rhianna was holding all the bags and bouncing on her toes with impatience.

"Ah. Are you refreshed from your meditation?" asked the handmaiden.

Branwyn shrugged noncommittally. "I appreciated having a few moments with nothing new to deal with, at least. Thank you."

"Of course. This way." The handmaiden led them out into the corridor, but it was different now. The walls were obsidian and rounded like a natural tunnel.

"Is changing the halls challenging?" asked Rhianna.

"Sometimes," said the handmaiden. "The Court itself is alive, and it must be directed. The Queen is the only one who can truly command its patterns. The rest of us merely request. Often it's less trouble to just take the long way. But that would be hard on you."

The corridor widened like the horn of a trumpet as they traversed it, ending in a broad arch that opened onto a cracked, flat landscape that stretched unbroken to the horizon. They emerged from the side of a cinder cone that wasn't much taller than the arch it contained. Nearby, a large, flat triangular rock dominated the view. A pavilion had been erected on the rock's upper surface and a steep white filigree staircase led from the ground to the rock's top.

"Our transport," said the handmaiden. "Please ascend."

On top of the rock, railings lined the edges, with cushions strapped to the rail at the wide end. Four low seats had been pulled from the stone in front of the pavilion. Severin lounged in one, his hands clasped behind his head.

Lazily, he said, "It took you long enough. And you didn't even take that bath, I see. You missed out."

"We looked at art," said Branwyn curtly. "We didn't wait very long."

The handmaiden stepped onto the stone's surface, then bent to retrieve the staircase. It folded into a small parcel as she lifted it. "There may be a jolt as we start, so please take a seat."

"This whole stone moves?" Branwyn asked. It seemed contrary to what stones did. When the handmaiden had mentioned transport, she'd imagined a carriage drawn by stone horses: something thematic, but familiar. This was just a big rock.

"It *is* a sailing stone," said the handmaiden. "It can travel quite fast."

Branwyn took the seat furthest from Severin and then regretted it when Rhianna plopped down right beside him.

"You look like you had fun," she told him.

He tilted his head back to watch the handmaiden. "I reminded some cave lions what it was like to be prey."

Rhianna laughed. "You mean you chased cats? Woof, woof."

Branwyn winced and regretted it as Severin's eyes slid over to her. He smirked at her discomfort. "It was something to do. I don't like waiting around."

The handmaiden said, "The beastmaster mentioned the cats were easier to handle after working with you. He seemed much amused." She entered the pavilion and touched the table within.

Somewhere, water began to trickle, growing in flow and sound until it was a low roar. Then, with a crackle and a pop, the water stopped. After a moment, the sailing stone gradually slid sideways and in a circle. It was far too much like being in a car that had lost traction. Branwyn spasmodically clutched at the sides of her chair, and even Rhianna swayed, but Severin, the jerk, laughed and kept his hands behind his head.

The sailing stone completed one lazy spin and started another, and Branwyn began to have worrying thoughts about teacup rides as faerie transport. Then, something clunked from the pavilion and the sailing stone shot forward at a rate that took Branwyn's breath away.

After a moment, both the sense of momentum and the impact of the wind faded. It wasn't quite like being in an airplane or a car, but it *was* a lot better than spinning their way to another Court. She could get used to it.

The handmaiden took the remaining seat. "Soon we will pass from the Queen's Domain into the wild Marches. That will comprise the longest part of this trip. It is ordinarily quite dangerous for even low fae to travel the Marches away from the Road, but the sailing stone makes such risks inconsequential." She gave them a sunny smile.

"Great!" said Rhianna. "Time for lunch." Before Branwyn could respond, she found two energy bars shoved into her hands. "You can have the chocolate ones and I'll have the peanut butter ones."

"Where's mine?" asked Severin.

Rhianna gave him a doubtful look. "Do you really need food?"

"Doesn't Umbriel eat sometimes?"

"He does," Rhianna conceded. "But he's nice. I figured a guy like you subsisted on sheer malice."

Severin laughed again, and Branwyn's insides roiled. Somehow Rhianna got along with all of them: her Advisor, Shatiel, the handmaiden. She even entertained Severin.

Rhianna always had possessed a knack for amusing those more powerful than herself. It had come in handy on their youthful joint misadventures, but the world was different now and at some point she would get hurt.

Branwyn realized she was just staring at her energy bars and started methodically eating them. She had no appetite, but she damn well wasn't going to let that stop her. As Penny had pointed out the night before, not taking care of her body meant her mind jumped all over the place, and she was tired enough as it was.

And by the time she'd finished with both bars, she *was* hungry. "Hey, give me some more," she said. "I know there's other stuff in that backpack. Give me one of those rice and bean packets."

"Uh-uh," said Rhianna. "My Advisor was very insistent we not eat faerie food, so this has to last us."

"Oh," said Branwyn, a dark thought occurring. "Handmaiden, what does happen if mortals eat faerie food?"

The handmaiden, who looked as though she was enjoying the sailing stone's speed enormously, dragged her gaze away from the horizon. "Many mortals who partake of our food find that mortal food can no longer sustain them. A smaller number find faerie food does not nourish, and those die if not returned to the mortal world."

Silence fell as Branwyn and Rhianna looked at each other. *The kids have been here for months.*

Severin slowly unclasped his hands from behind his head and brought them onto the arms of his seat.

Suddenly Rhianna said, "I'm not going to worry about this. I'm *sure* my Advisor must have a plan if the kids we rescue can't eat human food. Plenty of kids already have non-magical problems eating food. Which *sucks*, but technology can help with."

Branwyn said, "Plus, whoever took them from Tucker presumably wanted them to live, or why bother? So this isn't an issue."

Both sisters nodded firmly at each other, but Severin didn't relax again.

Shapes appeared on the horizon they sped toward: round hills rising like domes from a forest that started with unnatural abruptness. Near the edge of the playa, the sailing skewed to run parallel to the large, knotted old trees. When it reached the meadows beyond the forest, it spun again and gave a jerky hop, landing in the meadow. There, the sailing stone's locomotion was no longer smooth and frictionless, but as bumpy as a bad road.

"It will be bumpier as we get further from the Domain," said the handmaiden apologetically. "I hope it won't distress you. The Queen's son rather enjoyed it."

Branwyn turned to reassure her. The black diamond in her hammer started sparking again, whining in her mind. She fumbled it free from its loop on her jeans, a sudden premonition telling her she didn't want to have the black diamond that close to her body when a soul discharged.

She was right. As soon as she lifted the hammer over her head, the black diamond gave up trying to contain the energy and a dark shockwave expanded silently around her. Part of the shockwave passed through the pavilion's upper supports, leaving cracks behind. Rhianna said, "Oh!" and Severin's eyes narrowed.

"Uh," said Branwyn. "Hell. Damn. That was bigger than I expected."

"What was that, please?" inquired the handmaiden, rising to her feet. The sailing stone was still moving, although the pace had slackened dramatically.

"It means we've used up one quarter of the time we have to find these kids," said Branwyn.

"You're sure it's a proportional release?" asked Rhianna, her wide eyes narrowing in thought.

"Pretty sure," said Branwyn. "But don't ask me to explain the math, or how long we were in the belly of Death." She stared at her hammer. The energy going into the black diamond had been streamers of light. She really wished it returned the same way. She eyed the pavilion supports. The dark shockwave was dangerous.

But—"I think we're doing okay. No need to worry yet, time-wise."

Severin leaned forward in the chair, resting his hands between his knees in a posture that was more crouch than sit. He was on edge, but his hands were relaxed and his eyes, while narrow, were mostly human. When he glanced over and met Branwyn's eyes, his mouth twisted in a grim smile far removed from his normal shark smile.

The handmaiden walked to the pavilion and ran her fingers over the cracks in the supports. "This goes deep. It will have to be repaired before I can transport the Queen's son."

"Ugh," said Branwyn, standing up. It was bumpy, but she could keep her balance with a minor effort. "Maybe I can do something." Doing something was always better than worrying.

The handmaiden neither assented nor refused the offer, but remained touching the support, her mouth turned down. As Branwyn touched the other supporting column, Rhianna said thoughtfully, "I wonder what the price of breaking the Queen of Stone's private yacht is. It seems like it might stretch the expense account…"

The handmaiden turned quickly. "Price?"

"Reimbursement for breakages?" Rhianna suggested. "Is that not a thing here?"

Severin said, "That would make it so much harder for faeries to play with mortals."

Branwyn shook her head and concentrated on the pavilion. There was a purity about faerie materials that was distinctly different from traditional materials. In general, the Geometry of Faerie was more obscured, the mass of glowing lines and clusters she normally worked with replaced by the *thing* itself. She could still determine and adjust the properties of objects, but it was like translating from a second language she spoke imperfectly.

With the pavilion, it took concentration, but she could observe the damage the handmaiden had described. What looked like a crack from the outside was a *fracture*, and one that extended through the supports into the structure of the sailing stone itself. The magic of the stone still functioned, but there was a darkness coating the fracture that reminded Branwyn uneasily of the virus that had infected Titanone the previous year. She'd solved that by helping Titanone develop an immune system, but

Titanone was, magically speaking, alive. The stone, while a sophisticated creation, was not.

She pushed at the fracture for a few moments, trying to meld it together once more, then disengaged and asked the handmaiden, "How would it be repaired normally?"

"I… am not sure," said the handmaiden. "It should have been trivial to knit the stone together again, and then the magic regenerates naturally. But the energy of your… your *signal* lingers and cuts through the world."

Severin stood up. "Show me what it looks like, cupcake."

Puzzled, Branwyn said, "You want me to draw you a picture? I don't think it would mean much."

"Not that way," he said, moving over. He turned her back to the pavilion, raised her hand back to the support, and placed his over it.

Like this, he whispered in her mind.

Branwyn swallowed, keenly aware of Rhianna's sharp gaze. "W-Why?"

Just show me, cupcake.

For a moment, Branwyn yearned for a simpler time: when she had just hated Severin; when rebelling against both his commands and closeness was right and natural. She'd felt strong and certain then. Had it been so long ago? Or only yesterday?

He leaned his head forward, bumping it gently against hers. *Embellish your scrapbook later.*

Branwyn shook her head. He was right. Wishing for the past wouldn't bring it back. She focused herself and examined the structure of the pavilion and the sailing stone once again. This time, even when she concentrated, she couldn't escape the sense of Severin right behind her, looking over her shoulder. She'd never been a fan of being watched while she worked.

Severin's fingers laced through hers as they looked at the dark fracture. Once again her self-consciousness rose, threatening to take away her perception in a welter of emotion.

Shhh, he whispered. *Don't distract me, Branwyn.*

"What are you doing?" she mumbled.

In response, the fracture abruptly fused together, with a gleam of light that reminded Branwyn of Severin's molten glass weapons. The darkness that had limned the fracture fled from the light, twisting away and into the general Geometry.

"Ah!" cried Rhianna. The strange, startled sound from her usually unflappable sister jerked Branwyn from the Artificer trance.

"What?" said Branwyn, turning around and pushing Severin out of the way with one hand. Rhianna sat up straight in her seat, blinking frantically, her arms closed around herself. "Rhianna!"

Branwyn bounded across the jouncing sailing stone to her sister. Before she skidded to a halt, Rhianna had unclenched her arms. She shook her head. "That was... that was weird. I felt something move through me."

An ice spike rammed down Branwyn's spine. There was...

...a sparkle... on Rhianna's skin...

But she glinted strangely in the mirror, as if the dim light was striking angles instead of curves, and then scattering wrong.

She looked hollowed, like something had been taken away.

Branwyn realized that, somehow, the black energy had *damaged* her sister in a mysterious but fundamental way. She'd never seen anything like it.

Something brittle in Branwyn snapped.

"Fuck!" said Branwyn, but already in her head she was downplaying, downplaying, *don't show her how upset I am because...*

"Did it hurt you?" she demanded. "Are you all right?"

"Uh, nothing hurts?" Rhianna questioned herself as she patted herself down. "It was cold, but just for a minute."

"Son of a bitch!" Branwyn shouted. *Yeah, this was about right level of upset. This wasn't killing somebody, possibly herself.*

Rhianna scrambled back in her chair. "What? What happened?"

"What if it had hurt you?" *unforgiveable lie* "I keep screwing up!"

But Rhianna the liar would lie too. She'd keep smiling no matter how she hurt. She'd chased after Branwyn with both skinned knees dripping blood when they'd been children. She'd tried skating on a sprained ankle just so Branwyn's birthday party wouldn't be ruined. She'd once cracked jokes about a broken arm, denying her own pain until their stepfather had arrived to hold their anguished mother.

I cannot stand to see her pretend she's fine.

"Dammit! Handmaiden, check the stone? Can it speed up again?" Branwyn stood up, because moving was better than still-ness, action better than thought. Her gaze fell on Severin, who looking off the back of the stone.

Had he even noticed what had happened?

Then she thought *This was him, he did it, he did it on purpose, he distracted me* and she wanted to *kill* him. The urge swept across her with a strength she'd never before imagined. She'd stumbled a step in his direction under that drive before he turned and looked over at her.

Just a glance into his dark eyes and the bone-sharp guilt she'd started with resurfaced from the murderous rage. Whether he'd done it on purpose or not, it was her fault. She'd enabled him. She'd ignored the warning at the mirror. She'd learned artificing and dealt with Faeries. She, she, she...

Branwyn stopped.

She said, "No."

No. This was not happening now. This *was not happening* here. She *would not* break now, while she had work to do. She could break later after everything was done.

"What's happening?" she said icily to Severin. She'd be calm for now, perfectly calm. She *would*. It wasn't easy; the guilt and rage surged within her, telling her she was hiding, denying, *escaping*—but *later* she promised herself. *Later.* She'd solve everything else first.

"Something is following us," he said, an odd brightness in his voice.

Branwyn's brow furrowed. She couldn't, at first, see why it mattered, or how he could be so sure. Her thoughts raced wildly. Everything seemed like nonsense and noise. *Calm.* She would make herself be calm.

The handmaiden announced, "The structure has been adequately repaired, but the magic will take time to regenerate. We're almost halfway to the Domain of Summer, though."

"Great news!" said Rhianna, standing up and shading her eyes to look behind the stone. If she hadn't had that *glint*, Branwyn would have believed she was fine despite the black energy passing through her. But she did, and she wasn't, and Rhianna *couldn't know* her sister had done this to her... if she didn't know already. Bone-sharp guilt and hook-tooth lies, they'd fight to see who could destroy Branwyn first. But... *later.*

"Oh, wow," Rhianna added. "What *is* that?"

"I don't know," said Severin happily, like he was crazy, like it was the best thing he'd seen all day. "What do you think, lady?"

The handmaiden and Branwyn joined them. In the distance, the meadowlands were smoking.

Branwyn tried to concentrate. "It's a fire?"

"Something *on* fire," said Rhianna, an odd note in her voice.

They stared for a long while, until Rhianna said, "It's faster than we are."

"I know," said Severin, so cheerfully Branwyn wanted to stab him.

"I... don't know this beast," said the handmaiden. "It is not an aspect of Faerie I recognize." She looked up at the blue sky. "And it is dangerous."

Branwyn couldn't see anything unusual in the sky, but as it

caught up, she could finally make out the creature burning the meadow. It was very large; once Branwyn might have said 'enormous,' before she'd seen Night from a distance. It was easily the size of an elephant. While it bounded on four legs, it seemed to be constructed primarily of fire and thorns. Just looking at it made Branwyn uneasy.

The handmaiden returned to the table under the repaired pavilion and a moment later the sailing stone veered abruptly. In a clear response, the beast of fire and thorns altered its own course.

"Uh, how close are we to the Court of Summer?" Branwyn asked.

"Not nearly close enough," said the handmaiden. "The beast will catch us before we even enter the Domain."

"Nah," said Severin. "I'll deal with it. Be right back, cupcake." He hopped the guard rail, stepped off the back of the stone, and was immediately left far behind.

Branwyn looked blankly at where he'd dropped. Well. That was handled. She returned to her seat.

"Aren't you going to watch?" Rhianna asked.

"No."

"Oh." Rhianna paused to consider this. "Well, I am."

"Feel free," Branwyn said. "Cheer him on." She stared at the landscape ahead, but she didn't really see it. She *was* calm now, so next she made herself focus on something useful: the energy that had blasted through Rhianna, and how to avoid a repeat. There were three charges left in the hammer's Machine fragment. Random fragments of ideas floated through her mind, nonsensical thoughts that slipped away before she could grasp them and turn them meaningful.

Before Branwyn could cudgel a coherent plan out of her tired brain, the handmaiden joined her. "Do you not wish for your monster to delay the beast?"

Branwyn shrugged. "I don't have an opinion." Once she

might have scorned his bloodlust, resented him acting as rescuer, cursed his mere existence. Right now, all she cared about was avoiding further delay. The faster they completed their journey, the fewer opportunities for the dark energy to hurt somebody else.

She blinked and glanced narrowly at the handmaiden, wondering if she could see the change in Rhianna with that visor. She'd said she didn't have eyes like mortals did. "Do mortals and faeries and monsters all appear the same to you?"

The handmaiden tilted her head. "How do you mean?"

"You're one of the first faeries I've met who I could easily identify as 'not human' without using my magic Sight. Everybody else, monsters and angels and most of the faeries running around Earth, they… they may have a *look* but it's a hint, not a guarantee of what they are."

"Ah, mortal eyes." The handmaiden sounded enlightened. "I believe I see all you do, but without the requirement of light. All mortal bodies—and this includes my own and the monster's—have a unique composition of earthly materials, which is what I perceive. I can see both similarities and differences." She gave a little chuckle. "Though when I've observed crowds of mortals remotely, I tend to have problems seeing individuals."

Branwyn didn't understand why that was funny, and didn't care. Choosing her words carefully, aware of just how good Rhianna was at pretending to do one thing while paying attention to something else, she asked, "So you can see that Sev is what he is, while Rhianna and I are something else?"

"Oh yes. You both have natural mortal bodies, while his is a supremely crafted vessel. They're very distinct."

"How similar are Rhianna and I? Can you tell we're related?"

The handmaiden rotated her head between Branwyn and Rhianna. "You are *very* similar. Full-blooded sisters? But… there are… some differences…"

Branwyn could hear the frown developing in the handmaiden's voice and shook her head, holding her finger up to her mouth in a 'shh' gesture. Aloud she said, "I suppose there would be."

The handmaiden's mouth quirked to one side. Then she placed her fingertips on Branwyn's throat and whispered, "What is it? You may speak silently."

"The differences... has something changed very recently?" Branwyn mouthed.

"Yes," whispered the handmaiden. "The passing signal carried something away. Is that bad?"

"It's hard to see how it can be good," Branwyn managed. *Calm.* "Can you tell what it was?"

The handmaiden shook her head. "I can't. I am not much of a scholar of mortals."

"Not even by comparing to me?"

With a smile, the handmaiden said, "You're not *that* similar, Branwyn."

Frustrated, Branwyn sat back in her seat and pushed her hands through her hair. Behind her, Rhianna broke into a cheer. "Woo-hoo! I think it's down!"

She bounced to Branwyn's elbow. "He intercepted it a few minutes ago, but the fire kept burning. Just now, though, the wind took the smoke away, and nothing was left but the charred meadow. I wish I could have seen what he did. Will he be back soon, Bran?"

"How should I know?" Branwyn snapped and immediately regretted it. "I'm sorry. I'm worrying about the charges in the hammer, and what to do about them. Next time somebody could get hurt."

Liar, came Severin's voice in her ear, and, *Let's talk.*

Branwyn held up one finger. "Actually," she said, with brittle brightness, "Just give me a few minutes and I'll go get him."

Although she was expecting the *yank*, it came harder than she expected, and she sprawled backwards into the velvet darkness. Severin once again sat in the armchair. This time he had a ghastly burn on one side of his face and his clothes were shreds. But as she scrambled to her feet, the burn changed from a horrific mottled red, to shiny and pink, and then faded to his normal skin tone.

A single window floated at eye level, displaying Rhianna as she looked quizzically around the sailing stone. Her mouth formed a silent query, and then she flopped into Branwyn's seat and started talking to the handmaiden. Even via the window, Branwyn could still see the *glint* along Rhianna's form.

She dragged her gaze away to stare darkly at Severin. "What are we talking about?"

He met her gaze impassively, his eyes shadow-grey. "So calm for somebody who wanted to kill me a few moments ago."

"Later," she said. That was all she intended to say. Everything but calm and focus and action was for *later*. That was what she intended, but she was tired and her mind went in dangerous directions when she was tired. So instead she also said, "*Did* you aim the energy at her when you fused the stone?"

Severin leaned forward in his chair, and suddenly he was standing right in front of her. Softly, he said, "You want me to say yes, and you want me to say no. A double-edged knife to use against yourself." The shark smile passed over his face. "Ask me again *later*."

Her own rage came rushing back, breathtaking, overwhelming, and she felt an answering *creak* of cracking glass in her chest. Her rage called to his own. She wanted to *push him*, push that cracking glass until it exploded in shards around her. Her vision swam and the black velvet space flickered.

She reached up, pulled Severin's head down to hers and pressed her mouth against his. It wasn't a kiss so much as an invasion, opening up and pushing into him like he was one of her projects gone wrong and she was angrily looking for the flaw. She wanted to draw that world-ending rage of his over her and drown herself in it, punish herself with it.

But he was holding her face; he was kissing her too. His mouth and tongue and hands devoured her, and that was right. Not good, *so very bad, but right all the same. No matter how he touched her, or how good it felt, or how a part of her bleated about how she'd feel* tomorrow, *she couldn't stop because his rage was what she needed* right now: *the way it wove through the tightening of his muscles under her fingers and whispered under his words. It was a rage at the whole universe, a rage as great as her own and nothing could cut through it. But this, for just a moment, could transfigure it.*

Skin against skin and her nails on his back, and his teeth along her collarbone; his arms around her and his shoulders flexing. Then he was inside her, hard and moving, exquisite, exactly as she wanted, and she was still kissing him, wrapped around him, furious and hungry and aching. In her mind, she said, "Severin," and he whispered, "Say it again," and so she said it again and again. Then he said, "You don't really mean it," and she wanted to scream *as she clenched around him.*

Branwyn blinked.

Severin still sat in his armchair, and she stood in front of him, just as she had a moment before. As the fragment of experience flickered in her memory, she shifted her weight. She was fully clothed. So was he. Physically she felt... definitely uncomfortable... but not like she'd just...

"Did I just have a dream?" she demanded, scowling. She recognized her own dreams, influenced by the flavor of recent events.

One corner of his mouth tilted. "Back to the status quo?" Then he added, "It's not a good idea to visit me while tired, cupcake. Dreams work differently here."

She scowled, and the hate she felt was the old, familiar hate: the tip of an iceberg she knew how to avoid. That... other, purer hate, that murderous rage, was somehow tucked away now. The thought of *later* brought it close to the surface, but all she had to do right now was look away.

She looked at Severin instead. "You're a giant asshole."

"Aww, I like you too, cupcake. Did you want to talk about Rhianna more?"

"What is there to say?" If her glare was lasers, he'd be on fire.

Calmly, he said, "I see what you see. I don't know what was taken. I won't tell her. Is that about it?"

Branwyn drew her eyebrows together. After a moment, she said, "Thank you. Now let's go back before… before something else happens."

"Of course, cupcake." He grinned his asshole shark grin. "It sounds like you need a nap." And the window featuring Rhianna swooped over them.

11

The Domain of Summer

BRANWYN'S overnight bag made an adequate pillow, but the sailing stone was as hard as a rock. That about summed up her current sense of humor. She stretched out in the pavilion's shade and spent a few minutes trying to sleep. But she couldn't. She was too angry, too tense, and the memory of the Belly of Death was still too close.

"Sev!" she said as she sat up, because she didn't want any cracks about leashes.

He turned in his chair, giving her a skeptical look instead.

"When you do that forehead-sleepytime thing, are you just making people sleep normally, or is it weird?" She'd seen him put annoying people to sleep previously, and she'd heard how he'd used it as a supremely simple solution to calm Zachariah's panicking twins once.

"It's sleep," he said. Then he added, as if an irrelevant afterthought, "Dreamless sleep."

She was not amused. "Fine." Then she stretched out again and said, "Get on with it."

"Somebody's so cranky," he murmured, and crouched beside

her. She gave him her best laser glare until his finger touched her forehead. Then sleep swept over her, completely irresistible, peaceful. Dreamless, and nothing at all like the walk from Tucker to Faerie.

———

BRANWYN WOKE to Rhianna shaking her. "Come on, wake up, Branwyn!" But she'd been far too deeply asleep to just jump to her feet, or to even do more than frown at the worried note in her sister's voice.

"What...?" She shook her head muzzily and managed sitting up.

Rhianna moved behind her and started fixing her ponytail like they'd done for each other as kids. As she finger-combed Branwyn's hair, she said, "It's not an emergency, but the hand-maiden says we'll be passing into Summer's Domain soon, and Sev is off dealing with the beast again."

Sleep-drunk, Branwyn tried to process this. "Again?"

"Yeah. He's... he's had to put it down twice already since you fell asleep. He said it wouldn't be worth it to wake you."

"It keeps coming back?" Any minute now, Branwyn would get excited about that. Or possibly fall back asleep. That last sounded like a good idea.

Rhianna tightened Branwyn's ponytail, yanking on her hair. "No, no. Stay awake. Or, if you must go back to sleep, get him back here first. The handmaiden doesn't want to enter the Domain without him present. She said it would be improper."

Branwyn looked around. The handmaiden stood beside the control table, both hands placed on the surface. In the distance ahead of them, a green and golden flower the size of a mountain filled the horizon. The vast meadowlands were edged by a cliff-drop on one side and a barren field dotted with enormous trees on the other.

Directly behind the sailing stone, but far back, was the fire: red flames flickering through smoke, and the occasional flash of a long, curved thorn. Beyond that, Night moved across the land.

"You might as well look up, too," said Rhianna. "Get the whole picture. And then get him back here."

Obediently, Branwyn looked up. There was the brilliant blue sky, and the white sun that seemed somehow brighter, and, oh, there was the moon, too… and a plurality of rainbows… and a curving white band…

"A ring?" she asked, with simple amazement.

"The handmaiden called it the Binder," said Rhianna grimly. "One of the world-spirits. It's not supposed to be visible. But they're all very *interested* in our mysterious pursuit."

"Okay…" Branwyn shook her head thoroughly. "Right. Severin." She'd been trying to focus on the task requested of her, not call him, but evidently that didn't matter.

A little busy here, cupcake, he whispered.

"Come back," she whispered back.

Instead of arguing, he stepped out of the air. He wasn't burned this time, but blood dripped down both his arms from under shredded sleeves. Crouching before Branwyn, he took her chin in his hand and turned her head this way and that in rhythm with his words. "You should still be sleeping. What is it?"

Branwyn blinked at him, then pointed at the handmaiden. When he released her, she flopped back on her sister, sliding down to use Rhianna's lap as a pillow. "Wow, yeah. That was some sleep. Not good sleep for being on an adventure though. Dangerous. Gimme a minute." Her eyes drifted closed again.

"Yeah. I suppose he felt he could keep you safe while you rested," said Rhianna thoughtfully.

Branwyn's eyes popped open again. She stared at her sister's forearm and saw that awful *glint*. "Is there any coffee in that backpack? I'll eat it dry if I have to."

"I think so. Let me up."

Branwyn sighed and pushed herself upright again. Severin was leaning against one of the pavilion supports, looking back at the fire following them. Branwyn wondered if he'd figured anything out about it, but put off asking until she felt she could do something with the answers other than say, "Wow...."

Instead she looked at the sky. The face on the moon was different in Faerie. More real, somehow. And the rainbows more closely resembled beautiful dresses spilled across the sky than prismatic effects.

Rhianna appeared beside her again, shaking a dark fluid in a water bottle. "Instant coffee, liquid form."

It helped, some. Branwyn was standing, feeling more like the problem-solver she was supposed to be and trying not to dwell on the events immediately before her nap, when they passed into Summer's Domain.

There was no customs check, nobody to shake their finger at Severin and declare him contraband, despite the handmaiden talking of proprieties. The sailing stone simply slid through a wrinkle in one of the vast petals that walled off Summer's Domain, and the air itself changed. The air of the meadow March had been fresh, but Summer's air smelled *sweet*, full of the verdant perfume of a mild summer dawn, something Branwyn had experienced about three times in Pasadena, California.

That they were in a vast flower remained true within the Domain, with the golden petals curving into the sky all around them. In the far distance, what had to be the Summer Court shimmered: a second crystalline flower high on a twisting white stem. Between them and the high bloom were gently rolling fields, cultivated and dotted with clusters of round houses rising on squat stems of their own. But it was the same sky above, crowded with heavenly objects.

"The beast won't come through the wall?" Rhianna asked the handmaiden.

She shook her head. "It is very unlikely. And if it did, it would provide the Summer Knights with some entertainment."

Severin's mouth twisted sourly, and Branwyn wondered if he wasn't enjoying the fighting anymore, or if he just didn't want to share. Either way, tough luck for him. If Branwyn had to suffer, so could he.

She asked the handmaiden, "Did you ever figure out what it is? Or why it keeps coming back?"

"I have no answers. Your monster seemed to have the situation managed, save for the way the world-spirits are responding." The handmaiden looked up at the crowded sky. "That is more disturbing, and it is my happy thought that fae far greater than I must also be concerned."

"Hmm," said Branwyn. "I'll let that be my happy thought too."

She stretched, working the last of the sleep out of her muscles. She felt one hundred percent better than she had before the nap. The last twenty-four hours had been hard, cripplingly hard, and there were so many problems she still had to solve. But the deep sleep had let her mind get the filing done and safely tucked away the complex storm of emotions aroused by both monster and sister until she needed to bring them forth as tools and weapons.

Until then, well, she had Rhianna and Severin as allies, and within the context of this project, she trusted them to work with her: trusted Rhianna's basic humanity and Severin's strange desperation. After would take care of itself. Somehow it always did.

A road twisted through the cultivated fields, but it was well-trafficked by the rural residents of the Domain, and the sailing stone slid instead over a ditch between the road and the fields. The stone moved much faster than the wagons and carts pulled by draft animals that ranged from oxen to giant frogs.

The inhabitants of the Domain far more resembled what

Branwyn would once have expected of faeries: shorter than humans, brown-skinned, with large pointed ears and luminous eyes. They all watched the sailing stone with interest as it passed, and a few waved. Some of them were children.

Uneasily, Branwyn said to the handmaiden. "There are so many of them. Are they all... where did they come from? Are they changelings?"

The handmaiden looked at the residents indulgently. "It *is* a crowded Domain, is it not? They are the children of Harvest, a world-spirit, although I think changelings and mortals walk among them. I know some of the dreamborn who do not wish to be bothered by their changelings send them here. But most of the children of Harvest live as mortals do, albeit far more peacefully."

Branwyn looked back at a wizened elder driving a cart pulled by two gazelles. Once upon a time, Severin had dismissed her concern for Tarn's changelings by comparing them to video game characters. She'd personally seen Tarn's William killed twice, and he'd been restored each time.

"Do they ever come to Earth?" asked Rhianna.

The handmaiden paused, her brows rising as if the question startled her, then shook her head. "No, they could not."

Rhianna continued asking general questions about the inhabitants of Faerie in a chatty, friendly way. Branwyn paid attention with only half an ear as she returned to looking around. It was such a pretty fantasy land, but it made her skin prickle and she couldn't figure out why.

It didn't feel like a targeted threat though. She had enough personal issues to solve. Such as her hammer and its three remaining soul charges, and what to do if the Court of Summer proved a dead end toward finding the stolen children.

She sat down and put the hammer across her lap. It didn't take much analysis to see that there was no way to shape the discharge, so instead she had a firm conversation with the

Machine fragment about giving her more warning. It complained at her, in that wordless way of Machine fragments, letting her know how icky the soul energy felt. After a moment of commiseration, Branwyn withdrew her attention from the hammer and turned to the potentially solvable problem of tracing the kids.

She could probably do something with a compass, she decided. A compass attuned to mortal blood. Yes, there were other mortals in Faerie, but unless the kids had been split up, there would be quite a concentration of them. But... that was too uncertain, especially in such a short time frame. Not a compass, but a map and a dowsing crystal? She'd need a map of Faerie, and a crystal. But she didn't really understand dowsing conceptually. How accurate did the map have to be? Would she have to teach the crystal to read the map? Even in the modern age of faeries and wizards, it sounded too much like fuzzy thinking. No, she'd have to come up with something else...

She spent a while turning over ideas as the sparkling bloom of the Court of Summer grew closer and closer. Then something occurred to her, and she tilted her head back toward where Severin still stood.

"Sev, you can make charms, right?" She remembered the Queen of Stone, when she'd enacted the vision-sharing magic upon Branwyn at their very first meeting, saying it was a 'blessing,' not a charm, but Branwyn wasn't sure that was more than semantics. And she'd seen Severin doing Geometry-based tether magic.

He gave her an unfriendly look, possibly still cranky about being summoned back from his final fight. Or maybe he didn't like being called Sev. "I *can*."

"Did you put anything on Charlie?"

"No." His voice was chilly, his expression forbidding.

With a flash of dark delight, Branwyn realized that even in this grim mood, she was no more intimidated by him than she would be of a Senyaza monster hunter. It might have been because she had so many other tangled feelings that fear had simply dropped off the register. Or perhaps she just trusted herself to cope with any upsets. In either case that forbidding expression wasn't going to work on her now.

"Why not?" she asked. "The twins are loaded down with protective charms and I managed to get blanks set on my family too."

Every human had a minimum of seven Geometric nodes, and each node could host a charm that worked as a fixed or activated magical effect. Consent was *not* required to place them, and it was much easier for a charm creator to place their own than replace somebody else's. Since the magical effects could be nasty just as easily as they could be useful, unfilled nodes were *risky* if you interacted with the supernatural... and these days everybody was potentially interacting with the supernatural.

Severin stared at her for a moment and then looked away. When it became clear he didn't intend to answer, Branwyn rolled to her feet and moved so she was back in his line of sight. He looked over her head.

Branwyn looked at his hard jawline and resisted the irrational desire to stroke her finger down his throat. "I'm not going to make you tell me, you know. I'm just going to draw my own conclusions. Let's see..."

"Later," he said tightly. Something in Branwyn throbbed painfully, but he kept going. "Later, we can take out one of your charms and I'll make one for you. You won't like it very much, but then you'll have your precious answer. Doesn't that sound like fun?"

Blithely, Branwyn said, "Hmm. I don't think it'd help much. I was hoping you might have placed something I could use as a hook for tracking her down. Right now, I'm looking at a uniqueness issue."

She watched his expression change and took a step backwards. Not afraid of him, not afraid of the grimness fading from his face, just... managing herself and her desire to touch him.

"What else could you use?" he asked intently.

"Oh, anything concrete and unique to her. Got any vials of her blood tucked away?" She raised her eyebrows.

"No. I can find something else though."

"Yeah? Okay..." Branwyn stared off ahead for a few minutes. "If you won't do charms, it gets trickier. I can wake up something that *wants* to find her, and with your 'something else,' I can teach it to recognize her, but the mechanism of action is the tough part." She gave Severin a quick, distant smile. "Not impossible, though. I just need some creativity and the right materials. And oh look, we're coming up to the Court. This might not even be necessary."

Then she made her way to the front of the sailing stone, feeling his gaze on her, and proud of herself for treating him like a client instead of a complication. She'd used her time productively, too. That was just as important.

There was a cute little village at the base of the Summer Court: picturesque round houses with a hint of the mushroom about them, with gorgeously illustrated hanging signs indicating that here she might acquire a foaming tankard and there a pair of scissors, and oh look, there she could get potion bottles. *Actually, that pair of scissors might come in handy later.* She made a mental note.

The stem of the white bloom of the Summer Court was a broad translucent bole, surrounded by a white spiral staircase with absolutely no landings until the leaves began halfway up. The sailing stone spun to a stop in a little courtyard with a burbling fountain near the base of the stairs. Branwyn stared up. There was a dock on one of the giant leaves.

Airships? This really was a video game world.

Rhianna handed her the overnight bag. "I keep feeling like I've been here before. It's unreal."

155

"Yes," Branwyn agreed. "Parts of it, anyhow."

The handmaiden deployed the sailing stone's ladder and Branwyn headed to it. Once she was on the ground, she strode directly to the fountain, where the water forming a stone girl's hair rushed and swirled in a chest-high tulip basin before spilling into a wide trough. There, she dunked her face into the cold water and wished she had a bar of soap.

Rhianna said wistfully, "If they offer us a bath here, can we accept?"

Branwyn glanced at her from the corner of her eye as she slicked water off her face. "You can do what you want. You could have taken the bath before."

"Could I have?" Rhianna had a strange little smile, almost as disturbing as that *glint*.

"I wouldn't have stopped you."

"No." Rhianna sighed. "You would have just frowned." She shifted the straps of the backpack. "Are you ready for more stairs?"

The handmaiden approached, folding up the ladder. Branwyn noticed that Severin remained atop the sailing stone, crouched at the edge, looking down at them.

"What's up with him?" she asked the handmaiden.

"He wishes to remain for now. He said he would have no trouble joining you when you required him. But you were discussing stairs. If you wish to take them, you may, of course, but the Court of Summer has several elevators for public use within the bole, you see?"

Branwyn looked closer at the translucent trunk, and saw three green-tinted elevators moving up and down, all of them containing the faeries of one variety or another.

"The denizens of the Court and its Duchies enjoy pleasure-trips here. The view of the Domain from on high is considered... very satisfying. It isn't the grand view of my Queen's tower, but even some of the Court of Stone have expressed appreciation for it."

"Admit it, you love it," said Branwyn.

Primly, the handmaiden said, "When I first viewed this incarnation of the Domain, I was pleased enough. Will you come?"

"Well, with such high praise, how could I say no?"

Branwyn and Rhianna walked with the handmaiden along the trunk until they came to an ordinary-looking green door. Without fanfare, the handmaiden opened it and led them in.

The interior of the trunk had the three green-tinted transparent elevators around the perimeter, with a tiny but bustling marketplace in the center. The handmaiden ignored the marketplace and Branwyn caught Rhianna's arm as she swerved that direction, telling her, "You *might* have to choose between a bath and shopping."

Instead they went to one of the elevators. The loose line waiting for that elevator evaporated at the handmaiden's smile, and the three of them ended up alone in the rising room.

Thoughtfully, Rhianna said, "Is there no security here? You mentioned the Knights of Summer? Where are they?"

"Some are above, some below. But why do you speak of security?"

Rhianna frowned. "I had the impression the ruby knight functioned as a gatekeeper and guardian for your own Court. Is there nothing like that here?"

"Ah! The ruby knight is the Queen of Stone's champion. In all ways save one, he enacts her will. His own power is no greater than my own, but as her champion he channels the Queen's vast strength."

"And here?" Rhianna persisted.

The handmaiden hesitated. "It is different here. The Queen of Summer's strength is... is different."

Rhianna's frown deepened. "And is there any defense if Sev... if a dangerous enemy were to go on a rampage?"

"The Knights of Summer would engage him, of course, but they are sportsmen, not true warriors. As to your deeper question…" The handmaiden's mouth tightened. "The Court of Summer would be slaughtered. They have no true protection save for being what they are. Before the Covenant was broken that was enough. No faerie would harm a Queen Regnant. Now that Heaven and Hell have turned their attention to us again…" She shook her head, but didn't go on.

"I'm a little surprised the Queen of Stone let her son take a holiday here if it's so dangerous," said Branwyn.

"It is necessary while he is so young, for here is the Well of Time. And… the Queen can't imagine anyone harming him."

"But you can," Branwyn said.

The handmaiden's mouth twisted painfully. "Yes. He… he is so very easy to love. You will see. And when you have finished the Queen's behest, I will send you on to see the Queen of Summer, and you will see her, too. Maybe you'll even understand."

The elevator opened at the base of the flower and the handmaiden led them through an atrium-like space to yet another flight of stairs. Now that Rhianna had pointed it out, the lack of any kind of security, even something as basic as a reception desk, stood out to Branwyn. They simply walked through a door, up a flight of stairs, and down a hall. Outside curved double doors painted with many towers, the handmaiden stopped. She reached for the door handle, then stopped, breathing deeply for a moment. Her hand trembled.

There was a clatter behind the door, and a small child's voice said, "Down it goes!"

Sudden fear clenching her heart, Branwyn reached past the handmaiden and turned the door handle.

12

The Summer Court

BEYOND THE DOOR WAS A LARGE, airy playroom, where many children sat on a warm wooden floor, playing with blocks and dolls. Several adults loitered around the edges, as Marley did when she was supervising the twins. The adults were the tall, elegant faeries Branwyn normally saw, although most of them had brown skin instead of pale. The children were almost all members of the people called the children of Harvest, ranging from preschool-aged to early adolescence.

One of them was human.

They all looked over as the door opened, and the human boy who had been kneeling in front of a pile of wooden blocks fell back to a seated position, waving. "Handmaiden! Where have you been? I missed you."

"Oh no," said the eldest of the Harvest's children. "Is it time for Griff to go already?" She pounced on him, wrapping her arms around him and rubbing her cheek against his while tickling him. "He's too cute! I don't want to let him go!"

"Not... not instantly. But soon. His mother and... and the

whole Court of Stone misses him." There was a catch in the handmaiden's voice.

"I *suppose*," said the tweenish Harvest's child. "But stay a day or two. Who are these girls?"

The handmaiden said, "They have business with Griff for now. After that, I was going to send them to you, Your Majesty."

The young Queen of Summer jumped to her feet as Branwyn blinked. "All right." She clapped her hands. "Okay, babies, playtime's over. Say bye to Griff until next time he visits!"

The adults in the playroom mobilized, managing the crowd of children who wanted to kiss and hug Griff and herding or carrying them out of the room. The last to leave was the child Queen, who gave Branwyn and Rhianna a speculative look as she said, "I'll be waiting for you." Then she slammed the door behind her, and they were alone with the human son of the Queen of Stone.

Rhianna, who had stood, frozen, just inside the entrance the entire time, suddenly sat down hard on the wooden floor.

The handmaiden waved a hand helplessly. "The Summer Queen."

"Summer's my friend," said Griff proudly. "She brought the other kids to watch me make towers. And she helped me measure the Summer Court. Do you want to see how tall it is?"

Griff looked to be five or six years old, close in age to Zachariah's twins. As far as Branwyn could tell, he hadn't even noticed herself or Rhianna. He was wearing stretchy pants and a tunic embroidered with the Queen of Stone's aquamarine tower, and he wore a large oval locket set with a moonstone. His dark brown eyes were bright, his black, springy curls practically glowed, and his humanity radiated from him like a physical force.

The handmaiden said, "Later, Griff. For now, I want to introduce you to these mortals—"

Rhianna interrupted her. "I do want to see how tall the

Summer Court is. Can you show me, Griff?" She sent Branwyn an urgent look before crawling over to join Griff.

The little boy said, "All right! You sit there and watch!"

Branwyn caught the metaphorical ball and pulled the handmaiden to the far side of the room. The handmaiden followed her docilely, though she still had that catch in her breathing.

"Where did that kid come from? Who is he?" Branwyn whispered fiercely.

"He... he is the Queen of Stone's son," said the handmaiden uncertainly. "A mortal, yes. Did you not know?"

Branwyn kept remembering the Queen of Stone's odd behavior at the mention of stolen children and wanted to shake the handmaiden. "We did not. We did mention we were on a mission to recover stolen children, didn't we?"

The handmaiden's face stiffened and her voice grated. "Griff is not one of your stolen children."

"Then how did he get here? Where are his parents?"

"I don't know. In Hell, I hope. They didn't want him; they abandoned him, and he is *ours* now." A rim of crimson light appeared around the handmaiden's visor as her fists clenched.

The room itself trembled and Griff's tower collapsed. He frowned. "Is Mama sad? That shouldn't have happened. I had everything balanced just right."

"Try again," said Rhianna. "Sometimes that's all you can do."

"Listen," said Branwyn in a low voice. "You can't just—"

The handmaiden wrapped her hand around the shoulder strap of Branwyn's bag, tugging her closer, her words feverish and fast. "If you take that child... if you even *try* to take Griff, you would unleash a nightmare across both our worlds. Do not. *Please* do not."

Discomfited, Branwyn said, "Look, I don't *want* to take him away. He seems happy and healthy. There's just—"

That was when the handmaiden, the glow from under her

visor cherry-red, flung herself, sobbing, on Branwyn's shoulder. "He *does*, doesn't he? He *does* look healthy. He *is* healthy. He's so beautiful."

The handmaiden of the Queen of Stone was lighter than she looked. Branwyn was utterly flummoxed. She looked over the faerie's shoulder at Rhianna helplessly, and Rhianna made back-patting motions. Branwyn obediently duplicated them for the faerie.

I'm so, so glad Severin stayed behind, she thought.

Mmm? came his whisper.

"No!" she mouthed, suddenly frantic. "Don't come here. Stay where you are. You won't make things better."

Now I'm curious…

"No!"

I'll just find other entertainment, shall I? Ah, here comes something now…

Branwyn gritted her teeth and didn't rise to the bait. Instead she stroked the hair of the murmuring handmaiden and tried to figure out what she was saying. Something about a fire and how much it hurt watching a small child grow.

Griff, restacking his blocks, said, "The handmaiden is crying again, isn't she?"

"I think so," said Rhianna. "Does she cry often?"

"Six times since Mama adopted me," said Griff. "That I counted, anyhow. I miss things."

"Why does she cry?" asked Rhianna, stacking her own blocks.

Griff cast an expert eye over her little tower. "That's going to fall over at five blocks."

"Hmm," said Rhianna, and adjusted the base. "Do you know why the handmaiden cries sometimes, Griff?"

He shrugged. "She loves me. They all love me. Only Mama never cries." This, evidently, was the handmaiden's cue to cry harder. Branwyn stepped up the back-patting duties.

Griff looked up and noticed Rhianna for the first time. "Who are you? You're not a faerie."

"No, I'm human like you. That's my sister over there hugging the handmaiden."

"Are you?" he said. He reached out to brush his fingers over the back of Rhianna's hand. "Maybe you are. You're both different from the other human kids I've met here, though."

This cut through the handmaiden's sobs better than any of Branwyn's nebulous attempts at comfort. She raised her head from Branwyn's shoulder and pulled away. The glow under her visor had dimmed, and as she sniffled, it vanished. "When did you meet other human children, Griff?"

"Oh," said Griff. "Right. That was a secret."

"Griff," said the handmaiden. Branwyn followed her over to join everybody on the floor around the little boy. "Griff, if it's your secret, you can choose to reveal it, and if it's somebody else's secret, you must tell us who."

"Well…" he began. "Where I met them is Summer's secret, and how I met them, that's hers too. I think *why* is because we're mortals, and when… three times after the first. But *what* I did… that's *my* secret." He looked triumphant.

"Ooh," said Rhianna. "Are you going to tell us?"

"Maybe," he said. He put another block on top of an already impressive structure. "I thought people might be mad. But Mama sent me here for the Well of Time, and I figured other mortal kids needed time too. So I gave them some, using my locket." He showed it to them. The three women stared at the locket, spinning on its chain, until Griff dropped it and went to work on his tower again.

Branwyn finally said, "What does that mean, please?"

The handmaiden said quietly, "The locket carries enough time to enable a year of healthy growth. Griff came here to recharge it."

"Has he done something dangerous to himself by sharing it with others?" was Branwyn's next question.

"No, no. The locket has had enough exposure to recharge many times over. That isn't an issue."

"Griff, can you… tell us anything about the kids you met? Did you learn any of their names?"

Griff shook his head. "No. No names. They thought my towers were pretty. They wore mittens so they couldn't build anything themselves."

Branwyn took a deep breath. "Thank you. So… if this Well of Time is here, but the kids wore mittens and weren't benefiting from it, they aren't actually *here*." She recalled the vulnerability of the Summer Court and was glad she'd reached that extremely logical conclusion. She'd ask the Summer Queen, as gently as she could, and hopefully the monster would never have an opportunity to interact with her, or a reason to be angry with Summer's people.

Branwyn started to rise, then remembered her obligation to the Queen of Stone. "Have we now repaid the Queen of Stone, handmaiden?"

The handmaiden's voice trembled again. "I don't know. Are you going to take—"

Rhianna interrupted her in a cheery voice. "We don't have to decide that now. In fact, we don't have to decide that at all. That is what is technically known as 'above our pay grade.' I'll write a report. Somebody a lot wiser—and incidentally a lot nicer—than me will decide." She patted the handmaiden's arm. "It'll be okay."

The handmaiden sighed as if she couldn't believe that but had no other recourse. "Very well. And now you must attend upon the Summer Queen."

"Oh, no, not quite yet," said Rhianna. "First, selfies!" Then she pulled Griff and Branwyn and the handmaiden into a set of cellphone selfies and Branwyn tried to suppress her irritation.

She'd wanted to ask the handmaiden about the mysteriously childlike Summer Queen instead of taking goofy pictures.

It could just be her choice of vessel. Branwyn had met a monster called Candy, who also appeared as a preteen girl. But Candy was... terrifying, a predator perfectly designed to resemble prey. The Queen had behaved like a particularly authoritative classmate of Branwyn's youngest sister Meredith. Like a student council president, not a faerie queen. Given the surprise Griff had been, Branwyn really didn't want to walk into an audience with the childlike Queen while ignorant of important details.

"All right! These are great. I will do *my best* to get prints to you, handmaiden. Branwyn can probably handle it. It was great to meet you, Griff. Your tower-building skills are fantastic."

"Wait—" Branwyn began. "Can we find out more about—"

But the handmaiden only put her finger to her lips before turned to watch Griff start a new tower. Griff didn't even seem to notice them leaving. He reminded Branwyn very much of her brother Howl as a kid.

"One thing we've learned, Branwyn," said Rhianna in a low voice as she wrestled Branwyn to the door, "is that the Queens have way more information than their subjects. Or at least the Queen of Stone does. Let's *not* risk offending the Summer Queen by gossiping about her in her own castle. And—oh, these pictures of Griff *will* be useful for identifying him."

And in fact, when they opened the playroom door, the Summer Queen was sitting against the far wall, reading a book, all alone. She slammed the book shut and sprang to her feet. "Here I am! Would you like to come to my room?"

Branwyn wrinkled her brow. "Are you *really* the Summer Queen?"

The elfin girl gave them a mischievous smile. "Yes, I am."

"Don't you have... attendants or something? A throne room? Why were you waiting out here?"

The Summer Queen looked offended. "I *said* I'd be waiting for you. I told my attendants to go away. They're always trying to do things for me. It was boring. Come on, let's go to my room. Standing here is boring, too."

She tucked the book under her arm, took both their hands and started pulling them after her, walking backwards. "I'm so excited that you've come. I want so much to go visit the mortal world, and I can't. But you're here now, and we can have some fun."

"What kind of fun?" said Branwyn warily.

"Oh, this and that," said the Summer Queen airily. "We have to deal with a few things first. You didn't come just to entertain me, of course. I need to know what I'm selling before I tell you what I'm buying." That impish smile passed over her face again. "But we can talk about that in my room. For now, tell me your names? And how grown up you are? And where you come from? And what you do?"

"Will you tell us the same?" Rhianna asked sweetly.

The Summer Queen giggled. "Sure. I'm the Summer Queen. Griff and the other Queens call me Summer, and you can too, if you want." She continued walking backwards the whole time, leading them along the corridor, turning here, going up a ramp there. They occasionally passed other faeries and children of Harvest. The children of Harvest smiled at the Queen, but the faeries all appeared exasperated to some degree.

"I'm Rhianna Lennox," said Rhianna, and nudged Branwyn.

"Oh. I'm Branwyn. I'm... too damn grown up. I'm from Pasadena in California. And I'm... I'm an Artificer." It sounded weird to introduce herself by title.. She was used to people in the magic world knowing who she was.

Somehow she didn't feel much better about it when the Summer Queen wrinkled her nose and said conspiratorially, "Actually, I knew that last bit."

Rhianna said, "Oh, well, if we're doing everything all at

once… I'm probably not as grown up as I should be. I was born in Pasadena, but I live on the other side of the country now. And I'm an agent of the Office of the Unexpected."

Rhianna got the same nose wrinkle from Summer. "A spy, you mean. That's okay. I don't mind."

"I write reports," said Rhianna gravely. "Pages and pages of reports. It's actually pretty boring."

The Summer Queen stopped outside another pair of doors and flung them open into a room similar in size to Griff's playroom, but outfitted lavishly as a princess's bedroom. "Tada! Come in. Make yourself at home. Somebody will bring snacks. They're always trying to make me eat more."

There was a plush pink and gold armchair nearly surrounded by bookshelves, a giant canopied bed covered in topaz and blue pillows, a white wooden table with three chairs around it, a drafting desk with its own swivel chair, a window seat with more books, and, incongruously, a small television and a game console in front of a bean bag chair.

Branwyn went to the armchair while Rhianna put her bags on the table and sat there. The Summer Queen threw herself onto the oversized bed and beamed at them.

"Your turn for the rest of the answers, Summer," said Rhianna lightly.

"Oh right. Gotta get info for those reports, right? I'm not as grown up as I'd like to be. Where I come from… here, I guess? That's a tricky one for me. And of course, I'm the Summer Queen, which isn't any more exciting than writing reports." She looked between them. "What?"

Rhianna asked, "I don't want to be rude, but… are you *honestly* a kid, Summer?"

The Summer Queen pulled a face. "That *is* rude. But you don't know, so I'll forgive you. But yeah. I'm a kid. An immature person. This body does not yet have the boobs I aspire to."

"And why not?" asked Branwyn.

The kid Queen shrugged. "I can't do magic. I *have* to have a body, though, or everything would fall apart. And nobody else can make a body for me. So when I die, I start over again as a normal mortal zygote in the nearest available mom-type. It's very painful for me, and very scary for everybody else."

This caught Branwyn's professional interest. "Are you the same person each time? Do your memories carry over?"

"Well… I said mortal, but it's just the body, you know? I *am* the Summer Queen. So I know stuff. And I'm me. But I still have to be a fetus and a baby and learn how to use my body just like any baby does. It's *so boring.* They're always saying, *Be careful, Your Majesty. If you die, it will hurt, your Majesty,* but they have no idea what it's like to be stuck in a body that's practically always too young or too old for whatever I want to be doing." An old bitterness twanged in the Queen's final sentence, and Branwyn remembered the Queen of Stone's distaste for her courtiers.

"That sounds dreadful," said Rhianna with sincerity. "Not being able to use any magic in Faerie sounds like—"

"It sounds like any human in Faerie," said Branwyn. "Speaking of which—"

The Summer Queen's brown eyes hardened for a moment. "Not like either of you. Both of you have more magic than I'll ever have." Then she shrugged again. "But it doesn't matter. I still manage to have fun. Speaking of which, let's sort out one more thing and then we can get down to business. I've got one more important question, and it's your turn for answering."

"All right…" said Branwyn. There was a worrying light in the Queen's eyes.

The Queen rolled from her stomach to a sitting position, grabbed a big pillow to hug, and said breathlessly, "Which one of you is responsible for that incredibly hot monster downstairs?"

13

The Summer Queen

"WHAT?" said Branwyn flatly, shock temporarily blanking her mind.

Rhianna, frozen while digging through the supply backpack, said, "Uh, what does 'incredibly hot' mean when you use it?"

The Summer Queen looked between them again. "Did I get it wrong? Sexy? Amazingly attractive? Super cute? I don't like that last one, though, because it makes me think of Griff. Come *on*, which one of you is it? He said one of you was his mistress, he just didn't say which one."

Silently, treacherously, Rhianna pointed at Branwyn. The Summer Queen at once turned her full attention on Branwyn. With a big smile, she asked, "So, are you two, like, together? Coupling? Or is it just platonic?"

Branwyn clasped her hands in her lap and leaned firmly against the chair back. "You spoke with him?"

"I sure did! Right after I left you with Griff, I ran down to see what all the fuss was about. He was sitting on that stone. I said hi, and we talked some." She giggled. "I asked him if he was as dangerous as everybody said, and he said he was *more* dangerous." She fanned herself with her hand. "See? Hot!"

Branwyn decided they needed to push through to the business part of the agenda and out of the Domain of Summer *as soon as possible*. That meant providing the answers the Queen claimed they owed her. "We are not 'together, coupling,'" *because dreams don't count even if...* She pushed that distraction down. "And it is not platonic. We have... a business partnership at the moment. It's temporary."

"Ooh!" The Queen's eyes sparkled. "I wonder if I could form a business partnership with him, too. As, you know, a stepping stone to other things." As Branwyn opened and then closed her mouth, the Queen continued. "Well, we can talk about that more later. Tell me what you want from me, first."

Branwyn glanced at Rhianna, who motioned her to go ahead. "A faerie bound to Summer slaughtered a town on Earth. Most of the children of the town survived and, we suspect, were taken to Faerie. Do you know where they are?"

The Summer Queen pulled another face. "Gale. It was so tragic how he lost his love. And he still hasn't completed the task Honeychord set him to. I guess it'd be fitting if Honeychord unbound him, but that's *such* a sad ending."

"It was a sad ending for about four hundred other people, too, Your Majesty," said Branwyn, as neutrally as she could.

The Queen pushed her lips out in a pout. "Oh, don't get stuffy with me. I made sure the children survived, didn't I?"

"So you *do* know where they are?" For some reason, this made Branwyn more on edge rather than less.

"I do," said the Queen delicately. "What would you do if I told you?"

Rhianna took over briskly. "My employer would like to place them in the care of human families. Ideally, we'd like to arrange a controlled release so we can complete a full physical evaluation for each kid, but if we have to retrieve the whole crowd at once, we can work with that too."

"Hmm," said the Queen. "Well, that's not my decision. I arranged for their rescue, and I know where they are, but they're not in my care and I can't force their keeper to release them. You'll have to work that part out on your own."

"But you'll tell us *where* they are?" asked Branwyn eagerly.

The Queen waved a finger back and forth. "*That's* the favor you have to pay for."

"All right," said Branwyn and Rhianna simultaneously.

"Guys, you've got to be a little more reserved making bargains. At least ask before you agree to pay." The Summer Queen hopped off her bed and stood beside the window seat. "But I'm nice. I don't want much." She looked out the window. "That beast the monster mentioned is breaking through the wall. I'm calling Night to the Domain so Harvest's children will stay inside while everybody who wants to play with the big bad wolfie does so. I'll not only tell you where those kids are, but give you a shortcut to their location, once dawn breaks." She gave them a little smile. "Until then, we can have a slumber party."

Branwyn considered this. Then she considered her alternative solutions to finding the children. With Severin's help, she could *probably* put together an alternative. Travel might be an issue though.

Rhianna raised her finger. "Point of order? What determines when Night moves on?"

"See, that's the kind of question I want to hear!" The Queen spun in a circle. "I do. Or somebody else could call her, I suppose. But probably me. I won't keep her here for more than eight hours once she covers the Court. That's fair, isn't it?"

"And eight hours here is how long on Earth?" Rhianna asked patiently.

Breezily the Queen said, "Oh, we're at a one-to-one ratio here, because of the Well of Time. And there're clocks everywhere. I don't want to trick you. I just want to have a slumber party with some friends."

That big-eyed earnest look reminded Branwyn so much of Brynn wanting to tag along on this trip into Faerie. She suggested, "How about you tell us, and we get the kids, and after that we come back for this event? I can even bring along some friends closer to your.... More like you in temperament, anyhow."

The Queen pursed her lips. "Ohhh. That's really tempting. Like, we should make another deal just for that. But... this is too perfect an opportunity. I mean, you've got that monster downstairs, and I bet he's going to fight the beast of fire and thorns, and I want to seeeeee. And do makeovers with real makeup. You've got real makeup, right, Rhianna? And I definitely want to talk about boys."

"Can we talk about girls, too?" asked Rhianna, taking this far too seriously for Branwyn's tastes. A slumber party with Severin downstairs was way too dangerous an idea to be genuinely considering.

With a generous gesture, the Queen said, "Feel free, if you want. We can talk about hotties of all types."

"Good!" said Rhianna, evidently oblivious to Branwyn's attempts to signal her to slow down. "I do feel like I ought to tell you that the beast... it doesn't go down easily. Or rather, it keeps coming back. Do you know what it is?"

"Nope," said the Queen. "Maybe some angelic critter sent to cause havoc? They shouldn't be able to get past the Binder, but who knows these days." She joined Rhianna at the table and peeked into the open backpack. "Don't worry about it. Eventually it'll be destroyed, assimilated or caged. It's certainly not the first time we've had to deal with something like this."

The Summer Queen's lack of concern amplified Branwyn's discomfort with the situation. It didn't seem *right* that her personal territory was being invaded by a mysterious creature and she was more interested in a slumber party.

But she had to work with what she had. Her fingers moved over the gem in her hammer, tickled by the bubbling of the stored souls. As for herself, she'd napped well, but she'd exhaust herself trying to do what the Queen was offering to do for an objectively low price.

It was a tempting offer, despite the danger. She tried to remember the Queen's exact statements in her head. She should have taken notes. Actually, she should have brought Marley. Marley could have handled the notes *and* the worrying.

But no. Bringing Marley would have made everything more complicated, and depending on who came with Marley, might have constituted an act of war.

Rhianna and the Summer Queen were pawing through Rhianna's makeup case. Branwyn was pretty sure Rhianna had so far only implied future participation.

"Let's make the deal clear before we start the makeovers."

The Summer Queen looked up, surprised. "I thought I was pretty straightforward. You two haven't agreed yet though. I noticed that."

Branwyn grimaced. "We stay for a slumber party. In exchange, you tell us where the Tucker kids are, and put us on a shortcut there. I need one more thing though. Tell me that your shortcut will save us at least eight hours."

"I can't," said the Queen promptly. "How could I? I don't know what you might accomplish on your own. But I am not trying to trick you, and I do intend on helping you."

Branwyn blew out her breath. That was the best she was going to get. "Fine. If Rhianna accepts, so do I. You two work out the agenda while I go talk to His Nibs."

The Queen perked up. "Ooh, the monster? Can I come?"

"No, no," said Rhianna quickly. "Branwyn gets shy. Besides,

if you like him, you've got to play it cool. If he knows you're interested, he'll just jerk you around."

Her eyes widening, the Queen focused on Rhianna. "Yeah? Tell me more!"

Branwyn made good her escape. She encountered a faerie lady outside the door, with a tray of cakes and potato chips, got directions to the base of the Court, and started the hike.

It felt good to be by herself for a few minutes. The interior of the Summer Court was well decorated in pale greens and white, with pastel accents. Out one leaf-shaped window she saw the airship dock, where two faerie ladies were disembarking from a ship with moth wings.

She tried to enjoy the scenery instead of thinking about what was ahead or behind them. Without thinking about the next few hours, or the *glint* on Rhianna she hadn't yet managed to look at closely.

She realized that was something she could do at this slumber party. It was in the nature of three-person slumber parties that when makeover time happened, somebody would have time on their hands. Penny had performed plenty of makeovers on Marley while Branwyn had sketched or colored. This would be far more constructive.

She made her way to where the market was closing and was forced to refuse a crumbly cinnamon-scented pastry from a cheerful child of Harvest. Instead she walked outside, into the fragrance of wisteria and honeysuckle drifting on the evening wind.

After breathing in the fresh air for a moment, she strolled over to where they'd left the sailing stone. The courtyard had acquired a population while they'd been away, including a few male faeries in ornamented armor who seemed both self-impor-tant and ill-at-ease among the Harvest's children gawking at the sailing stone.

But Severin was no longer in his place at the top of the stone.

Branwyn eyed the armored faeries and decided not to summon him there. They seemed on edge enough without a monster appearing out of nowhere among them. Instead she returned to the row of blooming hydrangea shrubberies forming a narrow walk between the secondary courtyard and the front entrance to the Court.

"Severin," she whispered.

I'm here, he said, touching the back of her neck.

"Not busy?"

Not yet.

"Are you hiding in that place?"

No, just lurking in the shadows. There was a rustle of shrubbery, and he joined her in the greenery, looking at her impassively.

Branwyn stared at him for a long moment, trying to see him from the perspective of the Summer Queen. He wasn't nearly as beautiful as the angels, nor as attractive as most of the faeries. But that was just bodies, wasn't it? The Queen was a bored, semi-immortal teenager, and he was the sardonic, mysterious monster who would happily wipe out her people. It could make a sweet romance, but only if you cut away everything about it that was true.

He brought his hand up as if he was going to touch her face, then dropped it again. With an edge in his voice, he said, "Did you come down here just to look at me like that?"

Branwyn shook herself. "Night is coming to visit. We're going to stay here while she's in town. In the morning, the Summer Queen will send us to the Tucker children." She watched his face, but he remained impassive.

"Hmm. Will she now? She came down to see me."

"Yes," said Branwyn, keeping her face like stone, because two could play at that game. "What did you think of her?"

He gave her that shark grin. "I thought she looked very fragile. I wanted to snap her neck, just to see what would happen."

"Yeah, I'm not going to be telling her that when she

inevitably asks what you said about her." Branwyn ran her hand through her hair, then pulled out her ponytail and rubbed her head with both hands.

Severin watched her, an amused gleam in his eyes. "You could."

Branwyn gave him a severe look. "I have a feeling you know exactly what would happen if I told any sort of teenage girl that her crush was far too dangerous for her."

"I do," he said. "I always went with exposing their embarrassing personal secrets instead. Or just killing them, of course. But in this case, perhaps we could get that location a bit faster. I don't really trust the Wild Hunt."

Branwyn found herself actually considering the suggestion. Slowly, she said, "That might work. But I can't imagine you'd like it very much. You'd probably have to stay here a lot longer than eight hours while we did the kid-rescuing."

"Maybe. Maybe not." He gave her another one of those shark smiles.

Puzzled now, Branwyn asked, "Do you *want* to be her pet for a while?"

"Not in the slightest, cupcake. All I'd have to do is promise to be her boyfriend for the rest of her current life, and then make sure her life is very, very short."

Curiosity beat out horror. Branwyn said, "She's not dumb. I'm pretty sure her definition of 'boyfriend' would disallow any neck snapping."

With a ripple of his shoulders, Severin said, "I wouldn't have to do it myself. I'd just finish a couple of conversations."

Grimly, Branwyn demanded, "What have you been doing down here?"

He spread his hands. "She's got all these weak boys of Summer wandering around. I've been fixing some of them."

"Fixing them," Branwyn said flatly. The wind gusted, blowing flower petals between them.

"Well… I suppose it does depend on your perspective. Personally, I thought it might be useful if a few of them remembered how to be dangerous when that beast gets here, so I'm helping them understand their options. Really, they're all close to breaking anyhow."

Slowly, Branwyn started tying up her ponytail again, staring at him hard. "Go on."

He cocked an eyebrow. "You sure you want to know?" She tightened her jaw, and he laughed. "Apparently she's unusually trying this time around. Wise Sir Centri of her shining knights thinks she'd be much easier to handle as an infant. And the oh-so-passionate Sir Axis is *extremely* upset that she's been smiling at the likes of me instead of him. And that's just what I've discovered in the last hour or so."

Branwyn wanted to feel aghast, but she couldn't. It fit right in with her forebodings. "I bet she knows, too."

"Probably," Severin agreed. "But that makes gambling on me even more exciting for her."

After a moment, Branwyn said distantly, "I'm just thinking about the difference between telling a girl somebody is too dangerous for her, and telling her they've concocted an elaborate plan to murder her in order to get out of being her boyfriend."

He did touch her face this time, his fingers trailing across her cheek before he pressed his thumb lightly against her lips. "You've got it, cupcake."

Uncomfortable warmth rushed through her. She wanted to bite him, envisioned the likely outcome and instead just adjusted her head.

He dropped his hand. "Your call. Tell her whichever one you please."

"I'm not going to tell her either one. This whole conversation is a tangent."

"But you know she'll ask, cupcake," he said in mock surprise. "Are you going to *lie?*"

She glared at him. "In a red hot second. I might make up embarrassing personal secrets, too."

He laughed, and she thought wistfully about hitting him with her hammer. Then, in the distance, there was a long, low boom. Night was already creeping across the landscape, and she saw a flicker of red at the limit of her vision.

Severin looked toward the boom, too. "Ah, well. If you insist on staying here, it will still be an exciting night for the Court. I'll do my best to give you those eight hours."

"She wants to watch you fight," said Branwyn glumly. She hadn't intended to tell him the details of what the Summer Queen had planned, but after Severin's own dark confidences secrecy didn't seem as important anymore. "And get a makeover. She'll probably throw pillows."

"And French braid your hair. Hey, maybe you can get those baths, too."

Branwyn shivered. That last sounded better than she wanted to admit. "I'm going back. Don't get killed."

Have fun, said his voice in her ear. *Call me if you get bored and change your mind....*

14

Slumber Party

THE BASE of the Summer Court had emptied of visitors when Branwyn went back inside, and she had her choice of elevators. She picked the one that faced the incoming Night and watched as the elevator rose. When the elevator reached the top of its path, she remained, unable to pull herself away. There was something heart-twisting about the way it swept over the land, swallowing sunlight and rainbows and leaving behind only distant stars.

The land near Underlight had changed in Night, and it changed in Summer, too. Dense patches of forest squeezed themselves between cultivated fields and mist rose from the barrows that grew with the spread of darkness. Even the round structures of the children of Harvest changed, growing taller, narrower, and crooked. They all glowed with golden lights in the windows, though, which was comforting, .especially when considered against the red eyes she spotted moving in the nearest forest.

Far in the distance, directly along the road they'd followed, she could see the burning glow of the beast that had been following them. The Summer Queen had told her not to worry about it, that it would be dealt with somehow. She had to trust that.

From beyond the curve of the Court's trunk, a troop of knights in silver armor mounted on unicorns rode silently into view. The one in the lead raised a sword, and they galloped down the Night road. It made a pretty picture, but it didn't move her the same way Night's arrival had. Like the landscape itself, it was a vision designed to be looked at, rather than to express or accomplish something. Branwyn could understand why Severin disliked them.

That was not a thought she wanted to linger over, though, so she finally left the elevator and returned to the Summer Queen's room. The Court, now lit by foxfire, was eerily empty, although there were several faeries loitering in the corridor near the Queen's room. Two of them played musical instruments and one of them made towels dance before him with languid movements of his fingers.

Branwyn knocked on the Queen's door and Rhianna opened it. Her cheeks were flushed but her face looked a little drawn. "Hey. We were watching Night get settled in."

"Come in, come in!" Summer bounced up and down on her bed. "Though not for long. Rhianna was telling me how she'd skipped a bath at Stone. We have to fix that. Then I can dress you up! And play with your hair! I was reading a book on French braids."

Branwyn said, "Of course. I'm in. Let's do this."

Summer laughed. "You're expecting to be bored. Don't worry about *that*. Sit down and eat something and after that I'll show you my bathroom."

The windows over the window seat had been cranked open and a fresh breeze brought the scent of honeysuckle. Branwyn sat down at the table. It now held two trays of food. On one was a presentation of tiny filigree sugar constructions, candied fruit, paper-thin crisps curled in the shape of animals, and slices of what looked like uncooked pancetta. The other tray had the remnants of a bowl of ridged potato chips, a plate of chocolate chip cookies and some sticks of meat.

"They bring her food from Earth," reported Rhianna. "She said this tray was safe for us."

"They bought it at the supermarket," agreed Summer, hopping off the bed. "With money they earned performing. I made them do it right. Though now they've turned into real pests about making me eat food *they* prepare." She picked up a bird-cage of spun sugar with a crystal bird inside, sneered at it, then crunched it between her teeth.

Branwyn took a cookie and bit into it. She recognized the particular processed taste of the brand and made herself eat it anyhow. Then she ate a pressed meat stick. The tray of faerie food was far too pretty to have sitting there on an empty stomach. "Did both of you polish off the chips?"

Rhianna smiled while Summer laughed. "I can make them bring some more. They've got a whole pantry of junk food. Do you want pizzas later?"

"Sure, why not. Later, though. I definitely want to get that bath."

That made Rhianna's smile flicker and return larger. The Summer Queen looked between them. "You two really are sisters. Okay, let's go."

The Summer Queen's bath was more of a large inset hot tub, almost pool-like, with a single shower nearby to wash first. It suited Branwyn perfectly. Rhianna took the shower, giving Branwyn a few minutes of one-on-one time with Summer.

The Queen didn't waste a moment. Dropping her voice, she said, "So how was he? The monster, I mean? Did you mention me?"

Branwyn didn't hide her eyeroll because she wouldn't have hidden it from her sisters. "Of course I mentioned you. I was telling him we'd be staying the night as your guests."

"Well, did he *say* anything about me?"

Branwyn had prepared for this. "He thought you looked very young."

Instead of the pout of disappointment she expected, Summer squinted at her. "Did he? I can't quite tell." She tapped her mouth thoughtfully. "Your relationship with him is more complicated than you said, isn't it?"

"Yes," Branwyn admitted, because the Queen of Stone hadn't much liked Severin evading her direct questions, and evidently truth-detection was a general Queen trait.

Summer grinned. "That's cool. You can tell me all about it later."

"Who's next?" asked Rhianna, emerging from the shower, and Branwyn took the escape. And when it was Summer's turn and Branwyn and Rhianna had settled into the steaming water, she scooted close to Rhianna and hissed, "Was Truth or Dare on the agenda?"

"I couldn't figure out how to move it off," Rhianna whispered back.

"We'll just have to distract her, then."

The Summer Queen's shower was much quicker than either of theirs, and she splashed down into the pool beside them with a cheer. Then she backed away and inspected both of them frankly. "I definitely need to get a human body next time. Harvest's daughters don't develop nearly as much." Then she looked more closely at Rhianna. "How did you get those scars?"

Branwyn blinked and also stared at her sister. A number of recent scars pocked her ribcage and sliced across her stomach.

Rhianna gave a little smile. "I shouldn't say."

"Why not?" asked Summer bluntly. "I won't tell anybody else."

"Because I made a promise I wouldn't. If I broke my word, it would make it hard for me to face somebody I care about."

Summer gave Rhianna the same thoughtful look she'd given

Branwyn, and then said, disappointed, "Spy stuff." She turned on Branwyn. "You're not a spy, though. What's that mark on your neck?"

Branwyn instinctively covered Severin's mark with her fingers. "A bad memory."

"Hm. Okay," said the Queen, in the exact tone she'd earlier said, *We'll come back to that later.* She lifted one of her legs out of the water. "I have scars, too. This one's from when I broke my leg riding a unicorn when I was six."

Branwyn, still touching the mark Severin had left when he healed her broken arm, said, "They can't even heal you?"

Summer shrugged. "They can make things heal faster, but it was a bad break. The Harvest's daughter who took care of me said if they'd bother learning more about how bodies worked, they'd be better healers. But all they have to do to fix themselves is spend a day wishing."

"The door's open now. Make one of them go to medical school," said Rhianna firmly.

Summer laughed. "I don't know if I want somebody like that bossing me around, but it would be awfully fun to make somebody go to college for me. Maybe I will." She eyed Branwyn speculatively. "You know, that was a pretty strange thing for a human to say. Like you just sort of expect magic healing."

Branwyn shifted her weight so the warm water swished around her. "I don't expect it for *me*, but… somebody… I know is pretty good at it, I guess. I'm sort of surprised."

"The monster," guessed Summer. "Does he have a name, by the way? I know some monsters do and some don't."

Branwyn pressed her lips tightly together, and Rhianna stepped in and saved her. "We call him Sev. I don't think that's his real name, but I don't know what it is."

"Hmm," said Summer. She lay back in the water and floated, her hair spreading out around her.

Rhianna watched her and then said, in much the same way

Summer had asked about Sev, "So what's going on with the handmaiden? She couldn't stop crying over Griff."

Without lifting her head, Summer said, "Oh, Stone's always adopting mortal children. She makes sure they grow up properly, and then they die, because they're mortal. Then the whole Court falls apart so Stone doesn't. It hurts the handmaiden particularly because she's the spare."

Branwyn blinked. "You mean the heir?"

With a little laugh, Summer said, "Yeah, sure. The heir. You know, sometimes she's the only faerie in the world I can't hate."

As Branwyn tried and failed to sort through that explanation, the door opened and the faerie she'd noticed making towels dance appeared with a bundle of them. He deposited them on a shelf and gathered up the clothes scattered all over the floor.

"Clean those and return them in a couple of hours," ordered the Queen, with barely a glance. "And have the dressmaker wait in my room for us." She righted herself and looked between Branwyn and Rhianna. "Feeling better? Ready to play dress-up?"

"I wouldn't mind soaking a bit longer," Branwyn admitted. "It's a nice bath. I like the tiles on the ceiling." They were a slowly moving patchwork pattern that reminded Branwyn of her great grandmother's quilts and very peaceful to watch.

"Branwyn doesn't like to do things halfway," Rhianna said confidingly.

"Won't you get all shriveled up?" asked Summer.

"You say that like it's a bad thing," grumbled Branwyn. "All right, fine. What are we dressing up as?" She waded over to the edge of the pool and pulled herself out. Among the stack of towels were big fluffy purple bathrobes: two large and one smaller.

"Whatever we want," said Summer firmly. "My dressmaker will have a field day. I'm pretty sure she cries inside every time I put on a Harvest's daughter tunic instead of something she made."

Rhianna gazed at her thoughtfully as she toweled her hair. "What's your dressmaker's name?"

"Whirl," replied Summer, putting on her robe. "I like her, because she thinks clothes are more important than me. And she actually learned to sew a long time ago because she figured she'd make better designs if she had to work to produce them. But she won't be sewing tonight."

"Sounds like my kind of woman," said Branwyn, and Rhianna laughed at her.

As they went back to Summer's room, Branwyn looked at Rhianna walking ahead of her. She was remembering her sleepovers in middle and high school. When they'd happened at Branwyn's house, Rhianna, two-and-a-half years younger, had always joined them in the early parts of the evening, but she'd inevitably been sent to bed upstairs while Branwyn and her friends took over the den with sleeping bags.

Eventually, of course, Rhianna had sleepovers of her own, but all Branwyn really remembered of those was looming over 'the kids' when they made too much noise and she had an early morning.

God, even then, with all five of her even younger siblings running, or in the case of Meredith, crawling around, she'd still thought of Rhianna's friends as 'kids.' Those dumb kids that Rhianna liked to hang around with. The idiot boys and giddy girls, so much less interesting than Marley and Penny.

She wondered if Rhianna was in contact with any of them now. If so, she never visited them during holidays. The thought made Branwyn sad, and the realization that she hadn't noticed before made her heart clench.

"You're frowning," said Summer, as she held the bedroom door for her. "I wish I could fix whatever's troubling you."

"No, no," said Branwyn, hastily relaxing her face. "I'm fine. Let's see what Whirl can do."

Summer gave her that 'I spotted a lie' look again but only said, "All right. You'll be impressed."

The faerie dressmaker Whirl sat tailor-style on the swivel chair, wearing slacks and a jacket that was tight at the waist and loose at the shoulders. While she definitely looked like one of the brown-skinned faeries rather than the brown-skinned Harvest's children, she was smaller and more delicate than the other Court faeries, with flashing hands and an unsettling, measuring gaze.

"Will you let me make something for you that isn't glamour?" she demanded of Summer as soon as she closed the door. "And will you wear it when I do? And treat it with respect, instead of like those rags you normally call clothes?"

Branwyn couldn't repress a shiver. It was too much like getting a last-minute date to the prom and having to beg Penny for help acquiring a dress nice enough to show up that rich bitch who'd mocked Branwyn's overalls.

Hastily, Summer answered just as Branwyn had, because in that situation there was no other answer. "Yes, yes, of course. Anything you want."

Whirl surveyed her sternly. "Very well. Let me study your guests." She glanced at Branwyn and Rhianna in the purple robes. "Take those things off. Are you modest? I will give you chemises."

Neither Branwyn nor Rhianna were particularly modest, but they both accepted chemises anyhow. Whirl pointed at them each in turn and sparkles whirled out of her finger and condensed as silky bits of underwear. Branwyn's was green like her hair, and Rhianna's red like hers, and that was how Whirl addressed them for the remainder of her stay.

For a little while, they both acted as dressmaker's dummies for Whirl while Summer watched. Although she'd seemed cowed by Whirl's initial remarks, the Queen didn't hesitate to criticize Whirl's creations.

"Why the ruffles? Those ruffles look silly."

"Green stands wrong for that gown. Ruffles are necessary here. They emphasize femininity."

"They didn't always," volunteered Rhianna, then whispered, "Sorry, I'll just keep standing here."

"When is it our turn to dress up Summer?" asked Branwyn, who knew better than to have an opinion on her own dress. She wasn't even going to try to suggest less feminine garb for herself in this environment.

Whirl looked at her narrowly and then turned to Summer with an evil grin. "Stand up, child. Green wants to pick out clothes for you."

Looking delighted and embarrassed at the same time, Summer hopped up from the floor. Branwyn, suddenly on the spot, described the last outfit she'd seen Brynn wearing.

Summer flung open a mirror hidden by a sliding wall and looked at herself in long shorts and a cute t-shirt with lacing on the sides and her face fell. "This looks like kid's clothing."

"It looks much better than your favorite rags though," said Whirl nastily. "More practical, too, for what you get up to."

The Queen ignored Whirl and turned to Branwyn. "Describe something Sev would like."

God damn it. But at least she could answer this with absolute honesty. "I have no earthly idea."

Summer toyed with the lacing on the t-shirt. "We could bring him up here and ask. It'd be fun having a boy's opinion too."

"I don't think he cares about clothes. He'd be bored. Or a jerk." Branwyn took a chance. "He really is a jerk, Summer."

After a tiny pause, Summer said, "Of course you'd think so, but he was nice to *me*. Anyhow, let's try something else. Something more grown up."

Whirl, who was clearly as bored with the discussion of Severin as he would be with dress-up, looked up. "You do not have an adult's body. I could add the curves, but it would look false."

"Oh, come on," said Rhianna. "This is dress-up, not a fashion contest. The whole point is to put on the sexy firefighter costume you'd never wear in real life."

Whirl gave Rhianna the evil glance and waved her finger. With a spiral of sparks, Rhianna's classic Cinderella ballgown vanished, replaced by said sexy firefighter outfit.

Rhianna laughed. "No, I *would* wear this. You've got to put this on Branwyn. I'm not going to tell you what to put me in, but you should definitely give Summer a cute cat girl outfit."

To Branwyn's relief, Whirl ignored the suggestion to put the firefighter outfit on her and instead focused on dressing Summer. After that, Branwyn was able to fade into the background as a game rapidly developed between Whirl, Rhianna and Summer. Rhianna and Summer would suggest increasingly bizarre 'sexy' or 'cute' costumes to Whirl, and she would make them happen. At first, they were stock ideas Whirl had clearly seen somewhere before, but 'sexy unicorn' and 'cute window washer' both made Whirl's eyes narrow at the challenge, and then they were off to the races. Rhianna and Whirl were merciless at inventing weird sweetness to put Summer in, and Summer blushed and tried to hide her delight as best as somebody required to be honest could.

Branwyn occasionally threw out a suggestion, at first just to claim participation, and then when it was clear to her one of the others had made a suggestion that was not *quite* right. But as Summer and Rhianna got sillier, Branwyn curled up in the armchair and watched, brooding over Rhianna's scars and Rhianna's *glint*.

Finally, Whirl ended the escapade with a double snap. All outfits were replaced with long, silky nightgowns: green, red, and golden. "I am done," she announced. "You have outlasted the immortal; I have acquired a headache. Goodnight."

Summer collapsed onto the beanbag with a sated sigh. Then she lifted her head. "Before you go, sweet, wonderful Whirl, would you turn my other mirror into a view on the invading beast?"

Whirl gave her another stern look, but slid open a second section of wall and touched the half-length mirror there. Instantly, Whirl's reflection was replaced by crimson flames in darkness. She frowned, touched it again, and the exposure shifted so the brightness of the beast was dimmed and the darkness of the night lightened. What she saw there made her mouth tighten, but all she said was, "Enjoy your party, Your Majesty," and left the room.

Summer bounced to her feet and went to the mirror. "Hmm... Come see, you two."

Reluctant without knowing why, Branwyn nonetheless joined Summer, although not with Rhianna's alacrity. This was her first good view of the beast she'd only seen before as a distant fire. They called it 'the beast of fire and thorns,' but there was something of the wolf to it as well. It had great thorn-like claws and a crown of horns and its mane and tail and paws were crimson flame.

And it was big. Very big. Far, far bigger than an elephant, if the white figures around it were the knights she'd previously observed. The beast kept trying to step on them, but they dodged easily. They were doing something cunning with a net that was hampered by the way the net kept catching on fire. Each time the flames started, they were doused, but it was clearly a challenge.

Summer made a face. "My Knights. But is Sev out there? I don't see him."

Branwyn stared at the beast for a moment and spotted three red sparks making a regular circle above the beast: impossible to detect if you didn't have some idea of what to search for. "He's there." She scanned the area around the beast, then touched the mirror. "Right there."

She'd found the silhouette standing beside the edge of the

road. If she squinted, she thought she could see his hands in his pockets, in a stance she recognized.

"He's just standing there," said Summer.

"He's waiting until they need help," said Branwyn grimly.

Summer brightened. "Really? Aww."

Oops. "I don't think your Knights are going to like being helped by a monster, Summer."

Disdainfully, Summer said, "That's because they're meatheads."

They watched a while longer as the knights failed to do more than slow the beast. They got tossed this way and that, but there were enough of them that they were always underfoot.

But eventually, it was clear Severin was bored. After a particularly vigorous scattering of Knights, the three sparks over the beast's back accelerated until they were a blurred ring. Then all three of them shot downward. One impacted the beast's skull while the other two intersected with its spine.

The beast roared, collapsed like its strings had been cut, and then faded away, ending as nothing more than a burning outline that fizzled out. Severin's silhouette merged with the shadow of a tree while the Knights picked themselves up and shouted at each other.

Sounding a little disappointed, Summer said, "I thought he'd do... more. *Fight* it."

"I don't know," said Rhianna thoughtfully. "I thought that was pretty impressive. Though... he's been getting injured somehow, so he must not always be attacking at range."

The Knights regrouped and rode out of the frame. The mirror stayed fixed on the point where the beast had vanished. Summer touched it lightly. "It comes back."

"Yes," said Branwyn.

Summer was silent a moment. "It's a force rather than a true creature. It's still there, which is why the mirror hasn't lost focus."

Branwyn frowned. "How do you mean?"

"A force," said Summer vaguely. "Like Sev's bullets?"

"That doesn't make sense," Branwyn said. "If something stopped his bullets, they wouldn't start up again later."

"Maybe not in your version of the world," said Summer darkly. "It happens here all the time."

"Think of it like stopping something without absorbing the momentum, Bran," said Rhianna casually. "It doesn't bounce, nothing breaks, it just… stops. Where does the momentum go? *Somewhere.* And eventually it comes back, and the bullet starts moving again." She glanced over and met Branwyn's surprised stare. "I learn the strangest things at work."

"You've seen this before?" Branwyn demanded.

Rhianna hesitated. "Not… Not exactly like this. Something similar, though."

"How do you deal with those other unstoppable things?" Branwyn knew she sounded accusatory, and couldn't help herself.

"You let them get where they're going, and hope like hell you can clean up the mess after," said Rhianna with a shrug.

"Let's do our hair," suggested Summer. "We can watch the mirror while we do. Branwyn, I wanted to try giving you a French braid first."

Branwyn was really, *really* not in the mood to be a doll some more. But she'd agreed to take part in the slumber party, so she pushed down her bad mood and sat on the floor in front of the Summer Queen and let her brush and braid her hair.

Rhianna sat near the Queen, holding open the French braiding book she'd found. The Queen was mostly quiet as she worked with Branwyn's hair, occasionally muttering to herself, "Oops, missed one…" and other notes of the novice braider.

After a while, Branwyn, eyeing Rhianna as best she could without moving her head, said, "I hate that you can't tell me things anymore, Rhi. You used to tell me everything."

Rhianna shrugged and said lightly, "The cost of my mighty position, I'm afraid."

Branwyn considered this extremely unsatisfying answer. "Is it worth it? Don't you miss when it was you and me against the world?"

Rhianna was quiet for a moment. Then she took a deep breath and said, "It was never you and me against the world, Branwyn. It was you against the world and me trying desperately to keep up." She shook her head and kept going before Branwyn, stunned, could think of anything to say. "I wanted so badly for you to see me, but all you ever saw was your shadow. And now I'm out of your shadow. I've got my own life, and my own things I'm good at. I'm making different choices because I'm a different person than you. Sometimes I feel like I *have* to make different choices, just so I know I'm me. When I was a kid and did that, your disappointment always pushed me back into line. But... my Advisor likes me the way I am, Branwyn."

Weakly, Branwyn said, "You said he lectured you."

"Yes, and I like it! He *sees* me."

Branwyn didn't respond, thinking over Rhianna's description of herself, trying to decide if she was right. She couldn't tell. She was too hurt to tell. But... "I didn't *think* of you as my shadow. I thought of you as my sister."

Rhianna sighed. "I know." She squeezed Branwyn's shoulder in a ghost of a hug. "I know you did. It's okay."

Branwyn's hair was suddenly released from the gentle tugging. She shook her head, but it didn't feel like there was a braid. It felt loose against her back, sliding strangely over the silky nightgown. She felt the same way, as if she'd been unbound somehow.

"I don't think I can do this right now," said Summer, her voice melancholy.

"I'm sorry," said Rhianna. "I didn't mean to be a downer."

"Nah," said the Queen. "I think stuff like that's supposed to happen at slumber parties. But Branwyn's pretty bad at sitting still and I don't want to make her look ridiculous."

"Sorry," Branwyn muttered.

"How about I do your makeup, Summer?" said Rhianna brightly, as if she hadn't just… just what? Made Branwyn question their entire relationship? Confessed a secret? Calmly pointed out how Branwyn had accidentally hurt her? Branwyn was *sure* the brightness was false, but Rhianna was doing it anyhow, and doing it well.

And that's why I have to fix the glint before it becomes something worse.

15

Summer Nights

Branwyn said, "Yeah, you two do makeup. I'll do some sketching. I always used to draw at my slumber parties."

Summer perked up. "All right. There's art stuff in my desk. I think there's still some towers Griff drew me, too."

The desk contained everything Branwyn needed to draw, but she didn't want to sit there, turned away from the others. And Rhianna wanted a bright light for the makeup application, which of course the drafting table had, even if it was a particularly bright application of foxfire rather than an electric light. So Summer sat in the swivel chair and Rhianna sat in a table chair, and Branwyn sat across from them in the window seat with an oversized pad of luscious paper and a number 2 pencil.

It wasn't a conversable distance in the large room, but Branwyn wasn't in a conversational mood. Rhianna and Summer were quiet as well, except for murmurs about the makeup. From beyond the open window, she could hear snatches of faint music on a guitar and a flute: melodies she almost but not quite recognized. It was better than silence.

Branwyn concentrated on her breathing for a few minutes,

taking extra time before settling into the Artificer's trance. She needed to see what was actually there, not what she wanted to see. She had to get this right.

Even with her extra preparation, it was harder than she expected. She'd never looked at a Queen of Faerie with the Sight before. It was a mistake she never wanted to repeat. While everything else in Faerie was *itself*, the child was a mass of incandescent light bound into a loose human shape, and *cables* of the Geometry ran from her to the deep lines above and below Faerie. The slightest movement of her head sent tremors running up and down the cables and touched the deep lines.

Branwyn closed her eyes and turned her face toward the paper before opening them again. She set her pencil to work for a few minutes, sketching the mortal body of the Queen, blocking in Rhianna next to her. It kept her hands busy while the glory faded from her eyes.

It would be painful to look again, but she refused to give up this task or this opportunity. She'd earned this when she'd decided to not tell Rhianna about the *glint*, and when she'd avoided previous opportunities to study her sister. She could have done this on the sailing stone, but instead she'd slept. When had Rhianna last slept?

There was absolutely no room in her surge of determination for any small, pragmatic voices to point out she and Rhianna were different people, who had exerted themselves differently; that not sleeping enough had led her into a different uncomfortable situation. She shut them out. They didn't matter.

She turned the page in the sketchpad and looked up again. By angling her head, she could see Rhianna's shape but very little of Summer's. What little she did see made her head hurt, but that didn't matter as long as she could see what she'd done to Rhianna.

Branwyn hadn't looked at humans much as an Artificer. Her ability to work with a node network had capped out at four with

Titanone and she'd never yet repeated that feat. For most projects she stuck with one. The human network of seven was far beyond her scope.

But she wasn't trying to shape a human, or add a new node. All she wanted to do was *analyze* what was there. She wanted to figure out the source of the *glint*, understand out what was missing, and what that meant.

She spent the entire extended makeup session trying to comprehend what she was seeing. With or without the Sight, she could see that something was *missing*. But she couldn't see what that missing element *had been*. It was gone, and whatever it was, she couldn't identify it by comparing Rhianna to herself. Just as the handmaiden had said, just as *Rhianna* had said, they weren't nearly similar enough.

Her headache grew worse and worse, but she ignored it. Even when she could barely see through the agony, she couldn't separate it from the pain of what she'd done and what Rhianna had told her. All she could do was keep pushing, keep looking, work harder, find what was missing so she could learn how to repair it and make everything better again. She just had to keep pushing.

Something brushed against the back of her neck.

Whatever you're doing, stop. It's distracting, Severin whispered in her ear.

"Fuck off," she muttered, trying to wipe annoying blurriness from her eyes and flinching at the sudden sharpening of the pain.

Branwyn, if you don't cut it out, I'm going to show up and kill somebody, which would put a real damper on your little sleepover. I'm not in the mood to find out what happens to me if you have an aneurysm.

Suddenly explosive with fury, Branwyn turned to the half-open window behind her, and hurled the pencil, then threw out the entire pad of paper. Then she knelt on the window seat with her hands over her ears, panting as she finally really *felt* the pain in her head.

Distantly, she heard Rhianna say, "Bran?" A gentle hand, not her sister's touched her hair. She didn't dare look up. Rhianna sat beside her. Branwyn tried to focus, failed, flailed, panicked, all in her breath. Her sister's cool hand rubbed the back of her neck. So different from Severin's light touch.

It helped. Branwyn was able to visualize the pattern that shut off the Sight. The pain in her skull eased. She drew a deep breath, and another, and another. The pain kept fading. At last it was nearly gone, and she risked dropping her hands and raising her head.

Rhianna was as white as a ghost, while Summer hovered nearby, frowning. Branwyn took another couple of breaths, and said, "Um."

"Are you feeling better? What *happened?*" Rhianna demanded.

"Um," said Branwyn again, trying to figure out what to say. She'd accomplished *nothing* in exchange for all that pain.

Rhianna's eyes narrowed. "Branwyn, raise both arms to your sides, please."

Branwyn did so and then dropped them again. "I found out we shouldn't look at faerie Queens with the Sight. Or at least I shouldn't. Maybe you got a different charm. Uh, sorry about the paper, Summer."

Rhianna sighed. Then she put her arms around Branwyn and squeezed her tightly. "You're such an idiot, Branwyn. Why do you do such stupid things and keep doing them when they hurt?"

Summer looked between them with wide eyes as Branwyn said, "Hey, no pain, no gain, right? Don't you push yourself at the gym?" She squeezed Rhianna back, stuffing down the stress over her failure as deeply as she could.

"I have a *trainer*," Rhianna said firmly. "I don't just make it up as I go along and think, *oh this hurts, maybe I should do it some more.* And you do."

Branwyn was about to point out that *somebody* had to work out what Rhianna's trainer taught, when Summer said, "Oh! I think the beast is reforming." The Queen darted over to the enchanted mirror.

Branwyn amended her comment to, "I suppose we should watch this."

Rhianna kept one arm around Branwyn as she stood up, only dropping it once Branwyn had taken a few steps on her own. Walking wasn't a problem. Physically, she almost felt normal, except for the exhausting shadow of pain that made her want to flinch from things like a stray breeze and the light on the drafting table. As for her helplessness regarding the *glint*... well, whatever it was seemed stable, at least.

A burning glow filled the center of the enchanted mirror, tendrils of flame waving. Slowly they extended, becoming nebulous legs, a head, a tail. Finally, with a booming explosion that echoed outside the window, the beast of fire and thorns reformed.

Branwyn said, "Is it just me, or is it bigger?"

The red bullets of molten glass appeared over the beast once more. This time they didn't lazily circle, but plummeted down into the beast's skull and spine. The beast staggered, but didn't fall. Instead, it started bounding along the road, straight into the troop of disorganized knights that had turned back from their triumphant return to the Court.

Their tactics hadn't improved from the previous round. They slowed the beast but did not stop it. Severin's glass bullets punctured the beast several times, each time having a visible but non-lethal effect. One of the knights fell and didn't get up again; he was slung onto his waiting mount unceremoniously and the mount sent walking home. Neither Summer nor his companions seemed much concerned by this.

Summer actually turned away, once again bored and disappointed. "I know fights against giant creatures aren't the same as fights against ones your own size. I've got a video game about that. But it's not as fun to watch as it is to do."

"Video games?" asked Rhianna, eyebrows raised. "Here?"

"Yeah," said Summer listlessly. "Video games and lots and lots of batteries. They're okay." She trailed off, then brightened. "How about Truth or Dare?"

Rhianna said, "No, no, you can't bring up video games and then change the subject. I've always wanted to fight a giant monster myself. Games aren't the same thing, but on the bright side, you don't bleed as much." Then she lowered her voice conspiratorially and added, "Also, I think we should let Bran recover a little before Truth or Dare, because she's totally going to take the dares."

Rhianna was right; Branwyn *had* been intending on opting for dares over truth, until she saw the way Summer's eyes sparkled at the thought and realized all the ways dares could backfire on her, even if Summer thought they were harmless. Weakly, she said, "Yeah, I think I'll sit back down for a while."

She curled up in the armchair this time, sitting at an angle so she could see the enchanted mirror, the window, and, if she turned her head, the small tv. Mostly, she stared out the window, where she could see the distant flashes of red without the mirror. Eventually, the flashes stopped.

"Woo-hoo," said Summer when Branwyn told her. "Now you have to climb up its fur, Rhianna." Rhianna worked the control pad vigorously, but fell from the creature's back, and Summer clicked her tongue in dismay.

Branwyn chewed on her lip, then broached the downer question. "Summer, what will you do when the beast reaches the Court?"

Summer looked up. "Ooh, are you ready for Truth or Dare?"

After knocking her head against the back of the armchair, Branwyn said grimly, "Only if we can agree on some ground rules."

"Sure. You and I can do that while Rhianna gets the beast down. What's the first rule you want?"

Branwyn eyed Rhianna, and then slowly said, "No oath-breaking. If anybody says they've promised not to tell that answer, or not to do that thing, the requestor has to come up with something else."

Summer wrinkled her nose. "Okay. My turn! No picking the same option more than twice in a row. So you *can't* be all dares, Branwyn."

Branwyn hesitated, her gaze drifting to the mirror. Then she shook herself as she realized she was hoping for a giant burning beast to get her out of this. "Fine. Dares have to be actions, not an alternate way to get a truth."

Summer pouted. "I guess that's fair. Hmm. No physically harmful dares."

Surprised, Branwyn said, "Of course." She thought for a moment.

"Anything else?" said Summer, bouncing on her toes.

"No asking primarily for information on third parties," Branwyn said slowly. "Like, no asking me for the phone number of the cutest boy I know."

Summer frowned. "Sheesh, you're really limiting it. Okay, but this has got to be the last round of rules. And my last one will be 'no lies of omission'. We gotta share all the juicy details!"

"And... I'm down," said Rhianna. "This is a tough fight, Summer. Can I play Truth or Dare instead?" She rotated in the beanbag chair so she was facing them.

"Yeah, let's get started! All right, so... Branwyn's taking the first turn and I'm choosing Truth. And Branwyn wants to know what I'll do when that beast gets here." She settled herself on the bed, then tossed a pillow at each of them before hugging her own.

"Well... if they don't come up with a better plan, they're probably going to show up right before it does and try to get me to hide in the caves under the Court until it gets caged. And instead, I'll slip away from them with you two and we'll run around in Night having fun." She gave them a little smile.

"They?" Branwyn asked, the rest being an extremely unsatisfying projection. She exchanged looks with Rhianna. That whole plan might have to be modified somehow. Caves sounded a lot cozier than Night. Defeating the beast sounded even better. But cages....

Summer shrugged. "The Dukes and my other so-called guardians. Okay, my turn!" She looked speculatively between Branwyn and Rhianna and then said, "Rhianna, truth or dare?"

Rhianna promptly said, "Truth."

Summer gave her a mischievous smile. "I want to hear about your best kiss."

To Branwyn's surprise, for Rhianna normally had no trouble talking about her escapades, her shoulders and chest pinkened and she ducked her head. "Right. Okay." She peered at Branwyn through an overhang of red hair and then sighed. "Yeah. So, I have a roommate named Max, and once, after I sort of challenged him to, he kissed me."

Branwyn's fists clenched. "Max the monster?" *Max, Severin's buddy who could go places other monsters couldn't. Max, blond and bronzed and cheerful, with an ashen halo and bloody stubs for wings. Max who'd agreed Rhianna had to pay for 'betraying' them when all she'd done was her job.*

"Yes, that Max," said Rhianna, and that was all.

"What made it the best kiss?" prompted Summer. "Was it because he's a monster?"

Rhianna hesitated. "He was gentle, and he was clearly happy I'd challenged him, and he absolutely knew what he was doing. He didn't push. I felt like I'd jumped off a cliff blind and landed in a pile of feathers. I don't know if any of that was because he's a monster, or just because he's Max."

"Did it go anywhere?" asked Branwyn, and she tried so hard to keep the question light. From Rhianna's look, she'd failed.

"No. Just that kiss, that one time."

"Why not? If it was so good and he's your roommate?" Summer asked intently.

"Because it would complicate things with other people I care about, and he's never tried to convince me otherwise. And now it's my turn. Truth or dare, Summer?"

"Hey, shouldn't you ask Branwyn?" protested Summer.

"That wasn't in the rules," Rhianna said. "Don't try to wiggle out of it."

Summer grinned. "Okay. Dare."

"I dare you to go eat everything on the faerie food tray, as fast as you can."

The Queen's grin became a pout. "Really?"

"Yes, really. Stuff your face. Eat it all. You did ask for a dare." Rhianna was serene and firm.

"Finnnne," said Summer, and went to the table where she polished off the crisps, the candied fruit, the spun sugar and the sliced meat as quickly as any of Branwyn's teenage brothers. Then with her mouth still full she said, "Branwyn…"

"Dare," said Branwyn quickly.

After swallowing, Summer said, "You're an artist. Draw me a picture of Sev. There's more paper in the desk."

Judged objectively, this wasn't that bad. At least, it could have been so much worse. She didn't need to actually see him to sketch him. She seemed to have his face burned into her mind.

Somehow, despite how much worse it could have been, this bothered her. But… drawing was better than contemplation, even if sometimes they were the same thing. "I can do that. But I'm going to toss this right back at you while I work. Truth or dare, Summer?"

Summer laughed and grabbed her pillow. "Are you two ganging up on me?"

"You love it," said Branwyn, getting up to get the new pad of paper. "Pick one."

"Dare," Summer said promptly, just as Branwyn had half-expected.

She pulled out the sort of dare that Brynn would have secretly loved. "Sing your favorite song while doing a sexy dance."

It was nice when things worked out as planned. Even if they were very small things. Branwyn's skull twinged in remembered pain at the thought. But Summer gave an embarrassed, horrified laugh and leapt right to her feet. "I have to make sure they bring me one of those karaoke machines for my next party. This time…"

Branwyn smiled at her encouragingly and bent her head to her own dare. After a moment, Summer started singing and Branwyn paused for a long moment before she could draw again. Apparently Summer's favorite song was from Branwyn and Rhianna's step-dad's band.

It shouldn't have been a surprise. Jaime had been the lead vocalist for the song 'The Calling', which the Duchy of Nightwell had produced as the second breach of the tripartite Covenant keeping the faeries away from the mortal world. Album sales for Jaime's own local band had skyrocketed. It made sense that faeries would be fans. But… it was strange hearing a love song from her step-dad to her mother on the Queen of Summer's lips.

It wasn't particularly suited to sexy dancing, either, but nobody complained. Summer went to the window where she swayed while looking out into the night, and sang softly about waking up next to somebody she didn't deserve, who believed in her anyhow, and who she'd never stop loving.

Meanwhile Branwyn started three different sketches and discarded each of them. Her first attempt at his face had felt flat and wrong to her even though it was recognizably him. It was… empty, somehow. Then she'd tried a full-figure of him crouching on the sailing stone, but while she'd captured his compressed energy, the sketch was barely more than a few scribbled lines.

The third time, she'd focused on his eyes at their scariest, because maybe she could change Summer's mind that way... but she'd broken the pencil lead and torn the paper to shreds and that wasn't a good sketch either.

Summer finished her song and came over to see what Branwyn had accomplished. She looked at each of the discards, then brought Branwyn a new pencil. "It's tough, huh? But you can do it."

Branwyn accepted the pencil with a scowl that made Summer laugh. She told herself that she didn't need to capture Severin's *true spirit*, she just had to draw a picture of him that Summer would recognize. And hopefully one that would give her a better idea of what he was like. She doodled as she thought about this, then stopped and stared in horror before scribbling out the R A M I she'd drawn in jagged, artsy letters. What the hell was wrong with her?

Quickly she blocked in a new shape and started drawing a man with Severin's haircut and shark smile. That was the best she could do. Summer would have to be happy.

Meanwhile, Summer said, "Truth or dare, Rhianna?"

"How about a dare this time?" said Rhianna, turning back around from where she'd been poking at the video game menus.

Summer jumped up and down. "I've got the perfect one. You've got a cellphone, right?"

Rhianna held it up. "I do. But there's no cell tower in Faerie yet."

"That's okay. I mean, it's supposed to be a phone call, but I figured a way around it. Rhianna, I dare you to record an honest confession of your feelings for the person at the top of your favorites list, and then play it for them later."

Summer's previous request had made Rhianna go pink; this one made her go pale. She actually dropped her phone. "*What?*" Then she picked it up again. "Do I have to do it *now?*"

Summer nodded. "You have to record it now and play it later.

But… you could record it out in the hall if you really wanted to keep it secret. Because of that one rule Branwyn made."

Rhianna took a couple of shallow breaths. "No. No, I think I need the support. Uh, do you mind if I have a drink first?"

Branwyn watched with a dark interest as Rhianna dug out the little bottle of vodka from her bag and drained it. Then Rhianna looked up and met her gaze with bright eyes. "Bran? You remember how you were mad at me for kissing Max?"

"I wasn't *mad*, Rhi—"

"Don't be mad at me for this, okay? Please? Remember, it's Summer's fault! She's making me do this. We're doing this for the kids. Yeah. For the kids." She lifted the phone to her mouth, took a deep breath and pressed a button. "Hi, Umbriel. Um, I know this is really inappropriate. I know that. But working for you is the best thing that ever happened to me. I hate how much trouble I cause you and I am so grateful you've helped me grow and… and… I really like you. And I hope one day I can do something for you the way you've done so much for me."

Summer clapped her hands together, her eyes glowing, as Rhianna collapsed into the bean bag. "That was *so sweet*. Oh my goodness! That was amazing."

Rhianna stretched out a trembling hand to Branwyn and then melodramatically dropped it, her eyes clenched shut. "He's going to fire me, Bran. Will you be happy then?"

"No," said Branwyn, with a ruthless lack of sympathy. "*Then* I'd worry. The only reason to fire somebody after a 'confession' like that is if you wanted to make a move on them but were too ethical to do so while they worked for you."

Rhianna opened one eye so that suddenly she was winking. Then she shuddered. "You never know with him. I can think of at least four different excuses he'd have to kick me out after a speech like that."

"You have to play it anyhow," Summer insisted.

"She'll be fine," said Branwyn, maintaining her tough front.

But inside, something had eased, just a little. For the first time, she considered the possibility that Umbriel wasn't quite as much of a self-centered bastard as every other celestial she'd met. *Probably*, he was. Rhianna's speech wasn't *that* different from how Penny had felt about Ettoriel, after all. But there was a pretty important difference, in that Ettoriel had burned through Penny's soul, while Umbriel seemed to be protecting Rhianna.

"I'll play it," said Rhianna, sitting up again. "Possibly I'll press play and run away, though. No need to embarrass *him*. Hey, Summer, truth or truth? You've already had two dares."

"Oh! All right. Truth!" said Summer, flopping back on the bed, with the confidence of somebody who had nothing to hide.

Rhianna tapped her lips, her head tilting to one side. At last, she said, "*Why* are *you* the Summer Queen?"

Summer let her pillow fall and hugged her knees. "Hmm. It's odd talking to somebody who doesn't know. Faerie is so *small*. It's *better* now that we've reconnected to the world, even if not everybody is happy about it." She shrugged and when she spoke again, her voice was somehow older. "It's me because somebody had to be, and I... volunteered, in a way. It was a very long time ago, and the Pacts were scattered. If I hadn't picked up the Pact of Day, we all would have... vanished. *I* would have vanished. So I suppose I did it to save myself because I didn't think anybody else would." She laughed a little. "Most of them couldn't have anyhow. I don't blame them for *that*."

She raised her eyes and looked between Rhianna and Branwyn. Then she said, in her more typical voice, "Hey! The beast is reforming again! Maybe somebody will do something different this time." She added, "Okay, I've been talking a lot. Branwyn, truth or dare."

Branwyn stared at the picture under her fingers. It was basically done. Oh, there was plenty of finishing work she could do. But it was a sketch, and it resembled him. And it was all the strange little Queen had asked of her, personally, so far. It suddenly felt deeply unfair to try to hide things from Summer when she was bound by her very nature to honesty.

She glanced up at the enchanted mirror as the beast of fire and thorns roared. And at least if she answered a question now, Severin would probably be too busy to listen in.

"Truth."

Summer clapped her hands again. "Finally! So what's really going on with you and Sev? You said it was more complicated than mere business."

Branwyn pressed her lips together, tore the portrait off the pad and held it out to Summer. "Sev shows up in my life when he needs a catspaw. The first time was when he wanted to kill Tarn. The second time, he needed help killing an angel. This time... well, I think he wants to find a kid, but I wouldn't put any money on it."

"Are you skipping juicy details?" asked Summer suspiciously, taking the portrait.

"No," said Branwyn. "I'm thinking about how to explain them. ...I guess the simplest way is that while I take exception to his very existence, I also find him attractive to an embarrassing degree. He knows that and he enjoys teasing me about it."

"Does he like you? I mean, is he attracted to you?" Summer's eyes were big.

Branwyn's heart jumped into double time. "I... I don't know. All I know is that he likes to tease me. And that doesn't mean anything because tormenting people seems to be his... job or something."

"He was nice to me," muttered Summer, and looked down at the picture again. "Do you *want* him to like you?"

Branwyn scowled. "That doesn't matter. What matters is that he's an asshole."

Summer gave her a skeptical look. "Would that stop you from liking him if you thought he liked you?"

"Summer—I... I don't know. Feelings are hard." She pelted

the Queen with all her crumpled rejects save one. "I don't *want* to like him just because he likes me. There are better reasons to like somebody."

"Like what?" said Summer, uncrumpling each rejected start.

"Like… like their bravery, or their integrity, or their insight…" Branwyn trailed off, realized it, and hastily added, thinking of her friends, "Or their sense of humor, or their loyalty, or their gentleness…"

"Or because they help you pass English, or you just have fun with them," said Rhianna lightly. "Is it Branwyn's turn yet?"

"I guess so," said Summer dubiously. "That doesn't sound nearly as complicated as I expected, though. I thought they were exes or something."

"Sometimes all of Branwyn's relationships seem like war fronts. She's prickly like that. Your turn, Bran." Rhianna kicked a leg into the air, watching as the nightgown shimmied down it.

"Thanks. Truth or dare, Rhianna."

Rhianna looked at her from the corner of her eye. "Truth."

"Oh, good." Branwyn thought about how to phrase her question. "Does anything weird ever happen when you talk to Umbriel… or Max, I guess… on the phone?"

Rhianna frowned. "Not… usually. It's just a phone call. But I think I know what you mean. Sometimes, especially with my Advisor, it's like… like how I imagined praying to work when I was a kid. Like I can feel him there with me. Like he can hear me without the phone." She added hastily, "It's not actually praying. I'm usually reporting something to him, or he's mad about something. He can get very intense when he's mad."

"Okay," said Branwyn, deciding she'd rather feel better that it wasn't only her rather than annoyed that it was also Rhianna.

"My turn again! Truth or dare, Summer." Rhianna sat up.

"Dare," said Summer promptly. Branwyn could detect a pattern.

"Thank the next three faeries who help you with something," said Rhianna sweetly.

Summer squinted at Rhianna. "Your dares aren't very much fun."

Rhianna shrugged. "There has to be *some* incentive for you to pick truth, right?"

"Fine, fine… Branwyn, truth or dare?"

Branwyn protested, "Me again already?"

"You're getting off light, Branwyn," said Rhianna. "Get fortified."

"Well, I can't deal with any more feelings analysis. Dare."

Summer thought for a moment. "Show me how you flirt."

"Uh," said Branwyn. She tried to remember the last time she'd made a conscious attempt to flirt. "Uh. You're cute when you're not falling-down drunk? Want to come back to my place and see my magic hammer? That's a nice sword you have there, mind if I touch it? Get the hell out of my way, wait, actually, come back?"

They laughed at her and she didn't mind. It was good to get things back on a shallower and less personal track. With that in mind, she said, "So, Summer… Truth or dare?"

"Dare," said Summer. The Queen definitely had a pattern. But Branwyn was prepared.

"Order something *weird* from whatever passes for room service here. Something that'll really make them wonder."

Summer's grin made Branwyn smile back, especially when she said to Rhianna, "See, Branwyn does the kind of dares I like." She hopped to her feet, opened the door and spoke to somebody outside.

Rhianna called, "Make sure you say *thank you!*"

"And thank you *so much*, Sola," said Summer with exaggerated enthusiasm, before turning back to give Rhianna a dirty look. She was holding a stack of Branwyn and Rhianna's cleaned clothes, which she put on a chair.

Rhianna gave her a thumbs-up in response. "What did you order?"

"Dessert hummus. He had no idea what I was talking about," said Summer. "*Truth or dare*, Rhianna."

"Uh, truth. I feel like truth is less likely to make me lose my job."

"*Why* are *you* a spy?"

Branwyn watched the enchanted mirror while Rhianna thought about her answer. There were fewer knights now, but the beast was moving as if in slow motion. Branwyn's brow furrowed as she tried to remember where she'd seen that before.

"Well... first of all, I'm really *not* a spy, Summer, though I *wanted* to be when I was a kid. I thought it would be fun to pretend to be somebody else, and trick people for justice. I knew it would be exciting and adventurous and I didn't even think about *the reports*."

"It's not *just* reports," said Summer. "You're here now."

"That's true. It's also my job to go out and get the information before turning it into a report for the rest of my team. And sometimes I run errands, like this. But OX, especially my corner of it, isn't just an intelligence agency anymore." Rhianna looked at her hands. "Honestly, this is outside my usual line these days. I'm here because my Advisor wanted Branwyn involved. I think that connection is why he originally got me transferred to OX, too."

Branwyn's nascent positive feelings toward Umbriel abruptly faded.

"Ugh," said Summer. "Yeah. That's... I sympathize."

Rhianna glanced up. "Oh, he's made it clear he finds me, Rhianna, useful now. And what I do normally is better than I could have dreamed when I was in college." She smiled. "But no, I can't tell you details because of oaths. Hey, Branwyn, truth or dare?"

How did it keep coming back to her? At least it was Rhianna this time. "Truth."

Rhianna gave her an interested look. "When *was* the last time you had sex?"

The only sex that counts is real sex. "Um, there's a guy I've hooked up with a few times recently. The last few months?"

Summer gestured imperatively. "Juicy details!"

"All right. His name is Mack; he's one of Senyaza's monster hunters; we first got together at a party. He's nice, he's quiet, he doesn't distract me, we have our own lives."

"A booty call, not a boyfriend?" asked Summer, her gaze intent.

"Sure, if you want to put it that way." Branwyn glanced at Rhianna, who had a strange little smile. Something twinged in the back of Branwyn's mind.

"How did you first get together with him?" Summer asked.

That embarrassed Branwyn more than the other questions. "Uh, I think I said, *Hold still, I want to test out how well you kiss.*"

Summer howled with laughter. Rhianna said, "A little more casual than you usually go for, Bran? I thought you preferred partners in crime."

Branwyn shrugged. "I'm busy. I don't know him that well, but I trust people who trust him, and none of them have said a word. And he's pretty hot."

That twinge at the back of Branwyn's mind grew stronger, and suddenly she realized what it was. "Uh…" She sprang to her feet and staggered to the table on half-asleep feet, where she grabbed her hammer. "Excuse me, I just have to…"

She made it to the window, where she thrust the head of the hammer outside the window, angled so a dark energy ripple would hit the ground and the sky. *Plenty of time,* she told the Machine fragment. In response, the black diamond stopped holding onto the second charge and it practically detonated off the hammer.

But it was a ripple for only a fraction of a second, before it turned into a *swirl*, before it turned into a *line* that shot back into the room and arrowed straight into Rhianna.

Rhianna gasped, a wet little pained cry, and Branwyn was too horrified to speak. She flung herself beside Rhianna and wrapped her arms around her as she shuddered. Her sister was *ice cold*, and Branwyn's mind was blank with shock. She'd done everything she could to keep the energy away from Rhianna, and it had been meaningless.

"Is this a family trait?" asked Summer anxiously, and then, "Why does she look… *emptier?*"

Branwyn said, "Get over there, in the corner of the room, behind me, *right now*. Do it!"

Startled, Summer fell back out of Branwyn's line of vision, and Branwyn activated her Sight again, desperate to somehow *catch* what had been taken from Rhianna. Surely with a before and after…

Her head hurt again, but it wasn't as bad. She could bear it. It was just the memory of that mindless pain from before. She stared at Rhianna, stared at their hands side by side. All the lines were the same as they'd been before, but Rhianna's were… fainter. Thinner. She didn't know what it meant, except that it was bad. She swiped at them, trying to will them to expand again as she might expand a node from an intersection.

Rhianna yelped and pulled away from her. Branwyn let her go, pulling back herself. She watched, the Sight still glimmering in her eyes and echoes of deathly pain pounding in her head, as Rhianna stared down at her hands. After a minute, Rhianna looked up again, with a trembling little smile. "I guess it's half-time, huh?"

Branwyn wanted to throw herself around the room, wrecking things. She didn't. She stayed completely still. "We're doing fine," she said. "We're going to sort out the haunt and once we do, this is going to be fixed." She'd rebuild the divinity circuit and hand it over to Umbriel herself if she had to, if it would require that kind of miracle to save Rhianna.

But it was halftime, which meant there were two charges left. She didn't know why the second one had arrowed for Rhianna, but it wasn't an accident, and she couldn't blame Severin. How much of Rhianna would be left after the third one?

Hesitantly, she asked, "How do you feel, Rhi? Still cold? Weird in any way?"

"Truth," said Rhi absently. "I feel pretty weird, yeah. Like I'm not all here." She gave a little laugh. "I guess I'm not." Her eyes were too bright as she looked at Branwyn. "Truth or dare, Branwyn."

"Truth," whispered Branwyn.

"You saw this before, didn't you? On the sailing stone. You knew something had happened to me." Rhianna had the same quiet little voice.

"Yes," said Branwyn, wishing she was dead.

Rhianna sighed and stood up unsteadily. "Well. You saw it and you'll find a way to fix it, so there's nothing to worry about. You'll do it all."

"Um, guys?" said Summer worriedly over Branwyn's shoulder. "It's okay if we stop playing Truth or Dare now. Want to watch a movie instead?"

Rhianna picked up her clothes from where they'd been placed on the chair. "And hey, even if I feel weird and look weird... I can still do things. Maybe makeup can help."

Suddenly Summer was beside her, her face fierce, and Branwyn had to turn away. "You can do *anything*. Don't let anybody stop you. Even if they're stronger than you, they're not *you* and they can't understand what *you* need."

Branwyn held herself back from screaming. It wasn't the pain in her head. It was the terror for her sister and that awful rage against herself, for making mistakes and lying about them, for making it easier for herself because it was her *sister* and she couldn't bear it otherwise. But she should have done it anyhow.

There was the stomp of feet in the hall outside and Summer perked up. "The dessert hummus!"

But then the door was flung open and knights in battered white armor poured into the room. Summer and Rhianna were closer to the door than Branwyn, and it was Summer who shrieked in annoyance and made the weapons closing around her and Rhianna waver. "What are you doing here? Get out! Don't ruin my party! Centri, Axis, all of you *get out.*"

Eight. Eight faerie knights, all armed, all battered, and their expressions ranged from coldly determined—the one addressed as Centri—to the fervently passionate Axis. Branwyn saw past the glow of the Queen to their strange auras and the braided glows that bound them into the world.

"They're calling the beast, Your Majesty," said Centri. "We saw it respond when they sent the signal from your room. It's coming to them. We're going to save you."

One of them reached past Summer to take Rhianna's arm. Rhianna could have fought back, evaded, escaped. Branwyn knew she could have. But she didn't. Instead she blinked as if confused.

Summer smacked the knight's hand. "I don't care. Go away. I don't want you here."

Another knight shoved past the first one, pushing Summer so hard she staggered backward and fell over the beanbag chair. As he took Rhianna with both hands, Summer screamed, "How dare you!"

The braid defining the knight began to unwind. But it was slow, so slow. Dispassionately, because between the pain and the perception she had no longer had room for feeling emotions, Branwyn knelt down and put her hand on the floor. She felt the Court around her, and tucked that knowledge away for later, reaching down, down, further, until she could touch the deep root of Faerie.

It was, in fact, the world, from a different perspective. And the world was far too big for her to work with. It was out of her scope.

But the place where the faerie grabbing Rhianna connected to the world was... fragile, by comparison. It would have made sense to have scissors, but she didn't, so she turned tucked-away rage into a blade instead and cut the tie.

Now the faerie was unbinding from both ends, and it was much faster, so much faster that it was already *over*. The light dissolved into nothingness, and the faerie knight holding Rhianna dissolved in just the same way. There was only the scent of dried grass, sharp and fading.

Seven knights left, and they were all angry now. And Branwyn's head was killing her.

"I said she was too dangerous like this," said Centri, and two of the others stalked toward Summer, who scrambled backward with an almost feral gleam of excitement in her eyes. Rhianna finally stopped blinking and stumbled away from the knight closest to her. He lunged after her.

Branwyn tried to reach into the Court, to bend the structure itself to her will. It had nodes already. But her head *hurt*.

Didn't I warn you that if you didn't stop, I was going to kill someone? Severin whispered irritably, and stepped into Summer's bedroom. He looked like he'd been exerting himself, like he needed a shower, like he was annoyed at a naughty child. The first thing he did was step next to Branwyn and bring his finger to her forehead.

She ducked and backed away from him, gasping, "No. Them."

Without looking at what was happening behind him, Severin brought up his hand and his black diamond aura screamed to life. Static filled the room, and suddenly everybody else was moving *slowly*. "Shut it off," he said coldly. "Right now."

That was it. That was the choice she had. Sleep against her will, and trust she'd wake up again. Shut down the Sight voluntarily and trust they'd get out of this without her power. Or don't trust and trigger a catastrophic cascade of unpredictable but probably lethal proportions.

Trust *him?* Let *him* save them? She almost balked. But she hurt *so much*, and there was Rhianna to consider…

She visualized the shut-off pattern. The pain faded.

"Good choice," he said, his voice still cold. Then he flashed his shark smile. "Nice nightgown."

As he turned away, the *slowing* faded. Rhianna tripped, her pile of clothes flying everywhere. Summer bounded to her feet, clapping her hands. The seven knights crowded more completely into the room. Branwyn scrambled to her feet as her mind cleared, moving to put herself between Rhianna and the attackers.

"Oh, please, monster," said one of them. Branwyn couldn't tell them apart, save for the named Centri and Axis. "You're not going to fight seven of us."

Severin's gaze swept over them, and his expression of annoyance flashed into that same rage he'd had when the Wild Hunt had tried to destroy Imani. "No? But I'm going to kill at least two of you." The black diamond aura sharpened.

The speaker shifted, tensing against Severin's aura, but sneered. "Like we're afraid of your weak death, when our Queen is—"

"Nuh-uh, Revo," said Summer. "I told you not to wreck my party. Although it *did* bring Sev out to play. *Thank you* for that." She tossed her hair and glanced at Rhianna, who gave her another thumbs-up.

Several of the knights looked taken aback, including the speaker. They'd spread out now, clearly unused to fighting in ranks with those big swords. Severin didn't wait for them to regain their equilibrium. With one of those sudden darts, he was beside Revo, kicking the knight's legs out from under him even as he twisted his head so savagely that the oversized shoulder pauldrons slashed across his face. Then he dropped the knight, who collapsed onto the floor in a pile and didn't move again.

Before the first knight's armor had stopped ringing, Severin had skipped over to Centri in the rear. "Come on, don't hide behind them. Get out there. Show your Queen what you're made of."

He made as if to shove Centri, but Centri lunged forward ahead of him, twisting and diving over his fellow's body, revealing the knight's poniard Severin had swung at his back.

Meanwhile, three of the knights advanced on Branwyn and Rhianna, while Axis turned toward Summer. Branwyn kicked a chair at the knights while Rhianna muttered incoherently behind her about swords. Then Rhianna said, "Come on, Branwyn, let me deal with this, you go make us a way out."

"You?" said Branwyn harshly, and then "I can't." She and Rhianna were being backed toward the window.

"Bran—"

"No, I can't *make* anything right now!"

Summer squealed, "No! Get away, get out of my way! I want to watch Sev!" She bounded onto her bed and pushed one of the hangings over the knight pursuing her.

Rhianna knocked Branwyn down as her inner arm burned and a sword slid through where she'd been. Then Severin was between them and the knight, with blood on his face and his shirt thick with gore. "Can't you stay out of trouble for fifteen seconds?" He moved, flinging the closest knight away with superhuman strength.

Branwyn tried to get up, but Rhianna stood on her. And for all that she seemed half-translucent now, she weighed the same, which was more than Branwyn did. Rhianna snatched up a poniard from the ground—another? The same? Branwyn had lost track—and sprang off Branwyn's hip toward another of the knights. She didn't even try to dodge the knight's sword and Branwyn was *sure* it would impale her.

But somehow it didn't. It must have impaled her, yet she was fine, and the sword was clean, and then the knight, as surprised as Branwyn, had a poniard in the eye. Rhianna kept moving, through a spot where another sword most definitely was. But impossibly, she wasn't sliced in half as she went low and then that knight was falling as she kicked out the back of his knees.

As Rhianna smashed her fist into the fallen knight's face, Severin reached down and pulled Branwyn to her feet. His whisper buzzed in her ear. *Angel girl can move all right. Don't worry about her; Umbriel's got her back. Make yourself useful and convince the kid the party's over.* He was gone before the words ended, back to Centri.

Branwyn looked around wildly, found the Queen still on her bed and bounded over there. Axis was pleading with her rather than attacking her. No, not pleading with her, berating her. Ranting at her.

"—could you betray us like this? For *him*. I do everything for you. I've fought dragons for your entertainment. *He* is a murderer, a monster, without honor or grace or—"

"Shut *up*," said the Queen. "You're boring me. As soon as I have a minute, you're done, Axis."

"Uh, Summer," said Branwyn, watching the knight's face darken. "Don't you have other courtiers who might be able to help right now?"

Astonished, Summer said, "Why would I want them here, messing things up more? This is perfect!"

"You selfish little bitch," said Axis, his mouth twisting horribly. "Centri was right. We shouldn't ever let you get out of infancy."

"And yet you do," said Summer sweetly. "And for the

stupidest of reasons. You think I'll ever want you? You think I'll want *any* of you after all these years?" She laughed as she tumbled off the bed and hid behind Branwyn.

Axis scrambled over the huge bed after her and Branwyn backed up, shoving the Queen behind her. "See that blood on my arm, Summer? You really want Sev to die because you're enjoying the show?"

The Queen actually thought about it. "I want him to kill Axis and Centri for me. But I guess I can have somebody deal with the others. Whirl! Sola! Dawn!"

"Yes," said Severin, appearing on the bed behind Axis. "They're the ones I want to kill, too." He caught Axis in the drapery and yanked him back on the bed, tangling him in bedding. The black diamond aura suddenly compressed down to encompass just Axis, and the Queen gasped as its influence faded. Then Severin was sitting on Axis's chest, leaning close to him, pressing down hard on his mouth and nose while talking to him. Summer leaned around Branwyn to watch, and Branwyn got out of her way, too numb to be horrified.

Three other faeries had appeared in the room: Whirl, one of the musicians she'd seen earlier and the towel guy. There were only two other knights left standing; all three faeries closed on one of them, leaving Centri standing alone in the center of the room.

Outside the window, something roared.

Branwyn's head swiveled to the window and then the enchanted mirror. The red flames of the beast of fire and thorns were shockingly close, and it was moving fast.

Did it want them? Why? Branwyn's gaze went to Rhianna, crouched low and watching Centri. She thought of that first pulse of energy that had rippled through Faerie. She didn't understand. But there was no time right now to understand.

Centri's sword clattered to the floor. "It doesn't matter," he said to the three loyal faeries holding his companion. "Soon that beast will tear down the Court, swallow the Queen, and scatter the children of Harvest. One way or another we'll be starting over again."

The musician shrugged. "It's the way of things."

"Then we should embrace it," snarled Centri. "Control it! This weakness will destroy us now the Covenant no longer protects us."

Severin hopped off the bed, leaving a motionless, fading figure behind him. Rhianna skittered out of his way, still low to the ground as Severin said, "You've already let your weakness destroy you, boyo. Centri the Wise. Centri the fool."

"*You*," spat Centri, reaching for his sword only to discover he'd already dropped it. Severin's aura glittered around them.

"Me." Severin leaned forward. "You want strength, you want power, you want control, all for *your people*, but you won't *take her place*. But of course you can't do *that*. You're too weak, and you'd rather bitch and whine than grow. You've actually convinced yourself your fear means something. You're a waste of my energy and hers." He picked up Centri's sword and offered it back to him. "If you had a drop of courage or loyalty, you would still be fighting that beast, fighting until the dawn when *your people* would be safe. And if you were *worthy*, you'd respect the sacrifice she made just so you can *play*. But you're treacherous trash and all you can do is demand more, more, more." He closed Centri's fingers around the sword.

Dread emerged from Branwyn's numbness. "Severin," she whispered, and didn't realize it until he paused.

"Think about that a minute, will you?" Severin said, then turned and strolled over to Branwyn. His body language was smooth and calm, but his eyes were *savage*. He stopped in front of Branwyn, put his hands on her hips, and pulled her body hard against his. His voice in her ear said, *This time I am going to finish the job, cupcake, unless you feel like it's worth the price to stop me.*

Branwyn caught her breath and then shook her head. She

hadn't meant to say his name at all. She wasn't sure she wanted him to do what he was doing… but she wasn't his regulator. She wasn't his leash.

His fingers loosened on her hips but he didn't move from where he stood between her and Centri, except to turn his head. "So," he said conversationally, and everybody in the room stood as if spellbound. "No courage. No loyalty. But if you've got even a drop of strength in you, Centri, you know what you need to do. Do it right, and your precious Queen might even let you live again someday. Or you can leave it to me, like she wants. It'll take a while but eventually you won't have to worry about anything, ever again." He paused, then added, "Oh yes. You're more afraid of *that* than anything else, aren't you."

Branwyn twisted so she could see around Severin. The black diamond aura buzzed distantly as Centri stared at his sword, then placed the point under his chin.

If you really want to watch… Severin whispered.

She looked at him instead, at the shape of his profile as he kept his own gaze on the faerie knight. Quietly, she said, "Breaking them didn't work like you hoped, did it?"

His jaw tightened as there was a soft, wet sound behind him. "No," he said, and nothing else.

"Is it over?" asked Rhianna, her voice high. "Can I open my eyes?"

"That was *amazing*," said Summer, clapping her hands. "I loved it. Thank you *so much* for coming to help me, Whirl and Sola and Dawn! Take that jerk away and I'll deal with him—"

Something red filled the window, and slammed into the high bloom of the Summer Court. The whole structure swayed. Summer went tumbling across bodies that sparkled out of existence until she was caught by the musician. Whirl held her hands up and the furniture stopped flying. Rhianna slid across the floor, grabbing at her scattered clothes. Severin, annoying jerk, kept his balance, even when Branwyn clutched at him.

222

Sola the towel guy pushed the remaining knight into Dawn's hands and said, "Now it is time to go down to the caves, Your Majesty."

Summer looked thoughtful. "I... don't think so? I think we can come up with more fun things to do." The loud roar made her cover her ears, but she grinned wildly. "I'm sure we can. We can run around outside. I'm sure if we ride we'd be faster than it. Our unicorns are *really* fast."

Branwyn stared at her in dismay. "Summer—"

Summer gave her a sulky look. "It's barely halfway through the eight hours, guys."

The bloom swayed again and Branwyn pushed Severin away, saying irritably, "Do something about the way you smell. Summer, this has been a great—" The bloom swayed a third time.

Whirl sighed and left the room. Her magic remained, keeping the furniture fixed where she'd first caught it. Dawn left, too, hauling the shattered-looking knight behind him. Only Sola remained, looking at Summer with a desperate, pleading look.

Rhianna, stuffing her feet into her socks, said, "It's your turn, Branwyn."

Branwyn stared at her. "I'll get dressed..."

"No," said Rhianna, looking irritated. "It's *your turn*."

Branwyn blinked. Then, understanding, she looked at Summer, staring at the beast outside the window with a sort of horrified glee. "Truth or dare, Summer."

"Dare," said Summer instantly.

It was her third dare, but Branwyn decided it wasn't her responsibility to point that out. Instead, she said firmly, "Summer, I dare you to save your people and *let us go.*"

16

The Saint's Way

SUMMER STARED AT HER, a line appearing between her eyebrows. There was a protracted moment of silence, interrupted by another beastly roar. Then she gave a wry, old smile. "That's pretty good."

And suddenly she was the wildly enthusiastic teenager again. She jumped up and down and clapped her hands. "Come on, get dressed, hurry up, we have to go. Night won't stay long now that I've released her and I need you guys out of here before the children of Harvest come out and get stepped on!"

Rhianna rolled to Branwyn with her clothes and offered them. As Branwyn scrambled into them and sat to put on her shoes, Rhianna said softly, "I would have gone with 'end this night' but you went for the emotional appeal. Pretty good..."

Branwyn gave her a narrow look as she tied her shoes. "Thanks."

"Come on, come on!" Summer tossed their bags at them, then Branwyn's rejected sketch starts. "Don't leave anything here!" A moment later they were on their feet and following

Summer and Sola along the Court hall. Severin stayed behind, looking out the window at the beast, but Branwyn wasn't exactly worried about him catching up.

They hurried through the hall, descended three ramps, and stopped at the elevators. "Should we take the stairs?" Rhianna asked.

"Are you kidding?" said Branwyn. "Only if we have to, and we might be better off just jumping."

"These... should work?" said Summer. She frowned and winced, then stomped her foot. "Argh! Sola, fix it!"

Sola touched the elevator as well, then shook his head. "No. The Queen of Stone's handmaiden has pulled a small portion of her Domain here to protect the Queen's son, and it's disrupting the elevators."

"Can't blame her for that..." muttered Summer. "Um. Sola? Please? Help us down to the Saint's cave?"

"Of course, Your Majesty," said the towel faerie. "If you would let me bear you... and if you two ladies would *tightly* take my arms..."

This quickly arranged, Sola leaned forward and plummeted off the empty elevator shaft. Fluffy white wings burst from his shoulders, catching and braking them. Branwyn decided that once again, she didn't *really* need to watch, and closed her eyes and pretended she was on an amusement park ride until her feet touched rough ground.

Somehow, they were underground, in a beautifully lit crystalline cave covered with hanging moss and embraced by giant tree roots. There was an opening ahead of them shaped more by root than stone, with a white sand floor.

Sola gently deposited the Queen as his wings dissolved into blowing feathers. Summer caught one, pressed it to her mouth, and smiled at him before turning to Branwyn and Rhianna. "This is the shortcut I mentioned. Um... where's Sev? I think he should be here. You're going to be traveling somewhere beyond my Domain and it's improper for him to be cutting in as his first entrance."

Branwyn gritted her teeth and said, "Severin." She felt him behind her, but once again had to rely on the expressions of others to determine that he wasn't really there.

Why are you so trying? he whispered, breathing into her loose hair like he had at the Court of Stone.

"Come here," she snapped. Summer's eyes widened and Severin's arms slid around Branwyn's waist. Then he released her and stepped away. His clothes were clean and there was an aging scab on his cheek.

"So who has the kids, Summer?" asked Rhianna.

Summer dragged her eyes away from Severin. "Right. Um, I have a faeling... do you know what a faeling is? They're like changelings, except only my sisters and I can make them. They can't be unbound or unmade, so of course they're super annoying, and basically do whatever they want. I made this one a very long time ago and he hardly ever visits me, the jerk. But he really cares about kids. When I realized Gale was about to go postal, I felt bad for the little girl, so I told the Saint. Then he rescued her and the rest of them. He was so mad at me, and Gale, and that whole town." Summer shrugged. "He's mad a lot, though so no surprise there. Anyhow... let's go into the cave."

It wasn't sand on the floor of the cave beyond, but snow, and in the center of the sparkling snow was a mirror-like pool. Summer waved a hand. "So... yeah. That's the shortcut. Jump in there and you'll come out in the Saint's March. You'll have to figure things out from there yourself. As I said, he was really mad. It might not be easy." She glanced between Branwyn and Rhianna. "I bet you'll do it, though." She grinned. "I dare you to."

Gravely, Rhianna said, "Thank you. I hope we can keep in touch somehow after this."

"Me too," said Summer enthusiastically. "I want another party, with more people!"

"Uh, yeah," said Branwyn. "Are you going to be okay with your Court? Things got kind of… disturbing up there."

Summer shrugged. "It'll work out. It always does. Thanks for caring, Branwyn. And thanks for the picture."

"Sure," said Branwyn. She shifted her weight, uncomfortable, and then dug out her hair tie and pulled her hair back. "Uh. Yeah. Have I mentioned I hate long goodbyes?"

"Right," said Summer. She looked at Severin with her lashes veiling her eyes and said shyly, "It was really nice meeting you, Sev." She held out her hand.

Severin gave her one of his inscrutable looks, then ruffled her hair. "You're a cute kid. Want to know a secret?"

Summer nodded, eyes bright. He bent to her ear and started whispering. After a moment, as the whispering continued, Summer's gaze focused on Branwyn. She nodded occasionally, her eyes getting wider and wider. Finally, he stopped, and she said, "That's actually… kind of scary."

Severin nodded too-enthusiastic agreement. "Isn't it?"

"Thank you for telling me, though." Summer took a deep breath. "Okay. Oh. I'm sorry about this, but jumping into the Saint's Way is going to hurt a lot. Nothing gets damaged, but… it's the price he set." She hesitated. "Okay, I'm going so you don't feel pressured. But dawn's going to be here soon, so… don't take too long."

Then she ran out of the room, vanishing behind Sola's back in the other chamber.

"Severin…" said Branwyn in a voice like a thin wire. "What did you tell her?"

"I did say it was a secret." He glanced at her, grinned and added, "I don't really need a faerie queen as a stalker, cupcake."

"It was something about me, wasn't it?" she demanded.

"Why would something about *you* make her stop stalking *me*?" He paused, raising an eyebrow to see if Branwyn wanted to answer.

At that point, Rhianna pushed them both into the pool.

———

THEY SANK into the pool together as Rhianna jumped in after them. It was dark, it was cold, and it was painful, but it wasn't wet, or drowning. They floated down, Branwyn's eyes fluttering closed.

It really did ache, but after passing through the belly of Death and trying to fry her brain by working magic around a faerie queen, the *cold* pouring through her skin like a thousand piercing needles was… exhausting more than anything else. Not something she'd sign up for at the spa, that was for sure. But she was going… to save… some kids…. And maybe sleep…

Ice crystals grew out of her, tiny and sharp, and she raised her hand to look at them wonderingly. She breathed on it. They melted instantly, and the darkness exploded into white.

She fell to her knees in a snowy field at the base of a tall cliff that loomed out over her. It was as bright as day, but the sky was the old blue of a polar twilight. Rhianna sat beside her with a thump while Severin came down in a crouch.

"I should have asked how far we were traveling," said Branwyn. "I should have asked how much time we had before the beast caught up again."

"She would have just said she didn't know," said Rhianna. "I'm not sure she could know. Didn't that faerie say that the handmaiden had brought the Domain of Stone within the Summer Court?" She poked the snow. "We should have gotten coats from Whirl. That's what we should have done."

Branwyn pushed herself to her feet, then noticed Severin was still crouching. She brushed her fingers over his shoulder. "Are you okay?"

His shoulders tightened under her fingers and she pulled her hand away sharply. "I don't like this."

"What?" queried Rhianna.

"This snow. This climate. How there's nothing here." He gave them both a dark look. "You're both half-dead already." He stood up, wrapped his hand around the back of Branwyn's neck and tugged her to him. Before she could squirm away, his mouth dropped onto her forehead, right at her hairline, and the flashing coolness and warmth she remembered from when he'd healed her broken arm sank into her head and neck.

Then he released her, while her brain was still buzzing with the strange feeling of regeneration, and reached out for Rhianna. "I can't do as much for you."

Rhianna stepped forward willingly and submitted to Severin brushing her forehead with his lips. Her *glint* didn't change but her cheeks acquired a healthier color. She said, "What about you? You've been... exerting yourself more than I've ever seen Umbriel do."

Severin said impassively, "Your angel's spent the last few millennia kicking back in Heaven. I doubt he's focused much on designing or repairing his vessels. I'm *sure* he hasn't dedicated time learning to kill his brothers." He looked up into the sky. "Those knights were barely more than changelings, for all their dreamborn nature. Not much power, no tricks to extend what they had. Too long pretending to be other than they were. If Summer's Saint is on her level rather than theirs..." He trailed off before finally saying, "Don't expect him to go down easily."

"Talking is our plan A, plan B, plan C *and* plan D," said Rhianna. "It's not until plan E that we start with the violence, and *that* requires paperwork in triplicate."

Puzzled, Branwyn said, "I thought Summer had even less power than her knights, except that binding thing."

Severin gave her a thoughtful glance. "She's got almost as much power as the Queen of Stone. She just can't use it. I couldn't see why."

"It hurts her," said Rhianna quietly. "I'm cold. We might as well move."

———

"It's all very well to say *let's move* in a dramatic voice," said Branwyn a few moments later, "but do we have any *reason* to be walking this direction in particular?"

"Because if we need to walk along the cliff wall or climb it, we won't be able to see that while it's hanging over us like that," said Rhianna patiently. "And Griff didn't say he saw an empty snowfield. So this is the best direction to go."

Branwyn subjected this to more scrutiny than it really warranted, then turned around and walked backward. Severin stalked behind them, his hands in his pockets. The cliff was very tall, with icicles stretching from the ground to the cliff-top in many places. If there was anything atop it, she still couldn't see it. It curved away at the horizons where dark trees took over.

"Aren't you getting snow in your shoes?" asked Rhianna.

"It was going to happen anyhow," said Branwyn, but turned around again. "Did you have a plan for if Summer had remembered her own rule about taking more than two dares in a row?"

Rhianna rubbed her hands over her pale arms. "It was your turn, not mine. You would have come up with something."

"Your faith in me is terrifying," said Branwyn, annoyed.

Rhianna blew on her hands, and her warm breath went right through her fingers. Branwyn's insides twisted up, but all Rhianna said was, "*If* it had been me, I would have encouraged her to show us those caves and then set up a few more rounds until a dare came around again. She wouldn't have made it hard."

At that moment, something heavy and dark dropped over Branwyn's head, then slithered into her arms. She found herself holding an oversized navy parka while Rhianna struggled her way out from under a stylish black coat.

"You're not much use to me if I have to keep chasing away frostbite," said Severin acidly.

Rhianna slipped the black coat on at once, wrapping it around her and tying the belt. The crispness of the coat only emphasized the scattering of light under her skin that made her look half-empty.

Branwyn dragged her gaze back to Severin, who had swapped his most recent shirt for a long-sleeved gray sweater, and made herself imagine his laundry bill instead of Rhianna's condition. Or did he go to laundromats? She carefully arranged the navy parka over her arm. "What about you? Where's your coat?"

Rhianna said, "You know, Branwyn, from anybody else I'd call that *concern* but from you, it just sounds like you're picking a fight."

"She is," said Severin shortly. He put his extremely warm hand on Branwyn's cheek. "I'm a lot better designed than you, cupcake, and I'm not particularly trying to blend in here."

Branwyn scowled and reached up to pull aside his sweater neckline, revealing the scar her hammer had inflicted almost a year ago. "How come you still have that, anyhow? I've seen you heal from worse injuries a half-dozen times now."

He gave her an annoyed look. "I kept it as a constant reminder of the pleasure of your company." Then his eyes raised to the horizon, and he said in a different voice, "Put the coat on. Start walking again. That way." He started hiking across the snowfield again, at a slight angle from their earlier heading.

Branwyn said, "So what's the plan when we find the kids?" as she put on the parka. It was heavy and too big and smelled like

Severin. It also had huge pockets with absolutely nothing in them, not even lint. She wondered what had been there before he cleaned them out.

"We grab Charlie and get her back to Imani," said Severin, still focused on the horizon.

Branwyn, eyeing Rhianna's emptiness, approved of that idea. Presumably once the haunt shut down, the soul charges wouldn't be compelled to return to the ghost that had bound them.

Firmly, Rhianna said, "No snatching Charlie until we've worked out a release schedule."

Severin stopped, though he didn't turn. "That seems like a bad plan."

Branwyn said, "This is the worst thing I've ever said, but I think he's right. We need to get that haunt shut down."

Distantly, Rhianna said, "Just the day before yesterday, you said you wouldn't trade a kid to Severin to pay a debt. But you'd sell seventy to… what?" Her eyes sparkled unnaturally as she looked over at Branwyn. "Are you going to tell me this is about saving the world?"

Branwyn's hands clenched in the parka's pockets. She'd seen the Wild Hunt at work. They'd try to help the haunt as long as it remained harmless, but she didn't believe for a moment they'd take risks once it fully reactivated. "No. It's not."

"Watch out," said Severin as a vibration stirred the snow. He took one step backward as moving shapes Branwyn hadn't noticed before shot toward them. Then, with the sound of thunder, the herd of heavy-coated horses swept past them before wheeling and pounding off parallel to the cliff face.

"Playing," said Severin, flicking kicked up snow off himself. "There's people the way they came."

"We're going to find the Saint, and thank him for rescuing the kids, and talk to him about getting them home again," said Rhianna determinedly as she struck out in the indicated direction. "That's how we're starting this. Having Sev, who has a convenient wardrobe but a really bad local reputation, grab one of the Saint's wards and vanish with her is going to sabotage everything. Once we have a good working relationship established, we can extract Charlie first and directly." She shaded her eyes. "There *are* people. I think they're ice skating."

Branwyn followed Rhianna in silence. They didn't know anything about the Saint yet. And they had time. Rhianna would be fine. And *later*, she could deal with... everything else, everything else she'd pressed firmly down into the wells of darkness.

After a few minutes, they had a good view of the frozen pond where a dozen children skated. Some distance beyond the pond rose a large alpine lodge with outbuildings and cottages surrounding it. An evergreen forest filled in the far distance.

Beside the pond were two sleighs with empty traces. Two puppet-like figures sat on the sleighs, while three arctic wolves lounged on the pond bank.

Severin scanned the scene, then said, "No Saint there. You two make nice with the kids while I scout around." He dropped back behind Rhianna and Branwyn.

Rhianna kept hiking forward, but said quietly, "Will you stop him from attacking the Saint if it comes to that?"

Branwyn hesitated. "I don't think it will. He practically told us he didn't think he'd win that fight."

"Can you tell if he's lying?"

"I..." Branwyn's pulse quickened, and she shook her head. "No. But I've never seen him present himself as weaker than he is."

"Right." They both watched as the white wolves on the shore of the pond noticed them, grouped up, and started advancing toward them with a distinctly unfriendly air. "The Saint's... a werewolf? I'm confused."

"Let's stop," said Branwyn, taking Rhianna's icy hand. "I don't want to make them nervous."

The kids noticed when the wolves grouped up. The pond fell silent. Then one of the taller boys said something to another one, and they kicked something off their feet and started running after the wolves. A moment later most of the other children followed them.

Since the advancing wolves weren't running, soon the entire mass of kids caught up. The first boy darted in front of the wolves while the second one grabbed two of them by their ruffs and mostly failed to hold them back.

"Hi," said the first boy. "You shouldn't be here. You should probably go."

"Hi. I'm not sure we can," said Branwyn. "Although if your dogs are going to bite us, I'll at least run back the way I came."

"Uh… stop it, Snowball! They're not hurting us. They're not even that old." He knelt and wrapped his arms around the third wolf's shoulders.

Then the other children arrived, pouring over the wolves and surrounding Branwyn and Rhianna. They were all dressed in solid winter wear of natural origin, and they seemed well-fed and energetic, which boded well. The Saint clearly cared for their well-being.

A flurry of questions and comments avalanched over the women: Who were they, where had they come from, were they humans, they looked like humans, the Saint would be mad, could they ice skate, where were their mittens and boots, did they see the horses…?

"Hey, hey, quiet!" said the first boy. "Well, I guess it's too late now. I'm Matthew. Uh… our guardian will be here soon. I'm not sure if you're faeries in disguise or actually human, but… don't try to buy us from him if you want to stick around for a while."

"*Buy* you?" asked Branwyn. But as soon as she said it, she didn't need an answer. To some faeries, the Saint's March must have looked like a mortal ranch. "Of course not. I'm Branwyn. This is Rhianna." She stopped short, unwilling to introduce their mission when she didn't know the provenance of the children before her.

"We're human," said Rhianna lightly. "I take it you are too. How did you get here?"

Matthew said, in a noticeably neutral tone, "He rescued us." He turned and scanned the horizon. "He's coming now. You'll have to talk to him."

Rhianna responded by kneeling and talking instead to the smaller children, who hadn't stopped trying to seize attention. "Yes, I saw the horses. Are they your horses? What's your wolf's name? I'm a little afraid of ice skating. And I forgot my mittens."

Branwyn listened with half an ear while she watched the figure Matthew had identified. He was a big man, in a heavy brown coat with a fur-lined hood, and followed by a handful of children, another of the puppet-like individuals, and a fourth wolf. He walked swiftly and easily through the snow, unconcerned by the slower pace of kids following him.

As he passed the pond, Branwyn realized he had a neatly trimmed, full white beard. She'd never seen any faerie with a beard before, although she had no doubt they existed. But something about this beard bothered her. She felt, peculiarly, like it ought to be longer, wilder. She wondered if it somehow related to his faeling nature.

The Saint stopped abruptly to stare at them, then started walking again, his stride even longer. As he came into hearing range, the children crawling over Rhianna and staring at Branwyn suddenly scattered out of the way. It was like they were getting out of the line of fire, and Branwyn couldn't forget Matthew's first words: *you shouldn't be here.*

Even considering the white beard, the Saint was a surprisingly attractive older man. He was bulky, but it was the bulk of muscle rather than fat. His eyes were a striking dark blue, and not nearly as angry as the children had suggested he would be.

He stopped a few yards away from them as Rhianna climbed to her feet, inspecting them. Then he smiled, his white teeth dazzling in his weathered face and met Branwyn's eyes. "You are the wonderworker." He tapped a finger on the side of his nose. "I too, once upon a time."

17

Sainthome

BRANWYN STARED at the Saint and managed, "You… you are?" just as Rhianna tried to break her fingers. Judging from Rhianna's subsequent sigh, Branwyn was sure she'd scuttled whatever inspiration Rhianna had caught. But since she'd already she screwed up, why not ask more? "You're an Artificer? I thought…"

"I *was*, girl. It went with my humanity. Still. A pleasure to meet somebody from those days." His smile twisted wryly. "Clearly, you didn't come to beg for my ancient wisdom, though."

"I didn't," said Branwyn frankly. "But I would have." She looked around him at the puppet-like creature that had followed him and now saw it was a clockwork simulacrum of a human, with oversized joints. Simply from the way it gazed back at her, the gears in its eyes whirring, she knew it had multiple nodes. It took Rhianna squeezing her hand to remind her that here and now was *not the time* to study it.

"Well, if your sister and yonder boogieman had come calling without you, I would have sent them on their way. But… it'll be nice to chat with another wonderworker again, so you three can stay for a little while." He added in a lower, conspiratorial voice, "That'll give you a chance to make your case about the actual reason you came."

The Saint looked between Rhianna and Branwyn, not missing the clutched hands. "I'll have you walk in, though, while I take the children back to get washed for dinner. I expect you'll need the time to whistle back the dark one." He paused, then added, "I'm not inclined to be disagreeable right now. I hope that doesn't change. I don't like upsetting the children." He gave them a nod, half-turned and added, "Mind the horses."

With a thunder of hooves, the herd of furred horses swept around them, galloping to the pond and around it, where eight of them peeled off to skid to a stop near the sleighs. The Saint roared, "Time for dinner, children."

"Why do we have to walk, again?" asked Branwyn as the horses were hitched to the sleighs and the sleighs loaded with children faster than humanly possible. Then she glanced at Rhianna. "What's wrong?"

Rhianna had a ghastly grin, her eyes wide. "I will *end him*."

"Who?" Branwyn's anxiety spiked. Did this relate to Rhianna's empty *glint?*

"My Advisor," said Rhianna, like it was a filthy phrase. "My *Advisor* and his ideas on *information security*."

Branwyn let her breath out long and slow. "Oh." She thought. "Yeah. Imagine the schemes you could have come up with if we'd known from the beginning about this Artificer thing."

"We wouldn't even have had to pay you! You could have visited him for totally legitimate reasons and you would have gotten involved all by yourself!"

"Yeah—hey!"

"I would have come too, of course," added Rhianna. "Just like now."

"But you wouldn't have told me?" Branwyn demanded.

Rhianna patted her shoulder. "It would have been my job, not yours. And besides, *I'm* the trickster. My *Advisor* is the one who insisted we be as honest as possible so why does he... argh!" She actually stomped her foot in the snow.

Branwyn stared at her sister, mesmerized. It was somehow... *all right* that her sister would have done that, even though Branwyn would never do the same. That was *Rhianna*, who *was* more than Branwyn's little sister.

Except I did lie to her. And uselessly, only for myself. Who the hell do I think I am?

Branwyn shook her head hard. *Priorities.* She would save her sister and *then* deal with facing herself in the mirror.

"Now *you* look like you've swallowed a lemon. Why?" asked Rhianna, finally disentangling their hands.

"I'm worried about you," said Branwyn shortly, more honest than ordinary, because she'd lied before.

"Oh." Rhianna shifted her bags and turned away to scan the horizon. "Where's our boogieman, do you think?"

"I don't know and I don't care," snapped Branwyn, hurt by her sister's reaction. She started walking toward the sleigh tracks. Then she stopped. "I do care. I'm sorry. I just... *hate* being his leash."

"Yeah," said Rhianna, her voice odd. "It's pretty weird to feel like your main value is as a messenger between two other people."

Branwyn technically understood subtext was occurring, but she'd accidentally tapped one of her dark wells and couldn't stop herself from continuing. "I mean, I can say I won't call him all I want, but what does hiking downstairs *matter* if, as soon as somebody else asks, I just do it? Oh, sure, because it's *practical* or *easiest*, but where does that stop?" She caught herself and dragged in a deep breath, firmly closing the metaphorical tap. "Right. I'm sorry. You said something?"

Rhianna gave her a thoughtful look, then put her hands around her mouth and shouted "*Severin!!*"

An instant later, Branwyn felt the brush across the back of her neck. "He's coming," she said glumly. Her sister's effort was sweet, and just made her feel guilty.

A moment later, Severin stepped past her, hands in his pocket as he raised both eyebrows at Rhianna.

Rhianna came sharply to attention, ripping off a salute. "Commander Boogieman, I, Cadet Little Sister and First Lieutenant Wonderworker there have reports to make!"

"Hey, wait. Why is *he* a Commander?" Branwyn protested.

Rhianna covered her mouth so she could speak from the side. "*His ego.*"

"It's nice you feel like you had the time to put this act together," said Severin acidly. "I didn't catch what the Saint said because I was busy with his pets. Should I go back to that?"

"He used to be an Artificer," said Branwyn bluntly. "Out of… professional courtesy, he'll allow us to visit and ask him things."

Severin's left hand curled into a fist. "Isn't *that* convenient."

Rhianna jumped up and down, pointing at Severin. "You understand! You do! Isn't he *awful?*"

"Oh, come on, you two," said Branwyn, looking between them. "Obviously Umbriel didn't warn us because he could see the two of you would invent some trick, probably using me, and *just as obviously*, tricks like that will screw this up."

Both of them looked at her, with eerily similar dark looks. Rhianna scowled. "You *would* see his point of view."

"That only makes me want to kill him even more," said Severin. "Fine. I didn't see Charlie, but I saw plenty of other kids. Let's get over there and *ask him things.*"

They followed the sleigh trail. "Based on what he said, I'm sure he knows why we're here," said Rhianna. "And he's willing to negotiate with us as long as we behave."

"I'm not waiting around through another slumber party," warned Severin.

Rhianna grimaced. "Honestly, I'd rather slumber than party at this point. It's been a long day."

Briskly, Branwyn said, "No slumber parties. And you can nap while I grill him about Artificer stuff, Rhianna. I'm sure that was definitely on the negotiating table."

"You just want the excuse to talk shop," said Rhianna with a smile.

As they passed through the cluster of cottages in front of the lodge, one of the clockwork people opened the lodge's door and came out to wait for them. Once again, Branwyn resisted distracting herself with the Sight, but she did wonder if the proper term was 'robot' or 'golem.'

This one was bright brass, with polished wood inlays, and stood about five feet tall. Its gaze followed them as they approached. Then it inclined its head and spoke in pleasantly metallic voice, "Welcome to Sainthome. The boss is dining with the children. He has no interest in tempting you with dangerous morsels, so I shall invite you to the grand study, instead."

Without waiting for a response, the clockwork person turned and walked into the house. Branwyn admired its stride, noticing the springy movement of the hip joints. Rhianna shook her head and continued ahead of her, leaving Severin to murmur in Branwyn's ear, "Machines get you that way, huh?"

Absently, Branwyn said, "Blood in the water, right?" She glanced at him. "You notice when people get upset, right? Yeah, I notice something like that walking past me."

He studied her, then shook his head briefly. "Your skyscraper is more impressive than the automatons."

"Automatons, that's the right word! But I had so little to do with actually building Titanone."

Severin's eyes narrowed. With one hand, he pushed her toward the entrance. "Just imagine the treats in this grand study."

Branwyn sighed and trudged into the lodge. "I can't. I'm going to stay focused and not be seduced by all the shiny tools and trade secrets so I don't make stupid decisions. But I do wish I'd come here at another time, and for another reason." She viewed her near future darkly and added, "Maybe in another life."

The grand study was a large room that appeared to be half library and half playroom. There was a loft above the main floor with books and a desk, and many more books, tables and table-based activities on the main floor.

"This way, please," said the automaton, guiding them to the loft staircase. "After dinner, the boss spends time in the grand study with those children who wish to join him." The loft office was overcrowded to bursting. There was guest seating: a couch and two chairs, and all of them buried under books and documents. "Our apologies," said the automaton as it cleared off seating. "It's been a while since a visitor lasted long enough to make it to the office."

"That's not ominous," said Rhianna, and yawned.

"Most recent visitors from Faerie are primarily interested in the children, and the boss is very protective of the children. Please make yourself comfortable. Dinner will finish soon." The automaton started to descend the stairs again.

Branwyn said, "Hey! What are you called?"

The automaton looked at Branwyn for a long moment. "Kilter, miss." Then it continued its descent.

Branwyn threw herself in one of the chairs and bounced. "Kilter...."

Rhianna had flopped on the couch, her legs stretched out. She had her head tilted back and her eyes closed. Severin stood at the half-wall and looked over the space below.

Branwyn *had* to resist getting distracted by artificing shinies. She said, "You didn't hurt any of his pets when you were playing, did you?"

"I resisted the temptation," Severin said flatly.

Branwyn viewed him narrowly, then transferred her attention to Rhianna. "How are you feeling, Rhi?"

"I'm tired, Branwyn. I feel hollow, and it kind of hurts." She opened her eyes and saw Branwyn's alarmed expression. "It's like I'm drying out. It's only distracting when I sit still."

She didn't say, *Do you know what's wrong?* Or *Do you know how to fix it?* Or get upset, or even pretend she was fine. Branwyn knew she could have responded to any of those things. They all would have made her stronger, more determined. But Rhianna's calm, disengaged reporting made her feel helpless. Feeling helpless was her least favorite thing.

She slouched in the chair and stared at her hands until finally the door downstairs opened and a stream of children, wolves and automatons poured into the room around the big form of the Saint. They clustered around him for a moment. Then he waved the kids to their individual pursuits and came up the stairs.

Near the top, he paused, inspecting Severin. Severin didn't seem to notice, studying the kids on the lower floor instead. Shaking his head, the Saint finished his climb and moved past Severin to settle himself at his desk.

After looking at them, he said, "Well, I hope you've had time to come up with a gambit you're confident in?"

Rhianna slitted her eyes open, but didn't answer, so Branwyn said, "No, sir. No gambit. Just the truth. We're here because of Tucker."

The Saint gave her a faint, sad smile, touched his nose, then pointed with the same finger at Severin's back. As if cued, Severin called harshly, urgently, "Charlie!"

Branwyn shot to her feet to peer over the half-wall. Charlie was easy to spot: the only ebony-skinned child in a room of white kids, and the only one who looked up at Severin and determinedly back down at the book she was coloring.

Something creaked in Branwyn's chest. Severin's entire body

was a taut wire, his eyes pits and his mouth a forbidding slash. A few of the children, looking between Severin and Charlie, rearranged themselves so they were clearly between her and the 'boogieman' staring down at her.

Genially, the Saint said, "That's nice to see. Some of them have come a long way since I brought them home." He twiddled a fountain pen. "Charlie told me he might show up. I told her she wouldn't have to talk to him if she didn't want to."

The creaking in Branwyn's chest became a sustained hum. She stared at Severin. He wasn't moving, except for shallow breaths. His knuckles were white, but his fingers weren't denting anything. Nobody was screaming and crying. He was, she decided, regulating himself. *Good for him.*

Rhianna sat up, stretching her back. "Charlie's not the only kid from Tucker we need to talk about, sir. We're very grateful that you rescued them from that catastrophe, but we'd like to bring them back to Earth."

The Saint smiled faintly again. "Oh? What for? They've no homes to return to."

"We'll find them new ones," said Rhianna firmly.

"Your people have countless children already they can't find homes for," countered the Saint.

Rhianna winced, but had a prepared answer. "Unfortunately, fixing the rest of the foster care system is beyond my employer's power. But he can guarantee the Tucker children won't be caught in it."

The Saint said, "And instead they'll be caught in something like Tucker?" He laid down the fountain pen with a click. "Do you know what kind of place Tucker was?"

"A little," said Rhianna, calmly.

Branwyn was at a loss, until she remembered Gale saying *They killed her*, and looked down at Imani's ebony-skinned daughter. Small, insular towns were not famous for being safe if you were too different.

"Tucker wasn't unusual." The Saint's gentle voice had steel behind it. "I'm not inclined to send any child back to your world." He leaned back in his chair. "But I'll let you try to convince me. Convince me your world is a better place for children to grow up."

"*Will* they grow up here, sir?" asked Branwyn, finally reseating herself.

The Saint shrugged. "Eventually. And when they do, I'll let them choose what they want to do, or be."

"Why not let them choose now?"

The look the Saint gave Branwyn cut right through her. "You don't need me to explain that. Now, I know you're clever, because you're a wonderworker. You don't have to convince me right now. Take some time. Rest a little."

"Fine," sighed Rhianna and leaned her head back again.

Branwyn hesitated. "About Charlie…"

"She's a great kid," said the Saint. "Vulnerable, though. She's had it hard even here, because of what Tucker was." He glanced at Severin's back. "I don't want to let her go, but I will, the same as the others, if you can convince me."

Branwyn exhaled. *No gambits.* "Charlie's mom died in Tucker, but she isn't gone. She's become… very dangerous. If we could bring Charlie to her haunt, it would help her pass on."

The Saint looked pensive. "And is the Wild Hunt still flying about? I know there was a shake-up recently, but it seemed it was for the better."

"Yes," Branwyn admitted. "They're involved now."

"Ah, well then," said the Saint. "Better to let them deal with it than give a little girl nightmares, don't you think?"

Branwyn couldn't answer, but Severin turned around to stare directly at the Saint for the first time, growling, "She *already has* nightmares."

"Fewer now. Well, before you came along," said the Saint

evenly. "They'll fade again." He gazed steadily at Severin. "She's alive here, dark one. Isn't that all you really need?"

"What I need and what she needs are different things," said Severin and turned back to the overlook.

The Saint's eyes narrowed. "Is *that* how it is?" he said very softly.

Branwyn had a flash of déjà vu. Then Severin whispered in her ear, *I really, really want to kill him,* and the words carried such rage and hatred that she was breathless.

"Severin…" she whispered. He swiftly turned from the overlook and stepped behind her chair. Somehow, despite her chair, she could sense the pressure of his presence against her back.

The Saint said, "Well, take some time to think on it." He glanced over at Rhianna, who was now completely asleep. "Many of the children take a rest after dinner. Kilter will show you to a bedroom and you can rest, too."

"Can we talk to them?" asked Branwyn.

"I'd be a fool to say you couldn't," said the Saint. "But have some sense about it. Don't disturb them. For example, there's no need to mention Tucker."

———

A LITTLE WHILE LATER, Severin deposited Rhianna on one of the carved wooden twin beds in the room Kilter had escorted them to. It was on the ground floor and had an outside door, opening onto a patio with its own fireplace. As Kilter left, it carried away a bowl of dark apples that had been on a table, saying, "No indeed, no dangerous morsels for these guests."

Rhianna murmured, rolled over and curled up. She'd barely made a sound when Severin had slung her over his shoulder. Branwyn sat beside her and peeled off Rhianna's wet shoes and socks before tucking blankets around her.

She wasn't tired herself. Not really. Not enough to pass out like Rhianna had. The remnants of Severin's earlier healing still tingled in her mind. But Rhianna had been extremely energetic in the Queen of Summer's chamber when the knights had attacked. And she hadn't slept since being zapped by either of the signals.

Hesitantly, Branwyn considered that maybe… maybe sleep would help her recover. Maybe she'd recover whatever she'd lost naturally. Or maybe the Saint would know something about what had happened. But as soon as she thought *maybe it will be okay* a wave of anger swept over her. *Maybe somebody else will fix it,* she jeered at herself.

Severin put his hand on her head and said, "Later. For now, Charlie." He was staring out the window, his face hard.

Branwyn blinked and wiped blurriness from her eyes. On the patio beyond the window, Charlie was peeking around the stone chimney. But when Severin released Branwyn and moved to the window, she ran to the nearest cottage and darted behind it.

"How old is she?" asked Branwyn briskly, standing up and adjusting her—Severin's—coat.

He bit out the words. "Nine. *Still* nine."

"All right. Keep an eye on Rhianna for me and I'll talk to Charlie."

Severin looked at her. She looked back at him, patiently, in case he wanted to say more. A long moment passed. Then, without a word, he turned and threw himself onto the other twin bed, leaning against the headboard with his arms crossed so he could continue to stare out the window.

Wryly, Branwyn said, "Thanks for the vote of confidence," and went out the door.

She made a point of not obviously following the little girl. But she wasn't going anywhere else, either. She just ambled through the snow and somehow ended up behind the same cottage. But she went right past where Charlie crouched at the near corner and looked around the other corner before saying, "Hmm."

"What are you looking for?" asked Charlie in a small voice.

"My friend Severin said he lost something over here, so I was looking for it. Have you seen it?"

Charlie stood up and gave her a cross-eyed look that clearly said she was too old for such childish misdirections. Branwyn smiled back, because she'd conveyed the right message all the same. *I'm here. I know him. I'm not going to drag you to him.*

"Is he really your friend? I didn't think he had friends."

"I might be using a pretty loose definition," Branwyn admitted. "I've seen him with other friends, though." *Monsters all.* "Hi, by the way. I'm Branwyn." She held out her hand.

Charlie shook it gravely. "I'm Charlie. It's short for Charlotte." She glanced at the corner obscuring her view of Severin's window. "You came here with him. Why did he come?"

"Actually, I was hoping you could tell me that. He's not very talkative."

Charlie was quiet before abruptly saying, "Mom hated that about him. She used to get so mad after he visited." She frowned. "You honestly don't know?"

Branwyn shook her head. "No."

"Then I *really* don't get why you're here. It must have been hard to get here. I can at least guess why *he* came, but you came too, and you're not his friend?"

Branwyn wanted to explain all about the other kids from Tucker and Rhianna's mission, so this kid wasn't evaluating her relationship with Severin without all that very important context. But she had a handful of reasons to resist, so instead she shrugged and said, "He was very upset."

Charlie's delicate features twisted in a scowl. "I don't want to hear it."

"No," said Branwyn. "But you were going to tell me why you think he came."

After kicking some snow for a time, Charlie said, "Mom always said he was our evil fairy godfather. But he said he's not a fairy and not a godfather. He's been hanging around my mom's family for a really long time, though. Generations and generations. He named my super-great grandmother when she was a baby." She sighed. "Mom said taking care of us was his hobby now, like we were his pets, or a game. She didn't like it when I was really happy to see him. Once she told me we were just a way for him to stay busy. So I guess he's here now because he got bored."

Pets. Branwyn tried to reconcile this with the behavior she'd seen. Possibly for another *loose* definition of the word… But she knew how important it was to stay busy, especially when she was upset.

Shatiel's words, words she'd all but forgotten, came back to her. *"I hadn't realized how much of his remaining ability to care he'd invested in her…"* She imagined herself, bored and angry and immortal, focusing on a single project so her rage didn't consume her. She knew how *she'd* react if that project was stolen from her. But it was such a chilly way to think about the little girl in front of her that she wasn't sure she believed it.

"But you did see him?"

"Oh yeah. Lots," said Charlie. "I've known him since I was born. And mom did too. She didn't *always* fight with him. They just… disagreed a bunch." Charlie shook her head, her neat braids flying. "I don't want to talk about this. Not about him with mom. Only… what is he going to do now, please?"

Branwyn studied Charlie in the perpetual twilight of the Saint's March. "That probably depends on you. Do you want to keep living here with the Saint?"

Charlie shrugged tightly. "I don't have anywhere else to go, do I? Nobody else wants to take care of me."

Branwyn clenched her teeth until the rash urge to make promises for Severin that she wouldn't let him keep faded. "Where's your dad?"

"I don't know. He was just some guy from Kenya mom met

and liked for a while. They split up before I was born." She'd kicked through the loose snow to a packed layer.

Branwyn wrinkled her nose. "Yeah, my mom passed through that phase too. Though my dad lasted until my little sister was almost due. I don't even think of him as my dad. Just 'that guy.'"

"That sperm donor," suggested Charlie with a hint of a smile.

"Exactly." Branwyn waited. Annoying, but there were some things you couldn't rush.

After a few minutes of kicking her heel into the snowpack, Charlie said, "Do you think I should talk to him?"

Branwyn didn't rush her answer. "Personally, *I* think you should start by beating the crap out of him and go from there. But that might not be what *you* need to feel better. If talking's what will help, you should do that."

"Will you come with me?" asked Charlie shyly.

"Sure," Branwyn said, and held out her hand again. Charlie took it, and together they walked around the cottage corner.

18

In Darkness

SEVERIN HAD MOVED from the bedroom to the patio, where he was kicking back in one of the wooden chairs and twisting a piece of thin metal he'd ripped off of something between his fingers. Only the fact that Branwyn had never, ever seen him *fidgeting* destroyed his air of complete cool.

Well, that and the way he sprang to his feet as soon as he saw them and then froze, as if he thought moving more might make Charlie run again. That hurt his air of cool too.

Branwyn escorted Charlie over to the patio and stood there quietly. After a moment, Charlie extracted her hand and crossed her arms, scowling at Severin.

He crouched down. "Hi, mouse."

She gave him a nasty look. "You screwed up bad."

"Yes," he said. "I should have torn Gale apart as soon as he started sniffing around Imani."

"I wish you *had*," said Charlie. "And maybe everybody else in that stupid town too." A flash of conscience surfaced, and she added, "Well, not the kids. They're all right now. But all the uniforms, definitely." Her eyes flooded with tears. "And then you *left me here.*"

Branwyn got out of the way as Severin's arms closed around Charlie. He'd held Imani's ghost the same way, through similar tears, but with Imani's ghost, his face had been bleak. This time, he was furious, as if he was thinking about how Gale was *still available* to tear apart. He said something in Charlie's ear and she mumbled something back, shaking her head. He said something else, and she sighed and put her head on his shoulder as if unwilling to argue with him.

He stood up, picking Charlie up and balancing her on his hip like she was a toddler. "I'm taking her to Imani. I'll—"

Branwyn's burgeoning warm fuzzy feelings vanished in a rush of alarm. "No, you can't yet!"

Severin gave her an impatient glance. "And when can I? When you come up with an impossible answer to the Saint's challenge? He's never letting these kids go, cupcake."

"We'll come up with something." But panic yawned in Branwyn's stomach.

Severin said, "Will you? Before Rhianna vanishes? I don't think there will be much of her left after the next charge goes."

Branwyn wanted to keen. She *agreed* with him. She agreed with him completely. Except Rhianna *didn't want them to do this.* She wouldn't betray her this way. "Just... wait?"

He shook his head. "The faster I do this, the better it'll be, even for you."

"Severin..." she said haltingly.

His expression cool, he said, "You don't really mean it."

"Severin, no!" she said more urgently. Charlie lifted her head from his shoulder and looked at Branwyn with a resigned expression.

Severin turned away from her. "Give me a few minutes before you call again, cupcake. Otherwise you might interrupt something."

"Ramiel," she whispered, feeling as if she might crack in two. "Stop."

He stopped.

Then he put Charlie down. In a voice like a blade, he said, "I'll be back soon, mouse. This won't take nearly as long as I'd like." He turned around, his eyes molten with fury. Sick inside, just as furious at herself, Branwyn didn't move. Two steps and he had her by the arm. One more step and they were both in the windowed darkness that was his alone.

He'd said she'd pay a price for using his true name. The sick twisting of Branwyn's stomach suddenly became a dark anticipation, an *eagerness* for however he wanted to make her pay.

"Such love for your little sister," he said acidly. He turned her toward him and held her by the wrists, his darkly burning eyes boring into her. She saw herself reflected there: breathless, conflicted, unresisting. Waiting.

As he stared at her, the anger in his gaze faded and the usual veil dropped over his expression. Beyond them, something shifted in the velvet darkness: ghostly shapes moving and murmuring. She didn't know what they were and wasn't sure she cared. She couldn't seem to tear her eyes from him.

With an odd twist of his mouth, he released one of her wrists and brought his hand up to trail his fingers across her cheek and mouth, as he had in the Court of Summer.

This time she didn't move her head away. Instead, confused by his hesitation, she whispered, "Severin?"

Something reignited in his eyes. His fingers threaded through her hair. Then he was kissing her, his mouth closing over hers, his teeth nipping her lower lip. She gasped, and he brushed his lips over the corner of her mouth in a shadow of tenderness. What had been nervous anticipation transformed into a fire that swept over her, driving all thought away. She rose on her toes, leaning into him.

His hands in her hair tightened and now there was nothing

gentle about the way his mouth drove against hers, pushing her own open, his tongue moving as he held her head still. When he finally broke the kiss to push her coat off her shoulders, all she could do was blink up at him.

One of the ghostly images drifted through them. As soon as the phantasm touched her, she was back in the waking dream she'd had earlier: clutching at Severin, writhing against him, overwhelmed by a tangle of rage and passion.

The dream passed on and the fragmentary experience faded. But his hands were under her shirt now. The fabric snagged on her bra strap as he lifted it over her head. Things never snagged in dreams.

As excitement made her knees weak, she brought her hands down onto his tightly muscled shoulders. "I—"

Another dream passed through them. She was on a bathroom sink, her legs locked around him as she traded herself for help she hadn't needed. His fingers unhooked her bra. The dream drifted on, but his hands remained. His rough thumbs traced the thin line imprinted under her breasts by the elastic before pushing up on her nipples.

She gasped again, and he kissed her open mouth once before pressing his face into the hollow of her throat and kissing his way along her shoulder. One hand remained stroking her breasts, while he trailed his other hand down her stomach, unsnapped her jeans and slid his hand within. His fingers moved past her outer folds and brushed against the hood of her clitoris, and she moaned.

Branwyn's back was against a wall. One of the windows? Apparently solid when he wanted them to be. She squirmed against his hands, then tightened her arms around his head and shoulders so she could curl her fingers in his hair and enjoy the movement of his back.

Yet another dream slid through her mind. She was on top of him, riding him, and they were both covered in blood she could see, taste, but not feel. When the dream moved away, he was kissing her again as his hands made her wriggle and pant. She flailed at him, trying to remove his clothing like he'd stripped hers, but she couldn't figure it out and he wasn't helping her. Didn't he want to be naked with her? He was always at least a little naked in her dreams.

She eventually found the waistline of his jeans and fumbled at it. He laughed against her mouth and she pulled away to scowl at him. This was *his* punishment; didn't he want to do it right?

She thought that… and then she froze.

He stilled too, pulling away except for one hand drawing lazy circles against sensitive flesh, and watched her with his eyebrows raised and a crooked smile. Then she pushed him back, panting, "We shouldn't do this. Why would you do this?"

He moved the hand he'd just been touching her with under his nose and said lazily, "To distract myself from that thing you didn't want me to do. What was it again?"

Branwyn shook her head frantically. "No. You were furious with me. This is the price *I* want to pay, not the one *you* said I'd pay."

Severin gave her his predatory smile. "I'm all right with that."

Almost in tears of frustration, Branwyn said, "That's the part that bothers me! You never did anything like this before Shatiel. And now my dreams are here, and you're…" She remembered what he'd been doing, and shivered. Then her body registered a strident protest at the interruption of prior activities, and she threw herself at him.

He caught her, kissed her again, just as thoroughly. But his hands moved more slowly now, and when she pushed him away a second time, he didn't resist. She whispered, "Wouldn't it be nice if I could fuck you without feeling bad later? If I could fuck you and tell myself, *well, I had to, I did something to him?*"

"I'd be good either way," he assured her.

She shook her head. He didn't get it. "You're doing *exactly what I want*. And Shatiel bound your name to me."

He gave her an exasperated look so speaking she felt compelled to present additional evidence. "And you stopped! You stopped earlier, right after Shatiel did it, and you stopped now. Since when do you stop when I say stop?"

His silent exasperation was now a palpable force. Feeling sulky, Branwyn crossed her arms over her naked chest and said, "You were furious with me. Deservedly so. And now you're not."

"I could get there again real fast," he said dryly. He watched her for a moment. She let him, despite her skin prickling under the scrutiny. It was the least she could do in the circumstances.

"You've made several mistakes," he said eventually. "One of them I can't do anything about, and I'm sure it will continue to be entertaining in its own way. One of them is part of your charm. But one of them, I'll fix right now."

He moved closer to her again, and she couldn't back away because of the window-wall behind her. That was probably okay as long as he didn't touch her. But then he uncrossed her arms and cupped her breast and kissed her mouth lingeringly. And she let him. But at least she didn't cling to him—

He broke the kiss but continued to stroke her nipple slowly. "You thought I would harm you rather than simply taking something I want as my price. A mistake." He lowered his head and scraped his teeth over her breast before sucking at it, just for a moment, while she moaned and pushed her fingers through his hair.

After that, he looked at her again, stroking both thumbs over her breasts, and her hands dropped limply to her sides as she tried to control herself.

"But if you *want* me to hurt you? *I will.* I'll enjoy it." He released her breasts and ran his thumb over her lips. "But you have to ask first. Otherwise you're far too... *useful* to break."

Then he stepped away from her and tossed her shirt and bra

to her. "But since you have work to do, if you really want me to hurt you, ask me *later*."

Later.

Weakly, she said, "Offering to hurt me, but only if I ask isn't convincing me you have free will."

He settled back into his chair, watching her like he was at a show. "I did say you were making a mistake I can't do anything about."

Branwyn put on her bra. "Shut up," she said, and eyed him. He smiled at her and put his finger in front of his mouth.

She bared her teeth and pulled her shirt back on. "Why are you acting differently, then?"

"Am I?" he said, and that was all.

She sat on the nonexistent ground and put her head in her hands, trying to regain her equilibrium and her focus. He was there, of course, which should have made such a thing impossible. But what did she have to hide from him now? She'd thrown herself into his arms, and he'd still stopped when she asked him to. As long as he was quiet—and out of reach—all she had to do was breathe.

A distant sound made her glance up. "And why are my dreams here, if not because of the connection?"

He moved a finger and the phantasms and associated sounds faded. "Don't take it personally, cupcake. Anytime somebody dreams of me, the dreams linger here. I've got nothing to do with it." He moved a finger again and another dream appeared and faded: Imani, with her back to Severin and her arms crossed angrily. "I do try to keep them in a closet but sometimes… they get out."

Branwyn gave him a flat stare. He looked back at her, his face impassive but without the *on-edge* tension she had seen so often. She remembered him saying, in their first conversation in this place, *You can't even feel what you're doing to me.* She couldn't. She had no idea. That was the problem.

Her inescapable conscience twinged. It was a small problem, comparatively. Compared to Rhianna, compared to Imani, compared to almost anything else. *I'm annoyed for all the wrong reasons, because I can't stop wanting to sleep with a monster even when Rhianna might be dying.*

Biology sucked.

She sighed and put her head on her knees. Any minute something useful would occur to her. It was possible. In the meantime, it was a comfortable temperature here, and calm. She would let the overwhelming maelstrom of sensations subside until she could once again *act* rather than *react*.

"So what marvelous tale will you spin for the Saint?" Severin asked. "To convince him what a *fantastic* place the world is?"

No so calm. Branwyn raised her head. "Me? I thought my job was to hold down the fort until Rhianna woke up." Then she put her head down again. "I don't know. I'll think of something. I'll bribe him. I'll sweet-talk him. I'll put the fear of Umbriel into him."

"What did he say, now? You have to convince him Earth is a better place for kids than his house? You'd probably have a talking point if his house burned down."

Branwyn sighed. "I'll keep that in mind."

"Not a hypothetical, cupcake. Our big red playmate is coming." A window slid down, showing a snowfield stretching to the horizon—the top of the cliff, Branwyn thought. It wasn't completely empty; a single arctic wolf paced back and forth, head low and ears flattened.

Above the snowfield, a rose bloomed into existence, the petals growing into flames as once again the beast of fire and thorns respawned. Branwyn stared at it as the vestiges of her attempt to calm herself vanished. "Oh my god. It's the roses Rhianna fed. It's the *haunt*. She fed it and now she's part of it somehow. That's why the soul charges are going into her."

"Yes," said Severin, and she cranked her head around to stare at him. "I didn't see it either at first because it's dressed up in faerie nonsense. But it wants Rhianna and those other souls back, all the same."

Branwyn clenched her teeth, then grabbed up the parka. "Stop it. Keep it away from her. I'll talk to the Saint right now."

In response, a window swept over them. Branwyn stumbled into the bedroom where Rhianna slept. Severin brushed the back of her neck and vanished again.

Charlie sat on the other bed, hugging her knees. She jumped when they both appeared and stared at Branwyn in surprise after Severin vanished again. "You're still here."

Branwyn checked on Rhianna: still peacefully asleep. "And so is Severin, although he's a little busy right now. Do you know where I can find the Saint?"

"Uh... still in the study... I mean... you're still alive?" said Charlie, looking bewildered. "I thought he was going to kill you."

"No, I'm too *useful*," said Branwyn. The awe growing in Charlie's eyes was disturbing. "Charlie, do me a favor and stay here with my sister? She's ill and I don't want her to be worried if she wakes up and I'm not here."

"Oh, uh, okay. What's her name? Can I go through your bags?"

"Her name is Rhianna. You can peek through the backpack and that bag, but don't go through hers without her permission, please. Thanks, Charlie." She went out the interior door, waving.

Two birds, one stone. She wasn't *too* worried about Rhianna waking up alone, but keeping Charlie and Rhianna in the same room would reduce decision-making stress later.

It wasn't hard to find her way back to the grand study. The door was ajar, and the chatter of children was a reliable guide-post. She saw a few of them as she walked down the hall, mostly the older ones. They all looked at her as she passed. One of them, a rangy girl, called earnestly, "Good luck!"

The Saint was still in his loft office, although he now sat on the top stair, whittling something from wood. The shavings drifted down to a blanket spread on the floor below him. An automaton sat at the edge, reading to some of the smallest children.

When Branwyn stood at the base of the stairs and lifted a hand, the Saint gave her a nod of acknowledgement, finished a tricky bit with his knife, then stood up. "I thought you'd be along. Let's go for a walk."

Silently, Branwyn stood out of the way so he could descend. She followed him out into the hall, and then out of the lodge. She couldn't help a glance cliffward, but she didn't see the red glow of the beast of fire and thorns yet.

"It's out there," the Saint said, walking along a curved path that led to stables and paddocks. "The burning soul."

Branwyn crossed her arms tightly. "It wants my sister."

"Ah? Then it seems to me that soon you'll have to make a choice between a dead woman and a live one."

Branwyn didn't yell at him, though she wanted to, because the only reason it was a choice was his own scruples. She did kick some snow. *Would* ending Imani now save what was left of Rhianna? But she knew, *knew* that Severin would never agree with that, even if it was possible.

After they circled a paddock where four horses browsed a feed bin, she said, "You're the only supernatural entity I've met who doesn't seem to think that souls are as important as lives."

"They're not worthless," said the Saint. "I lost mine and poof, no more wonderworking." He snapped his fingers. "But I think the difference between a soul falling into the Horn of the Hunt and a soul drifting through the Fold to whatever lies beyond is… philosophy. Angels and what not, they're philosophy given form. It matters to them. But I lived once."

A horse came over to visit them, and the Saint pulled a slice of apple out of the air to feed it. "It's why I saved the children, you understand, when Summer and Honeychord just watched in play-horror."

"But you *only* saved the children," said Branwyn grimly.

"We all have our priorities and our limits." He cast a knowing eye over her. "Though they were hard for me to see, back in the early days."

Branwyn muttered, "I know some people in Tucker were… guilty, but they couldn't have all—"

"It wasn't about guilt or innocence, little sister," said the Saint, and Branwyn blinked to be so addressed. "Some of the children I pulled home were anything but innocent. How could they be, with the upbringing they had? But they had the shortest lives, save for those yet younger. They have the most ahead of them."

Chewing her lip, Branwyn stared at the fence railing. It was smooth, painted green, perfectly maintained. "You've taken them away from everything they know. And you don't have time here, do you? Not like at the Court of Summer."

"It drifts in, here and there. That time donated by the Court of Stone's child, they voted to give to the babies. But they all *will* grow up, eventually." He sighed. "They always do."

Branwyn shook her head. "But much slower than they would outside? Decades will pass there. When you let them go, what will there be for them?"

He gave her a knowing look. "You think there's something there for them now, but you haven't told me what that is." He pushed away from the railing and started walking again. "Would you like to see one of my workshops?"

"No, I— Yes. Of course." Branwyn trailed along behind him, telling herself she couldn't let him distract her. But she had to keep talking to him. She thought, then activated the reminder charm she had from long ago: *I am here to rescue children.*

The workshop was a machine shop in one of the stable-adjacent buildings, and it hadn't been used much recently. There was a fine dusting of snow over the threshold and on some bigger tools. The Saint went right past the machinery to a desk in the corner that was slightly less cluttered than the one in his study, where he began to dig around.

Branwyn wiped snow dust from the chill machines absently. Except for the snow, this place would be *paradise* for her. Meanwhile, the real world was full of hate, selfishness, bigotry, wanton destruction… everything she'd dedicated herself to fighting. Everything she'd been raised to fight. A world primarily focused on stepping on others, pushing them down, and it was her *duty* to rise up and knock the world on its ass so it could listen. So it could learn. So it could be better.

Well, she'd learned to make the *things* of the world listen, but she was no closer to fixing what was wrong with *people* than she had been at twelve years old. She didn't think about that much because what was the use? But the journey of the past few days had shown her exactly what *she* was. She was just as bad as everything she pretended to scorn: weak, arrogant, selfish, deceptive. And why shouldn't she be? She was only human, a product of a world irredeemably bad.

I am here to rescue children, whispered her reminder charm, and she laughed out loud because it hurt so much.

"That's a bitter laugh if ever I heard one," said the Saint. "Here. Take a look at this." He unrolled a diagram on the desk.

"Sure. Why not," said Branwyn. Lines covered the paper, each drawn twice in black ink and colored ink. The lines made patterns, even though all the patterns connected. It was pretty but meaningless to Branwyn.

The Saint unrolled another sheet. It had some of the same patterns, differently arranged. Then he unrolled a final sheet, this one clear. He laid it over the second one, and she recognized it as a turnaround diagram of one of his automatons. She compared the two diagrams, saw how the symbols were positioned, then said slowly, "It's a *vocabulary*."

It was a vocabulary. It was writing, writing that captured what she saw as an Artificer, and what none of Corbin's wizardry books had come close to understanding.

"Aha! You see it," said the Saint, beaming at her. "I hoped you would."

Branwyn looked between the two diagrams again. Then she sat down on the cold floor and burst into tears.

19

Devoured

"Ah," said the Saint. "You are tired." He patted Branwyn's head as she tried to control herself, frantically wiping tears away. "We can talk about it more later."

Branwyn struggled to her feet again. "Will you *please* let the children go back to Earth?"

The Saint's friendly expression faded into something neutral. "You should get some rest. And while you do so, I'd like you to think about why exactly you're asking that, and what it will cost those kids just so you can get what you want."

Branwyn felt like a spike had been rammed into her gut. She couldn't say a word. When the Saint flicked his fingers at her in a 'get along' way, she finally managed enough command of herself to turn and flee the workshop. She went out into the snow, away from the lodge and the cottages, and crouched down to hug herself.

This was very bad. She was moving further and further from the right answers, and time was getting shorter and shorter. And the Saint seemed to know her too well.

Severin touched the back of her neck and whispered in her ear. *Red is down for a little while. How was your chat?*

"Go away," whispered Branwyn, and the touch faded. She took a deep breath once it was gone and started thinking about whether she could betray Rhianna to save her.

But would it save her? Or was the damage done, permanent, irrevocable? Was rescuing these kids her last legacy, one her treacherous, selfish sister would ruin?

Branwyn knew she didn't care. She'd leave the kids in Sainthome forever, or turn them over to foster care, whatever would give her Rhianna back. Right now, that meant abandoning the rest of the kids while a monster took a traumatized little girl back into a horror story. And Branwyn would sacrifice any future chance to learn from an ancient master of her craft, the only other Artificer she'd ever met.

That should have been an easy choice. Her own enjoyment versus her sister's life. Who could think twice? But when she didn't know if it would matter or if it was right; when no matter what she reached for, she was choosing herself over her sister...

And then everything became so much worse.

Her hammer sang in her mind: a warning, a shout, and suddenly it was releasing the third charge, far too fast.

Far too fast, and much too early, because, after all, time was different here.

As soon as the black bolt leaped away from the hammer, she cried out and ran after it. Not to catch it, and not to see what was left, but because she'd realized as it sang that the Saint was *wrong*. When he'd suggested she'd have to choose between a living woman and a dead one, he'd implied letting the Wild Hunt eat Imani would save Rhianna.

But the Wild Hunt wouldn't merely eat Imani. It'd eat all the other souls bound into the haunt. Imani was the keystone, but she wasn't the structure, and Rhianna had become bound to the whole damn thing through the roses. Imani had to be redeemed, or Rhianna would be destroyed with her.

She ran to the bedroom, wrenched the door open, and found Charlie standing, terrified, beside what looked at first like an empty bed.

"This night lightning came through the window and hit her!" cried Charlie, but Branwyn barely heard her, leaping toward the bed.

Rhianna was still there, still bundled under the covers. Her chest was moving up and down in sleep. She was completely translucent. Ghostlike.

"It went *into* her and it's like it sucked part of her away, I didn't know what I was supposed to do!"

Branwyn gathered Rhianna into her arms, but she didn't awaken. And she was light, lighter than she had been hours ago when she'd stood on Branwyn's hip.

"Is she okay?" asked Charlie anxiously. Branwyn shook her head and rocked her sister.

"Severin," she said flatly. He brushed across her neck. She knew he was there because Charlie looked at him instead of her. She'd send them back to Imani—

That was when Rhianna opened her eyes. "Bran?"

Branwyn's heart stopped. "I'm here," she said quietly.

"You're warm..." said Rhianna. "That was pretty weird, Bran." She reached up to touch Branwyn's face with icy fingers, and Branwyn felt the cold rather than the pressure. "But don't worry. That was only three. You've got plenty of time. You just have to remember..."

Branwyn's grip tightened. "If you have some tricky idea, *tell me.*"

"Ouch, Bran... don't squeeze me. You'll figure it out. I don't know this time." Rhianna smiled. "I don't think my reason will convince him." She tugged a stray strand of Branwyn's hair. "I'm going to sleep a little more. I'm still here, though. Don't do anything stupid. I called dibs, remember?"

Branwyn let Rhianna pull away and snuggle under the quilts once more. After a minute, she turned around and was dully surprised to see both Charlie and Severin still there. They both looked at her, Charlie biting her lower lip, while Severin's black eyes reflected everything she hated about herself.

"Thanks, Charlie. I'm glad you were here. I'm sorry that frightened you. I'd like to get some rest now myself." Branwyn said the words mechanically, because they were the right words, the words to send Charlie away as quickly as possible.

Charlie looked at her, then up at Severin. Branwyn made herself say more words. "You should go with her. I'm just going to think for a while. She needs you more."

Severin kept looking at Branwyn. She looked back, waiting in case he had something to say. But he didn't. After a long moment, he took Charlie's hand and walked out of the room.

Branwyn shut the door gently behind them, and closed the curtains, casting the room into a deep gloom. After that, she curled up on the other twin bed, watching the tiny shadowed movement of Rhianna's shoulder as she slept.

At first Branwyn's mind was numb. She'd buried everything so she could listen to Rhianna and send Charlie away without frightening her. That meant it was Rhianna's remarks that bounced around her head, and the lies Branwyn had told Severin and Charlie followed. Eventually, all her other lies drifted out to join them.

All those lies about herself: who she was, what she valued. About what she believed in.

All those lies the Saint had seen right through. She believed in so much until it it was inconvenient. Until it cost her more than she wanted to pay.

When the first sob ripped out of her, she rolled over and pressed her face into the pillow. She couldn't solve this. No matter what she did, she was going to fail, and the only right way to fail came with too high a price. She'd do it anyhow, if she didn't die first, but she'd have to live forever with the knowledge that when push came to shove, she was a hypocrite. She couldn't fight for anything good in the world when she was, herself, so untrustworthy. She'd always been her own moral guide, always trusted her own sense of *right* and… it was, in the end, based around selfishness. There was nothing worth trusting there at all. She was as hollow as Rhianna looked.

It crashed over her that this was *later*. This was it. She'd been running from this nearly the whole journey but now here she was, failing, useless, treacherous, selfish, and breaking. She'd tried to put it off because it was inconvenient, but she *was* selfish, in the end. And now it was time to scream at the walls and throw things and collapse to the floor and wait for death.

But no. Rhianna slept in the next bed.

No melodrama, then: cry herself dessicate, get up wrecked, fail, fail again, lose what she loved and what she believed in, and go on to die slowly, day by day, year by year, just like the rest of the darkening world.

She realized there was another way. She knew his name. She probably wouldn't even have to use it.

When she rolled over, he stood at the foot of the bed, a shadow in the dimness watching her. Staring up at him, one arm across her abdomen and the other flung to one side, she called up every awful thought about herself. It was very easy to do. If she could just make herself appetizing enough, he'd *devour* her: eat up all her pain and wickedness until there was nothing of her left. She'd seen him kill before. She was sure he could do this.

He'd said he'd enjoy it.

When he moved alongside the bed and sat on the mattress, another sob escaped her, because she hurt so much and she didn't *want* to hurt anymore. Selfish, self-indulgent, and no matter which way she turned, everything was a betrayal of herself. Everything hurt.

She gasped convulsively. Silently, his dark aura tightly bound and her own chest creaking, his thumb traced the trail of her tears all the way down to her throat. His fingers brushed over the mark on her collarbone. Then he slid his hand under her neck and effortlessly pulled her to him, shifting her so she was in his lap once again. But this time he neither restrained her hands, nor caressed her. He simply wrapped his arms around her, his head lowered to press against her own. His breath stirred her hair and his hands were gentle against her back.

She remembered that he couldn't eat her, not really, because they were still connected. She cried harder, until she was breathless and hiccuping, remembering every time she'd used that connection, with or without a second thought. She was such a hypocrite.

He didn't say *a word*. His embrace didn't waver, even when she gagged on her own snot and wiped her nose on his shirt. Of course he was being kind. His current free will was debatable. But he didn't say anything, and she very much wished he would. Maybe if he did, if he teased her or mocked her or pushed her, she could be angry at him instead, and pull herself together. If he mocked her, she could kick this awful can down the road another few hours or days or years. Keep living the lie.

She *wanted* to live that lie, she realized, pressing her nose against his chest, inhaling the blood-tinged smoky-sweet scent that infused his shirt. His hand moved lightly, rhythmically, against her hair. Even if she wasn't good and just and brave and strong, even if she wasn't what she imagined she was, she *wanted* to be.

Did that mean anything?

It had to, she realized. It had to matter that she *wanted* to be better than she was. If people didn't reach for what they didn't have, if they didn't dream of a better world, how would a better world ever come to be? She took a breath without crying, contemplating that.

She'd been focusing on how she *had* to be better than she was, without remembering that the reason she had to be was that she *wanted* to be. Because she *wasn't*. Because she had limits. And bumping into them now didn't mean she couldn't reach beyond them later.

She drew a deep breath, let it out, and pushed herself away from Severin's chest. He looked at her, his face still shadowed. After a moment, he tucked a strand of her loose hair behind her ear. Then he shook his head, stood up and vanished from the room.

Branwyn pulled her legs up to her chest and fell over onto her side. She blinked in the dimness and realized a bottle of water and her hair tie were on the little night stand beside the twin bed. They hadn't been before. She stared at the water for a moment before rolling onto her back. She was worn out, thirsty, and red-nosed, but she wasn't dessicated. She wasn't broken. In a minute, she'd get the water, fix her hair, and figure something productive out.

But she wanted to lay quietly a moment first and reflect on what had just happened. Selfish, self-indulgent. Human. It was okay. She let herself have the moment. She let herself be every-thing she actually was.

She'd never really denied her attraction to Severin. Not *really*, not that it *existed*. She'd blamed biology, blamed hormones, dismissed it as something physical like cramps. She'd tried to accept that it was there and move away from it. She tried not to think about it more than she had to.

She'd always told herself she hated him. Hell, she *did* hate him, often.

But she didn't *only* hate him.

She'd called it weakness. But she *was weak*. And in his arms, as he'd kissed her earlier, she'd been ready to give into her yearnings anyhow, until she'd realized the catch.

Well, the catch was still there. But her feelings weren't only physical like cramps. And the catch didn't matter for the emotional part. Even before Shatiel had done his wicked work, she'd secretly, shamefully, *liked* Severin. He'd frightened her so much. He did awful things. He hurt people and enjoyed it. He was a terrible stain on the world. She couldn't forgive him, no matter how many crying girls he hugged.

But, at least for a few moments, in the deepest part of her mind, she forgave *herself* for liking him *anyhow*. He was perceptive and fearless. He was practically the definition of defiant. He didn't give a shit about the way other people expected things to be done. She *liked* him. She didn't have to be consistent.

And, hey, maybe she'd forgive herself for more than a few minutes. What Shatiel had done had changed things whether or not Severin admitted it. The passion, the catch… and this.

But if she did let herself keep liking him, she couldn't let him know about it. The jerk would only let it go to his head, and she had standards to maintain. Well. Standards to reach for. And she ought to reach for them even harder if she was going to relax her vigilance over her own emotions. He'd probably love to drag her down.

"Asshole," she muttered out loud.

Rhianna laughed softly from the other bed. "Oh, Branwyn."

Branwyn sat up. "Rhianna? I thought you were sleeping."

In a soft, sleepy voice, Rhianna said, "Great-gran was just saying how if you couldn't find somebody else to fight, you'd fight yourself. I think you'd bleed out if you didn't have somebody who loved you to spar with. How long did it take? Five minutes?"

"I'm so sorry I woke you," said Branwyn gently, choosing to ignore everything she'd actually said. She reached for the water, drank some, and lay back down again, looking at her sister's form.

"The creative process at work," Rhianna whispered. "I've been thinking, too." After a moment, she said, "Do you remember when you helped me go to that clinic when I was in high school?" She moved her head. "Of course you do. You've never forgiven me for it."

Branwyn lifted her head, staring at Rhianna incredulously. She remembered. "*Forgiven* you? What did I have to forgive?"

"Being a bad girl, maybe...?"

"You weren't a bad girl," said Branwyn firmly.

"Wasn't I? I had access to all the birth control I wanted, and I still ended up pregnant."

Despite her sister's illness, a scowl slid onto Branwyn's face. "Did I yell at you? Did I say anything other than 'okay'?"

Rhianna moved her head again. "No. You were really great then. But I think it must have been the first time you started... distrusting me. Believing I couldn't take care of myself."

"You're my *sister*," Branwyn said first, and then listened, and then considered. "I don't know. Maybe. If so, I'm sorry. You did take care of yourself then, and you didn't do anything wrong." She hesitated. "...Do you really believe I distrusted you after that?"

"You said it yourself back in Tucker... That I never did think about anything beyond my immediate gratification."

Guiltily, Branwyn said, "Oh. Well..." and then, because she was Branwyn, and they were sisters, she said, "Do you?"

"Oh, Branwyn. Of course I do. So does Sev. We just have our own priorities, so we make different choices than you would. And you love us, so that worries you."

"Shut your mouth. You thought you'd just slip that in there, did you?"

Rhianna laughed again. "Well, you might like him a little. But you love me."

"I do," Branwyn said firmly. She felt a little out of her depth in this conversation. She was seeing parts of her sister she'd never really looked at before. She was not the wise elder sister here. Nor was she ready to talk about liking Severin. But she was definite about loving Rhianna.

"I know," Rhianna agreed.

Branwyn forcibly relaxed her hands and sat up again. "I hated fighting with you, you know. I was always so happy when I could get you on my side. I thought you liked it too. I loved you and me against the world... even if you didn't see it the same way." Rhianna waved a hand weakly but Branwyn drove on. "I never wanted to fight with you. Not seriously. But I was afraid of your angel. I was afraid of what he might do to you."

"Past tense," said Rhianna lightly. "You're not afraid anymore, or you think it's too late?"

Branwyn bit her tongue, but it was indeed too late.

"The creative process," repeated Rhianna, waving a hand. Slowly she sat up as well. "Tell you what, Branwyn. Even if it is too late for me, you can... well... I won't tell you to trust him, and I won't tell you not to be afraid of him... but Umbriel makes *you* look evil, Branwyn."

"Probably not that hard," muttered Branwyn. She gathered her hair back and tied it up.

"Hah," said Rhianna. She took a deep breath, as if she was about to say something important. "I *like* being part of something bigger than myself, Bran. You don't work like that. You... you define *yourself* as something bigger than yourself and try to build toward that. It's like you're a lens projecting light on the world. But I can't do that. Trying to make myself big only made me... very small." She leaned forward. "I really want you to understand that."

"Okay," Branwyn managed. It was practically her definition of weakness. But Rhianna wasn't weak, and her angel wasn't making choices for her. He didn't give her a flowchart. He was... He was *trusting* her.

Bitter grief for all she'd never understood rose up, but weakly, weakly, from a heart still drained of tears. "I'll… I understand."

"Okay," said Rhianna. She exhaled. "And now I want you to help me get somewhere, just like in high school. Even if you disapprove."

"I *didn't dis*—never mind. Never mind. What do you want?"

Carefully, Rhianna said, "The beast of fire and thorns is back. I felt it before Sev left. I want you to take me away from this house, out there, so it can come to me."

"Why?" demanded Branwyn, her voice rising sharply.

"You know why, Branwyn. You're going to take me out there, and I'm going to stop the beast and you're going come back and use that to talk the Saint into releasing the kids."

Branwyn had no idea what she was talking about. "I'm not going to sacrifice you just to buy—"

"I'm not asking you to sacrifice me," said Rhianna breathlessly. "I'm asking you to *trust me*."

Oh.

"I see." Branwyn stared resentfully at her little sister. "I think maybe *I* should go distract the beast, while you go talk circles about the Saint."

Rhianna shook her head. "Nope. I called dibs on the stupid stuff, which means you have to be clever. What did you do with my shoes?"

20

Letting Go

THE POLAR TWILIGHT of Sainthome was unchanged, but the wind had picked up as Branwyn and Rhianna walked, hand in hand, out into the snowfield. Rhianna held her coat close around herself, but even so, the wind tugged at her like it was a sail.

Outdoors, it was even easier to see just how *faded* she was. Blowing snow didn't actually travel through her but Branwyn could see it on her far side. It was like she was a poor reflection in a darkened window. She left footprints as they walked, but they were lighter, and the snow didn't crunch under her feet.

In the distance, at the top of the cliff, the beast of fire and thorns roared and pawed at something tiny zipping around its head. Branwyn squinted and finally realized the pool of extreme contrast near the edge of the cliff was Severin. Darkness pinwheeled around his feet and extended upward to flare out from his shoulders.

Rhianna looked around, then back at the lodge. In her sleepy, quiet voice she said, "This is probably far enough. Bran, I'd shout again but I don't think he'd hear me right now…"

Branwyn hesitated, because trusting Rhianna was taking

everything she had. She'd already suppressed three alternative solutions that wouldn't involve Rhianna and also probably wouldn't work. "Rhianna, do you *know* something?"

"Oh, lots of things. But you don't believe me when I tell you. Come on, Bran. You can do this." Rhianna squeezed her hand.

Ashamed, because it was Rhianna reassuring her, Branwyn whispered, "Severin?"

What?

"Will… will you let it come now?"

After a pause, he whispered, *Do you want me to?*

No, she cried silently, but what she said was, "Rhianna does."

The tiny figure in the black pool turned. The beast struggled more with whatever was pestering it. But when the black pool vanished, the beast leapt forward. Another leap and it hopped down from the edge of the cliff like a dog jumping off a couch.

Then, in an odd, unbalanced lope, it lowered its head and headed toward Rhianna and Branwyn.

"You should get out of the way, Bran," said Rhianna, shaking off Branwyn's death-grip on her hand.

Reluctantly, Branwyn took two steps to the side. The beast was almost halfway to them now. Branwyn and Rhianna combined were the size of its foot.

Severin touched the back of her neck, then put his hands on her hips. Branwyn's vision blurred. She shook her head and stepped back another five steps until she bumped into a too-warm chest.

As the beast of fire and thorns closed on Rhianna, speeding up, becoming more like a fireball and less like a beast, Rhianna held up her hand, palm up. In a flash, it was beastlike again, and skidding to a halt. Through the snow flying everywhere. Branwyn realized its eyes were gouged out, and its feet like swiss cheese.

Red smeared across Rhianna's fingers. Delicately, the beast's tongue darted out and enveloped Rhianna's upturned hand. A flash of flame enveloped Rhianna and the beast, so hot it crisped the fine hairs on Branwyn's face. Water vapor exploded around them, freezing nearly instantly and falling to the ground with a tinkle.

Branwyn refused to look away. In the center of the inferno, Rhianna's hair rose around her face like a halo and what had been empty in her filled with flame. For a moment dark energy swirled from the beast to the woman.

Then both Rhianna and the beast of fire and thorns were gone. Branwyn stood with Severin behind her in a shallow crater in the snow that was rapidly becoming another ice pond. Her feet and the lower part of her jeans were soaked. She didn't care.

She brushed her fingers across the head of the hammer at her waist and felt the single remaining soul, the final part of the haunt where they'd started. She'd trusted Rhianna, and *this* is what it had earned her. This time. She couldn't even consider the idea that it wasn't worth it. She'd make it worth it.

Silently, she turned to hike back to the lodge, where she'd do... something.

"Wait," said Severin, harshly. She shook her head and walked away.

It's not over, he whispered. She glanced over her shoulder before whirling around.

In the air over the snow crater, a rose was blooming. As she stared in horror, the petals became tendrils of flame, which stretched out into limbs, a head, and many tails. The beast of fire and thorns was reborn.

As it settled to the ground, Branwyn looked wildly at Severin. He stood where he'd been, his arms crossed over his chest. He looked irritated, which told Branwyn nothing at all. She blinked and peered at the beast again and realized it was much smaller than it had been: perhaps only the size of an elephant now. It seemed more... solid than it had been when it had descended on Rhianna, too. The 'flames' were more 'tufts of hair' and 'too many tails' than flickering emanations of heat. And while it had been wolfish before, its proportions had shifted, making it far more foxlike, if foxes were elephant-sized.

With a single bound, the beast landed between Branwyn and Sainthome. As she gazed at it in bewilderment, it raised one paw and pushed her: the same quick, sharp motion Marley's cat did when she decided to shove something off a table. Branwyn fell flat on her butt in the snow, staring in astonishment. *"Rhianna?"*

Severin said, his voice dripping with scorn, "More faerie bullshit."

Meanwhile, the beast of fire and thorns nosed at Branwyn's feet, then picked them up in its mouth and started dragging Branwyn across the snow. "Hey, ow, that's *cold*, stop it!" howled Branwyn as snow slid up her coat and shirt. But her feet weren't freezing anymore.

Severin didn't do a damn thing as the beast released Branwyn's feet and rolled her through the snow. After that it lifted her by the parka and set her on her feet, mouthed her hair like it wanted to eat her whole head, and finally tripped her with a swipe of a paw and settled down in the snow with Branwyn between its paws like a chew toy.

As it settled its big vulpine head near her, looking at her with a vivid green eye, Branwyn said again, "Rhianna?" The eye didn't blink. Branwyn touched the beast's muzzle. It was warm and furry, as much a living thing as Severin. She looked over at him. He had his head down and his hands in his pockets again, watching her. At least he wasn't smiling.

"Uh, help?" she said. "Please?"

"You seem to be doing fine on your own," he said. But he strolled closer to the beast. The green eye moved to focus on him. Branwyn wriggled out from the paw pinning her and didn't get eaten, which she took as a good sign. She managed to get a few steps away before the beast's breath huffed out behind her as it sighed.

"I'm soaked and freezing," she said crossly. "Please tell me this is Rhianna? Somehow?"

"You sure like having things spelled out, don't you, cupcake," Severin said dryly.

"Yes. I do. If I didn't have contracts I wouldn't get paid," Branwyn snapped.

Severin sighed and put his hand on the beast's head, between its eyes. It submitted to this peacefully. He looked at it for a moment while Branwyn shivered. "She's in there. She's not alone." His eyes narrowed. "Stupid faerie bullshit. It won't last once we get back to Imani's haunt."

Branwyn struggled to parse this. "But she's in charge for now?"

Severin gave her an odd glance and pulled his hand away from the beast. It yawned, then licked the entire side of his body. He gave it a cold stare. It rolled on its back and waved its feet in the air, yipping in a way that sounded suspiciously like laughter.

"How many times did you kill it again?" asked Branwyn.

"Clearly not enough," Severin replied. "I don't know what you mean by *in charge*, cupcake. That thing isn't a platoon. Angel girl isn't the commander. She's just in there."

"And it's different," said Branwyn thoughtfully. Her shivering grew more pronounced. Severin was still looking at her with an odd intensity. "What?"

He glanced away, at the beast now tunneling into the snow. "I could have held it, you know."

At first she thought he was complaining. Then she realized, in his own indirect way, he was asking her *why*.

"Rhianna thought this would be better." She thoughtfully regarded the beast of fire and thorns rolling around in the snow. "I'm cold. I'm going to change clothes, and after that I'm going to talk to the Saint."

The clothing in her overnight bag had been selected with an eye toward tropical fun in the sun, not a sojourn in an offshoot of the Court of Winter, but by the time she arrived at the lodge, *dry* meant a lot. She looked back over her shoulder once. Severin had vanished again, probably to that nice, comfortable dark space of his, but the beast of fire and thorns was still playing in the snow, using its steaming breath to melt the snow, watching it refreeze into ice, and then skidding across it.

It was deeply strange.

After she'd changed into shorts and all three tops in the bag, she stepped out onto the windswept patio in one of her two pairs of dry socks and looked toward the stables. The Saint was over there, in one of the paddocks with some of the older kids, doing something with some horses.

If she waved and called, he'd come see her, and her feet could stay dry. He was nice like that. But if she did that, there wouldn't be any witnesses. So instead she put on her other pair of socks and her wet shoes, and trudged over to the paddock.

He noticed her as she leaned her elbows on the rail, and his twinkling eyes swept over her tropical garb. "I saw you playing with yon beastie. Kilter can find you warmer clothes than that, little sister. Winter doesn't quit here."

Branwyn shook her head at the offer and took a deep breath. "Let the kids who want to leave do so."

The paddock, previously full of surreptitious whispers, suddenly went silent. The Saint got that reserved, neutral expression again. "Have you finally found an argument, then?"

"For why my world is a better place for them to grow up? No. How could it be? But the world will be a better place *if they grow up there.*"

The Saint met her gaze for a long moment before looking off to the horizon. One of the kids hopped the fence and dashed to the lodge. Finally, the Saint said, very gently, "They're just children, little sister. You have millions like them back home."

Fiercely, she said, "Millions who have been *here* and walked away?"

The girl who had run to the lodge returned, other children behind her. They spread out around the paddock as if watching a fight. The Saint glanced at them and scratched his nose. "Well, they do miss their video games…"

Several of the older kids looked disgusted. The Saint smiled before looking at Branwyn again. "You think these kids are going to change the world? They're good, ordinary kids. Kendry there's handy with the horses, but she can be handy with horses here or there, and the world won't care one bit."

Branwyn scowled and pushed her hands through her hair. "Listen. My sister Rhianna showed me something. It was really hard for me to see. I don't know, maybe it'll be hard for you to see for the same reason." She opened her hands, showing empty palms. "You said they're ordinary kids. Were you an ordinary kid? I wasn't. I never even wanted to be." She shrugged. "And you know, I'm lucky enough to… to have the power to change the world. Right here in my hands, just like you did."

She paused as he glanced down at his own hands, then up at her again. "I'm still listening."

Branwyn tossed her hands in the air. "I'm just one person. So are you. A really *impressive* person, but you have limits. You said so yourself. What do seventy kids matter, you said. Steal them away and the world doesn't change at all." She paused for breath and looked around. Even more kids had arrived, including some in pajamas and boots. "But it doesn't have to be that way. You're a mountain. They can be the avalanche."

A ripple of murmurs spread through the children, but the Saint only gave her a thoughtful look and flexed his hands absently. "They're just children," he said softly. "I said I'd send them back when they're grown, if back they want to go."

Branwyn shrugged. "They'll be mountains too, by then. Mountains can't steer the avalanche. All they can do is let it go and hope for the best."

The Saint was silent.

One of the boys shuffled forward: Matthew, who'd stopped Snowball the wolf from biting, Matthew, who knew an opportunity when he saw one. "I'd like to go back, sir. Kilter and the others are great but I want to go to a proper school so I can go to college."

The girl identified as Kendry shook her head. "I don't. School sucks."

Matthew shrugged. "Mostly because of kids like I was, though."

"There was also homework," said Kendry darkly.

"I want to go back, too," cut in a smaller girl. "I want to put out flowers for my parents and learn how to stop other people from being mean. And I want to show my little sister dandelions."

A second boy said, "If I go back, I could cook the amazing things I learned here for people. I'd like that."

"I want to be a doctor," said another small kid, just as one of the older girls said, with a defiant expression, "I want to make video games, darn it."

Then the whole crowd was talking at once, pressing around the Saint. He looked over their heads at Branwyn and said thickly, "You've got them all riled up. I told you I didn't like upsetting them…" He trailed off, looking down at the upturned faces.

After a moment he looked up again. "That angel sponsoring your sister. He's going to be *personally responsible* for every single one of them?"

"Absolutely," said Branwyn, who felt that if they all had to sleep in Umbriel's living room, it was the least the angel deserved. Through the following cheer and excited scatter of children, she added. "I imagine he'll contact you to make arrangements." She narrowed her eyes, a suspicion occurring to her. "Maybe he already has."

The Saint looked over her shoulder rather than answering her. "What about you, Charlie?"

Charlie was standing a few yards away, holding Severin's hand with both her own. "I've got to go back," she said quietly.

The Saint raised his gaze from Charlie to Severin, but he said, "No. You don't. Not if *you* don't want to."

Charlie lowered her gaze to the ground, and Branwyn tensed for Problems.

Then Severin said, his voice raspy. "I want her to come back." His voice dried up, and he looked irritated when he spoke again. "She... means a lot to me. It would... it would be bad if I couldn't see her."

Charlie looked up at the monster beside her with bright eyes, then looked over at the Saint. "I've got to. I've got to say goodbye to my mom, but I don't want to say goodbye to him. Even if he is a giant jerk screw-up."

"Well then," said the Saint, and relaxed his hands at his side. "Well then."

Branwyn didn't have the optimism to smile. "We have an agreement? The children who wish to will be released? Charlie can leave now?"

The Saint didn't rush his answer. "In a moment. There's a few things left to resolve, don't you think? For example, yonder beastie. It can't stay here."

"It won't," said Severin, his voice still rough. "It has an unfinished task and fun in the snow can only distract it so long."

"All the same, I don't want it *here* when it runs out of joy," said the Saint evenly.

Severin's look of irritation intensified. He shook off Charlie's grip. "I'll be back in a moment, mouse. Go pack anything you want to bring out of fairyland." Without waiting for a response, he darted out into the snowfield toward the distant beast.

Charlie blinked, her brows lowering, but the Saint said, "Do as you're bid, child. He'll be back for you." She hesitated, then nodded and ran to a cottage.

Taking advantage of her absence, Branwyn said, "Will she be able to eat mortal food?"

"Probably not," said the Saint matter-of-factly. "That angel seemed to believe he could handle it. I'll give him twelve hours to sort that out before I come get her again."

Branwyn's breath hissed between her teeth. "Ergh."

"Yes, you do have some excitement ahead of you," the Saint agreed. "But now that Charlie's well beyond earshot, I have another warning for you: Be wary of easy answers. Do you really think the mother will be soothed to sleep by the child? In my experience, it's usually the other way around, if it happens at all."

Branwyn clenched a fist. "I don't know. I had to do something. If this doesn't redeem Imani, at least it…" She glanced in the direction Severin had gone, and didn't know what she wanted to say.

"Be wary of easy answers," repeated the Saint gently.

Suddenly Branwyn's eyes flooded with tears again. "*What part of this* has been *easy?*" she demanded.

"Well," said the Saint, as if he intended to be comforting, "It could have been much, much harder. As it might be for Charlie if she can't save her mother from the Hunt. That's quite a burden to put on a child."

"Why… why do you think it won't work?" Branwyn finally asked, very quietly.

The Saint scratched his chin. "Well, I'm not an expert on the realm of ghosts, of course, but I seem to recall that the lady was clinging to the mortal world even before that blasted faerie began his grand gesture. She was very angry, even then."

"Oh," said Branwyn. "And she might still be angry about her death… even though her lover punished them all for her?"

"Well, you'd know better than I on that front. I only glimpsed her at the beginning. Did you have a sense she was willing to let her murderers go free when you saw her?"

Branwyn thought of a town-sized hell, full of lost souls. She took a deep breath. "I'll come up with something."

The Saint quirked a smile. "If you do... and you survive the next few hours... I'll be in touch, little sister. You've done well here, and I appreciate that." His gaze shifted beyond her. "And here comes your boogieman, having banished the beast. Walking, I see. Well. Once Charlie gets here, you can be on your way."

Severin *was* walking back to them, his hands in his pockets and his head low. Branwyn picked her way through the remaining chattering children, too slowly, and met Severin at the corner of one of the cottages.

"What did you do?" she asked. He didn't appear injured, nor were his clothes damaged.

He raised his eyes and gave her a dark look. "I evicted it from Faerie. Can we go now?"

A chill ran through Branwyn, although she was already so cold that it was mostly in her head. "How?" If he'd somehow damaged her chance to get Rhianna back alive—

His mouth twisted and suddenly he was pulling her against his overheated chest and wrapping his arms completely around her. "You're too cold dressed like that. The beast will show up at the haunt again soon enough, dragging your precious Rhianna with it. I don't know what you'll do then, but I'm sure it will be stupidly dangerous." He brushed his lips over her ear and whispered, "But you won't be killing yourself for her, or anyone, while I'm around." It was a threat, not a reassurance.

"You're really warm," said Branwyn, deciding, with the emotional freedom granted by her earlier epiphany in the dark, to ignore what he'd said. "Thank you. I *was* cold." And then, because he deserved all her pettiness, she slid *her* icy hands under *his* shirt, pressing them against his deliciously warm stomach.

To her disappointment, he neither stiffened nor cried out, but he did inhale deeply, his eyes dilating before closing. She realized she was having a rather different effect on him than she'd intended when he whispered distantly *Can I fuck you yet?*

"Are you two *dating?*" said a disbelieving voice behind Branwyn. She turned sharply, like she'd been caught with her hand in the cookie jar, but of course Severin didn't release her. Why would he when he was now in his favorite spot?

Charlie stood with an embroidered leather bag, while two older girls held the bags Branwyn had left in her room. Charlie's eyes were wide with shock, but the other two girls were looking on with amused interest.

"No," said Branwyn, a firm answer to both questions. "I'm draining his body warmth with my icicle fingers." She waggled them.

"Are you *sure?*" demanded Charlie.

Branwyn pulled away from Severin completely and crouched down. "Charlie, he is way too much of a giant jerk screw-up for me to even *think* about dating him."

Charlie looked between them. "There's something weird going on between the two of you, though."

Severin said, "I'll explain it when you're older, mouse. Are you ready to go?"

Enlightenment dawned on Charlie's face. "Oh, *that.*" She frowned. "You promised you'd take care of me. You'd better not get distracted and forget."

"If you want your luggage, grab it, cupcake," Severin said, and scooped Charlie up again as Branwyn collected the bags from the two other girls. "And it's a little more complicated than *oh that*, mouse, but it's going to work out in your favor."

Branwyn was a little surprised he hadn't left it at the more embarrassing *oh that*. But it was good to know that reassuring Charlie was more important than annoying herself. Comforting. Empowering.

Be wary of easy answers, she remembered the Saint whispering.

She remembered that Severin hadn't told her *how* he'd evicted the beast of fire and thorns from Faerie.

She frowned.

"Can we go now, mistress?" repeated Severin, with a heavy note of sarcasm, holding out his hand.

Her frown turned into a scowl and she moved closer to him. She'd find out soon enough. She took his hand, and he *yanked* her into the darkness.

Part III

21

Complications

Long after they'd vanished, Brynn kept looking into the darkness that had swallowed Branwyn's crew. It irritated Amber, so she flicked the younger girl on the back of her head. "Are we going to do this, or stand around?" She glanced around at the rest of the Wild Hunt.

Jennifer was staring at the ground, chewing on the nail of her littlest finger, while Cat looked at the notebook he'd been writing in. AT crouched and scratched Heart's ears, which meant she was worried, and Yejun stood the farthest away, looking toward the center of town.

"Come on, already," Amber said. "Brynn, your mom is going to guilt-trip Jen again if we don't get this sorted out soon."

Jen lifted her gaze to focus on Amber, but what she said was, "Cat, how much of a problem do you think that celestial will be if we don't succeed here?"

Cat had looked up when Jen spoke because he always did. "Which one? I think as long as we make a good faith effort, Shatiel won't hold a grudge. I don't much care if he does, to be honest. The other one…" His eyes tracked to Brynn. "I can imagine him taking revenge."

"On Brynn?" Amber said incredulously, because the entire Hunt was pretty much invulnerable.

AT stood. "Her family matters to us."

Brynn dragged her gaze away from the blackness swirling outside the town and looked at them with a furrowed brow. "Severin? He won't hurt my family. He saved Meredith once."

Cat gave her an exasperated glance and snapped his book closed. "He was trying to hurt far more than your family before Shatiel restrained him."

Brynn gave him a funny look and Amber had that sense of dread she'd been getting lately, as if a fuse had been lit and she had to snuff it at once.

But before Brynn could say anything dangerous, Yejun said, "Key phrase: before Shatiel restrained him. Hey, does anybody understand what those rose petals are doing?"

AT said, "If we succeed, this isn't an issue." Her nose twitched, and she turned to look at Yejun. "What rose petals?"

Yejun frowned. "Those aren't rose petals?" He gestured at something in the air and AT lifted her nose.

Amber scented the roses, too. She'd seen them around the town: the only spot of real color in the gloom of the nightmare town. Now there was a breeze where there had been none since Shatiel vanished. It blew steady and cool, lifting Amber's hair.

"It's like a draft," said Brynn uncertainly.

Jen looked over Brynn's head into the darkness and breathed, "Oh, hell."

Yejun said, "Yeah, I don't think we should have let them leave the way they did, after all."

Amber felt the tickle of magic in the wind, and the cool mint-like bite of ghost essence. Since joining the Wild Hunt, she could function as a mostly ordinary mortal during daylight, but all the gifts she'd had as a monster's spawn came back when the sun was low in the sky… or when she was in a haunt as big as this one, apparently. "The haunt is *leaking?*"

Everybody was quiet for a moment. Finally Cat said, "Well, there's nothing we can do about it now, unless we're going to break our word and end things the old way."

"AT, what does it mean that the haunt is leaking?" asked Amber, going to the expert instead of the know-it-all.

AT walked closer to the darkness beyond the town, her nose still lifted to the sky. "I… don't think a haunt can *leak*, exactly. Grow, yes. In this case… I think they took something away with them that belonged here. Those soul charges in Branwyn's hammer, maybe. I can't smell them anymore, but if I have to track them down, I could probably use the rose scent."

Yejun said, "It's more than a trail, though. It's a path. I could practically walk it myself. I bet something else could too. And anything hungry for ghosts could come right in from the other side."

Jen was biting a nail again. "This is bad. This whole situation is bad."

Amber glanced between the other members of the Wild Hunt. "So… as I was saying, Brynn's mom is going to guilt-trip Jen if we don't get this done soon. Also there will be bonus fun with murder angels, invading monsters, and probably AT and Brynn will cry because we've flunked once again. Yes? Does that cover it?"

A melodious but unfamiliar voice spoke from above Amber. "So eloquent, Blondie! And I'll add, 'And so the Wild Hunt, still at the starting line, realized too late the great folly….'"

Amber stared, open-mouthed, at the beautiful woman drifting above them. She sat cross-legged in white yoga pants and a t-shirt, bending over a large book while she wrote with a quill. She had big earrings that were spinning horizontal rings, and long, wavy blond hair that carelessly tumbled over her shoulder.

Amber's eyes narrowed. Something about this woman

seemed familiar. Yes. She saw it in the mirror every day. But that reflection was a shadow compared to what she saw now. In those clinging yoga pants and that artfully casual fall of hair, Amber recognized that she was but an apprentice in the presence of a *master* of the unmartial art of "Fucking With You."

"Who the hell are you?" said Jen, in the flat voice of a woman whose patience with uninvited celestials had well and truly run out.

The woman, still muttering to herself, held up one finger while she finished her sentence.

Amber glanced at her companions: AT, ready to fight or run; Yejun, looking over his sunglasses; Brynn, looking cutely puzzled; Jen, with her face like a storm-cloud, and… and Cat, who looked momentarily enraged before his face went blank. Amber had never seen Cat other than calm, so it stood out.

The beautiful woman overhead finished what she was inscribing and straightened up. "Sorry about that, Skipper. I didn't want to lose my train of thought." She swung her legs around so she was lying on her stomach as she looked down at Jennifer. Her hair remained perfect. "What did you need?"

"Who are you?" repeated Jennifer, making an obvious effort to enunciate.

The woman waved a hand airily. "Oh, don't mind me. I'm only here to document the lead-up to the Apocalypse. You just carry on however you intended."

Jen stared, and then said slowly, "There's not going to be an Apocalypse, so you need to leave."

Pursing her lips delicately, the woman said, "Well, see, that's the thing, Skipper. We don't know." She raised her elegant eyebrows and glanced at the rest of the Hunt, before adding confidingly, "And either way, we'd want a record. We've got quite a library of failed Apocalypses by now."

"Haliel, Angel of Joy," said Cat, and Amber was only surprised it had taken him so long.

Haliel tipped two fingers to her brow in acknowledgement. "Nice to see you haven't forgotten everything, Slick. I'll just be getting back to work, shall I?"

Cat stopped looking at her, shook his head twice, then loped over to the campsite they'd started building at the rose house.

Startled, Jen said, "Cat?" When he didn't answer, she glared up at Haliel, and moved after Cat, followed by the three other members of the Hunt. Amber lingered, staring up at Haliel in an admiration she didn't think she could ever explain.

When Haliel noticed her, smiled and winked, Amber felt as if she'd caught the eye of an idol. Then the Angel of Joy pulled her book back in front of her and wrote, speaking slowly as she did, "Little did the Wild Hunt realize that even as their own smoldering tensions began to erupt, the pestilent demon Capricorn was feeding power back into the atrocity they'd refused to destroy."

Amber stared up at Haliel. Then she shouted, "Guys? Is the haunt getting stronger again?"

"Yes!" shouted Yejun explosively. "It is!"

Haliel's narration had stopped, but she continued to write without any more acknowledgement Amber was present. A moment later, Yejun joined her. "I can *feel* it but Cat and Jen are far too busy discussing Goldilocks up there to be interrupted by the likes of me. How did you know?"

Amber pointed with one finger up at the recording angel. Haliel kissed two fingers on her non-writing hand and flicked them at Yejun while remaining focused on her page. "You got there before me, Magic. Carry on, do."

Yejun's glance at Haliel was so contemptuous that Amber bristled on her behalf. But he turned away and Amber could sense the moment he tapped into the Horn that bound them together. His shout came through her spine instead of her ears. **"Hey AT! Find whoever's powering up the haunt."**

The distant figures over at the campsite jolted precisely as

Amber did, but AT, loitering halfway between the two groups turned her jump into real movement as her dogs exploded away from her.

"Yejun!" snapped Amber. "Did you have to do *that*? Words! Use your words!"

"It got their attention, didn't it?" Grim started his delighted 'treed-squirrel' bark, and Yejun shook his head. "Not hiding. Come on, you may have to help AT out." He took off running again, and Amber chased him.

"Haliel said it was a demon. I can't imagine what you expect me to do against a demon."

"Annoy him?" said Yejun. They rounded a corner in the ghost town and saw Grim barking and bouncing at two figures standing in front of a phantasmal ranch house. One was a ghost tied into the haunt, with a big cowboy hat and broad shoulders, while the other was a slim, dark-haired figure in stylish professional wear. They were clasping hands.

AT, approaching from another direction, got there first. She charged directly up to the pair, skidded to a stop within the phantasmal boundaries of the ghost and clasped the newcomer's hand herself, then used her remaining momentum to spin the slim figure away from the ghost. The shocked ghost promptly faded away.

As Amber joined her, AT released the figure, who overbalanced and fell into a seated position on the ground. Amber seized the opportunity and dropped herself right beside the newcomer.

She hooked an elbow around their arm, pleased to note that this celestial had a far more ordinary body than that kaiju monster Severin. While Severin always smelled unappetizingly customized, this demon seemed to have used the standard human template in constructing their vessel. He, or possibly she, smelled *delicious.* That was great news because Amber's monster-spawn strength depended on her hunger and she was still feeling embarrassed at how easily Severin had evaded her earlier.

"Oh wow," said the demon. "That *was* fast." Then the demon had an apparently happy thought, brightening. "Did Haliel tell you about me?"

"Capricorn?" demanded Amber.

"Oh yes, that's me," said the demon, and gave Amber a sweet smile. She, or possibly he, had a pixie face with a sweeping undercut black bob and animated hazel eyes. Literally animated? Amber squinted as the ring of fire around the demon's pupils flickered intriguingly. She couldn't decide if she was imagining it or not.

"Amber!" barked AT, and Amber jumped. "Yejun, grab Capricorn here. Amber, come here right now." AT sounded so hostile that Amber let Yejun take her place and skittered over to the curly-haired girl.

AT remained fixed on the sitting demon, her hands on her hips in a way that made her look like Jennifer. "He *only* smells delicious. There's nothing else at all."

"She?" Amber hesitantly suggested. It was so hard to tell. Even visually, all it took was looking at the demon to start instantly imagining the many potential ways to enjoy that deliciousness. It had been a *really* long time between meals of that sort.

AT shrugged. "Delicious doesn't have a pronoun." She glared at the demon.

Capricorn wasn't exactly struggling against Yejun's arm twist. Instead the demon gazed up at them with those animated eyes and a small, friendly smile. "He or she, whichever you prefer. Thank you for the compliment."

AT crouched down. "Listen, you, whoever you are. Stop trying to wake up this haunt, or I'm going to rip your head off."

Yejun grumbled, "Why would you even do something like feeding the haunt?"

Capricorn tilted her head to one side as if Yejun's question surprised her. "Well, one of my cousins had a very important decision stolen from him here, and I wanted to honor that choice by doing what he would have done. I thought it might kick off something interesting."

"Are you going to keep doing it if I let you go?" Yejun asked.

The demon's expression became pensive. "Technically, I should. I claimed this scene, so I have responsibilities."

AT's shadow, already unusually dark under the nightmare world's overcast sky, sharpened and changed, long claws extending from her fingers

"Wait!" said Amber, before AT got too caught up in the moment. "No, we need to do something to stop more of them from showing up."

"Oh my god," said AT, swinging around to stare at her. "What do you mean, more of them?"

Impatiently, Amber said, "We've already had four celestials show up to see this haunt. That's four more than we've had on any other call."

Incredulously, Yejun said, "It's a tourist attraction?" In the distance, Imani started singing, and he scowled.

"You're not wrong," said Capricorn ruefully. "This is a significant event. There's a lot of interest. Shatiel really sprang something on everybody when he unveiled it." She tilted her head. "I do wonder if there's a message in it."

"How do we stop more of you pests from showing up?" demanded Amber.

Capricorn shrugged awkwardly. "End it." Her eyes flicked toward Yejun. "All right, my friend. If I promise to at least warn you before I start undoing your work, can I have my arm back?"

Yejun released Capricorn to throw up his hands in frustration. "I'm not exactly the muscle anyhow. End it?"

"Well, sure. You barely got started last night cleaning up, and then you stopped and found some way to create this stasis instead. Finish the job, and there will be nothing left for anybody to come and see."

AT said, "Another way." Her head was low and her arms now crossed, but in her shadow the claws were still out. Possibly it might look scary to Capricorn, but it made Amber want to scruffle her curls, because even high school graduation hadn't done much to change AT's cartoon-cuteness.

Capricorn sat up straight, crossing her legs tailor-style, and put her index fingers together in front of her mouth. "Another way? Let me see… I could pull some strings, I suppose." Her eyes went to AT, and she smiled. "But not if it's just going to lead to my head getting ripped off."

AT's shadow flexed as she said, "Right, back to plan A—"

"—oh, come on, Capris," said Amber hurriedly. "Everybody is stressed enough. If you really want to support that psychopath's cause, hang around until he gets back and work with him then." She narrowed her eyes. "I bet you don't, though. I bet this is just some demon philosophy thing."

Capricorn sprang suddenly to her feet and brushed herself off. "You're not wrong," she said again. "Tell you what. I'll go spread a rumor that the main event doesn't start until next week. Then I'll pop back and we can discuss how I can philosophically support my oppressed cousin while preserving my own neck." She looked between Amber and AT inquisitively

Amber said, "Right. You do that," and waved. Capricorn gave her that sweet smile and vanished.

AT's shadow lost its unusual qualities, and she exhaled heavily. "Now can we please, please start helping Imani? We finally have a chance." She looked around. "Where's Cat and Jen? And Brynn?"

———

BRYNN STOOD ANXIOUSLY near Cat and Jen as they stared at each other in the rose house. Jen had followed Cat over and said, "What's wrong?" and Cat had only shrugged, which was so unlike him. And then Jen had said sharply, "Cat?" and that was when the horses of the Wild Hunt, resting on her arms, had started whispering in Brynn's head. When Yejun had blared a message through the horn demanding AT respond to actual trouble, the horses said, *stay, this is important too.*

So Brynn watched as Jen put out a hand to Cat as he sat on the cot, before pulling it back and looking away. She watched as Cat looked up at Jen with an intensity that always made Brynn feel like an intruder even at a family dinner.

"Is it… Do you remember Haliel?" asked Jen, still staring at a rosebush.

"I have never met her," said Cat slowly. "I'm sure Ettoriel knew her, though."

"She's not doing any harm," Brynn offered. "We could get to work?"

"That's a good idea, Brynn," said Cat. "Here's my notebook. If you find the others, you can get started. I just need to… take a few minutes." He flexed one hand and looked down at it.

Brynn accepted the notebook skeptically and silently addressed the herd psychically watching over her shoulder. *They seem fine. They've been fine since last year. They're coworkers, nothing else. This is the same as always.*

I'll bite you, warned Silver Horse, her own mount. *They'll get* romantic *if we leave them alone.*

Except for Jen chasing Cat instead of vice versa, and Cat giving me his precious notebook, and everything else going weird around here. Brynn sighed. 'No office romances' was practically the first rule the horses had laid down for the new Wild Hunt, at least for those with tendencies in that direction. Brynn, more interested in the girls at school, only knew because Brynn heard all the herd gossip.

Jen said anxiously, "Cat, I don't——"

He lifted the hand he'd been staring at and held it out to Jen, though he remained looking at the ground. Jen swayed and took a step forward so he could just touch her.

As his fingers brushed her long hair, Cat looked up sharply, his eyes blazing.

GIDDY-UP! shouted Silver Horse. *Go, go, go!*

Brynn shot into the air and came down saying, "Um hey so guys!" as Cat stood up, clearly about to gather Jennifer to him. Jennifer, startled by Brynn, twisted, catching and releasing Cat's hand in a firm leaderly reassuring squeeze.

Brynn crossed her horse-inked arms over her chest, making sure to grind her thumb in the rough location of Silver Horse's head. Staring at the dark ground herself, she said, "So, the horses have already told me more than I wanted to know about your private lives. They've, uh, deputized me to stand in for them while we're on this call. Literally. Except I don't think I can block line of sight between you two and I don't think it would matter if I did."

Jen's mouth became that worried line it had been since they'd arrived at this haunt. "Thank you for telling me of their concern. I'll... I'll be better."

"No," said Cat quietly, his gaze faraway. Brynn and Jen both stared at him in surprise, and he added, looking at Jen, "Brynn, I'm going to need you to exercise a little control over the horses for a few days."

"It doesn't work like that," said Brynn angrily. Cat had always had the most trouble working with the horses as partners rather than rider and beast, but he'd been getting along fine with Sunset Horse for months. "How can you *still* think like that?"

Cat gave her a sideways glance. "Yes, that is a problem, isn't it?"

From above came Haliel's narration. "And thus, despite the ticking down of the ingenious clock they'd worked onto their own skin, the Wild Hunt..."

"Haliel," said Cat, his voice the crack of a whip. "Shut up."

Haliel, drifting overhead, stopped mid-word. She peeked over the book at those below and gave Cat a lazy half-smile. "You're not my boss now, remember?"

Jen looked jerkily back at the rosebush again, and said, "Cat, take the time you need. Brynn and I will leave you alone." Without waiting for a response, she grabbed Brynn by the sleeve and hauled her out of the rose house.

Just outside the perimeter, Jen said loudly, while still pulling Brynn with her, "I hope you understand how unlikely we are to pull this off, Brynn."

"I'd like to at least *try,*" Brynn said, annoyed by the discussion topic but not the plan to retreat, because it made the horses relax.

"I mean, this *is* progress." Jen released Brynn to spread her arms wide. "This haunt stasis is… Sen would have been amazed. If Yejun can duplicate what Branwyn did, I think we'll eventually get there." She glanced at Brynn with a light in her eyes. "But haunts aren't simple. The emotions behind them aren't easily resolved."

Brynn squinted at Jen. "But they can be fixed. We *know* that now."

Jen said gently, "We've been lucky. Three successes in eighteen calls."

"We barely tried for some of those." Brynn kicked a phantasmal stone and sent it tumbling.

"We'll try here," Jen said. "But this is far too dangerous for us to hesitate on once the stasis ends." She sighed. "And I do need to call your mom again."

Brynn hesitated. Explaining Brynn's role in the Hunt to her family had been an unpleasant experience, but she and Jen had both agreed it had to happen. Holly had been distressed by the news, but had eventually framed it for herself as Brynn being in a special club, with Jen acting as the club's responsible advisor.

Brynn would much rather have been considered responsible for herself, but pretty much everybody else, even Branwyn, had told her not to push that on her mom yet. She was the only one Jen was officially responsible for, but Jen made herself responsible for the rest of them, too: feeding them, reminding them about bedtimes when they had early mornings, assigning chores at her farmhouse. AT and Amber and Yejun all accepted it unquestioningly. Sometimes they even seemed to welcome it.

But it bothered Brynn. She could see unexpected elements of her own mother in Jen, something more than the mother-henning. She wished Jen could see them, too. "Why don't you ever accept any of mom's coffee invites?"

Jen gave her a startled glance. "She's just being polite. I'm sure she doesn't want to spend time with the woman who lured her daughter into the Wild Hunt."

Brynn stopped pacing. "I joined *before* you."

"I don't think that matters. She doesn't approve of me. But I have to call her, all the same."

"She doesn't *know* you," said Brynn hotly. "But she'd like to."

Jen put her hand to her temple. "Just… leave it for now? Go through Cat's notebook while I tell Holly I'm stealing you for a few days this time."

Grumbling, Brynn looked around and up. The others were still out of sight but the barking had stopped. The recording angel Haliel drifted overhead, her head on her hands as she stared down at the ruins with a dreamy expression.

Brynn set her jaw and headed back to the rose house, where Cat was kicking back on the cot, his hands under his head. She tossed his notebook at him. "Get up. I don't know what's going on with you and that angel and Jen, but as the lady said, I'm a clock ticking down and that's not stopping while you angst."

Cat caught the notebook and sat up. "Have the horses demanded interference from you before, Brynn?"

"I said no angst!" said Brynn, ready to take it up a notch if she had to. Then she paused. Cat wasn't wearing or holding his glasses. Instinctively she glanced around and saw them, crushed, under the cot. She glanced up at Cat again, met his intense blue gaze, and said, "Not since last year, when I first took them to the farm."

Of course, there was the herd gossip. None of the herd seemed to consider it problematic to include Brynn in their conversations about their riders. Earth Horse and Sunset Horse had discussed the Situation Between Jen And Cat extensively more than once while Brynn found out how little putting a pillow over her head did to block their voices.

"She isn't happy, you know," Cat said. His hand moved as if to push up his glasses, and then he dropped it again.

Brynn lowered her gaze. "I do know. But I don't know what to do about it."

"I have some ideas," said Cat. "But you're right that we need to deal with the haunt first."

Looking sideways at him, Brynn said, "Is Haliel going to upset you more?"

Cat flipped pages in his notebook. "Possibly. She triggers strong emotions. I haven't yet managed what she raises for me. When this is over, if we make it that far, I'll resolve it. Gather everybody up, please, and I'll present my report."

Brynn bit her tongue and went to do her part.

22

Index

"FROM MY OBSERVATIONS, Imani has three issues she needs to resolve before this haunt unravels—and that's assuming Branwyn and Rhianna bring back the daughter." Cat's gaze swept the other five Huntsfolk.

"They will," Brynn assured him. It had been odd watching them vanish into the darkness. She'd had the awful feeling they were *going beyond her reach*. It had been hard not to run after them. But when she'd called Marley, Marley had said she was sitting on Corbin and felt like Branwyn would probably survive the next few days. Brynn wasn't sure why the TMI about Corbin was relevant, but believed Marley was more trustworthy than her own ungrounded fears. And if Branwyn survived, she'd bring the kid back. Simple as that.

"First, she's upset that the fire destroyed the research she was doing in Tucker. Second, she's displeased with her lover, and the punishment they've put together isn't helping her resolve that. And third, she was murdered; binding the souls of an entire town to her hasn't helped her resolve *that*." Cat presented his list in a cool, clinical tone.

"I wish it hadn't been fire," said Jen distantly.

Something squirmed in Brynn's stomach. Jennifer had all but died in the fire that had killed her lover and mentor Sen. "Don't worry about the fire-related ones."

Jen gave her a wry look. "I'll focus on the murder instead?"

"Haunts are never happy things," muttered Brynn, and wished she hadn't said anything.

AT heard her. "This one is. I mean, not when you remember how it happened. But parts of this haunt feel like a ghost-themed Disneyland now. It doesn't want to eat people. It wants to jump out and say *boo!*"

"That won't last," said Yejun. "Brynn's got all the depth on her skin."

"Maybe we can use that in the meantime," suggested Amber. Everybody looked at her and she waved her hands. "Look, if everything's simplified, maybe what she needs will be simple, too. Like, instead of needing somebody to take over her work and continue it for the next thirty years or whatever, we just need to show her a journal with IMANI'S WORK written on it."

"Are you suggesting we *trick her*?" Brynn demanded.

Amber looked annoyed. "I'm saying that if homegirl didn't have internet backups in this day and age, this is useless, and if she did, she's being irrational and we're not going to be able to reason her down."

"Ghosts aren't *usually* rational," AT protested.

"Well, Cat's talking about this like they are. Like we can just give her some talk therapy and it'll all be better. You've been acting like that, too, AT. I watched you following her around talking to her."

AT looked down. "It's all I know how to do."

"Bullshit," said Amber. "You were just telling a demon you'd rip her head off."

AT's head jerked up and her eyes narrowed. "You want me to rip a ghost's head off?"

"Sure, why not? Maybe that's what Imani needs. Maybe her whole problem is that nobody else ripped some heads off. Are you saying you wouldn't do it if it would help?"

Jen's voice cut through the growing argument. "You have good ideas, Amber. Go see if you can put them into action with Imani. Focus on the research for now. Cat can give you a journal if you think it will help." Her gaze shifted to Cat, and then Brynn. "You two go talk to Gale. See if you can bring back his wits. I suspect Imani's unsatisfied by his capitulation because he's refusing to face her as he was."

"Why us?" Brynn asked. She didn't want to talk to Gale. Gale was more of a monster than Severin. She didn't want to hear his excuses or justifications or whatever other vileness drove him.

"Because then your skin won't make things more complicated elsewhere." Jen's gaze moved back to Cat. "And because I think Cat might be able to reach him." She pressed her lips together. "AT and I will see what we can get from the other ghosts around town. I'd prefer to start that while they're simplified and easily engaged."

"What about me?" asked Yejun. "Want me to keep Amber on track?"

"Amber will stay on track just fine," snapped Amber, and turned to stalk away.

"Help her, don't agitate her, Yejun," said Jen softly.

"Their perfunctory planning session completed, the members of the self-sabotaging Wild Hunt split up to attend to the duties assigned by their... what's the opposite of intrepid? I'll come back to it... leader," came Haliel's voice.

Jen squeezed her eyes shut and shook her head, then said, "Come on, AT."

Brynn glared up at Haliel, who now had the book propped up on her knees. She couldn't decide if it annoyed her or pleased her that the so-called Angel of Joy didn't pursue one of the other pairs. On the one hand, she was really annoying. On the other hand, if she was annoying Brynn, she wasn't annoying Amber or Jen or AT. Brynn was certain she was better than everybody else at toughing out annoying people she couldn't punch, because she had three older brothers and the only one she could ever land a hit on was Howl, the least of them.

Cat watched Jen walk away. He looked odd without his glasses. "Come on," Brynn said. "Let's go see the mass murderer." She marched away, not missing that Haliel drifted after her.

After a moment, Haliel called, "Would you consider saying 'natural disaster' instead of 'mass murderer'? I think it works better."

Brynn applied years of skill development and ignored this.

Cat of the stupidly long legs caught up with her before she'd gone far, but he too now appeared capable of ignoring Haliel. Together they stalked over to where Gale was still bound to the whipping post Imani had dreamed into existence.

Whatever Severin had been doing to him before departing, it hadn't damaged him physically. He slumped there, staring at the ground. Even when Brynn smacked the back of his head, he didn't move. "Oh well, Severin broke him. Let's just get Honeychord here and get rid of him."

"Honeychord won't be coming for him," said Haliel. "I must not have mentioned that. Sorry!"

Brynn forgot her plan to ignore everything the angel said and looked up. "Why not? How do you know?"

Haliel tickled her chin with her quill's feather. "Faerie proprieties? Some rule of theirs about questers, I think. I didn't really pay attention when it was explained." She smiled brightly. "But don't worry. *If* this doesn't turn into the Apocalypse and he's still around, I'll deliver him to Honeychord myself. It was a personal request from their Duke."

Cat inspected the lightning-like restraints holding Gale, then pushed his hand into one. The lightning flared against his hand and continued on the other side, attenuated and weak. "His magic, not hers. Brynn, interrupt the other one and we'll get him out of this."

Grudgingly, Brynn did as requested. The lightning blazed into her palm and she gritted her teeth, because if Cat wasn't yelling, neither would she. It hurt, though, as if hundreds of needles were pricking her.

But as soon as she interrupted the flow, Cat reached over and yanked Gale away from the post by his hair, throwing him down into the shadowy road. He rolled as he fell, then curled up loosely.

When Cat and Brynn pulled their hands out of the lightning restraints, they shot forward and then fizzled out, sparking a few times before vanishing entirely. A moment later, the whipping post vanished, too. Brynn frowned at the absence. "Huh."

Cat crouched by the faerie, taking Gale's wrist in one hand. "What do you think he's afraid of, Brynn?" He asked it like a rhetorical question, but Brynn knew from experience that he always expected answers to his rhetorical questions. He was great at helping her with homework, but this wasn't homework.

Brynn knelt too, but only so she could see Cat's face. Looking at Gale's curled form made her feel sick. Cat, on the other hand, gazed at the faerie in the same clinical way he'd listed off the haunt's issues. It was strange without his glasses, but she'd grown very familiar with that expression over the past year. And looking at his face, remembering how he looked at Jennifer, she knew the answer to his question.

"Being ignored. Being ignored by *her*."

Cat looked up. "Good answer. That would be why he's woven himself through the haunt. *Mattering* means more to him than self-awareness."

"So we're going with 'natural disaster,' then?" queried Haliel. "Nice choice."

"No!" said Brynn. "Stop it. The next thing you'll do is blame Imani for what happened here."

"Oops," said Haliel and scribbled something out. "Are we not there yet? I may have gotten ahead a little." She tickled her chin again. "Although it does seem to me that this Imani *is* the one who chose to linger on, binding all her enemies into this wicked quilt, yes? I mean, what makes him so sickening that doesn't also apply to her?" She tossed her blonde hair like a shampoo commercial and added, "I hope you don't mind me asking. I just want to get motivations down properly."

Cat said, "Brynn, if you keep talking to her, I'm going to have trouble controlling myself. That would be distracting. Shall we focus instead?"

Brynn unclenched her fists slowly. "Right. Actually…" She rolled Gale over so that his blank face pointed up at the angel and said to him, "She's going to take you away. And you can't use the haunt to stop her, because I'm suppressing it. If you want to fight back, you'll have to pull yourself together."

Gale blinked, but his face remained slack. Brynn sat back on her heels, annoyed. Cat tapped Gale's forehead thoughtfully. "That might work if he had enough of a mind left to understand you."

"Well, how do we do that?" Brynn asked shortly. "Could we use your knife to cut him loose from the haunt?" Cat had a knife he called the Ragged Blade that he'd described as having *unusual powers of separation*.

"Ooh," said Haliel. "I'd like to see that."

Cat did glance at Haliel then, but all he said was, "Perhaps. We'd have to find the right surface to place the edge on. And I don't think it would be good for Imani."

"Well, what are your ideas? Jen said she thought you'd be able to reach him. Is she wrong?" Brynn was breathless even suggesting the idea. Jen could totally be wrong, but Cat might not appreciate the idea.

But Cat smiled faintly. "Brynn, you're the nice one. What would you do if you cared about him?"

"Ew," said Brynn. "Ergh. I guess I'd get him somewhere warm and cozy, and then I'd start asking more questions. Why was he here in the first place? How was he involved in Imani's death? Why did he do this?" She frowned at the faerie. "Everything's all wound together. I don't know if there's a yarn end here."

"It's tangled," said Cat. "Those are good questions. Personally, I'd ask: Are there any more of those lightning flows of his magic around town that we can interrupt?"

Brynn blinked. "That's… a good idea, too."

Cat nodded. "Let's go explore, shall we?"

———

AMBER STRODE through the haunted town ahead of Yejun, following Imani's distant song through the phantom buildings and the chained ghosts. As she moved farther away from Brynn, the structures simplified and the faces of the ghosts became indistinct. A building Amber had recognized as a general small-town mercantile when she'd passed before with Brynn was now a butcher shop, complete with sausages in the window. Grim, frisking back and forth between herself and Yejun behind her, paused for a long stare at those sausages before racing back to Yejun.

Imani's song lost none of its substance, though. It was a complex piece of music: mostly pure vocalized notes in a classical style, with occasional lyrics. Amber wondered if she'd composed it, or if it had come along with the ballgown when Imani had become a Hellqueen.

Amber had written her own bit of magical music when she'd been bound to her master, although 'hacked together' was probably a better description. It wasn't art, but it had done the job, and nothing else would have worked. Imani's song had seemed like a complete inversion in those shattering moments before

Shatiel had locked her down; while Amber's song had been a lullaby, designed to soothe both prey and her master to tranquility, Imani's song had been an anthem of rage, calling the world to wake up and riot.

Now, while the haunt was drained and suppressed, it was… pretty. Just pretty.

Amber walked down a blackened road with ghostly ranch houses on either side until she came to a crumbling church with a fire still burning in its depths. Imani sat on a bench across the street, her hands demurely in her lap, humming as she watched other ghosts desperately scurry around the church.

"Hey, Imani," said Amber. She'd watched AT talking at the ghost in exactly the same way she talked to her mother's ghost. But Denise knew AT, was bound to her, and AT didn't have to work to get her attention. Amber was pretty confident just talking wouldn't work here.

"They ran here," said Imani dreamily. "When the fire came. I was waiting for them. They'd always wanted me to come to church, so I did."

"What a treat," said Yejun, slouching up to Amber. "So what's the plan?"

Amber watched Imani sway back and forth, her red ballgown flickering and her dark, translucent skin glowing. "Do you think ghosts are people?"

She could hear Yejun's surprise. "That's, uh… an unexpected question."

"Brynn and AT think they are. I'm not so sure. Do you think *I'm* a person?" Amber glanced at Yejun.

With a disgusted twist of his mouth, he said, "You'd damn well better be, given the work I put into saving your ass."

"Me or Denise: who would you rather have a conversation with?"

Nastily, Yejun said, "Isn't there a third option?"

"Me, of course," continued Amber blithely. "I'll remember what you said ten minutes from now. Why is that?"

Yejun pushed his shaggy hair away from his face and looked at Amber over his sunglasses. "I think I may have liked you more before you started attending college lectures."

"I had to keep from falling asleep in Philo 101 somehow." Amber looked at Imani again. "If you ever tell AT this, I will skin you. But I don't think a ghost is a person. I think it's a prison."

Slowly, all expression faded from Yejun's face. "How do you figure?"

Amber smoothed her hair away from her face. "If I'm ever unbound from the Horn, I'm going to stop existing. No soul. AT says she doesn't have a soul either. Though I tell you, if somebody like AT doesn't have a soul, I'm not sure what the point is."

"Get to the point, Amber? Please?"

"You'd get lost if I didn't draw you a map, you dropout," Amber said sweetly. She tapped her foot on the ground. "Last night we learned something pretty important: that energy can be drained from a soul. Yeah?" Yejun's gaze went far away, and he frowned. Amber paused. Despite her snide remarks, she knew Yejun was brilliant. If he disagreed with her, she was probably on completely the wrong track.

"Why did you stop?" he demanded. "Keep going with this lecture of yours."

Amber relaxed. "I think a soul is composed of two parts: a self and a bundle of energy. And I don't think a soul can stick around in the world unless it's been… stabilized somehow. Like in a body." She took a deep breath. "I think when they say I don't have a soul, or AT doesn't, it's because that energy isn't bundled up with our selves anymore. It got used up, or used differently, or something. We're still ourselves, though. Unlike Denise or Imani here, who are supposed *to be* souls but don't act much like people."

Yejun frowned, looking at Imani. "Get back to the prison part."

"Well, if a bodiless soul wants to stick around, it needs to be stabilized, right? So it *makes* a ghost to inhabit, like a tiny little haunt. I think the *self* is inside the ghost, unable to manifest properly because ghosts are pretty shitty vessels. So unless they're really good at making their ghost, they just walk around like animatronic versions of themselves, only able to respond to certain stimuli."

Yejun swung his gaze back to Amber. "Hmm. And where does this get us?" he said, sounding so much like Cat that she wanted to punch him. Really, it would be much better for everybody if Yejun lied his way into college and had teachers other than Jen and Cat.

Instead she said, "Jailbreak her, Yejun. Just like you jailbroke me. Get the person out of the ghost." He didn't say anything so Amber kept talking. "I think she'll still be stabilized by her haunt, but we can communicate with her. And if the haunt doesn't hold her, she goes away and most of our problems are solved."

"You're kidding," Yejun finally said, his voice flat.

"Oh, come on, Ye."

"No, you come on. I didn't 'jailbreak' you, I stopped you from evaporating when your boyfriend dumped you."

Amber blew out her breath. "But you saw what happened to me when he tried to unbind me. And you rebound me to yourself. Yes, ew, gross, but I *know* you can do this."

Yejun looked away. "If this worked, somebody would have done it before."

Amber furrowed her brow. "Why? Who? When?"

"Philosophy *and* journalism. Haven't you been working hard?"

Amber grabbed Yejun's arm. Farm work had left it nicely muscled, but he was still basically a twig in her hands. "Yejun, you can do this, but that doesn't mean anybody else can, or would. The last Wild Hunt certainly didn't care. What is your problem?"

Yejun yanked himself away from Amber and took a few steps away, looking up at the church. "I don't like how we keep coming up with ideas that require *me*. Jen and AT believe I can copy what Branwyn did last night and now you want me to… peel ghosts open." He did a complicated shrug and Amber could smell the magic pouring off him.

"Yeah, well, you're special. Why is this a problem?" Yejun *was* special. He'd been born with an entirely different node structure than any other human, as well as a native ability to see the magical Geometry. Magical experts hadn't expected him to survive childhood. His religious family had believed he was a witch they were obligated to shelter until he died. But he'd grown up instead, and he could do things with the Geometry that regularly blew Cat and Jen's minds.

Yejun looked up at the sky. "I don't want solutions that mean I have to stay in the Wild Hunt forever."

Amber went cold all over. "What does that mean?"

"Come on, Amber, who's being dense now? I don't want to stay in the Wild Hunt forever. Some day I'd like to get out. Do other things."

"You can do anything you want now," snapped Amber, feeling that familiar dreadful sense of a lit fuse she had to stomp out.

Yejun gave her a pointed look over his sunglasses. "Not *anything* I want."

Amber shook her head fiercely. "You're talking about—"

"I'm saying we've already bumped into some boundaries. We might encounter more. Someday I might want out."

"But the Hunt requires six riders," said Amber urgently. "We can't break the Hunt or I'll *die*. Jen probably will too. You *can't*."

Yejun shrugged and looked up at the sky again. "I wouldn't leave without finding a warm body as a replacement. I don't even know *how* to leave right now, Amber. It's just… hypothetical. But if everything we do depends on me *in particular*, replacing me is going to be a lot harder. I don't want to be trapped."

Sullenly, Amber said, "*I'm* trapped."

"And it hasn't bothered you one bit, has it? You love it. You and Brynn both love it, and AT's happy to have a family."

"Have you told AT this?" Amber demanded.

Yejun gave her a sharp glance. "Hell, no. And you'd better not either, or I'll tell her *your* theory that her mom's in a prison."

"Have you told *anyone* other than me?"

"No! And this is why!"

Amber waved her hands. "Then *why* did you tell *me*?"

Grim, looking between the pair, whuffed questioningly, and Yejun crouched down to rub the dog's ears. "Because I saw how to do what you wanted and I didn't have time to come up with a lie."

Amber tightened her mouth. "If you don't do this and we have to devour the haunt, Brynn will cry. You know how she cries. She tries to be brave, but her eyes get all shiny and she wipes them a lot. And AT will growl and say she's a monster and then she'll hug her pillow in bed and *sob*. I've heard her. It's heartbreaking."

Yejun's eyes were hidden behind his sunglasses as he looked up at her, but she could feel the glare all the same. "You're scum, Amber."

"I'm not the one who'd rather destroy souls than risk his future ability to kiss one particular girl."

"I don't want to destroy—gah!" Grim yelped as Yejun's hands tightened and Yejun pushed himself away to sit on the ground. "You're the soul expert all of a sudden. Can't you come up with something else?"

"No! That was already really hard!" Amber took another deep breath and tried cajolery. "Come on, Yejun. Try this here and… and I won't tell anybody what you did. Even if it works."

She brightened. "Maybe if it works, you can figure out how to make a ritual out of it. Something anybody can do."

"Hah," said Yejun hollowly. He hunched his shoulders, folded his arms under his knees and stared off into the distance. Irritation surged through Amber as she looked down at him. He had no right to look so... so *young*. He was almost her own age, dammit, and Brynn and AT were even younger. Cat, too, if you were being technical about it.

Amber didn't enjoy thinking about how she was the second oldest person in the group. It made her feel upsettingly responsible. Usually Cat was a pleasant reminder that chronological age wasn't everything; his body and identity might be fresh from the factory floor, but his mind and personality belonged with the tenured senior professors at Amber's university. He'd been strange lately, though. Between him and Yejun that fuse just kept relighting.

"Fine," said Yejun suddenly. "Don't say a word to anybody." He rocked back and sprang to his feet.

"Oops," said an unwelcome but familiar voice. "Do I count for anybody?" Capricorn was leaning on the back of Imani's bench, looking extremely stylish in her dark suit. While she'd been away, she'd picked up a curly-brimmed hat that only made her look more delicious.

"Great!" said Yejun, clapping a hand to his head angrily. "Just great. This is all your fault, Amber."

Capricorn's eyes widened. "Oh no. I'm very good at keeping secrets."

"For a price, right?" Yejun said.

"I *sell* secrets for a price," corrected Capricorn. "And other things." She gave Amber a particular smile and Amber shook herself out of unconscious dreams of indulging herself.

Capricorn then looked back at Yejun. "Why don't you give whatever you were going to do a try? Perhaps it simply... won't work?"

"Yes, thank you for the suggestion, I'd already considered that way out," said Yejun, stretching his hands.

"Ah, but the sadness of our friend who rips heads off will bother you. I understand that!" Capricorn looked around and up into the sky. "We all have people we want to please. Well, go ahead, then." She stepped away from the bench with a flourish.

Yejun walked over to stand directly in front of Imani and took his sunglasses off, tucking them in his shirt. She gradually frowned, looking up at him, the spectral planes of her face shifting glacially towards anger. He didn't wait for her to get there, but put his left hand on her forehead. With no more warning than that, magic exploded off him. What was normally a tickle against Amber's skin and a tang in her nose became exponentially stronger: an all-over itch blown from Yejun, and a scent so sharp her nose burned.

Capricorn swayed back, holding onto her hat. "Wow! I'm lucky to see this!"

"Amber…" said Yejun, through clenched teeth. "She's fighting back. Sing to her or something."

"Oh!" said Amber and darted behind the bench. She bent her head close to Imani's and started crooning her lullaby. It didn't obviously soothe the ghost, but it at least seemed to be a distraction. Yejun's eyes flickered everywhere. The buzz against Amber's skin came from many directions at once.

As if they were actors interrupted, all the ghosts at the church stopped their scurrying and turned to watch Yejun and Amber. Normally Amber felt like she was the hunter and ghosts her prey, but what she and Yejun were doing made her feel peculiarly exposed.

Then Yejun made a gesture that was half-shove, half-throw, and the lashing of magic stopped abruptly. "There," he said, breathing shallowly. "It won't last."

Imani blinked as Amber stopped singing. The spirit looked

human again, as she had when that bastard Severin had hugged her. "What's… what's happening?"

"Uh," said Amber, looking over Yejun's shoulder. "Yejun, what's that?"

Something was forming in the middle of the street. It started as a spinning circle that extended crimson lines, and then the lines tangled together to become thicker strands.

"Hell," said Yejun, looking back and then hopping over the bench. "That's what I peeled off her. I said this wouldn't last!"

"Imani, we want to help you," said Amber rapidly. "We want to help you recover your work and deal with… everything else." Amber wasn't sure why a ghost would need to breathe hard, but Imani was. It probably wasn't a good sign. "Oh god, what the hell is that?"

The crimson tangle was extending a head like a chisel.

"That's basically a bane," said Capricorn apologetically. "I've never seen one form from a ghost before. Of course, I've never seen anybody do what you just did, either!"

A tail, long and whip-thin, emerged from the other end of the crimson shape. "It can't hurt us, can it?" asked Amber apprehensively. "Ouch!"

Capricorn, who had pinched Amber in response to her question, said, "It probably can. It might not be able to *damage* you, of course. But all a bane really wants to do is recombine with its source. They'll keep going until they do."

"Right," said Amber. "Yejun, stall your bane. Is it a mouse? Oh, ew, it *is* a giant mouse. Stall it while I talk to Imani!" And she scooped Imani into her arms.

Yejun said, "Hey! I'm not the muscle! What do you expect me to do?"

Amber didn't stick around to listen. A mouse, really? If Yejun hadn't wanted to be the one to delay it, he should have carried off Imani first. As she sped away, Capricorn's voice drifted after her. "Would you like my help, my friend?"

Amber ran to the rose house where Imani had died and set her on the cot. The spirit looked up at her in bewilderment. "I don't know you."

Impatiently, Amber said, "You're dead. You're a ghost. A very angry one. Except right now, only for a little while, you're not. Do you remember that asshole Severin?"

Imani's face clouded. "He didn't come." She hesitated. "And then he did? I was sleeping but I remember that he came and told me he loved me."

Amber didn't remember that phrase but conceded that the ghost might have been reading between the lines. "And that your kid Charlie was still alive. You remember that part, too?"

Imani's face tightened, but didn't shift into the planes of the Hellqueen as it had when Severin had told her about Charlie. "I didn't want to. It hurts. He lies sometimes. If he thinks the truth will upset me."

Amber hesitated. But Jen had asked her to focus on Imani's work. "We'll come back to that. We're going to help you."

"I'm already dead," said Imani, looking away. "And angry."

"Good," said Amber. "Don't forgive those assholes. But you're not just angry at them. Remember Gale?" Imani turned a look on Amber that should have stripped her flesh from her bones. Amber rushed on. "You kept saying Gale *destroyed your work. Please* tell me what your work was?"

Instead of answering, Imani's gaze moved beyond Amber. She turned and saw Yejun running up, holding a hat and a dark jacket over his arm, Grim darting ahead of him. "What are you doing here? You were supposed to stall that thing!"

Yejun squinted at Amber as he stopped. "What did you expect *me* to do? He said he'd hold it back for a while if I held his coat and hat for him."

"He?"

"That Capricorn guy. When I got out of there, he was telling it they needed to have a nice chat over tea while stopping it with one hand."

"Uh…" Amber said weakly. This was getting a little beyond her. She looked worriedly over Yejun's shoulder, but whatever Capricorn was doing must have been working for the moment.

"I came here at first because there used to be a concentration camp here and I wanted to write about it," said Imani quietly, and Amber and Yejun both swung around to look at her. "Several camps, actually. An internment camp during World War II, and a youth boot camp a few decades ago. I think there was a prison camp for natives in the 19th century too, but most of the evidence for that one is long gone."

Yejun pulled a stained little notebook from his pocket along with a pen and started writing. Amber kept a wary eye out for any giant mouse invasions while trying to appear attentive.

"I had to do my research locally. The town's been here all that time," continued Imani. "So many of the other towns in this region were abandoned when the mines dried up."

"I guess they found something else to profit from," said Amber sourly.

Imani's gaze focused on Amber. "Yes. I was investigating that, eventually. That's how Gale and I met. But they didn't like either of us. Not the way we looked, not what we were doing. When the town elders realized I was going to publish what I'd discovered, they came—"

An unearthly shriek echoed through the ghost town. Amber recognized it immediately as the cry of a giant, angry mouse, and quivered.

Urgently, Yejun said, "Imani: You had backups of your research, right? Online somewhere?"

"What…? Yes!" Her eyes widened. "Let me—"

"Yes, yes!" said Yejun, crouching beside her with the notebook. "Amber, your turn!"

"Ack, me?" Amber looked wildly at the horrible creature

waddling around a building. It was a giant, crimson rodent, with huge round ears and an enormous quivering nose and terrifying front teeth. It smelled *horrible*. Had it *eaten* Capricorn?

The thought infuriated Amber. Such deliciousness shouldn't have been wasted on that monster. Angrily, she ran to intercept the beast, bounding over its chisel head and catching its disturbingly smooth tail. That nightmarish screech echoed through the town again as Amber pulled hard. Grim barked at the monster furiously.

The tail was too smooth. It slid out of Amber's hands as the giant mouse escaped and galloped away. A moment later, there was a flash of flame from the rose house and the mouse vanished.

Imani the Hellqueen soared into the sky and started singing again.

23

Focus

"Yejun?" asked Amber, alarmed, zooming back to the house again. Yejun was crouched down beside the cot, his head down. He gave her a thumbs-up while scribbling something.

Capricorn jumped down from atop the rose-wrapped ruins and picked up her jacket from the cot. "That was an unusual experience. Did you get what you needed?"

Amber blinked. "What happened to you?" She hadn't *really* thought the mouse had eaten the demon. Of course not. Even the hounds of the Wild Hunt couldn't properly digest a demon.

With that sweet, mild smile, Capricorn put on her jacket and picked up her hat, twirling it before placing it on her head. "I held it until my shoes started getting scuffed. I thought that would probably be enough time. Was it?"

Yejun stood up. "Well, we can get into her accounts now. It's a start. I think we *should* get that journal from Cat and make a prop, though. Something she can take with her." He tucked the notebook back into his pocket and looked at Capricorn from under his shag of hair. "Why did you offer to help?"

"Oh, my goodness. You'd just done an astonishing piece of

magic, all so you could get a few words with a trapped soul. It would have been very poor-spirited of me to just sit and laugh, don't you think?" Capricorn bounced on shiny shoes and waved up at Imani cheerily.

"Yeah, but I thought you were here to advocate for that asshole Severin's choice to break the world or whatever," said Amber, also looking up at Imani. Whatever drove her now didn't seem to hold a grudge about the magic performed on her. Instead, she drifted toward the center of town, singing her pretty anthem of blood, possibly looking for her faerie lover to torment.

"Oh, *that*," said Capricorn. "Well, yes." She tapped a well-manicured square fingernail on her chin. "Oh, I know! He wanted to support his adopted child, yes? So I'm sure he would have done the same thing."

Yejun gave Capricorn a long stare that she met placidly before he finally said, "Yeah…. So let's hear what else do you intend on doing along those lines?"

"Oh, I don't have a PowerPoint or anything. I'm sort of making it up as I go along." This time her smile had teeth. "Just like you."

Evenly, Yejun said, "All right. But if you start trying to undo anything we're doing here, I will personally tether you down while AT rips your head off."

Capricorn gave a theatrical shiver. "Ooh, I wouldn't want that to happen. I'll be good! Didn't I say I'd warn you before I started any of that again?"

"Yeah, okay, you're a demon who just said you'll 'be good', so I'm going to go ahead and keep taking everything you say with a grain of salt." Yejun pulled out his sunglasses and put them back on.

Amber had an important question she needed answered at this point. She phrased it carefully. "Can you do that to Haliel, too? The tethering?"

Capricorn's eyes rounded and she looked between Amber and Yejun as if she also found the answer to this question vital.

Yejun shook his head. "That one's mostly a projection. There's nothing much there to tether. Unfortunately."

Capricorn's sigh of relief was much more dramatic than Amber's, allowing Amber to keep her idol-worship secret for a little longer. That was good because everybody was definitely going to yell at her when she ran off later to learn at the feet of the master.

"Why do you care if an angel gets tethered, demon?" asked Yejun as he started to walk backward out of the rose house, his hands in his pockets. It was an annoying trick of his, but it worked to make Capricorn and Amber follow him. Grim, who had furtively claimed the cot, sighed and hopped down to trail behind Amber.

"Oh, my friend. Demons aren't the *enemies* of angels. I just want to help them understand their choices." Capricorn hopped on a barely visible fence-railing and strolled down it with the grace of a tightrope walker. "And Haliel is charming, don't you think?"

"Where is she, anyhow?" said Amber, looking around. If she was going to be forced to watch people other than her be preternaturally graceful, she'd much rather it was the Angel of Joy instead of Miss Delicious and Yejun.

Capricorn had an immediate answer. "She's watching the ex-angel and the horse girl walk around. They must be awfully interesting. Shall we go find them?"

"Sure," said Yejun. "You lead the way."

———

"Is this really the best way to be spending your time?" asked Haliel as Cat and Brynn picked their way through the ghostly town. "It doesn't make for very good narrative."

"Would there *normally* be visible flows of energy in a situation like this?" asked Brynn.

"I don't know," said Cat. "There's never been a situation like this, as far as I know. But one can see the connections between a celestial and their soul-born servants in the Geometry, if one knows what to search for." He bent down and looked in a storm drain. "And there's more *under* to this town than I would have expected."

They walked more. Haliel said, "Maybe I'll go check on the Skipper and Curls. I bet they're hearing some great stories. They're probably making real progress. I'll just head over there, shall I?"

"Haliel," said Cat, stopping. "Don't."

With a lazy smile, Haliel said, "We all have jobs to do, Slick. You have this wild goose chase, and I have to document interesting events."

Cat looked up. "Do you *really* want me to be 'interesting', Haliel?"

"Oh, *yes please*," begged Haliel. "I volunteered for this gig *entirely* because I hoped you'd be interesting."

Driven by an instinctive dread, Brynn was already moving when Silver Horse and Sunset Horse both shouted *Stop him!* in her mind. She slid her arm around Cat's, reached up and tweaked his nose, covered his eyes with her fingers, and tried but failed to trip him.

He scooped her up in one arm, then peeled her off him and set her down. "No," he said, giving her a steady look. "I know how dangerous the consequences could be. But thank you."

Adrenaline-induced jitters made Brynn's voice shake as she said, "*I* don't. I don't understand what's going on at all. What were you going to *do?*"

Cat spread his fingers and put them on her head. He was quiet for a moment. Above, Haliel's pen scritched on paper.

Finally, Cat said, "The Wild Hunt is made of mortals. Originally shards of celestials, but mortal ones. We killed them, after all." He lifted his hand from her head. "What do you think would happen if a full celestial joined its ranks?"

"I don't know!" Brynn decided it probably *would* be better for Haliel to go off and bother somebody else. Amber and Yejun would be best.

"Neither do I," said Cat calmly. "Let's not find out." He started walking again.

Brynn caught his sleeve. "No. You don't do this. You tell me what's going on *right now,* for real, no Cattishness."

He looked back at her, still calm, like he was making a decision in a grocery store. "I want to talk to Jen without the horses' interference."

Don't you dare, said Silver Horse.

"I live in California!" said Brynn fretfully. "Do it when this is over. Go inside the farmhouse, shut the door, ignore their shouting and talk. Or whatever."

Cat smiled wryly. "The only time Jen can ignore the wise counsel of Earth Horse is when he's on your arms."

You let us out right now, Brynn, said Silver Horse furiously. *I have to kick somebody.*

Do it and I'll kick you, said Sunset Horse. *He's mine and I'll see to any kicking, if you please.*

Brynn put her hands over her ears, even though that *never* worked, and then said, out loud, but to everybody listening, "I'll think about it."

Haliel said, "The mounts are bothering her, aren't they? That's what it means when she covers her ears like that, am I right? Would you like to tell me what they're saying? No? That's fine. My own dialog will be better anyhow."

"Can't we let her go somewhere else?" pleaded Brynn to Cat.

"Nah, you've finally gotten interesting, Ink. I mean, you'll never find anything just walking around down there, but you two keep arguing and we're going to get right to the meat."

Cat shook his head, turned away, and kept walking. Brynn looked up at Haliel, narrowing her eyes. Then she said, "Cat, what happens to a celestial if we kill just their bodies? I know they can come back, but... what happens right away?"

"They become much harder to talk to," said Cat, in the most Cattish of ways, without stopping.

Brynn glowered and stomped after him. She was increasingly convinced this *was* a dead end: maybe the result of Haliel's needling but also true. They hadn't seen any other lightning flows. Cat kept looking into storm drains and scuffing through dead gardens, but if he had a reason he was keeping it to himself.

"This isn't working," she persisted. "We need to try something else."

Cat wheeled around. "Feel free."

"I *am*," said Brynn. "I'm trying to *talk to you*." *Scritch scritch* came from overhead but Brynn ignored it.

"I'm not a faerie, Brynn. I didn't destroy a town in a fit of pique. And I'm not going to engage in the thought exercise of what I'd do in Gale's situation."

Brynn's fists were tightly clenched. She remembered the stories she'd heard from Branwyn and Marley about who Cat had used to be. Nobody seemed sure what exactly had happened, except for the bare facts: the angel Ettoriel had vanished, defeated by his own rampant emotions, and some time later, his vessel had reappeared, calling himself Cat and declaring he was his own person.

According to Branwyn and Marley, Cat *wasn't* an angel, not according to their magical Sight. And according to Cat, Ettoriel was simply gone, never to return. He'd suggested the Ragged Blade was involved, without ever stating it outright, in that Cattish way of his.

And Haliel's attitude supported the idea that the only version of Ettoriel out there was... Cat.

Silver Horse said, *Less talking, more trampling angels.*

Earth Horse added, *We need to end this haunt and go back to the farm. Jen is unhappy enough.*

Brynn said, "I think you already did, Cat."

"Did what?" he said coldly.

Biting her thumbnail, Brynn said, "The angel version of you was going to do something awful, before Marley stopped him. Then you—I mean *he*—did something with all that angel power. Sent it away somehow before becoming *you*. Isn't that kind of like what Gale's done?"

Cat drew a deep breath, clasped his hands behind his back, and said in his best professorial voice, "Puns aside, do I look catatonic to you, Brynn?"

Brynn crossed her arms and refused to get drawn in to the rhetorical question. Instead she waited.

After a moment, he said, "Are we done?" and turned away.

"Sure," said Brynn. "I'm going to go talk to Jen." She glanced up at Haliel, who gave her one of her little salutes. Brynn nodded an acknowledgement and began to walk away.

"I *can't* do what she wants, Brynn," called Cat. "And it wouldn't help if I could."

Brynn schooled her face before turning around, her eyebrows raised in polite inquiry. "Did you say something?"

The look of pure annoyance Cat gave her made it even harder to keep triumph off her face. "You're right. It's 'kind of like what Gale's done.' But I'm *not going to be him again*, while Gale isn't willing to let go of *her*. Similar road. Different choices. Jennifer never has understood that."

Haliel said, "I like that, Slick. No rewrites. Care to go on?"

"What about before?" asked Brynn uncertainly. "Just a few minutes ago, when you said you knew what the consequences would be?"

Cat hesitated, then said very deliberately, "I don't need to be him to pick up what he left behind."

Brynn's skin prickled as a surge of fear partially her own and partially the horses' ran through her. Backing off, she said, "Let's get back to Gale. So you can't figure out how his power separation is working because he took a different route there?"

"Boo!" said Haliel. "Go back to talking about Ettoriel!"

"I can't know, but I can make educated guesses," said Cat evenly. "I don't think he could have spread himself this much without a focus."

An unearthly shriek echoed through the town, passing right through the unreal structures. Haliel shaded her eyes, peering into the distance. Then she said, "No, no, nevermind, it's nothing important. Go back to discussing Slick's secret identity."

Brynn closed her eyes and paid attention to how she felt: not emotionally, but magically. The haunt hadn't changed in any significant way; the flow of soul energy off her skin was steady; and while she didn't quite know what it would feel like if one of her fellow Huntsfolk were in danger, she was sure it would feel like *something*. Whatever the shriek was, presumably somebody else was handling it.

"A focus," she said. "And that's what you're looking for with all the *under*? It might have helped to have explained this earlier."

Cat only shrugged, but Haliel said, "Oh, Ink. He was doing his best not to think about it. Poor, confused Ettoriel."

Another shriek resounded through the haunt. Cat said calmly, "Ettoriel is gone."

Haliel smiled. "Is he? Too bad. I know where his Nina is, too."

Cat looked up at Haliel. "Who?"

Her smile broadening, Haliel said, "You're just straight-up lying now, Slick." She started writing in her book again.

Brynn rejoined Cat and said softly, "I could throw a brick at her."

"I appreciate the thought, but not your inevitable concussion. Let's just find the focus."

"Is it really going to look like lightning flows?"

Cat sighed. "It's going to look like something real, and it's going to influence the surrounding Geometry."

Brynn said, "Oh. And I can't see the Geometry." When the demon Tia had sent Brynn to help reboot the original Wild Hunt, she'd outfitted her with a full set of charms that all turned out to be part of one big spell: the magic that let Brynn carry horses—and souls—on her skin. Being able to see the Geometry would be *useful*, but it just wasn't in Brynn's line.

"You're useful in other ways." He didn't need to glance up at Haliel for Brynn to understand what he meant. "I apologize for being difficult." He hesitated, and then added softly, "I would really like that conversation with Jen, though."

"Oh, come on, don't whisper or I'll just have to get creative," complained Haliel.

"Would you like some help, Haliel?" said a pleasant, unfamiliar voice behind them. Brynn turned to see Amber, Yejun, and a black-haired stranger in a dapper suit with a hat.

Brynn shook her head, staring at the stranger. Capricorn, she guessed, of the variable pronouns and the delicious smell. Brynn couldn't smell him, but he confused her all the same. *Him*, but the first *him* who'd ever attracted her.

"Oh my god, Capricorn, go away!" said Haliel, with more irritation than Brynn would have predicted.

"I can only go so far," said Capricorn cheerfully. "I'm here for work!"

"You wretched little beast, you're going to mess everything up!"

Brynn decided to blame her strange reaction on Capricorn's androgyny and looked at Amber and Yejun, who were watching the exchange between the demon and the angel.

"That's certainly a valid point of view," agreed Capricorn, still gazing up at Haliel with sparkling eyes. "I'll look forward to your critique later?"

Haliel slammed her book shut and floated higher. "I don't

have to put up with this. I have options. There's a whole filthy town to document here."

As she flew away, Brynn said weakly to Cat, "Were they having the same conversation?" Then Capricorn turned his brilliant gaze onto Brynn, smiled, and her knees went weak. "Uh, Cat?"

Amber appeared by Brynn's other side, looking wistfully in the direction Haliel went before nodding toward Capricorn "I know. It's creepy how yummy she looks, right?"

"She?" said Brynn, grabbing at whatever she could.

"Whichever you prefer," said Capricorn, with a sweet smile.

"That's the *problem*," wailed Brynn.

Suddenly Yejun was standing between Brynn and Capricorn: not like he meant to do it, just like he was being accidentally rude. "Cat, we need that book Jen wanted you to give us."

Brynn pulled herself together. "You're really going to *trick her*?"

"No, brat, we're going to make her a prop so she can remember what we've already done," said Yejun patiently.

Cat pulled out the notebook he'd been writing in and tore out the pages already inscribed. When he proffered it to Yejun, the other young man was too shocked to accept it.

"It's just a notebook, Yejun," said Cat quietly.

Yejun took it, shaking his head. As he pulled out his own tiny notebook and started copying information from one to another, he said. "I don't know, man. No notebook, no glasses, how am I supposed to recognize you?"

"What did happen to your glasses?" asked Amber, frowning.

"They annoyed me," said Cat.

Amber's eyes narrowed. "Yeah… About that—"

Quickly Brynn said, "So what did you do? What happened? What was that awful noise?"

Amber stopped looking at Cat as if she was about to start something and shuddered. "It was a giant mouse."

"That's… unusual," said Cat, his eyebrows going up.

"Not really," said Yejun, too quickly. "Anyhow, we managed to communicate with Imani for a very brief period, and she told us about her work. We've got access to online archives, so it's no longer technically lost."

"What *was* she working on?" asked Brynn.

"History," shrugged Yejun. "I don't know how much it matters now. Where's Gale?"

Capricorn inserted himself into the little group and stood listening politely with his hands behind his back: just one of the team. Brynn eyed him warily.

"Gale is locked down. We're looking for a way to unlock him." Cat surveyed Amber and Yejun. "Maybe the two of you can help."

Grim, who had been investigating Capricorn's hands, suddenly sprang into the center of the group and started barking and wagging his tail. Then he grabbed Yejun's trouser leg and started tugging.

"Hark, it is the Grimphone," said Yejun. "Does she want all of us or just me, Grimwhiskers?"

In response, Grim nudged each of them, and even licked Capricorn's hands, so everybody strolled after him to where a phantasmal post office stood. Several figures moved around the post office. As they got closer the ghosts sharpened into individuals and the old-fashioned building resolved into something built in the last century. Haliel drifted high above, visible but not audible.

"Brynn's here," said AT, from somewhere within the building. "And everybody else." She came through the building wall, noticeably dirtier than she'd been last time Brynn saw her. "Come see what we found!"

Within the dark structure, a pale light shimmered from below ground level. The ground beneath the building had collapsed into a deep pit, and Jen stood at the bottom, gazing at a boarded up door in a stone wall. There were four small balls of foxfire floating in the corners of the pit, and Brynn recognized them as originating from one of the utility charms Jen had put on AT.

"It's a sub-basement," explained AT, sliding down a loose ramp of rubble. "Jen found it."

Jen glanced up at them. "I think there's far more than four hundred ghosts here, and some of them are much older than others. There's something *old* down here, along with strange patterns in the Geometry."

Brynn sat on the edge of the pit while Amber jumped down and Yejun followed AT down the rubble ramp. Capricorn sat beside Brynn, while Cat stood on her other side her, his hands loose at his sides and his head low. Softly, he said, "Even more *under*."

Jen looked up at Cat, and then quickly shifted her gaze to Capricorn. Her eyes narrowed, but all she said was, "This isn't obviously related to Imani, but it may tie into why this haunt is so powerful. So I'd like to see what's in here."

AT said, "Do you want to do the honors, Amber? I already got plenty of exercise excavating."

Amber curled her fingers around one of the thick planks over the door and gave a yank. Nails popped out, and the board splintered and broke. "Ugh," said Amber. "This will take me a while. Did you learn anything from the ghosts themselves?"

Jen sighed. "Yes. More from what they didn't say than what they did. A conservative town, xenophobic, especially these days. Mixed feelings about Imani, but they didn't like Gale at all."

"Obviously warranted," said Amber, yanking off another board.

"Mixed feelings, huh? But who actually killed her?" Brynn pulled her knees up to her chest.

"One ghost said it was an accident," said AT, tentatively. "But they really didn't want to talk about it."

"Hah," said Amber. "Yejun, tell them about what you did."

Quickly, Yejun sketched out that they'd managed to somehow have an open conversation with Imani; how they'd found out her account data, and how she'd been working on a history of the town's shadowy past.

When he was done, Amber pulled the final piece of board off the door and said, "I'm guessing if it was an accident, it was the kind of 'accident' where, after a heated argument, a gun 'accidentally' went off. Or maybe the kind of accident where an anonymous caller reported her to the cops as a threat to the town."

Before anybody could reply, she pulled hard on the door's ancient metal handle and very, very slowly, it opened.

24

Labyrinth

AMBER SQUINTED as she pulled the door open, for the other side was lit. At first it seemed as bright as morning, her least favorite time, but as the door opened wider the radiance dimmed, until it was no more that the foxfire that lit the sub-basement.

The passage beyond was wide and stone-hewn, unlit except for a gentle glow from lines engraved on the floor. A side passage interrupted one wall only a few yards down, with a four-way intersection visible past that. In the distance, the main passage curved.

AT surveyed the tunnel beside Amber and said doubtfully, "Do you think it leads to the Far City?"

"Hah hah, very funny," said Amber, shuddering at the memory of the horrific hallway they'd encountered on their journey to reboot the Wild Hunt.

"What's that?" said Brynn, and she came slipping down the rubble ramp. As she joined them in crowding around the entrance, two new side passages opened. The lines engraved into the floor multiplied and the entire complex grew brighter.

"Whoa," said Yejun. He brushed between Amber and AT to

step into the tunnel. He looked up, down, and at the walls. Then he walked to the first intersection and peered down it.

Amber watched him like a hawk, ready to spring or flee at the slightest out-of-place muscle twitch. But he stared for a moment, pulled off his sunglasses, before stepping back, frowning. Eventually he walked back to them, arriving safely in about the expected time.

Amber exhaled, letting go of a bit of tension.

Yejun flipped his sunglasses around a finger. "It's a lot of tunnels. And big, focused magic around… something." He shook his head. "There's some serious strangeness going on here. I think I can unravel it, though."

"Oh, I wouldn't," said Capricorn, from the back of the crowd. "That would probably be counterproductive."

"Capricorn, stop meddling!" said Haliel, who was now hovering right above the pit, somehow visible through the shadowy phantom roof of the post office. "Go play in traffic or something."

Capricorn glanced up at Haliel with a fond little smile. Jennifer said, "Explain, please," but far more nicely than she'd spoken to Shatiel, Severin or Haliel.

Capricorn's smile faded into a thoughtful expression, though she continued gazing up at Haliel. Then she lowered her gaze to Jen. "Should I?"

"At least give us a hint," begged Amber. Haliel might disapprove, but Amber was far too wary of mysterious corridors to care after her time in the Far City. As a member of the Wild Hunt, she might be physically invulnerable, but the endless nightmare corridor in the Far City hadn't been *physically* dangerous.

Capricorn brightened, her cheerful smile returning. "That's a good idea." She glanced at Cat, still on the pit's edge, and back at Jen. "Do you know what a relic is?"

Slowly, Jen said, "An implement used in a magical ritual that has acquired magic of its own."

Yejun leaned out of the passage. "Like the Horn?"

Capricorn bounced on her toes. "Yes, exactly!" She looked between them again and stopped bouncing. "Hmm... You must need another hint."

Jen put her fingers to her temple, her brow creasing. Her gaze traveled to Yejun, and then the glowing engraved floor behind him. "I don't know if anybody has ever tried to remove the natural charm from a relic. I suppose some researcher must have, sometime."

"Oh yes," agreed Capricorn. "They always discover something quite unexpected the first time, too." She bounced again, looking between them hopefully.

Yejun said, "Bro, at this point, if you don't tell us, we experiment and find out, and this whole conversation is a waste of time."

"Experiment on *what?* The Horn?" asked Brynn sharply.

"The tunnel," said Yejun, as Jen said, "The labyrinth."

Capricorn gave Jen a delighted smile, swept a low bow over her hand and then brought it to her mouth. "You are truly dazzling."

Jen flushed, but didn't withdraw her hand. Out of the corner of her eye, Amber noticed Cat jumping into the pit. It was far too high a drop for normal humans to make, though Amber supposed if Cat wanted to rely on the not-painless Wild Hunt invulnerability, that was... actually, it was typical of Cat. So typical.

Haliel drifted down, too, a perfect scowl on her perfect face. "Since you're ruining this, you might as well get it over with quickly."

Without releasing Jen's hand, Capricorn smiled sweetly at Haliel. "My friend Yejun made a very good point."

Cat said, his voice icy as he joined everybody, "What do they discover, Capricorn?"

Capricorn gave him a round-eyed glance, then brightened

and released Jen's hand. "Yes, of course. One of their discoveries is that the natural charm of a relic doesn't fall apart once it's removed from the relic. It continues to exist, but in a different form."

Amber shuddered and said without thinking, "A giant mouse...?"

"That was unusual, friend Amber, but in essence, yes. Of course, it's not always a mouse. Sometimes they can be quite dangerous."

Yejun frowned. "You said all those things wanted to do was return to their source."

Capricorn looked embarrassed. "You know, I didn't mean to do one of those technical truths. I mean, talk about living down to the stereotype! Because, see, that's *technically* true. But depending on their purpose, the route they take to get there might be quite... convoluted."

Haliel said loudly, "I heard a tale once of a bane that had to harvest twelve livers before it returned to its wand, *every time* it was released. Another one had to murder all invaders... in Minos, was it?" She covered a giggle. "There was even one that had to be *killed*, which was hilarious, because as you know, normally that does very little to stop them." She peeked at them over the hand covering her giggle. "You did know that already, right?"

Capricorn gave Haliel an chagrined look. "That wasn't very nice."

Haliel's sweet smile warmed Amber's heart. "How does it feel, having your fun ruined?"

Cat said flatly, "You both seem to know much more about relics and banes than I do. I find that... curious."

Amber blinked, then recalled that Cat had been the vessel of an angel before he'd stolen his own leash, and with it, much of the angel's esoteric knowledge.

Haliel and Capricorn both gave Cat eerily similar looks of

amusement. Then Capricorn said eagerly, "It's a rather obfuscated branch of study, but it's very rewarding!"

"I just read something somewhere, that's all," said Haliel airily. They both gave the Wild Hunt expectant looks.

Yejun said, "Hey, I have a great idea, how about I *don't* untangle the mysterious spell complicating the mysterious tunnel system in this weird fucking haunt? I'm sure somebody can come up with a better plan."

Cat, who had been staring blankly at the demon and the angel, pivoted to address the rest of the Hunt. "Yes. It's not hard. Brynn will go back to the other side of town, and the haunt will simplify. Jen will go with her, and we other four will coordinate on exploring the tunnels as fast as possible."

"Cat—" began Jen, her voice catching. "Brynn doesn't need me to babysit her and—"

Cat gave her a little smile that was almost smug. "Go with her so that when the rest of us accidentally activate whatever ritual is carved into the labyrinth halls, you can unravel it, or pull us out via the Horn."

Jen's eyes narrowed. "Somebody else could take the Horn. Amber, for example.

Horrified, Amber said, "Oh my god, no."

Cat stepped forward toward Jen meaningfully, and Jen backed up, toward the edge of the pit. Cat said, "It's your job, I'm afraid."

"You could do it," said Jen angrily.

Cat took another step. "I can't. I have the wrong priorities."

Jen stepped back again. Brynn got a distant expression on her face, then darted over, grabbed Jen by the hand, and said, "Come on, Jen. Earth Horse is worried."

Jen's shoulders instantly slumped, her angry spark guttering out. "Right. All right. I'll work on Imani and Tucker."

Brynn said desperately, "We can get the camp set up properly.

Branwyn and Rhianna could be back any minute, after all, and they'll need someplace safe to rest."

Brightly, Capricorn said, "I'm going that direction myself. I'm looking forward to speaking with you more, my friends."

As they climbed out of the pit, Haliel called, "And good riddance!" She transferred her glittering gaze to the remaining four members of the Hunt. "All right, team, what's the plan?"

AT gave her a withering glance under lowered eyebrows, then said to the others, "Grab a dog and spread out. Give me your notebook, Yejun, and I'll do that fancy-pants pack magic Cat suggested last month and draw a map. If you get disoriented, your dog will get you back onto a true path."

"Uh, no," said Yejun. "I mean, yes, take the notebook." He paused. "Actually, Grim! Take this to Brynn, go go go boy!" He sent Grim off with Yejun's tiny notebook in his mouth before resuming. "We have to protect that notebook for Imani. But I meant to say, *please* don't try drawing a map in that tiny thing." He held up both his hands as AT tried to reply, then put his sunglasses back on. "But wait, I've got this anyhow."

Looking up at Haliel, he said, "Hey, Goldilocks. Tear out one of those big beautiful blank sheets for us now, and you can have it back once we're done with this haunt."

Haliel gave him a disbelieving stare. "Why would I—oh. *Oh.*" She tickled her chin with her quill. "An actual document from this event inside my book. That's... that's an interesting offer, Magic. Absolutely impossible, but..." Her gaze turned distant. "Y-ess. I can see how to sell it." Then, briskly, she turned to the back of her big book, tore out a page with a sound like rolling thunder, and held it out to Yejun. Though she still seemed to be far more than an arm's length above them, somehow Yejun had no problems reaching up to accept the gift.

As he pulled his hand down, Amber whispered, "I thought she was a projection?"

"She is, but this isn't," said Yejun. "Here, AT. Map away.

Amber, you and Cat get started. I'll be in as soon as Grim gets back."

With a wistful glance up at Haliel, Amber sighed and went into the tunnels with Nod trailing behind her.

———

AFTER ACCEPTING Yejun's notebook for safekeeping, Brynn and Jennifer walked across the town, with Capricorn strolling in the same direction a few yards away.

Unable to escape the memory of Jen's shoulders slumping a few moments ago, Brynn said wretchedly, "I am so very sorry I did that to you, Jen. And the worst part is, it wasn't even true. I wanted to get you out of there and Earth Horse had just made a remark…"

Jen had been listening to Brynn with an expression of bewilderment shading into confusion, but at that she smiled wryly. "And what did he say instead?"

Brynn bit her lip, and then dropped her voice a register and repeated, "I'm not quite sure how to feel about what's going on here."

Jen blinked before bursting into a laugh that continued a little too long. When she calmed herself, she said, "Earth Horse is a good friend, and you did just as you ought."

After hesitating, Brynn asked carefully, "Do you ever argue with Earth Horse?"

Jen considered the question. "We disagree sometimes, but I don't think we've argued. He's very wise, so I try to pay attention to what he says."

In Brynn's own opinion, Earth Horse had the best sense of humor of the more verbal horses, but he was also even more possessive of his rider than Sunset Horse was of Cat.

That's what she's used to, said Earth Horse defensively. *All she wanted when we bonded was for somebody to make decisions for her.*

Hush, Brynn thought fiercely. *Go to sleep.*

Aloud, she said, "Why were you arguing with Cat? It seems like a good plan."

"It is," said Jen, her gaze dropping to the ground. "I don't always think very clearly where Cat is concerned, though. He can be so... frustrating."

Brynn walked in silence beside Jen for a moment before saying, "How?" It felt a little disingenuous to ask since she herself sometimes found Cat so frustrating she'd assigned the term 'Cattish' to his behavior. But she desperately wanted to find out how Jen felt about him, and direct inquiries had only ever elicited generic responses.

Jennifer sighed. "He tries to... protect me. He only ever makes decisions, like he just did, if he's trying to protect me somehow, or if he believes some decision of mine requires reinforcing."

Brynn nodded. "And you don't want to be protected. It can get pretty stifling when people think you can't take care of yourself," she added pointedly.

"Yes," said Jennifer. Then she shook her head. "No. No, that's not it at all. I was never a rebel, Brynn, not even at your age. If Cat wanted to take over leading the Hunt, I'd be happy to follow. I was so *happy* following Sen," she added wistfully. "But he doesn't. He won't." She frowns. "He says he *shouldn't,* and he's probably right. But I get so... confused by him."

The campsite at the rose house came into sight and Jen slowed. "And I shouldn't be inflicting this on you, Brynn. I'm sorry. The last thing you want is to hear the muddling of a dreary middle-aged woman."

Brynn stopped dead and then grabbed Jen's hand again. "Jen, the *first* thing I want is for you to *stop treating me like a kid.* You're not my mother. I don't *need* you to be my mother. Maybe Yejun and AT and Amber do, I don't know. But I have a mother, and a grandmother, and five elder siblings, and you're my *teammate.* You don't have to protect me from your feelings. And I really, *really* think you need somebody to talk to other than Earth Horse."

Jennifer blinked at Brynn. Her hand in Brynn's tightened. "Thank you," she said after a moment, before pulling away and turning back to the rose house. Silently, hopefully, Brynn followed her, but by the time they'd pulled another tent upright, Brynn's hope had dimmed. Jen may have thanked her, but it hadn't been an acceptance of Brynn's offer.

"Fine," said Brynn. "I'll start, then." She sat on the cot and crossed her legs, watching Jen fuss with knots. "Cat loves you."

Jennifer flinched visibly and dropped a rope. "He believes he does. For now," she muttered, and glanced up into the sky. Haliel was nowhere to be seen although Capricorn walked along an invisible fence at the nearest phantom house.

"You care about him, too," said Brynn, silently daring Jen to go with the *I care about everybody in the Hunt* approach.

Instead Jen sat on the ground and put her head in her hands. "I don't know. Once I thought—But it doesn't matter now. We're colleagues. Teammates, as you said." She rubbed her forehead. "I keep trying to remember that."

Brynn remembered Cat stretching out an arm to Jen earlier, when he'd been sitting where she was now. "But he keeps reaching for you, which makes it hard?"

Jen glanced up, her blue eyes shadowed. "This morning? That was... that was the first time he'd ever done that. He never wants *anything* from me. I've never known how to deal with that. This morning..." She sighed. "I suppose I'm glad you were there."

Brynn clenched her teeth, very unhappy she'd been there. She stretched out on the cot and put her arm over her eyes. She demanded of the horses, *Why won't you let them figure this out?*

The Hunt would be twisted again, said Gold Horse, one of the quieter ones. *Mortal passions so often turn toxic. Look around.*

Sunset Horse said, *He can't help it. He was* made *to love somebody.*

I thought explaining that to Jennifer would help, said Earth Horse. *But it didn't.*

Brynn put her hands over her ears out of habit. When she'd first adopted the horses, using the magic Tia had given her to pull them out from under their abusive previous riders, she'd been so happy. She had finally found a way to contribute, despite being the most ordinary person in the team. The horses had needed her, and she'd been able to save them, like a hero in a story. In return, they'd been wise guides and teachers to their new riders.

Over the past year, she had never regretted becoming their keeper, no matter the inconveniences of her magical tattoos or the late-night herd gossip sessions. But she was becoming increasingly convinced that their 'wisdom' was based on a very narrow view of humanity. And Earth Horse telling Jen that Cat was 'made to love somebody,' didn't seem very wise at all.

She lowered her hands and made a crabwise attempt to pry more answers out of Jennifer. "Does Cat's origin bother you, Jen?"

Jen, who had been digging through some storage cubes they'd hauled over that morning, paused while pulling out some foil bags of freeze-dried food. "Brynn, why are you so worried about this right now?"

"Because you and Cat are both being strange today, and because I *always* worry about you. I just… didn't know what I could do."

"You can't do anything," said Jen gently. Then she glanced up in the sky again. "I'm sure—" Her voice caught again. "I'm sure once we're done here and we get away from this place, things will go back to normal."

Brynn stared at her. "Are you *afraid* of Haliel?"

Jen wrapped her arms around herself. "I… I really wish she wasn't here. Except the part of me that thinks it would be better for Cat to stop pretending he's something he's not, and then I want her to go and take him with her. And that thought hurts a *lot more* than it should."

Brynn set her jaw and sat up. She'd heard enough to come to a decision, although she was still feeling out exactly what it was. In the meantime, she said, "Can I at least give you a hug?"

Jen gave her a pained smile and unfolded one arm for Brynn. "Of course."

Brynn squeezed her for a moment, then kissed her cheek. "Everybody loves you, you know. Not just Cat."

Capricorn unexpectedly said, "Sometimes love can be very frightening to the beloved." He was perched on the camp chair, watching with a small smile. "Especially if they're beloved for reasons that don't match their self-image."

Brynn gave Capricorn a scathing look. "Why are you butting in?"

"Oh dear, I've been rude, haven't I? I thought perhaps the clever Jennifer might wish to reflect on something else. So I came over to help." His smile widened, and Brynn stared at the way his lips curved and his eyes danced until what he'd actually said sank in. At first, she was angry, but then she realized he was being kind where she'd been cruel.

"Oh," she said, subdued. "Yeah. Do that." She went back to the cot and stretched out again, laying her head on her hands.

"Is it insulting if I compliment you on how well-read you are, my friend?" Capricorn asked Jen.

Jen, staring at the freeze-dried packets she'd laid out, raised her gaze. "Not at all. Thank you. My master was an old nephil, and I loved finding little pieces of trivia she didn't know." She smiled at a memory. "Or, more likely, that she'd forgotten."

"Did that include trivia about relics?" asked Capricorn.

Jen tilted her head. "I don't remember, but I doubt it. The basic concept is a common topic, and as you saw, I don't know much of the more obscure details."

Apologetically, Capricorn said, "I haven't looked into mortal writings on the matter in some time. Is the ritual for destroying a relic included in that basic concept?"

Brynn sighed and rolled over as Jen and Capricorn started a scholastic discussion that was even more obscure and technical than the conversations Jen had with Yejun and Cat. Eventually, bored, annoyed, and lulled by the gentle murmur of voices, she drifted off to sleep.

———

IT TOOK Amber and the others what seemed like *hours* to get through the labyrinth of tunnels beneath Tucker. As soon as Brynn walked away, the extra corridors vanished again, but even at its simplest, the tunnel complex still ran under the entire town and seemed to have boarded-up entrances all over, as well as inexplicable dead ends, confusing loops and unexpected joins.

Amber met Cat at a T-intersection and they both turned toward the unexplored branch and walked together for a while, following Nod and Heart.

"This is really, really boring," Amber complained. "I tried going faster but Nod had a fit."

"Poor Amber," said Cat, and she glared at him.

"I suppose *you* find this fascinating. I bet all these stupid lines mean something to *you*."

"They mean we're getting closer to being able to resolve this haunt."

"That's just a guess. This could be a red herring."

"Yes, it *is* much easier to complain about somebody else's plan than make your own, isn't it?"

Amber stopped dead, but Cat didn't. When she caught up with him again, she said, "Why are *you* so cranky lately?"

At first she didn't think he was going to answer, but then he said, "I think joining the Wild Hunt was a mistake."

Instantly Amber clutched at Cat's arm. "What the hell is

wrong with you guys?" she cried. "Jen and I would be *dead* without the Hunt. I thought you cared about *her,* at least."

Cat turned on her swiftly. "What's wrong with *you,* Amber? You're so dependent on the Hunt but all you want to do is complain while other people solve problems."

This struck Amber as so deeply unfair that she was speechless. She wanted to point out that she'd developed the theory and made the plan that had gained Imani's account information. But she'd promised Yejun she wouldn't share details.

Then Cat turned away again. Heart came back from down the corridor and put a paw on his leg, and he crouched down to scratch her shoulders as she leaned on him. "In any case, I didn't mean rebooting the Hunt was wrong. But I'd be more help to Jen if I hadn't stepped in."

"It needed six," said Amber, sullenly.

Cat shrugged. "There were other mortals there. It didn't have to be me."

Amber's brow wrinkled. "Jen held out her hand to you. I remember that. She wanted you with her."

"She didn't know then what I would turn out to be, or what taking responsibility for the Hunt would do to her." Cat stood up again.

Amber wasn't having it. "You never hid what you were, except maybe by wearing those stupid glasses."

"That's what I *was,* Amber. Not what I am." He started walking again, Heart remaining close by his side.

Nod glanced back, his ears flat, and Amber understood exactly how he felt. "You know, if I could, I *would* vote you off the island right this minute," she snapped, matching Cat's stride. "What the hell are you, then?"

He didn't answer. When, shortly after, they came to another intersection, Amber was all too ready to return to the boredom of ambling after Nod. Some time later, when she briefly passed Yejun, she told him, "You and Cat both make me sick!" His hurt, puzzled look made her feel better, until it made her feel worse.

She could only guess at the passage of time, but she thought it took an hour before she and Cat once again walked together. Possibly it was even the same corridor. This time, she resolved not to speak to him at all.

Then he said, "I make her unhappy, and I don't want to do that. But I can't understand what she wants from me, and she won't let herself tell me, because she's convinced it's wrong."

So much for resolutions. Cautiously, Amber said, "I always thought Jen was sort of... *naturally* unhappy. She seems like a worrier. I thought she enjoyed it."

Cat glanced at her. "She wasn't unhappy when I first met her. Those first few weeks, before Sen died, she was... satisfied with her life. She thought I made things more complicated, but she wasn't afraid of what might come, because she trusted Sen. Sen made all the important decisions, Sen took care of her, and Sen liked me."

"Oh," said Amber, digesting this. She found herself re-evaluating Jen, re-examining all of Jen's behavior since the Hunt had reformed. Suddenly it was no longer the natural behavior of a middle-aged woman. She saw in Jen somebody trying desperately to be something she didn't know how to be, not because she wanted to do it, but because somebody *had* to do it.

They reached another T-intersection and from down one of the other two passages Yejun called, "Hey! I think we're close."

They paused to wait for him to join them, and then all three dogs trotted ahead, down a long corridor crammed with parallel lines like a circuit board. On their left hand, they passed a rounded room with empty, broken crates, similar to others they'd passed, but the corridor continued on.

"I can't believe this has taken so long," said Amber.

"Well, we've been making a map, haven't we?" said Yejun. "Not just trying to solve it."

"AT was right to try to get the whole pattern before taking us to the heart," agreed Cat. "Especially if it's magical."

The gentle curve of the tunnel straightened and at the end was a wide opening. A sound came from beyond the brightness that filled the opening: *scritch scritch.*

"You know, I'd wondered where she'd gone," said Yejun gloomily.

Amber's spirits lifted, and she sped up, going so far as to outpace Nod in her eagerness. The black dog growled and chased her, which caused the other dogs to chase him, so that Amber arrived in the central chamber in a tumble of canines.

She had a glimpse of Haliel sitting cross-legged on a box in the center of the room, her book open on her lap. Then scarlet lightning flashed around the box, passing harmlessly through Haliel and crawling along the walls. One of the tendrils passed through Amber with an unpleasant tickle, and then the lightning was gone.

Unfazed, Haliel said, "Careful, Blondie. Tripping over a dog isn't something you should be famous for. Take a minute, get yourself together. Maybe comb your hair."

Amber held her hair back from her face and said, "What was that light? That was too much light. I didn't like it."

Behind her, Yejun said, "Um." His voice had a worried, embarrassed note that Amber didn't like either.

"Despite Capricorn's best efforts to ruin everything, you kids released a bane anyhow." Haliel's smile was a work of art, but Amber couldn't properly appreciate it.

She whirled on Yejun. "You! You are the worst—"

He held his hands up. "I didn't know! It's not the *labyrinth* bane. I didn't even touch that spell! All I did was tidy up some of the tangle as I passed it!"

"Oh, you all completed the pattern together. Go team!" said Haliel.

Cat said, "That box is another relic." He stepped past Amber and Yejun and entered the room.

The central chamber was a large and nearly empty room. There were two gray stone slabs in the center; one was empty while the other held the box Haliel sat above. It was a little larger than Amber's college trunk, but made of carved white stone, with poles at the top on the long sides.

Amber stared at the box, momentarily distracted from yelling at Yejun. But it was Yejun who said, "Is that… is that the Ark of the Covenant?"

Haliel laughed merrily. "*An* ark of promise, in any case."

"More meddling, Haliel?" Cat asked.

Haliel floated up to the ceiling. "Pooh. If you don't know what it is already, I'll eat this book."

Cat's eyes narrowed and Amber guessed he was sorely tempted. But his commitment to sincerity apparently won out, and he said, "I had suspicions."

Haliel nodded. "That's exactly how I'll record it." She bent her head to her book and narrated, "As usual, the artificial persona embraced his self-imposed restrictions and announced: I have a suspicion."

Yejun said, "So where did the bane *go?*" He stared up at the curved ceiling of the chamber where Haliel hovered.

Haliel smiled and kept writing. Cat advanced on the box and circled it. The dogs sniffed around the corners of the room. Amber finger-combed her hair for a moment, and then followed Cat.

The white stone of the box had roses sculpted in mid-relief on the sides, twining around the corners, with tiny thorns extruding here and there. The lid was slightly domed, and unornamented. Amber put her hand on it, and then yanked it away, frowning.

"There's char here," said Cat quietly. He nodded at the soot-blackened ground around the stone pedestal under the ark. "But not on the stone."

Abruptly, Yejun said, "I don't like knowing what's up with that bane. I'm going out to check on AT." Grim whuffed as Yejun turned away and galloped over to him.

Amber's frown deepened. Annoyed, she called, "Bring her down here, so we can move this thing to the surface."

Cat and Yejun both looked at her in surprise. Impatiently, she said, "We're certainly not leaving it here now."

With an unusual hesitance, Yejun said, "I don't want to screw anything up worse than I have."

With what she felt was great strength of mind, Amber let this go by without the snide remark it clearly deserved. There were more important things to say. "I don't care if moving it screws something else up, because leaving it here will be worse."

Cat narrowed his eyes. "Why?"

Amber gave Cat a long, steady look. "Would you be asking Jen that?"

There was a crack of laughter from Yejun as Cat blinked. "I'll bring her down." He vanished into the tunnels with Grim.

Amber called after him, "Don't set off any more magic coming back!"

After a moment, Cat said acidly, "Jen knows far more about magic than you do."

"But she knows exactly the same amount about the Hunt that I do," countered Amber. "And this box should have had our attention long ago. I guess it was hidden by the labyrinth though. The Horn's detection abilities definitely have some holes."

Cat frowned and traced his fingers over the relief of a rose. "Oh." He frowned. "It's not a normal haunt."

Amber idly looked up at Haliel, writing away. "Well, it's also an 'ark of promise,' whatever that is. And it was put down here on purpose, so I'm guessing the haunt is artificially constructed. I can see why you'd miss that, though."

Haliel gave her a thumbs-up while continuing to write, a

small smile curving her mouth, and Amber bit her lip to keep from smiling back.

"An ark of promise is—" Cat began, but Amber waved her hands.

"Save it until we've got it back on the surface. You don't want to explain it over and over again. Why don't you check out the magic around the room instead, and I'll keep an eye out for any returning red glows?"

Cat gave her a very strange look before turning his attention to the floor of the room. As he moved slowly around the slabs of stone, Amber leaned against the wall, secretly marveling at the way Cat was doing what she'd said. She wondered how far she could push that.

It was a very strange feeling, telling somebody else what to do in their own field. She'd always assumed bossy people were born, not made. She'd never been one of them, except in those situations where she had the marked advantage, like telling AT how to dress. She'd certainly never *wanted* to be one of them, because they clearly had special knowledge. Was it really as simple as directing people to do the obvious?

No, it couldn't be. She was missing something. But she intended to experiment more until she figured it out. If nothing else, the look on Cat's face was worth it.

25

Ark

AFTER AT and Amber eventually got the heavy stone ark out of the labyrinth and the excavated sub-basement, with much swearing and complaining on both ends, they put it down, not very gently, on the ground level and took a rest.

"Should somebody go get Brynn and Jen?" asked AT, after a moment. "We've been over here a long time."

Cat, who was loitering around with Yejun like the under-worked weaklings they were, shook his head. "Not yet."

Amber, sensing an opportunity, sat up and jumped in. "They should stay put for now. Cat's idea about having Jen as a failsafe was a good one. And we should figure some things out before we bring Brynn over." She pulled her mouth to one side. "I wonder how similar they are."

"That's only got the one node, and it's empty," said Yejun. "So not that similar."

"They both hold souls, though," countered Amber. "Or some part of souls."

AT shook her hands. "Carrying it was not fun, guys. It's a contained haunt, but it's a powerful one."

"It's all tangled up with Gale and Imani's haunt, too," said Cat. "Jen was right. This is why Imani's haunt is so overwhelming. Gale did something…"

"Oh, come *on*, open it already!" Haliel demanded.

AT said, "Do you already know what's inside?"

"No," said Haliel, annoyed. "If I did, I'd already be writing."

"How did you get there before us, anyhow?" asked Yejun.

Haliel hesitated. "If I tell you, will you open the damn box?"

"Yes," said Amber firmly.

With a shrug, Haliel used her quill to sketch a vague round pattern in the air. As it glimmered and faded away, she said, "Magic would have found it too, if he'd looked down from up here."

"Thanks!" said Amber, and she pushed the lid off the ark before anybody could stop her.

Within the stone box was a coarse, dark brown powder, with larger chunks scattered throughout. Amber knew instinctively what she was looking at. "Bones. Or bone dust, anyhow. I guess that makes sense." Something pale glinted on one side of the box and Amber reached in and pulled out a yellowed binder. "So tell us about an ark of promise, Cat."

Cat put his hands behind his back, eyeing the binder Amber held. "You can extrapolate what they are from the story of the Ark of the Covenant."

"Wait," said AT. "The Covenant in the Ark of the Covenant wasn't the faerie Covenant, right?"

Haliel laughed but didn't say anything. Cat said, "No. Ancient history is full of covenants. The faerie Covenant was framed as an agreement that the faeries would stay away from the mortal world and then made magically binding. Many of the others were simple promises. There are traditions where a gift accompanies an exchange of promises." He tapped his foot on the lid Amber had removed. "When the promise was between a celestial and a group of people, this was a common way to preserve the gift. Amber, are you going to open that binder or just hold it?"

Amber said, "I can just imagine what you would have done if I'd read this while you were lecturing. Yejun, here. You read this, and you do it without setting off any more magical traps, please." She gave Cat a speculative look and then went for broke. "Cat, you and AT go fetch Gale and bring him here."

Cat returned Amber's earlier long, steady stare with interest. While he was giving her the hairy eyeball, AT said wonderingly, "Wow, you *are* being bossy suddenly. What's up with that?"

Amber hesitated, and then said, "Ask me later? Cat, you have a question?"

Yejun hissed between his teeth and for a moment, Amber wondered if she'd gone too far imitating her professors at college. But Cat merely said, very calmly, "And what will you be doing, Amber?"

She gave him a reckless smile. "I'm going to keep an eye out for Imani and distract her if she shows up to meddle. After all, Yejun and I already successfully interacted with her once."

Cat stared at her for a moment more, then shook his head and turned away. "He might have recovered enough from Severin's little talk to resist, so you'd best come too, AT."

AT looked between Cat and Amber with wide eyes, then gave Amber a furtive grin before scampering after Cat. Amber watched them until they rounded a corner, and then sagged against one of the phantasmal walls of the post office.

Haliel said, "Interesting game, Blondie. Are you sure it's worth it?"

Amber looked up worriedly. "You don't think so?"

Drifting lower, Haliel said, "It's always seemed more like trouble, less like fun. But *you're* clearly enjoying yourself."

Amber shrugged self-consciously. "Yeah. I mean, why not?"

"It won't last," said Haliel darkly. "It'll turn into Dullsville. I've watched it happen."

Amber frowned. "If it does, I'll stop."

Haliel shook her head. "*You won't be able to.* That's the trap. I mean, look at the Skipper. She acts like she's got a constant headache but does she just walk away? No! And don't even ask me about how staid Umbriel's become."

Yejun glanced up from his binder. "Aren't your sort usually pretty boring? And that's why we have Capricorn and so on running around?"

Coldly, Haliel said, "If you're going to talk about that wretched demon, I'm going after Slick and Curls."

"No!" said Amber hurriedly. "Forget Capricorn. I mean, I wish I could, that's for sure."

"Good girl," said Haliel approvingly. She sighed. "Magic is right, though. The boys upstairs are far too busy and important to enjoy the simple pleasures." She studied Amber. "I suppose it might go differently for you, with this lot. They're far less stuffy, and you've at least got some potential, unlike the Skipper."

Amber glowed. "Thank you!"

"Be careful saying that around Cat, Goldilocks," said Yejun. "Amber, I think we have another problem."

As Amber straightened up, Haliel gave her a pointed look that she didn't quite understand. "What's that?"

Yejun tapped the binder. "This mostly reads like a bad translation of a bad translation, but it's pretty clear about the bane associated with the ark. It's a creature of some sort. The shape seems to vary, but the results of releasing it are pretty consistent. It goes out, it acquires twelve souls, and it returns to the box."

"And now you clarify 'acquires,' right?"

"Well... it generally leaves the dead bodies behind."

"The souls of the living, then," Amber said gloomily. She sighed. It was best that she was the one hearing this first. Any of the other girls would be really upset by this, but Amber herself had been a monster of the 'go out and fetch me tasty souls' variety before she'd decided enough was enough.

"It doesn't say, but the last few times they've summoned it, twelve bodies were left behind…" Yejun was giving her the same expectant look he gave Jen sometimes.

Amber looked around the ghost town. "And they wouldn't have any idea of its range because they would have always summoned it right here in the center of town. Wonderful." She shook her head. "What else does the binder say?"

Yejun blinked. "You're not worried about a monster going out and hunting down the twelve closest people who aren't us?"

Flatly, Amber said, "We can't do anything about it. We didn't release it on purpose. So, no, I'm not worried. I *am* getting angry though. What else is in the binder?"

"Uh, there's the bad, bad translation of the ark's ancient history, which is almost complete gibberish. Mixed up Christianity and sacred weddings and guardians. But it was with the families who founded Tucker long, long before they settled here. They were the descendants of… chosen ones? Come on, guys, these aren't even proper sentences." Yejun scowled at the binder.

"Anyhow, here's records of when they used it. No records within the past thirty years or so, except a note about sealing up the labyrinth. Before that, they… really had no idea what they were doing, except that they knew they could summon the monster by crossing certain thresholds of the labyrinth in a single night, and they thought some of those who had their souls taken by the bane would be revived in immortal bodies a lot sooner than Judgement Day."

He hesitated. "I think they used victims from the camps as sacrifices to pave the way for whoever they were trying to consecrate to the ark. But almost the whole document was retyped when they put together the binder and some notes are annotated like a feral Wikipedia article." He ran his fingers over a page. "I can *feel* how much the typist hated what they were recording."

"So they tried to lock it away and forget about it, until Imani got too close," said Amber grimly.

"Speak of the devil..." whispered Yejun, looking up.

High above them, Imani hovered, in full Hellqueen regalia, staring at the box with eyes of fire.

"Hey, Haliel," hissed Yejun. "How do you feel about mice?"

"Don't try to involve me in your deviant magic," said Haliel sweetly.

Amber moved to the open ark, reached in and stirred the bone particles with her hand. Imani moved lower, Haliel scooting out of her way.

"What *is* that?" Imani breathed. "So strange... so familiar. I feel it in here." She pressed a hand against her chest. "But I've never seen it."

Coming to earth, she knelt and traced the shape of the sculpted roses without actually touching the box. "I know these roses, though. Gale's roses. He grew them after it was far too late. To please me, he said." Her face became harsh. "But I already spent far too long letting him please me and see the price I paid for such pleasure."

"How exactly are you distracting her, Amber?" asked Yejun nervously.

"I'm *listening* to her, Yejun. In a bit, possibly I'll sing. Hush." Then Amber said to Imani, who had raised her head, "Men, yeah?"

Imani's face darkened further, her eyes blazing. "Men. Wicked men, so quick to promise, so quick to betray. Every promise, broken. Where is Severin, who promised me my daughter?"

Quickly, Amber said, "What did Gale promise?"

"To protect me, of course," snapped Imani. "These men, so powerful, promising to protect me but when I needed them, where were they?" A horrible smile stretched her face. "But I'm the powerful one now."

Amber frowned. She knew Imani only from a few moments, but this didn't seem like it fit her script. Her voice was wrong.

Amber remembered the ghosts at the burning church, breaking character to turn and watch them pull Imani's true self from the ghost. What was going on? Was it something about Gale?

"Did he trick you?" Amber demanded. "Did he lie his way into your bed?"

Imani's smile faded, and she hesitated. "He sneered at me, at first. Looked down on me. Demanded my help. I surprised him. He said he fell in love. He said he loved me! We spent days… he said he loved me. And then he abandoned me and burned Charlie!" She sobbed, and Amber found herself in the uncomfortable situation of wishing Severin was there.

But it was only her. She started humming: not her usual lullaby, but a tiny variation, created on the spot and intended to soothe pain rather than hunger. Imani kept sobbing, but she grew quieter, and the flames around her faded to embers.

"And here comes Slick with the man of the hour," announced Haliel. "Maybe now we can get some of the sordid details."

Amber, still humming, circled Imani so she could see both the ghost and the others. Gale staggered between AT and Cat, looking dazed. The moment he saw Imani, his expression twisted in agony and he lunged toward Amber, only to fall on his face as Cat tripped him.

As he lifted his head from the ground, he saw the ark. "Oh," he said. "You found that."

"Why don't you tell us about it, Gale?" said Cat.

Gale pushed himself up to a seated position and looked up at Cat. "It's… it's why I came here? I knew it was here some-where, but I couldn't find it." He looked between them. "All right, all right, storytime. She… she laughed at me when I found her. Me! Her! Wasn't frightened at all. Wasn't *impressed*. Not like the other mortals. She'd been here a year reading about this evil town. Didn't know what she'd found until I made her help me. She was *so beautiful* when she helped me trace it… she *laughed*."

Cat crouched beside Gale and grabbed his hair. "Honey-chord made a promise and sent you? What was the promise?"

With a drunken giggle, Gale said, "Twelve dancing princesses, promised brides. My lord and my brothers swore to turn them into changelings once we were free." He closed one eye. "But things got *very strange* with these mortals. Corrupted. Broken. Banes. But that's all right…" He trailed off and closed his eyes.

Cat's fingers tightened. "Why is it all right?"

"Ouch!" Gale's eyes remained closed. "'Cause it doesn't matter anymore. 'Cause Imani's dead. 'Cause I fed the princesses and all the other souls the box had caught to Imani, and Shatiel incubated her and all we need is Severin to come back and do his thing and *crack* goes the egg."

Imani stopped crying during this monologue, raising her head. The flames faded from her dark, brilliant eyes. "And all I wanted you to do was protect my daughter."

"Oops," said Gale. "You were too beautiful. I loved you too much. Dangerous for my kind to love… somebody must have warned you."

Suddenly Imani was incandescent. "You are a *coward.* You give me roses and blood and souls and power but *you're* hiding from me. But I'll find you eventually, my love. That proud face! I'll tear it off. Those elegant hands! I'll break them. Your cock, so long and thick—"

Amber realized she'd stopped her song and picked it up again hastily, while AT announced, "Imani, I think I hear Severin near the church!"

Imani's rant faltered and she glared at everybody. Then she pushed an ice-cold hand against Amber's mouth and soared into the sky, once again singing her own song.

"Augh! What is wrong with you people?" shouted Haliel, her gorgeous hair in slight disarray. "The kid with three brothers isn't even here! It was just getting good!"

"Why don't you make it up like you usually do?" asked Cat, without even looking at her.

Haliel threw her quill at his head. It passed right through him before shimmering and reappearing in her hand. "I'm going after her. Maybe I can get an exclusive interview. And if I do, you can bet I'm not sharing the secrets I uncover with any of you losers." She flew off in the same direction as Imani.

Yejun blew out his breath. "That was terrifying."

"Was it?" said Amber distantly. "I was kind of cheering her on. We've really got to get Gale here back to his old self. We can give him to her wrapped with a bow."

"I think now's the time to bring in Brynn and Jen, AT," said Cat, still holding Gale by the hair. "I'd like to see what Brynn brings out." He paused. "AT?"

AT jerked and woke up from a reverie, staring in the direction Imani had gone. "Right. I'll go get them." She dashed off.

———

Brynn slept and dreamt of the horses. It wasn't the first time she'd dreamt of the horses, not by any means. Silver Horse, irritated by her ignorance, had given her extra riding lessons in her dreams, and sometimes she dozed through their late-night gossip sessions. It was hard to ride all day and not ride in her dreams, in any case.

This dream wasn't like any of those. She sat at one of the big tables in a diner, with six other people. She knew them instinctively: Gold Horse, lightly built but all corded muscle, with amber eyes and white hair; Black Horse, with skin that matched the dark hair waving down to her hips and huge brown eyes; Silver Horse, with pale skin, shaggy black hair, blue eyes, and an ice cream sundae in front of her; Red Horse, tall and lanky, with spiky red hair and darkly tanned skin. Sunset Horse beside him looked like his sister, with cropped auburn hair, freckled lighter skin and fierce eyes. And then there was Earth Horse, with his chocolate skin and flaxen hair as long as Black Horse's. Other than Silver Horse, he was the only one who'd ordered more than a drink at this dream diner: he had a stack of peanut butter sandwiches sliced in triangles. He winked at her as he took a big bite.

"Why… why are you all humans?" Brynn asked weakly.

"Why are you a horse?" countered Silver Horse and ate a big spoonful of sundae.

Brynn brightened. "Oh, cool! Am I a pretty horse?"

Silver Horse snorted. "You're a shrimpy little filly with wild hair. You make a much better human." She scooped syrup off the side of her dish and licked her finger.

"This is your dream, Brynn," said Earth Horse. "Why did you make us human?"

Brynn looked at them, puzzled. "I don't really understand."

Gold Horse said, "If you did, would you be having this dream?"

That was when Heart, Brynn's favorite dog, started licking her face. Brynn tried to brush Heart away, tried to roll over and go back to the strange dream, but she didn't have any blankets to pull over her head and another pair of paws were on her hip and AT was saying, "Come on, wake up, Brynn."

"Nooo," groaned Brynn. "That was important…"

AT, looming over the cot, paused, then asked, "What was?"

"Talking to the horses!"

We haven't gone anywhere, Brynn, said Earth Horse.

Brynn blinked and finished waking up. "I—oh. I was having a dream."

Not much of one, said Silver Horse with a silent chortle.

Leave her alone, said Red Horse. *She has other work to do.*

The other horses went silent, just as surprised as Brynn was. While Red Horse had no hesitations about dominating Amber ruthlessly, he usually stayed out of casual herd chatter and deferred to both Earth Horse and Silver Horse.

"Will you bring the horses out before the day is done?" asked Capricorn hopefully. He was standing behind AT, with Jen kneeling at work nearby.

Brynn glanced up at the sky; it was once again full dark. "Uh, I don't know. How long was I asleep?"

"Oh, that was hyperbole. Yesterday is over already." Capricorn bounced on his toes. "I suppose I meant, 'before this adventure is over.' I'd quite like to see them!"

Feel free to let us out at any time, said Silver Horse sweetly, and then *Ouch!*

Could they genuinely fight each other while patches of magical ink on her arms? Brynn would have to ask later. "Did you solve the labyrinth already, AT?"

"Yeah. And we found what was at its heart. And now you and Jen need to come and see. Uh. I take it you don't want to ride?"

Brynn stood up and stretched. "I'd love to ride, but, uh, there's herd strife at the moment and I'd rather not bring it into the real world."

"I can imagine. This must be boring for them," commented AT. "Jen, are you ready?"

Jen finished something she was doing beside a tent and stood up. She tucked a small bag into her pocket and gave Brynn a crooked smile. "I think you're going through a growth spurt, Brynn. You slept like a rock. Are you hungry? I've got freeze-dried beef stew ready to go." She opened another, larger plastic bag, and a savory scent wafted out.

Brynn was a little hungry, but judging from the way AT winced, not nearly as much as her friend. "I'm okay. I think the Hunt magic is tiding me over. Give it to AT?"

Worriedly, AT said, "Oh no, I already had some."

"Yeah, but you need more than *some*, AT…"

Jen looked exasperated and closed the bag again. "I'll leave it here. Somebody will eat it eventually."

"Me!" suggested Capricorn. "My goodness, field rations have come a long way. That smells so good!"

Graciously, Jen said, "Yes, you, if nobody else wants it."

AT stared at Jen and Capricorn and then gave Brynn an incredulous glance. Brynn shrugged as Jen continued, "I'm going back to the post office now. AT, stay with Brynn until she's ready to go. Coming, Capricorn?"

"Thank you, I will," said Capricorn brightly, and they set off side by side.

"Ready to go?" muttered AT, confused. "Are you not ready to go?"

Brynn bit her lip. "We might as well let them get ahead. I think Jen might be mad at me?"

AT shook her head slowly. "No. She doesn't smell angry at all. She... she's more relaxed than she's been in a long time."

Prickles ran down Brynn's spine. "Capricorn. When I fell asleep, she was talking to Capricorn about magic." Urgently, she asked, "AT, can you tell if she thinks Capricorn is... delicious-looking too?"

AT's nose twitched, and then Heart dashed after Jen, falling into step between her and Capricorn. "Uh. She likes him, for sure. I don't know if it's, uh... sexual. Jen doesn't react like that unless she's touched."

Brynn blinked. "You just *know* that?"

Defensively, AT said, "I can't turn off my nose, all right? And it's awfully hard to miss when Jen and Cat brush hands while passing the rolls at a family dinner. Anyhow, are we going over there or what?"

Guiltily fascinated, Brynn lingered. "What happens, exactly?"

"Brynn..." AT shook her head again.

"You want to tell me it's none of my business," countered Brynn. "But it is. The horses have *made* it my business."

"It's not their business, either," muttered AT, looking down.

"Are you happy with Yejun right now?" Brynn demanded.

"What? Yes! Why are you asking?" AT was so startled she took a step away from Brynn.

"No suppressed longings? No resentment, no regrets about joining the Hunt?" Brynn persisted.

"What?" AT repeated. "No! I like Yejun a lot, and I know he likes me, but I think things are good right now." Her dark skin took on a hint of red. "It's hard to get seriously interested in any of the local guys, but I've gone on a few dates as practice and Yejun introduced me both times." She frowned. "I told you about them, too."

"Yeah, and I wondered about it then, too," said Brynn. "But I didn't want to complicate anything by asking nosy questions."

"So why are you asking now? Sheesh, Brynn—"

"Because…" Brynn closed her eyes, thought of Cat's broken glasses, and opened her eyes again. "Because Cat and Jen aren't happy and if I can't sort it out, we might all pay for that. And Capricorn may have just *really* complicated things. Actually, yeah, let's go. Let's go fast."

AT's brows lowered as Brynn walked past her, and she fell into step. "This is what the horses were worried about."

"Yeah and *look* how well their meddling has worked. Jen doesn't even seem to know how she feels anymore. Which is, by the way, why I'd still love that blow-by-blow description of the roll-passing hand-touching scentfest."

AT sighed. "She's a mess."

Sorry… said Earth Horse, very quietly. Brynn clenched her jaw and said nothing as AT continued.

"She wants to touch him more, and she's guilty and ashamed about it. It's a lot like Branwyn and Severin, really. Like, she's hungry, but she's trying to be this image she's built up and just by being hungry she's failing."

Brynn tripped over her own feet and AT caught her arm, looking at her in concern, and asked, "You're surprised?"

"Don't worry about that right now," Brynn said hastily. "Uh… is it the same for both of the other sides?"

AT pursed her lips. "Severin's hard to read, but he likes Bran a lot. He *reacts* to her, which is more than he does to anybody else. It was creepy how he gave Amber that *look* but scentwise he was totally inert. And when he was pissing off my father, he might have been feeding birds in the park."

Brynn filed this away without letting herself think about it too much. "And Cat?"

"Cat *could* be hard to read, if he wanted to. But he doesn't care. He's tuned to Radio Jen all day, every day. He's not as calm as he likes us to believe, though." AT hesitated. "I don't know how to describe his reaction. It's not like Jen's hunger. I'm not even sure it's human. It's big, though. I think he acts calm because that other feeling takes up all the rest of the space in him."

Brynn bit her thumbnail. "This is not as helpful as I hoped it would be."

"Sorry," said AT, not particularly sincerely. "What were you hoping for?"

Floundering for the right word, Brynn waved her hands and said, "Equity? No, that's not right. Balance? It was when you said *It's not like Jen's hunger* that I started worrying."

"You wanted me to tell you they both felt the same way?" AT guessed. "But I don't know how they could. Jen's got a whole life of memories behind her, and Cat is… Cat."

"And I'm fifteen." Brynn sighed.

"They can probably work it out on their own…. Maybe?" AT suggested.

"You missed out on middle school, didn't you?" asked Brynn darkly.

"Yeah, pretty much," said AT, a bleak note entering her voice.

"Do you think there's room in Cat's big vast whatever for

jealousy?" Brynn eyed how close the post office was and said, "No, I'm gonna ask more pertinent questions before we get there. Do you think Cat, tuned to Radio Jen, is going to notice what you did about how much more relaxed she is after a long chat with Capricorn? And have *you* noticed that Cat seems a little more... on edge lately?"

"Yes, absolutely, and yes, I have. It's Haliel." AT answered briskly, without even needing to think. Then she stopped walking and took Brynn's elbow. "*What* aren't you telling me, Brynn? You're making me nervous."

Brynn tried to work out how to explain her worries to AT. Finally, she said, "As I see it, the best possible scenario is that Jen has found a friend who will help her with some chill, Cat will feel better about the new chill Jen without caring how she got that way, the horses will also acquire chill because Cat and Jen are so chill, and the Hunt won't explode." She nodded firmly. "That would be ideal. And I wouldn't have to do a *thing*."

Sunset Horse said *Or I could kick Capricorn into next week.*

Brynn put her hands over her ears. *You don't want them to be together! What's* wrong *with you?*

I don't want to lose my rider, either. I've worked far too hard training him.

Brynn sighed. "And Sunset Horse doesn't think that's very likely. How about you, AT?"

Slowly, AT said, "I wasn't entirely honest earlier. Yejun's actually been a little jealous of my dates. I... I haven't been jealous of the girls he's flirted with because I've got something with him they can't replace, and that's what jealousy is, right? When you're upset about being replaced? I'm not worried about somebody replacing me, but I guess Yejun does worry. I haven't asked him about it because he hasn't told me and it's not... eating him alive or anything. I can just smell it sometimes, under his smile." AT let out a long breath. "I don't know if Cat will be jealous the same way as Yejun. If he makes her unhappy and Capricorn makes her happy, what is he losing?"

Brynn stared at AT. What she'd said was so... *rational* that Brynn had trouble believing it, just because... since when were emotions rational?

Then AT's gaze turned inward, and she said, "Uh... or maybe I'm... uh, let's run the rest of the way."

Brynn ran.

26

Triangles

When Brynn and AT skidded to a halt near the modernizing post office, Jen was looking at Cat with a sad little smile, while Cat looked blankly at the space between Jen and Capricorn. Amber and Yejun were standing close together on the far side of a stone box, Yejun holding a yellowed binder.

"Good. You're here," he said to Brynn, and pivoted toward the opened stone box behind him. Brynn could sense the bound souls, although they now wandered freely through Imani's haunt. "Although nothing has changed with the ark. Apparently I've wasted your time, Brynn."

"Uh, no. I was only sleeping," said Brynn. "What is that box?"

Yejun cleared his throat and rushed through a description of the binder contents, along with the red light of the bane that had escaped when they'd completed the labyrinth. Brynn tried to focus on Yejun, but she couldn't stop watching Cat.

He kept staring at nothing, his hands twitching occasionally. When Yejun wound down, Amber said without any attempt to disguise her naked anxiety, "Cat?"

"Yes?" He glanced up. "You've been doing so well, Amber. Don't turn to me now."

Jen said quietly, "We'll have to extract Gale. Yejun—?"

Yejun shook his head. "Not unless everything else fails, Jen. My technique won't be healthy."

"Do we care?" asked AT. "He killed a town."

"Imani does," said Amber.

"Your knife, Cat," said Brynn. "You said you might be able to separate him from the haunt but it wouldn't be good for Imani. How about using it to cut him away from the ark?"

Cat was quiet for a moment too long. "I don't think that will work. I need to focus and I can't right now. I probably shouldn't even be here." He stared off into space again.

Jen looked puzzled. "Cat?"

Capricorn touched Jen's hand. "Sometimes unexpected developments can trigger unexpected feelings! It's all right, my friend. I'm sure you'll come up with another plan."

Flatly, Cat said, "I'm sure you will. There are new options."

From above, Haliel said, "Did I hear somebody praying for me—Capricorn, you worm! What are you doing now?"

Capricorn beamed up at the Angel of Joy. "Giving you a present, my love!"

Haliel scowled. "Don't call me that."

Capricorn's face fell ludicrously. "Did I? I'm so sorry! I forgot!"

With a surprisingly mild gesture of dismissal, Haliel said, "What's this... oh." Slowly, she smiled. "Slick, are you having a meltdown?"

"Shut up, Haliel," said Cat. "Jen, I'm having trouble concentrating. I don't want to do anything counterproductive, so I'm going for a walk." He started walking away.

"I'll go with you, Slick," said Haliel enthusiastically. "It's not your fault, anyhow. Leaving is the right idea."

"Cat," said Jen in a small voice. Capricorn took a step closer to her, so he was standing just behind her as Cat turned back to Jen, his eyebrows politely raised.

She said, "Just a walk?"

Evenly, Cat said, "Probably a bit farther than a walk."

Amber squeaked and gasped, "Cat, no!"

Cat gave Amber an impatient glance. "You'll be fine, I promise."

Haliel said, "Very true. They don't actually need *you*. You're just going to make things complicated for her. You already have, from what I hear."

Jen's mouth was a thin, small line as Cat looked up to Haliel. "Yes. I think you're right."

"You were an experiment, that's all."

"A failed experiment," said Cat bitterly.

"So come with me, and we can figure out what went wrong." Haliel's voice was sweet and soothing, as if she was talking to a wounded wild animal. Sweet like poison, soothing like morphine, and so, so wrong.

"Haliel, *shut up!*" Brynn shouted, her fists clenched. "Can somebody *kill her*?"

"Brynn," said Jen, exactly like a teacher giving her a warning in class. She exhaled. "Cat…" she repeated, then again stopped.

Once again, he looked at her, and his expression was no longer controlled, polite interest. It was hungry, desperate, hurting. "I'm trying to do the right thing, Jen. If I stay, I can't promise I will. I don't know how to—" He moved a hand convulsively and his gaze went to Capricorn standing behind Jen, and back to Jen. "I can't be who I need to be."

Jen hugged herself. "Stay until we solve this haunt. Then I'll help you find a way to leave the Hunt safely. You can go be whatever you please."

As Cat's expression turned bleak, Sunset Horse said, anguished, *Why couldn't she have stopped at 'stay'?*

Because I broke her, said Earth Horse bitterly.

What happens if we just tie him onto Sunset Horse forever? asked Silver Horse. *It'd be uncomfortable, sure, but you'd make that sacrifice for the Hunt, right, Sunset?*

Cat said quietly, "As you wish," and for once, Haliel had nothing to say. She only smiled like a cat in the cream.

"Um," said Yejun. "I'm not usually a meddler, but I want to suggest nobody make any permanent decisions while under the influence of Goldilocks and Delicious." Neither Cat nor Jen even glanced at him, and he sighed. "But what do I know?"

"Exactly, Magic."

"So noted, Yejun," said Cat, belatedly, and walked over to the box. The Ragged Knife shimmered into existence in his hand. "AT, Amber, hold Gale, please."

"Now you can focus?" asked Amber sourly, but came around the box to grab Gale from where he'd been dozing on the ground. AT took his other arm.

"Bring him closer," instructed Cat. "Hold him parallel to the box. Yejun, I need you to spot me. I can see what I need to with the Blade, but none of us want to find out what happens if I make a mistake. Brynn, get as close as you can, just in case."

The Wild Hunt, sans Jen, crowded around the ark. Brynn eyed the Ragged Blade, which could sometimes cut through a shadow and sometimes failed to cut a slice of cheese. Cat had demonstrated both possibilities in the past. Now he placed the blade along one of the sculpted roses. "It's a triangle," he said. "The ark is connected to Imani's haunt and to Gale; Gale is connected to the ark and Imani's haunt. I cut one corner, and it becomes a line: Gale to Imani, Imani to the ark. The haunt will weaken, but not enough to fall apart. Still, I don't know what the impact will be for you, Brynn."

"I'll be fine," said Brynn.

"Why not cut all three corners?" Yejun asked intently.

"Because it still wouldn't weaken Imani's haunt enough to matter, but it might unbind Gale from his body. And because if we can solve Imani's haunt while she's entangled with the ark, we can dissolve them both without feeding the horn." There was no hint of the lecturer in Cat's voice. His words were precisely delivered, but he was reading off instructions, not teaching.

"Let's get on with it," said Amber.

Cat flexed the fingers holding the knife's handle and slid the blade through the stem of the stone rose. The stone remained unmarked, but a vividly colored phantom rose parted from the stone and fell to the ground.

For a moment nobody moved. Nothing seemed to have happened. Then Gale said, "Wha…?"

Cat picked up the phantom rose and pressed it against Gale's chest. The thorns drew blood and suddenly sank into his chest.

Brynn felt the result: the slow trickle of soul energy returning to the haunt shifted gears. It was a changed pattern and she couldn't immediately tell if it had accelerated or slowed, but the odds that it had slowed seemed low.

As Brynn tried to evaluate the new pattern of dispersal, Gale *changed* too. He straightened his posture, and his eyes cleared. The wind picked up, bringing the scent of rain and wood smoke. He looked around coldly, then stepped out of Amber and AT's grasp as if he was smoke. Even in his rags, he was suddenly beautiful. Not like strange Capricorn, no, but like a work of art in a museum, and just as untouchable.

"You should not have done that," he said, in a resonant, brittle voice. "Not that it matters. Imani has grown enough to take my power directly now."

"Why don't you ask her if she wants it?" suggested Amber, an edge in her voice.

"She wants to punish me," Gale said. "She will."

"You're really going straight back to what you were?" said Brynn, marveling. "I have no idea how she could have fallen for somebody like you."

Jen stepped among them. "Hello, Gale. Do you hate Imani so much that you want us to devour her?"

Gale's fine brows developed a crease. "I love her."

Calmly, Jen said, "Then you're going to help us save her, rather than returning to your hiding place."

Gale studied Jen for a long moment. The sweet, thick scent of honey joined the scents of rain and wood smoke in the breeze. Then he gestured at her, his long fingers moving invitingly. She tilted her head, and he looked from her to Cat before he laughed, long and rich. "I remember now. Just a few moments ago. Yet *you* think *I* can redeem Imani."

Doubt flickered across Jen's face. "I think if you love her, you'll try."

Gale gave her a mocking smile. "And what if she doesn't want to be redeemed?"

"She's suffering," said Jen sharply.

Capricorn moved out from behind Jen. "I'd be pleased to be of assistance, my friend. I'm *certain* my principal would do so if he were here."

Gale looked down his nose at the smaller, slighter demon. "Your principal?"

"Oh, I'm acting on behalf of a certain person whom I feel was unfairly stymied. I believe you met him earlier?" said Capricorn. "Dark fellow, very attached to the lady."

Gale's golden skin paled a shade. Capricorn stepped to his side and put his hand on Gale's elbow. "This way, if you please." When Gale jerked away, Capricorn's eyes widened. "You don't want to make this *difficult*, do you?"

In a hungry voice, Yejun said, "Can I hold your coat for you again, Capricorn?"

"Oh, thank you, my friend, but I'm sure that won't be necessary. After all, Gale loves Imani. Love can be so motivating." Capricorn never removed his wide gaze from Gale. He once again placed his fingers on Gale's elbow, and this time Gale started walking in the indicated direction, looking surprised by his own movement.

Brynn watched uneasily. She wasn't sure what she'd expected from an unveiled Gale, but this elegant, arrogant, bitter man wasn't it. That he'd killed four hundred people, she could believe. But in a fit of psychotic rage? He didn't seem that different from any other celestial she'd met. He didn't even seem that different from Amber when she'd first met Amber. It was all very worrying.

"Well?" said Amber. "Clearly she knows where Imani is. Let's get going and see if we can get this sorted out." She fluttered her hands and circled the rest of the Hunt like AT's dogs, until everybody else was following behind Capricorn and Gale, even Haliel. Chewing her lip, Brynn went with them.

———

CAPRICORN LED THEM ACROSS TOWN. After only a short distance, Gale once again jerked away from the demon, but kept moving of his own volition. Brynn and AT fell into step together, exchanging looks, while Jen walked on Capricorn's other side. Cat kept trying to fall back behind everybody else, but Amber was determined not to let him escape so easily, and she walked beside him.

The phantom town shifted and changed around them as they approached what appeared first as a single square building with a bell, but eventually morphed into a contemporary school. Imani sat on a swing, moving idly back and forth as she sang quietly.

To Amber's surprise, she wasn't singing her blood anthem, but something very similar to Amber's own lullaby. She looked up as they approached and the creaking of the swing stopped as her humming faded away. Her eyes glowed like coals.

Gale stopped, too. "I gave her that dress," he said, his voice so low even Amber's sharp ears almost missed it. She left Cat to his own recognizance and moved closer, a leaden weight in her stomach. She suddenly had a bad feeling about this whole endeavor.

"Where's Charlie, Gale?" asked Imani, in a soft, dangerous voice.

Gale's face twisted. "I don't know. I can't remember."

And there it was. It was the same conversation they'd had before, when Gale had been nearly senseless. Giving him back his mind and power hadn't given him back knowledge he simply didn't have.

"She's alive," said Jen, in her supernaturally calm voice. "She's safe."

Gale glanced down at Jen in surprised silence. Annoyed, Amber hissed, "Tell her that, you idiot."

He hesitated. "I won't lie to her."

Imani drifted closer, her features morphing into their more angular Hellqueen form. She reached out for Gale with a taloned hand, though he was yet beyond her reach. "Gale…"

"Oh well," said Amber, stepping away from him. "I guess we'll go with Imani's plan of ripping you to pieces."

"I deserve it," he said flatly.

Brynn said acidly, "Too bad for Tucker that you didn't feel this way before you wiped them out."

Gale looked back at Brynn. "Child, if you think—"

Imani's talons lashed out, her arm elongating as she reached for Gale's throat. Without flinching or looking away from Brynn, Gale caught her wrist before she reached his throat, pulled, and spun her to hold her back against his chest with his arm was around her waist. She didn't fight or struggle, although her chest rose and fell rapidly.

Gale bent his head down to hers and breathed, "In a moment, beautiful. They think we care for the filth that killed you. We can't have that."

She looked up at him. "I hate them. I hate you more for

not killing them before they killed me. I hate them more because I screamed and died and my neighbors closed the blinds. I hate them the most. You burned them, and that was right..."

Tears in her eyes, Brynn said, "It was a whole *town*. They couldn't have all done it."

"She's dead, my young friend. And so are they," said Capricorn, without her usual bounce. "Caring about the death of strangers is the province of the living."

"And they pretty much failed her there," said Amber, moodily.

"Well, it's clearly possible to distract her from her other concerns," said Jen, as Imani turned in Gale's arms to face him. "And if our friends return successfully, we'll be able to resolve one..."

She paused as Imani used her talons to slice off Gale's rags, and added, "Or possibly two of her concerns... but I don't know what to do about the town..." Jen trailed off as Gale and Imani's embrace became more intimate.

After several moments, Amber said resentfully, "That's not what she said she'd do to him at *all*."

"Brynn..." said Jen in a shaky voice, lowering her eyes. "Cat, don't let—"

"I'm a member of the Wild Hunt, not a kid," said Brynn, her eyes very wide. Cat didn't move from where he stood, although he was watching Jen, not Gale and Imani.

Yejun, his back turned, said, "Is *everybody* but me really into voyeurism or something?"

Above them, Haliel's pen scritched away, and she growled, "If *anybody* interferes here, I will make the rest of your lives *miserable*. Wow. I can't wait to show this to the boys upstairs."

"I won't let anybody stop them, my—Haliel!" said Capricorn.

AT sat on the ground and patted her dogs. "Uh, yeah. This isn't the first time. They, uh, did this earlier, right after we drained the haunt. She doesn't *just* hate him. I think their relationship must have been... very sexual..."

"Apparently," said Jen dryly, and added, "All right, well, let's leave them to it and maybe this will help exorcise some of those pent-up emotions now that he's back to the man she knew..."

"We're not going to leave him here unsupervised so he can pour his power back into the haunt again," said Amber flatly.

Jen gave her a wry look. "Then you can stay, watch and interfere if necessary. But everybody else who is uncomfortable can take a break."

Brynn shook herself and glanced between Jen and Cat. Amber once again thought of lit fuses. Brynn was up to something, and it was going to go wrong. But what could Amber do? She didn't trust this faerie an inch.

"I'll stay with you, Amber," said AT, and for a moment Amber thought, *Yes, you monitor them and I'll stop Brynn from doing something stupid*, but she let the thought die unsaid. "Thanks," she said instead, watching as Jen and Yejun walked away, followed by Cat and Brynn. Then she sat down and glanced at AT. "You're not uncomfortable?"

AT shrugged, drawing in the black dust with a finger. "Ghosts live in a world of their own. I've always been able to see them. They get up to some embarrassing stuff. And... our first haunt was a couple like those guys. The one we ate too quickly. I feel like I owe it to them."

Amber glanced at the current couple out of the corner of her eye. Gale was bleeding in several places now as Imani took what she wanted from him. But he didn't seem to mind. He had his gaze fixed on her with a passion that was unnerving.

Her own lover, her master, the monster who had taken her soul had never looked at her like that. He'd killed hundreds, maybe thousands of people, too. As far as she knew, he was still out there. Jen and Cat had discouraged her from confronting him at first, and since then, she'd been too engaged in her new life to think about what she'd left behind.

When she'd been mortal, she'd truly believed she loved him. She'd given herself to him as completely as a human could. She hated him now, but she wondered if, upon seeing him again, she'd react as Imani had.

Her stomach churned at the thought. But Imani hadn't given herself the way Amber had, and as far as Amber could tell, he hadn't asked her to. It was a marked and important difference. Amber had been looking forward to Imani's bloody punishment of her lover. But now, when comparing Gale to her own lover, she realized what she'd *really* wanted was the same punishment on her ex-master. It was food for thought.

"As far as I know, faeries can't be tethered and executed the same way as angels and demons and monsters," said AT, half musing to herself. "Somehow they found a way around that while they were exiled." She hugged Nod. "I'm glad I'm not a judge."

"It's tricky," said Amber slowly. "I bet Honeychord doesn't care very much, or they wouldn't have let him hide out here for the last year. Somebody with leverage over them would have to insist." She thought about it more. "Yeah, I'm glad Rhianna's boss is taking responsibility for that."

———

BRYNN QUICKENED her pace to catch up with Cat. "Hey," she said anxiously.

He gave her a quick sideways glance. "Are you all right?"

She shook her head. "I'm *fine*. Are *you* all right?"

"Not really, no," he said distantly.

"Because of Capricorn?" Brynn twisted her hands together.

"Am I jealous of Capricorn, you mean?" he said dryly, and then sighed. "How could I be? I'm glad she's found somebody to talk to. But it does underscore how little I can do for her."

"You should talk to her more," said Brynn firmly. "Just like you wanted. Here. Now. No horses, and while the busybodies are distracted."

"It's a little late, don't you think?"

"No," said Brynn.

What are you doing? Silver Horse demanded.

Sunset Horse said, *Do you think it matters anymore? The flaw was there from the start.*

Gold Horse said, *I don't like this. Let it be and things will settle down.*

I made a mistake, Earth Horse whispered.

You all did, said Brynn. *You only ever see the worst result of human love. How could you not?*

As they approached the campsite, she called, "Jennifer! Cat wants to talk to you."

In a low, angry voice, Cat said, "And what do you want me to say, Brynn?"

Jen and Yejun glanced back, and Jen said, "Of course," with only a little tremble in her voice.

Brynn stepped away from Cat. "Just the two of you."

"Whoops," said Yejun and turned away. He called as he speed-walked back into town, "I'm going to go inspect those magic rose bushes."

Brynn started to follow him, but Jen said, "Brynn! Stay, please."

"Um," said Brynn. "I don't know——"

"It doesn't matter," said Cat. In a few long strides, he crossed to Jennifer, put his hands on the sides of her head, and kissed her. After a moment, Jen put her hands on his elbows and leaned in. The kiss continued just long enough for Brynn to regret not escaping, and then Cat released Jen.

"I love you," he said roughly, and turned away.

In a quiet voice, Jen said, "I wish that were true."

Cat froze, his head down, but Brynn could still see the look of anguish spasm across his face. Slowly, he turned back to Jen.

She lowered her gaze and stumbled over her words. "I wish you loved me for real? I wish you loved me freely. Not because you were made to love somebody."

His eyes blazing and his voice furious, he said, "I was made to love somebody, and it *wasn't you*."

Tears spilled out of Jen's eyes. She wiped them away with her palms, but kept coming. "I know it wasn't me. How could it have been somebody like *me?* I'm nobody. I was never anybody. A wizard's assistant, that's all."

Jen's tears wiped Cat's anger from his face. He twitched toward her and pulled himself back. Blankly, he said, "Why won't you believe I love you?"

"Because you're a dream, Cat. You're… you're too perfect." Jen said and gasped as she tried to suppress her tears.

"Bullshit," said Cat, his voice hardening.

Brynn wrapped her arms around herself, rocking on her heels, completely uncertain of what she ought to do. Why had Jen asked her to stay?

Don't do anything, said Earth Horse.

"You're a dream," Jen repeated. "And at some point you're going to *wake up*."

Cat's jaw clenched. "Is that what it will take?" A silver sizzle traced itself around him and there was the first hint of the pressure of a celestial's active aura.

Do something! cried Sunset Horse, and Brynn agreed.

"And then what?" she blurted. "What happens once she believes you love her? Does that solve anything? Does she fall into your arms? Is that what you want?"

The silver sizzling vanished and Cat gave Brynn a startled look. "No! I've never wanted that."

Liar, whispered Sunset Horse, but Brynn didn't repeat *that*. Jen fixed her gaze intently on Cat. She barely seemed to be breathing.

Cat dragged in a deep breath. "She's not a prize," he muttered. "She's not *mine*. I'm hers."

"What if I was?" asked Jen abruptly. Her tears were gone.

"What?" said Cat, completely off-balance for the first time in all the time Brynn had known him.

"What if I was *yours*?"

"You're not an object," he said weakly.

"And you are?" Jen said, very calm now.

He brought his hands to his hair, digging his fingers in. Then he dropped them and said, "If I have to be."

"What if I was yours?" repeated Jen, inexorably.

"Don't!" His hands twitched, and he stepped back and half-turned away.

But Jen wasn't letting him get away. She advanced on him, and his breathing became fast and shallow. "You never want anything from me," she said. "Not even a cup of coffee. How can you love me if you don't want *anything* from me?"

She didn't reach out for him, didn't touch him, but she stood close enough to embrace him if he reached out. He stood frozen, save for the rise and fall of his chest.

Finally, he spoke, his voice barely more than a whisper. "If I thought you were mine, I would want *everything* from you. Better we not go there."

Masters, said Sunset Horse, in exasperation.

Jen looked at Cat, unmoving. Waiting.

He brought up his hand to her cheek, ran his fingers over her skin, tucked a strand of hair behind her ear. "If you were mine, no horse, no word, no law could keep me away from you. If you ran, I'd find you. If you died, I'd still go after you. I'd tear down Heaven itself to get to you." He dropped his hand back to his side. "So. Better we not go there. Better I'm yours, and you're free to do whatever you please."

Still, Jen looked at him. Almost pleadingly, he said, "Tell me again I don't love you."

"No," Brynn burst out. "Ask *her* if she loves *you.*"

Silence fell. Jen stared at Cat, searching his face patiently.

Cat seemed paralyzed, color draining from his face. Only his mouth moved as he reached toward different words and fell short. *I don't… Do you…*

At last, very pale, he said, "What do you want from me?"

"*Hold me.*" The words broke out of Jen like water from a dam, and she leaned into his chest.

Bemused, Cat wrapped his arms around her.

Humans are too complicated, complained Silver Horse.

Are we letting this happen? asked Gold Horse.

We didn't stop anything, Earth Horse said.

I did, responded Gold Horse firmly.

Then Jen lifted her head from Cat's chest and put her hands on his face. "Be *more.* Sen always wanted me to be more, and I never understood. I do now. Be more and see if you still love me then."

Oh hell, said Sunset Horse.

———

THE BLOODSTAINED FAERIE and the burning ghost cuddled near the swing set of the school, while AT and Amber had invented seven variants on tic-tac-toe in the black ash, including the 'Nod wins via paw print' version.

Above them, Haliel frowned at her book, her quill continuing to scritch as she embellished what she'd already written. Capricorn sat stylishly on a jungle gym below her, watching Haliel, the lovers, and AT and Amber, her head moving like a curious bird.

At one point, Haliel raised her head, looking into the distance. At the same moment, Amber felt an unwelcome *pressure* against her bond with the horn. She froze.

Haliel said, "Is that…?"

"Not yet, Haliel!" said Capricorn. "But if you want to go see,

I'll go with you!"

Haliel narrowed her eyes. "You'd ruin it somehow. You're like a destiny vandal or something. I'll stay here, thanks."

Capricorn smiled and bounced on her toes.

AT shook her head and whispered, "I'm not very impressed by the Angel of Joy up there."

Amber gave AT a shocked look. "She's amazing. Look at how she gets everybody wound up."

AT shrugged back. "I don't like the demon either, but I'd put my money on him in a fight between the two."

Amber completely failed to parse this, and settled for, "It's not always about fighting, AT. Also, why did you settle on 'him'?"

"Seems better than 'her' for 'too delicious to trust.'" She gave Capricorn a narrow look, and Capricorn gave her a cheerful little wave.

Then Imani partially rose, looking down at her lover sprawled beneath her. She once again appeared human, although fire flickered like wings along her naked shoulder blades. "I remember this too well," she said softly. "Days of passion, days of distraction, while Tucker's hatred grew. And then it all came tumbling down, and you left me to their attacks. How *could* you?"

The school playground shimmered around them, faint traceries of a house twinkling and fading. Shadows of people moved across the ground, and male voices jeered. A moment later, a siren's wail and more male voices, and five gunshots, rapid-fire.

Imani tilted her head, listening, and stroked her nails down Gale's bloody chest. "Was this your love?"

"It was my failure," he said flatly. "I was in the labyrinth on my lord's quest. I didn't know until too late."

Silence reigned for a long moment, Imani drawing designs in the blood. Then she sighed. "Words I've heard before. Such unlucky gods." Bending her head, she kissed Gale lingeringly, before saying, "Shall I punish you only because you were unlucky, handsome god?"

He put his hands on hers, and Amber tensed in case this was the precursor to Gale once again empowering the haunt.

"It would be a gift," he whispered.

Imani was still. Something in the haunt shifted, and afterimages danced around Imani and faded. In an odd voice, she said, "Punishment…"

Then, slowly, the ghost shook her head. "You are, and always have been, a distraction, just as you first told me I was."

"I was wrong," he said fiercely. "You are *everything*."

Imani was still, and then she rolled her head back, lifting her face to the sky. "Sometimes. Sometimes I am." The fire at her back flickered into her Hellqueen dress, though she remained kneeling atop Gale. "What was your love when I died, Gale?"

He exhaled. "My love was the fire." For the first time, regret tinged his words.

Imani pulled her hands free but once again bent close to him. "I never asked to be your *everything*. I won't be. But I was *everything* to her, to the child I chose, and carried, and nursed and dressed and taught. They took *everything* from her, everything but her life, and then you, who said you loved me, took that."

She stroked his hair away from his anguished face. "I would hurt you forever, but you want it *so much*. Unlucky god, with so many roles to play…"

"I want to be with you," he whispered. "I want to die with you."

"Do you think I want to be with *you?*" Imani said. Her face shifted, and he reached up to touch it.

"Yes," he said gently. "I know you do, or this would be much easier for you."

She pulled away from him and stood up. "Where's Charlie, Gale?"

Amber sighed and muttered, "Here we go again."

But before Gale could give his traditional answer, a new, young and clear, said, "Mom?"

Part IV

27

The Return

THE VELVET DARKNESS of Severin's space was different, even in the brief time Branwyn was there. It was warm, of course. But the scent of roses filled her nose, and the old armchair that had resembled hers was gone. And then a window swept over them and the dim dreariness of Imani's haunt replaced everything.

A woman floated in the air above a spectral playground, her legs curled under her, and it wasn't Imani. She had perfect blonde hair and a giant book on her lap, in which she was writing with a feathered pen. Except for the lack of wings and the presence of yoga pants, she was practically the stereotype of an angelic observer.

Below her, leaning on a jungle gym, stood a black-haired figure in a hat and a snappy suit that Branwyn would have happily worn herself. That one saw their arrival and lifted a finger to their mouth with a secretive little smile as they turned their head.

Beyond them, Imani rose over Gale as he sprawled in the dust. Nearby, Amber and AT watched them intensely, while AT's dogs all twisted toward Severin with flattened ears.

Silently, Severin put Charlie on the ground, but kept his hand on her shoulder as he looked over the angel and her dark-haired companion.

"Where's Charlie, Gale?" asked Imani, in a high, sweet, dangerous voice.

"Mom?" said Charlie.

Everybody—Imani, Gale, the angel, AT, Amber—looked at Charlie. Imani's mouth yawned open as if she was about to wail. Instead, as if a magic curtain had been opened, Imani Hellqueen vanished, replaced by Imani the woman, in a pair of old cut-off jeans and a faded t-shirt. She had warm brown skin, hazel eyes and a pensive look.

"Charlie," she said softly. "Come here."

Severin's hand stayed on Charlie's shoulder and the little girl hesitated. "You're dead, aren't you, Mom?"

Flames flickered in Imani's eyes. "I died... They took me from you, Charlie."

"But I'm okay, Mom. Nobody hurt me." Charlie's voice trembled. "You were so worried for me, right?"

"Gale burned you," Imani whispered.

"No!" said Charlie urgently. "No. I'm right here."

"Come to me, then," said Imani, and stretched out her arms.

But Severin kept his hand on Charlie's shoulder, even when she tried to pull away.

"You can come to her, Imani," he said harshly. "But she's not going to you. You can't take her with you."

"I can't reach her," said Imani plaintively. "She should be with me. She needs me."

This was not the beautiful reunion Branwyn had been hoping for. She remembered the Saint's warning and pulled out her hammer, holding it lightly in one hand as she started trying to imagine alternative solutions to the problems arrayed before her.

BRYNN SHIFTED UNCOMFORTABLY as Cat and Jen stared at each other. Jen said, "I loved Sen so much, Cat, ever since I was barely more than a child. I was so happy with her: taking care of her, helping her, being with her. And she loved me as well. I know that. But when you came along... she... she cared for you too."

Cat opened his mouth, and she put her hand over it, her words speeding up. "That was fine. You weren't the first. But I... wanted you too. And that made her so happy! She said once she wanted to send the two of us on a trip together, just us... and I didn't understand. I never understood when she tried to encourage me to be... more. More than just *hers*."

Jen dragged in a breath, and there was a sob breaking under her words as she said, "But I *don't* want you to—"

The haunt *changed* and Brynn squeaked despite herself as the flow of souls off her skin shifted again. This time, it was very definitely moving faster. Much, much faster.

"Something's happened," she cried, as Cat and Jen looked around and broke apart. She saw a flash of Imani in her mind's eye and realized at least part of what was going on. "Branwyn and Rhianna are back with Imani's daughter!"

Then she took off running, pulling the full power of the Wild Hunt over her for the first time since they'd drained the haunt. She could feel Cat and Jen following her, feel Amber and AT ahead of her, and Yejun coming in from the north.

Skidding to a stop near the ghost of the school, she stared hard at Imani as the rest of the Hunt pounded up behind her. She was vaguely aware of Branwyn and Severin standing with a little girl, distantly noticed that Rhianna had wandered off some-where, but otherwise, Imani and the haunt filled her senses.

"This isn't good," she said. "I think cutting Gale free broke something." She clutched at her arms as if she could stop the soul energy from escaping.

Imani was strange now. The shadow of the Hellqueen version hovered behind the human version, attached to her but not driving her. But the human version was *wrong* too. Though it looked like her true self, it too was part of the corrupted haunt, and the haunt was *hungry*.

"It's dangerous for mortals. Branwyn and the kid shouldn't be here," added Brynn. "And where did Rhianna go?"

Amber darted over. "Should we just eat her now, then?" she said sarcastically. "I mean, if we're not going to let her talk to her kid…"

Brynn covered her ears. "No! That's not her talking, anyhow. It's the haunt, it's a trap."

Amber frowned. "That may be… She didn't talk like that before when she was herself. I was wondering why…"

Cat said, "Severin brought them; he can take them away again. They'll be safe."

"But *will* he?" asked Jen. "Or is he going to feed them to her?"

"I might be able to help the real Imani talk," said Yejun slowly. "But I don't know if it will last. I don't know if it will *matter*. If Brynn's right, Imani may not be driving this thing anymore."

Frustrated, Brynn said, "But who is?"

"Tucker," said Amber flatly. She glanced around the town. All the other ghosts were gone, but the shadows had become far more substantial.

"A whole town?" demanded Jen, frowning.

"That might explain some things," said AT moodily. "We never really dug into whose haunt this was."

Flatly, Cat said, "It's Imani's. She's the one Shatiel cared about. She's the keystone. We're not freeing anybody else until we free her."

Amber and Yejun exchanged a pointed look. Then Amber said, "You might as well give it a try, Yejun."

BRANWYN TOUCHED the gem in her hammer thoughtfully and watched as Imani's image flickered and wailed, "I want my daughter."

Off to one side, the Wild Hunt coalesced into their collaborative huddle, speaking in those rapid, incomprehensible half-sentences they'd used before. Clearly they'd also detected some kind of snag in the proceedings.

Charlie watched the ghost of her mother with a puzzled expression. Branwyn said, "Not how she usually acts?"

Shaking her head slowly, Charlie said, "My mom should be a *good* ghost. She'd want me to be safe. She'd be yelling at Severin for bringing me here, I bet." Charlie looked up at Severin. "Where's my mom for real?"

"She's here," he said grimly. "Trapped under all the bullshit Shatiel and Gale piled onto her."

"Trapped by her own rage, too," said a friendly voice. The androgynous figure in the suit stood on Severin's other side.

Severin snorted. "Imani? Never."

"No? Then perhaps she's been trapped by the silencing of her rage? I'm Capricorn, by the way! I'm here to help you."

Severin gave Capricorn a sidelong look. Capricorn tilted their head and smiled. Branwyn was pretty sure more passed between them than a glance, but also sure that it had resolved peacefully because Severin merely looked back at Imani without trying to kill anybody.

"So she's stuck?" inquired Charlie. "What can I do?"

"Call her," suggested Severin. "She's in there. She can find her way out for you."

Charlie looked apprehensive. "But then she calls me, and I *really* want to go to her."

Severin shrugged. "Say you can't. Tell her I'm keeping you from her."

Capricorn cleared their throat. "I don't believe that would work out to Imani's benefit. In fact—"

Suddenly Yejun was at Capricorn's side. "Hey, Delicious, how do you feel about more mouse-wrangling?"

Charlie and Severin both looked at Yejun sharply.

"Mouse?" said Severin.

Yejun said, "Oh, uh. Stay tuned? I think I can pull the real Imani out of what's holding her, but there's a side effect and it may only be temporary anyhow."

Capricorn carefully took off their hat and jacket and offered them to Branwyn. "Would you be so kind as to hold these, please?" Branwyn took them, bemused, and Capricorn glanced down at their polished shoes as they rolled up their sleeves. "No, I couldn't stand it if I scuffed them," they said decisively, and stepped out of them.

"What about a mouse?" said Charlie. "Do you mean me?"

Yejun looked at Charlie over his sunglasses. "Are you a mouse, too?"

"Um," said Charlie, and fell silent, clearly out of her depth.

"Mouse is her nickname," said Branwyn briskly. "Also apparently the form of the side effect. Are we all clear now? You're confident about this, Yejun?"

"Uh, mostly," said Yejun, and his eyes, still visible over his lowered glasses, darted to Severin. "It might be… a little upsetting but she'll be *herself* when I'm done. It seemed to help last time. She's stopped wailing about her work, anyhow."

Branwyn could feel the softest creak in her chest. Then Severin looked at her, his expression twisted. She had the surreal experience of feeling his touch at the back of her neck while he stood in front of her.

Then Capricorn stepped between them to adjust the folds of the jacket over Branwyn's arm. Softly, they said, "You have been acting as his filter recently, yes? But he mustn't leave the child now."

Branwyn opened her mouth to deny acting as Severin's 'filter' and then paused as she remembered Severin stepping behind her when he wanted to kill the courtiers of the Court of Stone; when he was enraged by the Saint; even his sardonic remark in his space about using her as a distraction.

"Capricorn!" shouted the recording angel, above them. "*Stop meddling.*"

"It's my job!" Capricorn called back, happily, before half-skipping out between Severin and Branwyn as if shoved.

At the same time, Severin said silently, *First angel I've liked in a while, that one. I don't want to… make things worse, cupcake.* Her chest creaked again, and she saw his own breathing become shallow. *I don't want to overreact like the kid's afraid I will.*

Branwyn exhaled slowly. "You've got this." Then she deliberately adjusted her position so she stood behind him. He watched her as she moved, until he was craning his head, watching her from the corner of his eye.

"Get on with it, Yejun," Branwyn commanded, and then, more quietly, "Focus on Imani and Charlie, Severin." She bared her teeth. "You can hide behind me again later if you have to."

His eyes narrowed. Then his shark smile flickered across his face as he faced forward again.

Branwyn watched over his shoulder as Capricorn and Yejun both strolled up to Imani. The ghost paused her wailing to glare at them, a bloom of flame swelling around her. Neither the demon nor the young man seemed particularly intimidated by this, although Amber trailed after them in a protective sort of way.

Yejun began to do his magic, which looked from the outside more like Branwyn's magic than Corbin's. Capricorn stretched their clasped hands out in front of them, like they were about to engage in a light bout of tennis.

From somewhere, AT said, "But what is he *doing?*"

Brynn muttered, "It's like he's *dissecting* her. How can he do that?"

Severin's shoulders tightened as Charlie asked, "Is this okay?

I don't know…" and Branwyn locked her own hands behind her back so she didn't touch him, didn't distract him.

"It's okay," she said instead, answering Charlie. "Yejun knows what he's doing." But as the ghost's form began to shift toward something even more horrific, and Amber darted forward to hum a song that carried oddly in the crackling air, Branwyn wondered just how much of a lie she was telling.

Then Yejun ripped something faintly visible away from the ghost and tossed it aside. As Capricorn sprang toward the spinning magical mass like a dog after a tennis ball, Imani turned toward Severin and Charlie. She was once again the woman in jeans and a t-shirt, with wisps of hair flying wildly around her face.

She took one step toward them, and then blurred forward until she was kneeling in front of Charlie, tears streaming down her cheeks as she opened her arms to the little girl. "My baby."

"Mom?" said Charlie uncertainly. "Can I hug you? I can see right through you, Mom."

Severin lifted his hand from Charlie's shoulder and reached out to pull Brynn in from somewhere nearby. While Brynn stumbled, she didn't protest, instead kneeling down beside Charlie and Imani and putting a hand on each of their shoulders. Then, carefully, Imani hugged her daughter, like she was fragile porcelain.

A glint of red pulled Branwyn's attention away from the touching moment. Back where Imani'd been and Capricorn still was, a crimson circle was extending tendrils in an unpleasantly familiar way. She drew in her breath sharply, but before she could say anything, the tangle of lines abruptly became an unpleasant-looking elephantine mouse.

Capricorn immediately put their hands on the mouse's big head and began to talk to it very quietly. The mouse tried to shake its head, but Capricorn's grip was like a vise and all the mouse managed was a full body shimmy and long claw-marks in the cinders of the school.

Then Imani stood up. She glanced once at Capricorn and the giant mouse, then crossed to where Gale still lounged on the ground near the swing set. "Get up," she said to him crisply.

Slowly, his gaze burning, he rose to his knees.

"Up," Imani repeated impatiently. "You've done far too much kneeling, and it's accomplished no more than a baby sucking its thumb."

He opened his mouth, then closed it and stood up. He towered over her, but as she put her hands on her hips and tilted her head to look up at him, she somehow seemed the larger one.

"You let me die," said Imani quietly. "You distracted me from the danger around me and then let me die." She paused, then went on. "That's what I believed all this time, but I was wrong. You were wrong, too." She reached up to trail her fingers along his cheek, and he flinched. "You wanted a story where you were in control. But that's not this world, handsome god. Not even now."

"It hurts," he whispered.

"It's going to hurt more before you're done, Gale," she said seriously, her hand curling against his face. "You didn't kill Charlie, but you might have. You've got to pay for that. Not with blood and tears and regret, which don't do anybody any good, but with *work.*" She inspected him sternly.

His mouth moved, but Branwyn couldn't hear him.

Imani shook her head. "Even if it was possible; even if your lord obliged you, what good does dying do? You've got lives to pay for. You can't do that as a thunderstorm." She dropped her hand from his face and turned away. "But it's up to you. You can decide whether you made a mistake, or whether you were never more than a liar."

Gracefully, she stepped away as he reached for her and finished turning her back on him. With another glance at Capricorn, whose discussion with the crimson mouse was growing more heated, Imani surveyed the array of observers.

When she met Branwyn's eyes, Branwyn felt a jolt at the simple fact that the ghost was *seeing her*. This was a woman who could do that: look past her guardian and her daughter, look past the psychopomps trying to exorcise her haunt, and see the random woman in the background, just as she saw everybody else.

For the first time, a genuinely *personal* grief that this woman had been murdered hit Branwyn. She leaned her head against Severin's back, thought of Rhianna, of her hammer, of sacrifices and love, and bit back the tears Imani and Branwyn both considered so useless.

———

AMBER TRIED to split her attention between Imani, Gale and Capricorn, which meant Imani's inspection flitted over her like a change in the light. Gale was swaying like a tree in a high wind. Meanwhile, Capricorn's remarks to the mouse were increasingly urgent, but—and this mattered to Amber—was it her words or her supernatural strength holding the mouse back? Capricorn wouldn't always be around, but there might be more monstrous mice in the Hunt's future.

"Now what?" said Imani, her chin raised a little.

AT sighed. "It's all still here."

Brynn said, "The haunt is still holding the souls of the town. Won't you please let them go, ma'am?"

"Why?" asked Imani. "Why are you doing this?"

"We don't want to destroy you," said Jennifer bluntly.

Imani laughed, and it wasn't a happy laugh. "I've already been destroyed, lady. My life and death were both stolen from me and my work... all my research and writing about this town is now worthless."

"Your death?" said Brynn, confused.

Imani spread her hands. "The story of this town, its life and death, has been silenced, and me with it. The injustice doesn't matter as much as the *peace*." She rolled the word around bitterly.

Branwyn raised her head and growled, "Umbriel. Umbriel and his cover-up."

Brynn frowned. "Where is Rhianna anyhow?"

Jennifer cut across Brynn's question. "Peace is what we'd like to give you, Imani. But you have to help us out."

Imani crossed her arms. "I think peace is what you'd like *me* to give *you*. You'd like me to go quietly, just so you can sleep well at night. But I'm not going to lay down what little I have left just to make you feel better."

Jen blinked in response to this, but AT and Brynn both flinched hard before bowing their shoulders. Amber shook her head in frustration and tried to add Severin to the people she was monitoring. He was standing very still, but Branwyn was at his back and the little girl in front of him and *probably* they'd slow him down if he tried anything sudden. Probably.

"Do you realize what will happen if we don't resolve this?" demanded Jennifer harshly.

"You do what you have to, lady," said Imani calmly. "But I won't make it easy for you. I'm not going to show my daughter how to give up just because people like you don't want to sweat." She laughed again. "If I was that kind of person, I wouldn't be dead now."

She turned toward Capricorn and the mouse. Capricorn was now leaning into the 'discussion' with the mouse, her stocking feet digging into the ground.

"Wait," called Cat, and Imani turned back, her eyebrows raised politely.

"What if there was another option?" Cat said. "Something between a nightmare and nothingness? Something with a voice. Would you release the haunt then?"

Branwyn stepped around Severin, her bright eyes suddenly

sharp and attentive. She held her hammer tightly in the hand not holding Capricorn's hat.

Imani studied Cat for a moment. So did everybody else in the Hunt, because unlike Amber, they probably had no idea what he was talking about. She chewed savagely on her lip and wondered if her little magic song could just put *everybody* to sleep while she thought things through.

The moment went on too long, that horrible space between looking at a clock and waiting for the first tick. At last, Imani shook her head and said, with a tinge of regret, "I can't."

"Can't? Or won't?" asked Cat, unruffled by her refusal.

Lightning crackled across the dark sky and all the ghostly structures of the school and playground took on a malevolent glow. Brynn squealed and hugged her arms. Imani looked past Cat, then tilted her head. "Can't, I'm afraid."

"Why is that?" asked Cat, moving closer to her.

Imani opened her arms wide. "If I let them go, how could I be the villain of their story? No, they're going to stay, just like they stayed in town when they were alive. And they're going to keep me here, so they can be my victims, because in their story, that erases what they did to me." She shrugged. "All I can do is take us out on my terms."

Amber shivered. She could feel the hostility of the haunt all around her. It hated them. Although Imani truly had begun the haunt in her initial surge of ghostly wrath, it was maintaining itself now. It wasn't, after all, going to be salvageable. They'd failed before they started, because they hadn't understood just how twisted things had become.

And Shatiel had helped it happen. How *could* he—

Amber's brief flare of rage was interrupted by Cat saying something softly to Imani. Amber couldn't hear him, but she didn't need to, not while they were all connected via the Horn. His exact words were lost, but he was offering her something wrong and terrifying.

All of Amber's bad feelings came crashing over her at once, and she gasped, caught in the grip of a terror she hadn't felt since her master had discovered her betrayal. Without conscious effort, she darted over to join Cat and Imani.

"Cat—" she said, anguished. She could feel the perturbation of the rest of the Hunt, but they didn't understand, they didn't really *believe*. They whispered to each other but what was the use of that?

Cat gave her a steady look. "Amber." Then his face twisted into something that matched Amber's own feelings and he said very softly, "Help me save her."

Amber stared at him, feeling as if her heart was being wrenched out of her.

Imani glanced between the two of them. "I have to go now," she said quietly. "I don't have time to understand. But if you destroy me, save somebody else."

Then she slipped away, just as Capricorn said loudly, "Well, darn!"

A flash of heat and flame surrounded Cat and Amber as they looked at each other. It rolled off them harmlessly. As it faded, Imani the Hellqueen reformed, gave both of them baleful looks, and then darted toward Branwyn and Charlie.

Brynn, who had been standing as if frozen, moved abruptly, catching Imani by the wrist as she passed, holding her as if Imani was flesh and blood and Brynn was steel. At the same time, Severin twisted, picking up Branwyn bodily and depositing her beside Charlie and behind him.

Bitterly, Jennifer said, "Well, we tried, kids." She was holding the Horn. Darkness pooled around Severin's feet as he took a step toward her and then stopped.

"Amber..." said Cat, and Amber winced.

Then she said, "Fine. Be that way. I never liked you anyhow." His mouth quirked, and she added, "Don't fuck this up."

Then she darted over to Jennifer as the older woman raised the Horn. "Jen! Wait!"

Jen lowered the Horn and gave her a tired look. "We don't have much time, Amber, and drawing this out is only going to hurt the kids more."

"Absolutely," said Amber. "Just… give me the Horn."

Jen blinked. "What?"

Amber took a deep breath and used the bossiest voice she could. "Jennifer, *give me the Horn.*"

And Jennifer handed it over. "What do you want it for?"

Amber held the Horn close to her chest. It had changed since she'd first stolen it from the original Wild Hunt. It was no longer *malevolent.* It was part of her, part of all of them. But the one who held it had *responsibilities.*

Breathlessly, Amber said, "I want it so you don't have to carry it, Jen."

Jen's eyes widened. "What?" but behind her, AT was smiling through teary eyes.

Amber waved one hand airily. "Go work some magic or something. Do a job you love. Taking down this haunt isn't your call anymore. It's mine. I've got the Horn."

In a strangled voice, Jen said, "It's all of our responsibility, Amber. You can't just…."

"Then why were *you* the one about to blow the horn, despite AT crying and Cat having an actual plan?"

Jen stared at her in consternation. Above them, Haliel laughed. "I think I'm still going to call her the Skipper, though. I mean, what else about her really stands out?"

Amber found herself treacherously wishing the Angel of Joy would use her powers elsewhere. But the remark shut Jen down completely.

She glanced at Cat, glanced down, and stepped back. "Fine. You want to carry the Horn? Be my guest. I'll be here if you change your mind."

Doubt attacked Amber. But suddenly Capricorn was beside her, and Jen's hurt feelings had to be a problem for later.

"There *is* a plan!" said Capricorn cheerfully. "It sounds very dramatic. You'll like it, Haliel!" The demon's gaze went to Jen and her expression sombered. "I'll even stay over here!" She glanced at Amber. "Go, go!"

Amber looked around, saw Cat talking to Branwyn and Severin and Yejun, and went to join them, holding the Horn close. It felt nice under her hands.

28

The Hard Work Of A Miracle

WHEN SEVERIN PICKED Branwyn up like she was no larger than Charlie and moved her behind him, she very properly resisted her instinct to kick him. But it was a bit of an effort. She liked her feet on the ground.

Brynn, holding the angry ghost by one hand, said in a trembling voice, "Branwyn, where is Rhianna? You need to tell me right now so I can make sure she's safe——"

"She's not here," said Severin curtly. "She'll be showing up later." And once again, Branwyn wanted to kick him. Then again, the answer was complicated. At least, she *hoped* so.

"Hold that thought, Brynn," she said quickly. "Hopefully we can get this sorted out before she gets back."

Charlie peeked around Severin and said sadly, "Mom..."

The Hellqueen Imani stilled her monstrous thrashing at the sound and turned toward Severin. "Why is she still here, Severin? Why? Do you hate us both? Did you bring her here to torture me?"

Severin said acidly, "I *really* wish I'd dealt with Tucker before

Gale. They wouldn't have needed *any* other villain for their little story."

Cat joined them. "In that case, I have good news for you."

Capricorn and Yejun entered the huddle, Capricorn pausing to take back their hat and jacket from Branwyn. She hadn't been particularly careful holding them, but as soon as Capricorn put them on, they looked perfect again.

Severin gave Cat his flat look. "Oh?"

"I'm going to cut Imani out of the haunt," said Cat, twisting his hand to show off his weird super-dense knife. "The haunt will fight back. We need to weaken and distract it." He met Severin's gaze. "Previously we treated the haunt as an extension of Imani. But it's not, is it, Brynn?"

Brynn, still outside the huddle because she was keeping Imani away, said, "It's more than four hundred additional souls, most of which are fully charged up again." She swallowed. "It's a town that killed to keep its secrets, even the secrets they hated."

"Imani isn't holding them anymore, either," said Yejun. "Well, not tightly. They could escape if they really wanted to."

"They just don't want to," said Brynn, her eyes dark. "How can they be so—" She clamped her mouth shut as Imani turned toward her.

"They're wicked," hissed Imani. "Slow and weak and small, but all twisted up and see the chains they weave for each other."

"All of them?" asked Brynn in a small voice.

"Let's find out," said Cat, and his voice was almost cheerful in comparison. "Those that have lingered because they feel bound by the community might move on if staying became particularly unpleasant."

"You still talk like an angel, remnant," said Severin, but his shark smile was cracking across his face.

Scare the shit out of them, Severin, Branwyn thought, remembering the Court of Stone again.

Cat's eyes narrowed. "Be the true devil of this hell they've constructed, kaiju."

"What's going on?" demanded Amber, popping up where Capricorn had been standing a moment before. AT wriggled in beside her.

"Severin and AT are going to divide the ghosts into those who'd like to be free, and those who prefer the haunt," said Cat. "I'm going to cut Imani from the haunt. You're going to blow the horn once Imani is safe." His gaze went to Brynn.

"And I keep holding Imani?" Brynn guessed.

Slowly, Cat shook his head. "She's resisting you. She can't resist this." He lowered his gaze until he was looking at Charlie, still peeking around Severin's back. "Can you help us, Charlie?"

"Um," said Charlie nervously. "Help how?" When Severin tried to push her back behind him again, she dodged his hand. "How?"

"Hold Imani's hands," said Cat simply. "Tell her you love her."

"Um," said Branwyn. "Isn't Brynn trying to stop exactly that right now, because the haunt wants to eat her?"

"She'll need protection," agreed Cat. He looked at Severin, who was still smiling, or at least baring his teeth. "Some protective charms would help."

Severin's smile vanished. "Not from me, they wouldn't."

"Ah," said Cat. He glanced around, spotted Capricorn talking to Jennifer, and looked away.

Yejun said diffidently, "I could probably protect her. Not with charms, but, you know, my way."

Severin gave Yejun a hard stare. "How the hell did you make it through childhood, kid?"

"I relied on spite," said Yejun casually. "Are you going to let us do this?"

Severin crouched down beside Charlie. "What do you think?"

Charlie scowled. "You brought me here 'cause we were going to sort this out. Now you're waffling?"

Severin countered, "I said I'd take care of you. Right now, taking care of you means getting you out of here, not letting some freak babysit you."

Charlie shook her head. "He's not a freak. He's *cool*. Unlike *you*." She pushed her way past Severin and took Yejun's hand. "All I have to do is hold my mom's hand, Mister?" she asked Cat.

Yejun, startled by Charlie's hand in his, turned his head to Severin. But Severin seemed unbothered by Charlie's words or choice. He rose to his feet and looked past the group, out at the haunt, his shark smile creeping back onto his face.

"That's all you have to do, but you can't let go, no matter what," said Cat.

"Okay," said Charlie. "I'm good at that."

"Do you have a role for me, or should I improvise?" Branwyn finally asked, holding her hammer in both hands. It still had a single remaining soul charge in the black diamond, and it quivered on the edge of release.

Cat shrugged. "You and Brynn hold on to what you've got and be ready for things to go wrong." He glanced up at Haliel, who gave him a thumbs up as he added, "They probably will."

"I'm going," said Severin. "Don't dawdle, AT." He darted away, his glittering aura cutting through the haunt's gloom. In the distance, a low moan rose.

AT hesitated, glancing at Cat. When he nodded, she and her dogs ran off in a different direction.

Branwyn studied Cat. Something about the Wild Hunt had changed since she'd gone into Faerie, and it centered on the tall blond man. Everybody else watched him like he was a bomb about to go off. Everybody except Jennifer, who had her gaze firmly fixed on Capricorn.

But Severin had accepted his plan. And Branwyn knew she'd need to do *something* whenever the beast of fire and thorns returned with Rhianna. Probably best to reserve her strength for that. But it left her uneasy. Cat had a plan for her, she was certain. He was too smart to leave her power on the shelf. But he obviously wanted to keep that part a secret. Why?

"All right, Charlie," said Cat. "Your turn. Go to your mother."

Charlie looked at the apparition in the ballgown. "It's like a Halloween costume, right? Like she's put on a costume and forgotten how to take it off?"

"Smart kid," said Amber.

Yejun took off his sunglasses and said gently, "I'm going to keep my hands on your head, Charlie."

Charlie nodded absently and walked over to her mom, Yejun close behind her. As soon as she was within reach, Imani reached out for her daughter: not the mother's embrace, but a hungry, mindless flail.

Charlie flinched as her mother's hands passed through her. But a line appeared between Yejun's brows and faint luminescence flickered around the little girl. Then Charlie took a deep breath and grabbed her mother's hands.

Before, Brynn had clearly been serving as a channel for the ghost and the living child to touch each other. This time, Yejun was doing something different. Charlie's faint glow deepened, coming from beneath her skin. Branwyn was uncomfortably reminded of the *glint* she'd seen in Rhianna, although she couldn't identify why.

"Come out, mom," whispered Charlie. The ghost twitched more, but didn't pull away from Charlie. "You can do this, mom... Mom?" Hesitantly, she started singing a lullaby.

Slowly, the real Imani emerged from the Hellqueen version, like she was surfacing from deep water. The Hellqueen dress shredded away from her, but the pieces hovered behind her, each one reaching out for the woman.

The real Imani, but not entirely. She didn't speak this time, and her gaze was far away. But she quieted, until she was still, her hands limp in her daughter's. Branwyn's skin crawled at Imani's blind eyes, as she remembered her journey through what the faeries had called the belly of Death, remembered clinging to the pain of her burning tattoo.

Quietly, Brynn slipped her hand into Branwyn's. Branwyn hadn't even noticed her releasing Imani, so caught had she been by the memory of clinging to life. She dragged in a breath, her fingers tightening on Brynn's. She hadn't felt Rhianna in the belly of Death. Hopefully the bond between mother and daughter was stronger.

Cat moved behind Imani, his blade out. He stood there for a long moment, before saying, "Branwyn?"

"Already?" muttered Branwyn and glanced at Brynn. Her little sister's face was pale and when Branwyn tugged at her hand, Brynn didn't let go.

"I'm not letting you wander off too," said Brynn fiercely.

Branwyn tightened her hand again. "All right." She towed her sister closer to Cat. "What's wrong?"

Cat looked down at the strange blade in his hand. "It's... resisting." He offered it hilt first to Branwyn. "You've done well with blades before."

Amber, still clinging to the Horn, called, "I *warned* you, Cat —" and shut her mouth.

Branwyn almost laughed at his description of her past with blades. "I don't like working with weapons," she warned him. "I probably can't do any more than you can."

"The Ragged Blade isn't a weapon," he said. "It's a tool. Please take it and see if you can do what I can't."

Branwyn closed her fingers around the hilt.

It was neither artifact, nor Machine. If there were nodes buried in the blade's wildly dense layering of Geometric lines, she couldn't detect them. But despite that lack, there was an *awareness* in the blade. It spoke to her, and she didn't understand. It felt good in her hand though.

It needed something. Not the forge of her soul, which it didn't seem to notice. Something else...

She thought she heard Severin's distant whisper. It didn't matter though. She'd been asked to do what only she could do. She just had to understand how to connect to the Blade. Connect to the Blade, like Rhianna had connected to the haunt.

Dreamily, she wrenched her other hand away from Brynn and brought her palm to the blade. It had been her unscarred palm, but now the edge of the Ragged Blade delicately parted her skin and tasted her blood. Then it spoke to her again.

Is this right?

She saw new lines all around her: lines completely independent from the Geometry, lines where the indivisible could be sheared apart, never to join again. But although there were lines through *everything*, the Blade found most of the lines repulsive. A few were neutral, and even fewer attracted the blade.

She could see the line to separate Imani from the haunt. It repelled the blade as she focused on it.

Is this right? asked the Blade once again, the words carrying their own context. Cat had an ulterior motive in separating Imani from her haunt, and the Ragged Blade refused to be used for its wielder's benefit.

Yes, Branwyn thought.

Then help me, said the Blade, and Branwyn leaned on the Blade, driving it against the repelling line.

———

BRYNN TWISTED her hands together as Branwyn went off into her *working* headspace and cut open her own hand. This was not what she'd signed up for. This was not what she wanted to watch. And

Rhianna was—but surely she'd *know*, right? If Rhianna was dead, she, Brynn of the Wild Hunt, would *have* to know. Truly know, not just have a horrible suspicion that wouldn't go away. Right?

I hate this, she whispered to the horses.

There is nothing good about today, said Earth Horse mournfully.

This isn't what we're supposed to do, fretted Gold Horse.

Sweat along her brow and blood flowing freely from her hand, Branwyn pushed the knife out and down. It moved slowly, and Imani's flickering resumed as Branwyn cut.

"Steady," whispered Cat. "Keep holding her, Charlie. This will work."

Branwyn cut and cut. It took what seemed like hours. The moaning of the haunt became a low howl, and Brynn could feel terrified souls fleeing into the sky and the great beyond. Technically, that was good: a goal achieved. But she couldn't feel like it was *right*, not the way it was being accomplished.

"Mouse alert," said Amber nervously, and added, "Oh, I guess that's me." Brynn looked where Amber was looking. A red rose of fire was blooming deeper in the town.

Sharply, Cat said, "That's not a mouse. Amber, you have to keep it away from Branwyn and Charlie."

Amber sighed and tucked the Horn away. As she did, Brynn said, "What about me? What is it?"

"I don't know," said Cat, hurriedly. "The bane from the ark, I think. And if it comes to it, yes, you keep it away from them too, if you can."

Twelve souls, Brynn remembered. But shouldn't it have them already? Why would it come back without them? She looked closely at the creature forming: long legs, long nose, bushy tail, a mane of fire. Her breath hissed between her teeth as she *saw*.

It had four souls: four souls that had escaped the Haunt and it had recaptured; three souls from Tucker... and Rhianna. And now it was back where it'd started, following the last soul in Branwyn's hammer and ready to acquire seven more souls after that.

Amber ran over to the bane and then hopped backward as a paw came down where she'd been planning to stop. "That's a lot bigger than a mouse!"

Brynn stood, stunned into stillness. How could Rhianna be one of the bane's souls? Why hadn't Branwyn told her? Why hadn't Brynn herself *known*? What good was any of this?

"Oof," said Branwyn, as she finished her long cut. "Ouch…"

Imani shuddered all over, and Charlie's song hitched although her grip on her mother's hands never faltered. Abruptly the shadows of the haunt grew long and thick, and Brynn felt the last of the soul charges on her skin lift away. Darkness flashed from Branwyn's hammer, too. She hardly cared.

"Branwyn," she shrieked, furious, terrified, despairing. Amber was struggling with the bane, but the bane seemed to be playing with Amber rather than truly hampered.

"What?" said Branwyn, startled. "Oh," she added as she saw the beast. Anguish twisted across her face and her grip tightened on the Ragged Blade. "Maybe I can…"

Cat said, "And now is exactly when I need Amber. Hmm."

The Ragged Blade vanished from Branwyn's hand. She stared down at the absence. "Oh, come on!"

"You'll have to run, Branwyn," said Cat. "Bait it away. It can't interrupt Charlie."

"Is it dangerous now?" asked Branwyn, surprised. "I thought Rhianna… oh." The bane knocked Amber over and looked around.

"It's dangerous," said Brynn, wiping her nose. "It needs eight more souls, Branwyn."

Branwyn shivered before plunging past them all. "Hey," she shouted. "Over here!"

Let us out, said Earth Horse, and suddenly he was commanding rather than depressed. Now *you let us out, Brynn*.

"Yes," Brynn said. She raised her arms, and color exploded around her. The horses emerged from her running, all but Sunset

Horse. Silver Horse charged to Branwyn and slid to her knees, scrambling to her feet when Branwyn was only half on.

Black Horse and Gold Horse followed Silver Horse, but split around the giant bane, circling it and then charging it. Red Horse went to Amber, Earth Horse bucked in place and only after that did Sunset Horse step out, and stand absolutely still.

Brynn, please, said Earth Horse. *Jennifer.*

With a jolt, Brynn realized Jennifer was barely visible in the distance, running away from the school with Capricorn beside her. No, not away from the school, to the post office where the ark rested still. "What's she doing?"

Something scary. Something related to the demon. She won't listen to me. Brynn! And Earth Horse nudged her so hard she almost fell down. She caught his mane, and he started moving, dragging her with him as he followed Jennifer.

"But—" began Brynn. *But Branwyn. But Rhianna. But Cat...* But Earth Horse was frantic, terrified. He needed her.

Go, said Sunset Horse. *You've done all you can here.*

Brynn went.

———

HER SISTER's horse danced under Branwyn, and she tried very hard to stay on. The beast of fire and thorns bounded forward, and the silver-maned horse skittered to one side, staying out of reach.

When the horse had first knelt for Branwyn to mount, she'd thought the creature meant to help her flee. But apparently that would have been too easy. Instead Silver Horse was using her as *bait*, just like Cat had suggested: staying close enough to keep the beast more interested in Branwyn than Charlie.

Branwyn was still dazed from her experience with the Ragged Blade. Her hand hurt, and her chest ached. For a moment she'd thought she could use the Ragged Blade to free

Rhianna from the beast. But no sooner had she thought it than the blade had vanished from her hand.

Silver Horse hopped to one side as a taloned paw flashed out, and Branwyn almost toppled off. The beast sat back on its haunches, looking puzzled. Its nose twitched, and it turned back toward Charlie and Imani. Silver Horse stomped her foot, and suddenly Black Horse and Gold Horse charged in from the sides, whirling and kicking the beast.

It was a well organized attack, but it had little impact on the beast. It growled like thunder and caught Gold Horse with one paw, sending the horse flying. He recovered like a gymnast, but stayed away, moving warily. Black Horse dodged another paw and backed off.

Once again, Silver Horse danced in place, but the beast gave her a confused look and once again turned toward Imani and Charlie.

"It can't see me very well when I'm on you," Branwyn whispered. Silver Horse flicked her ears back and somehow sidled right out from under Branwyn. She landed awkwardly on her feet and stumbled as the beast's attention snapped back around.

What do we do? Branwyn didn't know. She'd recovered a little of her wits on Silver Horse's back, but she knew just how unstoppable the beast of fire and thorns was. Brynn had said it needed eight more souls. Was that the only way to banish it? What did that mean for Rhianna?

The beast sprang forward, and Branwyn knew one thing for certain: she wanted to live longer than the next minute. She fled across the ghostly school playground. She wasn't anywhere near fast enough, but when it didn't immediately catch her, she figured the horses were doing their best to slow it down.

The beast screamed, and Severin whispered, *I am going to kill Shatiel someday.*

Branwyn didn't stop, didn't look back until the beast

screamed again, from farther away. Then she dared to stop for breath, and a glance over her shoulder.

Severin was on top of the beast, and he wasn't alone. A mass of black shadows entangled him, and it took Branwyn a moment to realize it wasn't *his* darkness, but the shadows of the haunt. The evil in Tucker *had* fought back against Imani's separation, and what it had fought was him. Severin looked awful, scarcely human. His eyes were so dark and his face so pale that it was as if the flesh had been flayed from his skull, while the fire of the beast's mane licked around him.

Branwyn caught enough of her breath to move again and didn't. She thought she ought to stay with some member of the Hunt because she felt very *exposed* out here. But the only Hunts-folk she could see was Amber and Cat and Yejun, all standing around Imani. Where had Brynn gone?

Then Amber shouted, "Dammit!" and Cat shouted, "Bran-wyn!" and Branwyn realized that the whole Ragged Knife thing hadn't been what Cat had expected to use her for. No, that was now. Of course.

———

"THIS IS ALL GOING WRONG," snapped Amber, keenly aware of her torn blouse. That bane had been a lot more *physical* than she expected. "You have no idea what you're doing. This only worked before because of the Fiddler."

"No," said Cat. "This part always would have worked. Let me see the Horn, Amber."

Scowling, she brought it out. It felt nice under her hands, but now that she was angry and in pain, she realized it felt nice the same way her master's skin had felt nice against hers. The Horn was a new master, and she couldn't help wondering if she'd claimed it or it had claimed her. Haliel had tried to warn her, but had she listened? Of course not. She'd done this so Jennifer would be happier, and she'd done this for Cat, and she was just realizing there was a paradox hidden in the depths like a treacherous reef.

Cat stroked his fingers along the brass shine. He sighed, and once again Amber's heart hurt like it was being wrenched out of her. She loved the whole stupid Hunt: Brynn and AT, of course, and Jennifer, and obnoxious Yejun and even annoying Cat. She loved him and he wanted to leave them and the *Horn didn't care*. It was a piece of magic metal with a single purpose

"Dammit!" she shouted, as Cat shouted, "Branwyn!"

"Guys," said Yejun. "The Horn's strength isn't really helping me here. I can't protect Charlie for much longer, and the haunt wants them *both* now."

"Nothing's going to happen to Charlie," snapped Amber. She had the damn Horn. She'd at least make sure of that.

Branwyn ran up, panting. "Now what?" Amber sprang forward and came down with both feet on a pitch-black shadow writhing across the ground after Branwyn. It twitched under her toes.

Cat said, "In a moment, there will be a vacancy in the Hunt. I need you to use the tool that will become available to bind a new Hunter to the Horn, please."

"What," said Branwyn flatly, which is about how Amber felt, even though she'd known it was coming. Glumly, she noticed Yejun wasn't surprised either. Maybe everybody knew, and she was the only one who cared.

Then Sunset Horse shouted silently. Amber had never heard Sunset Horse's mental voice before, but it was unmistakably her as she pushed her way between Branwyn and Cat. At her words, tears sprang to Amber's eyes.

Did you think I would just let you go?

Cat stopped breathing for a moment. Softly, he said, "Sunset."

Sunset looked at him steadily, her head turned. Amber

couldn't hear what she said next, but Cat brought his hand up to her nose. "You'll have a better partner."

Sunset Horse pushed her head forward and stepped on Cat's foot. "Ouch," he said mildly. "It will be all right." He hesitated. "Please, Sunset Horse. If you refuse, I won't. I can't. But please…"

Sunset Horse knocked her head against his shoulder, and whirled away, and Cat's shoulders relaxed a fraction.

He'd stay for his horse? Amber wanted to screech. But Red Horse bumped her from behind and she blew out her breath instead. The horses had worked hard on training them. It said something that even Cat hadn't been immune.

Also, if Sunset Horse rejects his replacement, we acquire new problems, said Red Horse dryly.

Is this going to work? Amber asked Red Horse plaintively. *Aren't you afraid?*

You know, I'm not, said Red Horse. *Gold Horse is, and the others. But… sometimes things change. You're not the Hunters-Who-Were. We shouldn't expect you to be.*

But what if everything goes kaboom?

Why are you helping him if you're afraid of that?

Amber sniffled. *Because I love them.*

Red Horse nudged her again. *Brynn has worked to convince us mortal love isn't always bad. And Cat loves you, too. Maybe that will make the difference.*

Cat finished saying something to Branwyn and looked around. "I'm glad Brynn and AT aren't here right now."

Amber glanced up at Haliel, who hadn't budged. The Angel of Joy was no longer writing, but staring down at Cat with glowing eyes.

Cat went on, staring at nothing in particular. "I really think it will be okay. You'll all be fine. It's…" He stopped, frowning, and Amber realized abruptly that Cat, too, was frightened. She left

Red Horse standing on the animate shadow and Sunset Horse trampling another one and joined Cat.

When she put her hand against his shoulder, he glanced down at her. "I really hope I stay me," he said conversationally. "As long as I stay me, I think it will work out."

Yejun said roughly, "If you don't know, man... I *warned* you about making decisions under Goldilocks' influence, you dork."

"I don't know," said Cat quietly. "I'm not doing this for Haliel." He waved a hand at Imani. "And it's far too late to go back now."

Then Cat closed his eyes and spread his wings. The Hunt dissolved as he became what he was not allowed to be. The dogs howled and AT yelled, but Amber only closed her eyes.

For a moment, the Horn still held her together. Amber could no longer feel her found family around her, no longer sense the haunt as anything other than a concentration of magic. She was *so hungry*. But she was bound still to the Horn.

Would it last? Would *she* last like this? She couldn't tell. The magic of the Horn was shifting wildly. But she had this moment, at least. Hopefully, she wouldn't need more.

———

ONE OF THE few things Branwyn would casually admit to having in common with Severin was their mutual dislike of angels. Shatiel was the closest she'd come to meeting one she'd liked, and he'd had to ruin that by demonstrating his really terrible ideas about *boundaries*.

And Umbriel had, *okay, probably hadn't* brainwashed her sister, and Hadraniel had tried to steal her volition, and the blonde overhead just seemed *annoying*... but you never forget your first.

And there he was, standing in front of her now. The wings of light that arced up and over them called up the memory of the wildfire that had surrounded them when the angel Ettoriel had tried to kill Marley and Penny and two little girls.

Branwyn backed away a step, and caught herself as Amber said, "Ouch! Branwyn, hurry!"

But Branwyn wasn't sure what to do. She could just barely sense the strands binding what had been Cat to the Horn of the Wild Hunt, but the Horn itself was vast, old magic and even if she could catch its attention, she didn't know if she had the strength to make it listen. It wasn't a created artifact but a natural one, and those worried her.

The angel opened his eyes, and they were blue, Cat's eyes. His gaze swept across everybody and he raised one hand above his head. "Old friend…" he whispered and his voice was music.

Motherfucker Severin whispered, but it didn't appear that the angel had been addressing him. A horizontal wheel larger than a man appeared overhead, toothed like a gear and spinning in triplicate. Haliel clapped her hands in delight even as she skittered quite a distance from the wheel.

Branwyn had seen the wheel before, too, although last time she had no idea of what she was looking at. Now she understood, and she swallowed hard. She was used to working with Machine fragments, and once she'd molded one of the Machine Swords. This, drifting right above her, was a partial manifestation of an actual, unbroken, complete Machine. She couldn't help but marvel at how close the angel came to touching it.

Then he said, "Artificer," and spread his other hand toward her. Branwyn remembered what he'd said about an *available tool.* "Oh my God."

The angel smiled faintly. "Not exactly." The celestial wheel moved from hovering over him to hovering over Branwyn, descending as it did so. Branwyn stared at it, giddiness gradually taking the place of all her other emotions. She looked at Imani, staring at her daughter with wide, blind eyes and frozen by Charlie's broken humming. Charlie was trying fiercely to concentrate on her mother, tears streaming down her cheeks.

Branwyn had saved Penny's life with a key she'd cobbled together from three Machine fragments. A wild exhilaration filled her. She could *do so much more* with this full Machine.

"The Horn, Artificer," said the angel.

The descending Machine came to rest right above Branwyn's head. Incandescence filled her, overwhelmed her. Unlike BELIAL, this Machine didn't try to impose its name on her, or if it did, she couldn't retain it. But that previous experience helped her still. She surfaced from the incandescence knowing her own name. That was what mattered. That, and the forge of her soul.

She looked around and clearly saw the Horn of the Wild Hunt, with strands flapping freely. And there was Imani, free from the haunt, a naked soul held to the world by nothing more than her daughter's love. She deserved better. Branwyn could give it to her, and after that, she could do so much more…

Charlie's tears became sobs, and Branwyn blinked at the direction of her own thoughts. Then she spread out her hands and took up the strands of the Horn, fed them through the Machine touching her soul, and tied them to Imani's nodes, one by one, so that once again the Wild Hunt had six riders.

When she finished, the Machine lifted away from her and returned to the angel. The incandescence that filled her faded, and Branwyn was both bereft and grateful. She staggered, and Amber caught her.

"You've done well, children," said the angel, touching Charlie and Yejun as he circled them. "Just a little longer." He placed both his hands on Imani's head and brightness flashed around them both.

Son of a bitch, said Severin, but weakly.

The brightness faded and Imani blinked. She was still a ghost, but full awareness had returned to her eyes. She looked up at the angel. "I… Yes. Yes."

Branwyn looked around. Severin still entangled with the shadows and the beast of fire and thorns. AT and the dogs were also harrying the beast, but the shadows stayed away from them. Where the shadows did move on the ground, deep cracks opened, and stars glinted within them.

"Is the Hunt working?" she demanded. "Everything required in place?"

Hesitantly, Amber nodded. "I think so? There's something—"

"Then *deal with the haunt*," Branwyn shouted.

Amber stared down at the horn. "I've never..." She shook her head, then lifted the Horn to her mouth and blew.

The sound was just as sweet as when Jennifer played, which seemed to give Amber confidence. For the third time, the haunt shuddered against the power of the Horn. Yejun and Amber and Imani all developed that superreal quality, and somehow Jennifer and Brynn and AT were right there, too, while doing something else entirely.

Jennifer glanced up as she stood in front of something, gave a strange little smile, and looked down again. AT fell back with her dogs. Brynn held Earth Horse's head and cried. Something flickered between all of them: dogs, horses, people.

Then the haunt that had been Imani's prison and Imani's revenge shuddered apart, until it was nothing more than black dust that streamed into the horn. A soul howled as it was taken away, but Branwyn didn't feel an ounce of sympathy. They could have left. They didn't.

As the haunt vanished, the original ruins of Tucker returned, although the deep, strange cracks in the ground created by the haunt remained. It was dawn, but Branwyn had no idea what the day was.

The angel spread his wings wide and looked up at the deep blue sky. Then he walked over to where Gale still stood, shoulders slumped, forgotten and apparently content with that. The angel put his hand on Gale's forehead and murmured, "Since I'm here..." There was another bright flash and Gale twisted away from him.

"Stay away from me," he snarled. "You have no right—" He stopped, pushed his hands through his hair, said, "Fuck," and walked away.

The angel turned back to the others. "Just a little enforcement of Imani's judgement. He'll do what he needs to," he said pleasantly. "And now..."

His wings swept down and his eyes closed. Lightning flashed in the clear sky, and his Machine companion rose back to the heavens again. "And now...." The angel repeated, and this time he sounded troubled. "What's my name?" he asked, honestly bewildered.

"Cat!" shouted Amber, as Haliel crowed, "Ettoriel!"

"Cat," said Yejun, shaking his hands as he lifted them from Charlie's head.

"You'd better damn well be Cat," muttered Branwyn.

"Cat," said AT, fiercely.

"Cat," whispered Brynn, her voice like the wind.

"I love you," whispered Jennifer through the same wind.

"Oh," said the angel. "Yes."

His wings vanished with a pop, along with the glory that surrounded him. Cat stood in the dust of Tucker, blinking a little.

"Poop," said Haliel. "Well, Slick is Slick no matter what anybody else calls him." She started writing in her book again.

Good enough, said Severin, and slid off the bloody beast of fire and thorns to land in a pile on the ground. *Stay alive for a minute or three, cupcake, and I'll get you and Charlie away from that thing.*

The beast looked around. But it didn't notice Branwyn or Charlie. It noticed Cat. Cat, who somehow wasn't an angel anymore, but wasn't a member of the Hunt, either. Cat, who was mortal.

He turned to gaze at it, his mouth crooking in a wry, sad smile.

———

BRYNN CLENCHED her fists as Jennifer stood in front of the ark. She'd refused to help Jen put the lid back on, but ever so helpful, ever so strong Capricorn had been there. Brynn didn't even know why she refused, except that Earth Horse was frantic and convinced that whatever Jen was doing would hurt her as nothing else could. They'd both watched sullenly as Jen drew a magic circle around the ark, with Capricorn walking along beside her and fixing it in place.

And then Cat had broken the Hunt, and Branwyn had reforged it, and you'd think that might have given Jen second thoughts. But she'd turned her attention back to the ark almost immediately.

"Like this?" she said to Capricorn, placing her hands on the replaced lid.

"Almost," he said. "Yes, like that!" He kept his hands over hers. "Remember how I explained that only a mortal could destroy a relic?"

"Yes, of course," said Jennifer, giving him a wide-eyed look.

"I sort of rounded the truth, there," Capricorn said, with a guilty expression. "So I do need to warn you that there's more to destroying a relic than the ritual. There's a price that has to be paid, too. A price only mortals can pay."

Amusement flashed across Jennifer's face. "There always seems to be. What is it?"

"It varies," said Capricorn delicately. "But it can be overwhelming, if you don't have courage. I thought you did, as soon as I saw you. But only you know."

Jennifer, please, said Earth Horse.

Cat, screamed Sunset Horse, and Brynn jumped. Instinctively she reached for him through the Horn, but found only a stranger.

Why won't he run*?* demanded Silver Horse.

We'll get him, said Red Horse. *Whether he likes it or not.*

Jen glanced at Earth Horse and moved a hand as if trying to soothe him. "I never thought I was particularly brave." She exhaled. "But I know how to do what I have to. And I have to do this."

Magic flared around her. With a resounding crack, the ark shattered. The bone dust within the ark rose into the air, spiraling around Jen and becoming the red glow of roses. Then, all at once, the light flowed inside Jen.

With a tiny little smile, Capricorn said, "I rounded the truth. Nobody can break a relic, Jennifer. But mortals can become one."

———

As HORSES and dogs did their best to interfere with the beast of fire and thorns, and Amber and her red stallion argued with Cat, Branwyn kept her gaze on the slumped form of Severin. He hadn't said *anything* since telling her he'd remove her and Charlie. She wanted very badly to demand, to force his attention. But she resisted, she resisted. She'd keep on resisting until the beast was bearing down on her and Charlie, after it had consumed Cat. At that point, well... she wanted to live. She'd do what she had to.

Then, without any warning, the beast of fire and thorns exploded into rose petals which faded into nothingness. Everybody stopped moving, except to look around in confusion.

Branwyn had been still long enough. She ran over to Severin. He sprawled on the ground, a physical wreck. His eyes were open, though, and glinting as he looked up at her.

"Why aren't you healed?" she demanded.

"I did say that next time you made me bleed, I'd need you to kiss it and make it better," he said lazily. "I happen to be bleeding quite a lot."

She scowled down at him. "Kiss or kick? I did not make you bleed now any more than the other times you tangled with that thing. You had no problems healing yourself when you had half your face burned off."

He gave her his shark grin. "Sit down beside me, anyhow, cupcake."

Begrudgingly, she sat down tailor-style beside him. "The haunt was pretty nasty, huh?"

"Oh yes. That's Imani for you."

"All those other assholes, too," Branwyn noted.

Severin chuckled creakily. "But it took Imani to make them dangerous to *me*. I'm glad you saved her."

Alarmed at this confession of feelings, Branwyn said, "You aren't dying, are you?"

"Nope," he said. "Though I'll tell you something. When you use a celestial's true name, they don't simply hear you. They get stronger. Just for a little while. Like a surge of adrenalin." Branwyn's scowl returned, and he eyed her in amusement. "I don't need you to say my name to get that effect, cupcake. All I need you to do is touch me."

Branwyn narrowed her eyes. "Are you lying to me?"

"Try it and see."

She looked him up and down. Not only did he have numerous hideous burns and long gashes, but the horrible blackness of the haunt's attack shadows lingered on his arms and legs. He *had* healed a little as she spoke with him. But it had been much faster before.

Sighing, she put her hand on his forehead and stroked his hair. He closed his eyes rather than gloating, which further convinced Branwyn that he was at the kaiju equivalent of death's door. But his injuries did heal faster, and after a moment or two, the black taint faded from his extremities.

"What happened to the beast?" he asked, eventually, his eyes still closed. "I felt it vanish, but that's all."

"That's... all. It vanished. I assume it'll be back again. I'll have to figure out how to get Rhianna out of it. Maybe Brynn can help..."

Severin opened his eyes and looked up at her without speaking. She didn't like it, so she looked away, twisting her fingers in his hair. Then, surprised, she said, "Here comes Jen. She's... different."

She stood up, pulling Severin after her for an instant. "Oops," she said, released his hair, and ran over to where the rest of the Hunt—and Cat—stood around Imani and Charlie.

Jen walked beside Brynn, with Earth Horse on her other side. Capricorn trailed behind them, smiling cheerfully.

"I should have known," said Haliel darkly.

"She's not just 'Skipper' now, Haliel!" said Capricorn.

"She'll always be Skipper to *me*, you vandal."

Jennifer had her own set of tattoos now, and the way she walked was... *different.* There was something almost animalistic about her. Her hair had changed color, too: it had been dull brown before, but now it glinted a metallic copper. As she got closer, the marks on her arms and neck resolved into thorny, twining roses.

Those damn roses.

"Jennifer?" AT said hesitantly. "What happened? We felt *something* after the bane vanished. What did you do?"

Jen held out her arms, showing the marks on her skin. "I had a bit of an argument. But don't worry. I won."

Brynn blurted, "She broke the ark, and then she absorbed the bane. It was amazing. I thought for a minute the bane was going to be part of the Wild Hunt in her place."

"Oh my god," said Branwyn, alone in her distress. "What happened to the souls inside the beast?"

Jennifer tilted her head. "Let's find out."

"Wait!" said Amber urgently. "If you're about to summon that thing like Brynn calls the horses, remember about the twelve souls it has to eat?"

Jennifer gave her a little smile. "I'm a wizard, not a spell, Amber. I have slightly more control than a stone box." The roses leapt off her skin and writhed together above her, and a moment later the enormous beast of fire and thorns landed on the ground beyond.

Once again, it was different. A wolf, or possibly a fox, and now it had it had the wings of a dragon, too. It sat down and lifted a paw as if to shake hands. Gently, Jennifer said, "Let them go."

The beast inhaled, then exhaled flame. Four figures appeared in the flame, and three of them almost instantly faded away. One lingered as the flame vanished.

"Rhianna," Branwyn whispered, and ran to her sister. She looked just like the other ghosts, just like Imani did still. Branwyn reached for her, and her fingers passed right through.

"Well, that was odd," said Rhianna, looking thoughtful.

"You're a ghost," said Branwyn wretchedly. "You're really dead?" Suppressed panic rose up.

Rhianna tapped her lips with a finger. "I don't quite know."

"She's—" began Amber behind them, and then, "Ouch!" Brynn came up and took Rhianna and Branwyn's hands, bringing them into contact with each other. Her head was low, her hair in her face, but Branwyn didn't need to see anything to know she was crying.

All Branwyn could think was that their mother would cry too. *Everybody* would cry. And Branwyn would have to say *She volunteered,* and it wouldn't mean a thing, because she was Rhianna's older sister. How could this be happening?

"That's a neat trick, brat," said Rhianna fondly. "But I don't think it's… oh yes. You should probably stand back." As she said that, she started to sparkle.

A celestial numina spread itself over them: not Ettoriel's, not Severin's, but one that felt vaguely familiar to Branwyn. She glared around, looking for the angel that had led her sister to this stupid sacrifice. But save for his numina, Umbriel did not appear.

Rhianna smiled up at the sky as the sparkling became flashing, and then each sparkle became flesh and blood and bone. For a moment, Rhianna glittered like a galaxy, and then the sparkles faded away, leaving behind a nude but very much alive Rhianna.

"Hmm," she said, inspecting her hands and arms. Then she spread her arms wide. "Witness the magic of expense reports, Branwyn!"

Branwyn stared at her sister, and then leapt upon her, gathering her into a fierce, physical hug. Brynn burrowed in between them and both elder and younger sister cried on the middle one, who looked up at the sky and said, "Thanks, boss."

"I don't believe it," said Amber faintly. "How did she do that?"

"He," said Cat helpfully. "The angel Umbriel. And very expensively, I suspect."

"This is his body," confided Rhianna to Branwyn, who was wiping tears from her face with one arm while hanging onto Rhianna with the other. "I mean, it's my body now, and I do think he's done a very good job of adjusting it for me. But he'll have to make a new vessel for himself, so it'll be awhile before I can get my safety charms refreshed. I'll probably be stuck on desk work until then. Maybe I can take a vacation!" Then she blinked. "Oh, right. Excuse me."

Rhianna extracted herself from between Branwyn and Brynn and walked over to where Imani and Charlie stood close together. "I've got something for you from my boss," she informed Charlie. Rhianna put her hand over her heart, extracting something that glowed to Branwyn's Geometry vision, and pushed it into one of Charlie's nodes. "That'll help when you get hungry." She glanced back at Branwyn, her mouth twisted wryly. "No vacation for a while. Apparently the budget's been all used up. I've got to be my Advisor's hands for a while."

She looked around. "Ooh, are those our bags? I have an emergency minidress in there! Come on, Bran-Brynn!"

———

AMBER SHOOK her head as Branwyn and Brynn chased their very strange sister through the remains of Tucker toward the campsite. A moment later, Severin strolled after them, pausing only long enough to give Imani a long look. Then he said, "I'll be back, Charlie," and continued on after the Lennox women.

"She still has a soul," Amber complained. "If her angel had made her a spawn or changeling or whatever they call it, I could understand what just happened. But she's got a soul. I can see it."

"Oh, hush, Amber," said Yejun impatiently. "Jen, you've got an extra node now. That's so… cool. *Ten nodes.*"

"Do I?" asked Jen, vaguely surprised. "I suppose that makes sense." She held out her hand, and the big red bane turned into colored light and streamed back onto her skin.

"Well done," said Cat, smiling. "And thank you." Jen looked at him, but didn't smile, or say a word.

"And you, man," said Yejun. "What happened to you? For a minute you were an angel and now you're just… you. Still not a normal human."

"You should talk," said AT. "He *smells* the same. That's good enough for me."

"No, I'm not what I was," Cat said slowly. "But the power of a celestial is tied to their name, and my name is Cat."

"Doesn't really matter," said Haliel, sniffing. "You took the power. It'll keep coming back again. Although there might be a way to make it really yours." She smiled slowly. "Nina could probably help. I hear the girl has quite the knack for naming things."

Cat looked at Jennifer instead of Haliel. "Before you were interrupted, you were about to tell me what you *didn't* want me to do. Will you finish that?"

She studied him and then glanced down at her tattooed arms. Behind her, Capricorn bounced up and down on her toes gleefully.

When Jennifer answered, it was without any of her usual hesitance. Instead, very matter-of-factly, she said, "I didn't want you to go away with Haliel. Perhaps that's wrong of me, but I don't care."

"Then I won't," Cat said happily. "I'll stay with Yejun, instead."

Amber felt a lump rise in her throat, and blurted around it, "Oh thank God. He'd never wear clean clothes again if you left."

"And maybe I can bring Sunset Horse carrots sometimes," Cat added.

"This is all very sweet," said Haliel coldly. "But I warned you that power isn't going away. It's probably going to show up *just* as you're hanging out underpants to dry, and it'll do something *really embarrassing*." She surveyed them all, and added, "*And then I'll write it down.*"

"Haliel?" said Capricorn. "Let's go find some coffee! You can show me your book and tell me what you thought of my work!"

"Get lost, Capricorn," growled Haliel.

"I can't! But I *can* bring *you* coffee if you don't want to go out! You still like cinnamon dulce lattes, right? I know where I can get that!" Capricorn stepped backward and vanished.

"Oh sweet heaven," muttered Haliel. "I can't deal with Coffee with Capricorn right now. All right, kids, I'm heading out. I'll be expecting that map in the mail, Magic. And Slick…. We'll be *talking more*."

"Talking's fine," said Cat. Haliel gave him a nasty look, and also then vanished.

AT nudged Amber. "Told you so."

Amber understood exactly what she meant, but couldn't agree with her. "You can't call *that* a win."

"Depends on what you were trying to accomplish, I guess," said AT.

Jennifer looked back at where Capricorn had been. "That's a dangerous demon. Yes, yes, Earth Horse. But you're a dangerous friend too, aren't you?" She patted the horse absently on the neck.

Then she turned and knelt beside Imani and Charlie. "Hi."

"Hi," said Imani awkwardly. "Is it odd that I know *what* I am now, this whole Wild Hunt thing, but not why I'm…" She waved a still translucent hand.

Jen sat back on her heels and glanced over at Amber, her eyebrows raised. Guiltily, Amber remembered what she'd done to Jennifer, and hurried over to join her. "Uh, hi. You're still a bodiless soul, just like I'm still a bloodsucking fiend. But you'll probably eventually get the hang of being just like a human some of the time. But if you don't, that's okay, too. Isn't it?" She ended on a note more hopeful than authoritative and slumped a little.

"I'm speaking and you're hearing me," said Imani. "I'll make it work."

Jennifer patted Amber on the shoulder and rose to her feet again.

"Jennifer?" said Amber quickly. "Uh, do you want the Horn back again?"

"I don't think so," said Jennifer with a little smile. "I think you'll learn a lot carrying it."

"Great," said Amber glumly.

"Hey, Amber, maybe there's a class you can take next semester," said Yejun. "I'm sure your fancy college offers a class in everything, right?"

"Why don't you start by helping Imani decide where she and Charlie are going to live now?" suggested Jennifer, her gaze moving to Cat.

"Yeah..." muttered Amber, but she continued watching Jennifer and Cat instead.

Softly, Jennifer said, "Laundry and carrots, huh? Anything else?"

"Yes," said Cat steadily. Then he brushed his fingers through her hair. "Let's talk about the details later, though."

"Yes, please," said Yejun. "You do that. Later. I'm getting pretty tired of oh never mind Jesus Christ," he finished in disgust as Jen stood on her tiptoes and kissed Cat. "I hope that redhead is wearing clothes by now," he added, and stalked away.

Amber sighed and looked back at Imani. "Our work isn't usually this exciting," she said.

"I don't mind exciting," said Imani.

"I kind of do," said Charlie. "Mom, if you can't touch stuff, you can't make dinner. Are we going to have to live with Severin?"

"Severin doesn't live anywhere, kiddo," said Imani sweetly. "He's got nothing but a dirty bed and a big closet in a locked room. I've seen it. Disgusting."

"Ew," said Charlie. "Really? So what are we going to do?"

"Don't worry," said Amber. "Your family's a lot bigger now. And those two lovebirds cook really, really well."

———

BRANWYN WAS the last person Severin delivered home, after some complications regarding Imani and Charlie's disposition. At first, they'd been set to move into Jennifer's big farmhouse, but as soon as they got there and looked around, Imani and Charlie had both become nervous.

"I don't want to live in the middle of nowhere again, Mom," said Charlie. "I want to go to a school where nobody's going to stare at me."

"It's not that bad here," said AT, and she might have convinced them if Severin had given her a chance. But he hadn't.

"Plenty of opportunities to visit," he'd said, and yanked them away again, only to step through a window targeted on Branwyn's family home.

"You've got a focus here, too?" she said, outraged.

"It's useful," he said. "So, your mom's been bored and lonely lately. You think she'd put them up?"

"Where are we?" demanded Charlie.

"Pasadena, near LA." said Branwyn absently, and Imani nodded in approval. Branwyn shoved aside her annoyance at Severin monitoring her family home and considered his question. "She'd love it, although she might need some time to get used to Imani."

The introduction had been a little complicated, but as soon as Holly understood that Charlie and the flickering spirit beside her needed a safe place to stay while recovering from trauma, all of Holly's nurturing instincts kicked in.

"I'll make my way from here," said Rhianna brightly, as Severin held out a hand to her. "I'm never going to get used to that space of yours. You know, Branwyn's place isn't that far. Unless you're going somewhere else?" she added innocently.

Before Branwyn could respond, Severin gave Rhianna a shark smile and yanked Branwyn away.

They lingered a moment in the velvet darkness. She held her breath, wondering if once again she'd have to explain to him why she couldn't do what she really *wanted* to do. But he only pressed his thumb against her lips, gave her that grin, and pulled her into her studio.

"Well then," she said, briskly. "I guess that's that." She thought for a moment. "Are we still going to have to fight over Rhianna's punishment in a month or so?"

"Nah," he said. "She died five times already. I think that's enough. I bet Candy'll be impressed, too. Max certainly will be."

Branwyn shuddered. "You like giving me nightmares, don't you?"

"I prefer your dreams." He gave her a darkly hungry look, and her mouth burned where he'd touched her. "However," he added, and then stopped.

He never took his eyes off her, but his expression changed to one she'd learned to recognize as *wants to say something but doesn't know how*.

She gazed back at him, patiently, in case this time he figured it out.

Finally, he said, "I know you're eager to… explore the possibilities, but… don't be in a hurry to ditch Shatiel's charm."

She raised her eyebrows. "Don't you hate being my dog?"

He shrugged and said, "Not as much as you hate being my leash."

"Tell me the real reason," she demanded.

His eyes glittered as he looked down at her. Then he exhaled and looked over her head. "Shatiel said some things when he first told me about what he'd done. I didn't pay much attention at the time. I'd… like to now. It'll be easier with a regulator."

"I'm not going to manage you," she warned. "I'm not going to call you. You're 'Sev' forever now."

"Keep telling yourself that, cupcake," he replied, with his smallest smile. Then, without another word, he stepped backward and away.

The End

Author's Note

Thank you for reading **Fury Convergence**! I hope you enjoyed it. I also hope you'll consider writing a review on Amazon. Every one single one helps.

More Senyaza Series stories lie ahead. Turn the page to find out how to hear about those as they're released.

About the Author

Chrysoula Tzavelas is a word witch specializing in SF novels and video game content, as well as an amateur digital artist. She has a long-running interest in interactive storytelling, mythology and complex imaginary worlds.

When she's not writing or wrangling two children, she can be found thinking out loud on Twitter. Her latest book, Fury Convergence, is the sixth volume of the cybermagic urban fantasy Senyaza Series, while her epic fantasy novel Citadel of the Sky was Book of the Month at the F-BOM SF&F Feminist Book Club.

More detailed information on what she's working on at any given time can be found at her Patreon.

facebook.com/chrysoula.tzavelas

twitter.com/chrysoula

amazon.com/author/chrysoulatzavelas

Acknowledgments

As always, a big thank you to my alpha and beta readers, Ailsa, Suzanne, Jenna, Rachel, Kiva and Michelle. Without them these books would never be finished.

I used a template provided by Ravven for the cover, and DAZ Studio and Photoshop to produce the art. Both the print and ebook editions were produced in Vellum.

Also by Chrysoula Tzavelas

Senyaza Series

Matchbox Girls

Infinity Key

Wolf Interval

Etiquette of Exiles

Divinity Circuit

Thrones of the Firstborn

Citadel of the Sky

Green Wild

Other Stories

Bramble Child

Nightlights

www.ingramcontent.com/pod-product-compliance
Lightning Source LLC
Chambersburg PA
CBHW021120260626
47169CB00005B/1373